Northbound traffic was moving smoothly on the Golden Gate Bridge. They were nearly across the bridge when Craig felt a slight dizziness. In the next second, vertigo engulfed him and he couldn't feel his hands on the wheel or his foot on the accelerator. Awareness of his boys in the backseat, of the car hurtling at close to fifty miles per hour on a bridge packed with other cars, screamed alarm through him. Something huge pressed upon his consciousness. He frantically tried to maintain focus on the road, to regain control of his muscles. Helpless rage battled against the numb tingling that stung his body. A surge of panic, then consciousness left him.

And billions of others.

A CATCH IN TIME

DALIA RODDY

MEDALLION
PRESS

Medallion Press, Inc.
Printed in USA

A CATCH IN TIME

DALIA RODDY

DEDICATION:

In memory of my father and my mother, Muzhir and Inge Gailani.

Published 2010 by Medallion Press, Inc.

The MEDALLION PRESS LOGO
is a registered trademark of Medallion Press, Inc.

Cover design by James Tampa

Typeset in Adobe Garamond Pro
Printed in the United States of America

ISBN: 978-160542103-2

10 9 8 7 6 5 4 3 2 1
First Edition

ACKNOWLEDGMENTS:

My deepest thanks to Kimberley Cameron, agent magnifique, whose good cheer, constant support, and near-superhuman perseverance guided me to this tangible result.

I want to thank my sisters, Camilia and Jasmine, for their unshakable belief in me, my father, my nieces and nephew, Megan, Neil, and Daisey, for their enduring optimism during setbacks, and my friends (you know who you are—and, yes, Dee and Andy, you top the list) for their stalwart conviction that I would "do it."

To my children, Melanie and Nicholas—you're the best. Thank you for never doubting this day would come.

And finally, to my husband, Bill—there are no words. You know what I mean . . . and more.

PROLOGUE

TUNISIA, 7:00 P.M.

Mohammed Al-Kujbahan perched on the hump of ground rising several feet above the bank of the watering hole. His sharp gaze darted through the darkness, picking out the shadowy forms of his charges as they lumbered, wheezing and cough-grunting, to the water's edge.

"Hammudi." His younger sister's sweet, high-pitched call came through the night. Mohammed scowled. How many times had he told her to stop calling him by that childish form of his name? "Hammudi. *Yehla, yehla*," she called, closer now.

What was she doing out here? And why tell him to hurry? He was doing his job. Who could hurry a camel?

"Here," he answered softly, not for her, that softness, but for the camels. He was a good camel herder, the best, he told himself.

Aida, despite the darkness, lithely clambered up beside him. "The lamb is ready, Hammudi," she said.

"I'm hungry."

"Go eat, then."

"Mother says we must wait for you. Ah, Hammudi, please. I am so hungry." Aida tugged his thin arm.

Mohammed shrugged off her touch. Aida's tone irritated him. He was hungry, too, but the food they ate cost money. He nudged her roughly. "Go back to the tent. Do something useful. I will come when I come. You know nothing of my duties."

The rich American who had contracted the camels was shrewd, far more watchful than other contractors. And freer with coins.

Calling him mean and spiteful, Aida scrambled away. A camel bellowed, and something in its tone brought Mohammed to his feet. Other camels milled, shifted, bumped each other and rumbled noisily. Mohammed pinned his gaze to Aida's fleeing form as camels edged before and behind her. He tried to call to her but sudden blackness filled the world and he collapsed, unconscious, not seeing tiny Aida drop to the sand or the camels trampling her, their small brains filled with terror.

PART I

CHAPTER 1

SAN FRANCISCO, 11:00 A.M.

Craig Thomas glanced at his two boys in the rearview mirror just as he merged with traffic on the Golden Gate Bridge approach. Ignoring the dread that pitted his stomach at his glimpse of five-year-old Lucas's guileless expression, he distracted himself with thoughts of John Thomas.

By age three, his oldest son had no longer responded to being called John or Johnny. John knew his mother was Mary Thomas and his father was Craig Thomas and that he was John Thomas. He required everyone to call him John Thomas, though his mother was allowed to call him Honey. Craig smiled at the memory.

Perhaps it was time to relocate to a family neighborhood beyond the fringes of the city. He and Mary had talked of such a move after Lucas was born. John Thomas had fit well into their life in the heart of San Francisco, but somehow Lucas's arrival had pushed them off center. Then Mary had died and thoughts of relocation vanished.

In the backseat, Lucas was chattering to John Thomas. Another glance in the mirror showed John Thomas looking out his side window, ignoring Lucas. *He knows,* Craig thought suddenly, and could no longer shunt aside his dread. He felt again the chill that had frozen his heart the day the truth about Lucas had slammed into him.

He and his sons had just crossed Fulton Street, bordering a playground in Golden Gate Park, when they heard a car horn blare through the screech of tires, and saw a golden retriever tumble into a convulsive heap. Ear-splitting yowls pierced the air. A young boy, maybe eight years old, like John Thomas, dashed to the dog's side, his screams broken by hysterical pleas for help. Passers-by rushed to them, milling helplessly.

The howling of both dog and boy evoked such misery that Craig was momentarily stupefied. Hands trembling, he drew his boys to his side and caught his breath at the sight of John Thomas, face twisted in empathetic pain too large for him to understand. Craig dropped to his knees and folded John Thomas to his chest. Turning to Lucas, ready to absorb his pain as well, he stiffened in shock.

Lucas was smiling.

Craig stifled rising panic. *He's too young to understand,*

he reasoned, as fear thudded through him. *It's a blank smile, not one of pleasure.* But Lucas was staring at the hysterical boy, the piteously screaming dog, and his smile didn't waver. Craig frantically scanned the faces of children in the crowd, seeking reassurance in their expressions. But not one was smiling. Even a toddler, clutched in its mother's arms, had tears rolling down his round cheeks.

Worse yet, Craig's fear felt familiar. Lucas's cold smile only strengthened what he'd suspected for quite some time; there was something dreadfully wrong with his younger son. There'd been too many hints in the past year that Lucas's emotional reactions weren't normal. For one thing, Lucas was indifferent to John Thomas, something that had always puzzled Craig. He'd assumed younger siblings tagged behind older ones like orbiting planets bound by gravity to their sun. But Lucas ignored John Thomas's activities. And John Thomas didn't tease Lucas.

Craig wasn't sure whether their odd relationship was due to Lucas's strangeness or to John Thomas's precocious maturity. But was John Thomas mature enough to recognize a problem with Lucas?

Craig now knew he had lost all trust in Lucas. *That cold smile.* How was it possible? Then it struck him: *Should I even leave John Thomas alone with Lucas?* He was horrified at such a thought about his own flesh and blood.

Northbound traffic was moving smoothly on the Golden Gate Bridge. They were nearly across the bridge when Craig felt a slight dizziness. In the next second, vertigo engulfed him and he couldn't feel his hands on the wheel or his foot on the accelerator. Awareness of his boys in the backseat, of the car hurtling at close to fifty miles per hour on a bridge packed with other cars, screamed alarm through him. Something huge pressed upon his consciousness. He frantically tried to maintain focus on the road, to regain control of his muscles. Helpless rage battled against the numb tingling that stung his body. A surge of panic, then consciousness left him.

And billions of others.

Vertigo and unconsciousness were indiscriminate. Every highway, bridge, and street was filled with horrific accidents as drivers slumped over their wheels.

In their Volvo, Craig and his sons plowed through a narrow opening between careening cars, bounced off the side rail of the Golden Gate, then received the impact of the vehicles piling up behind them. The blow carried them beyond the cement boundaries bordering the end of the bridge and bounced them to a halt on the shoulder of the bay-side exit to the Vista Point parking lot.

The horrific collisions took less than a minute, and were followed by the sounds of still-running engines, several stuck horns, and an occasional upturned wheel spinning out its slowing force.

For three minutes, not a whisper of consciousness flickered in the minds of any of the survivors trapped in the distorted metal wrecks.

United States, est. population (pre-blackout): significantly above 300 million.
United States, est. population (post-blackout): 198,500,000.

CHAPTER 2

SAN FRANCISCO, 11:00 A.M.

PREGNANT. LAURA TOSSED THE TELLTALE STICK INTO a small wastebasket next to her bathroom sink.

She stared into the mirror. Her hair was thick, honey-colored, unkempt after the night. She scrunched her nose. Someone had told her she had Meryl Streep's nose. *Great. Chipmunk cheeks and Meryl Streep's nose.* At twenty-six, she felt she was fading and wondered what Mack saw in her. Her brown eyes watered and nausea buckled her over the sink.

You're a mess. You're pregnant, Mack's gone (thank God). Leaving the bathroom, she stopped at the threshold of her apartment's living room. She could no longer put off calling the clinic for an appointment.

Sinking into her chair, she reached for the phone and resolutely batted away her fear. She had to take care of this, and recover, before Mack returned from his overseas trip. He'd never know.

She'd had boyfriends before, but never one like Mack. Older than her by at least fifteen years, Mack was both rugged and charming, an adventurer, a real-life Indiana Jones, and she was flattered by his attention. He could have any woman he wanted, but four months ago, he'd chosen her, and their relationship became all that a small-town girl like herself dreamed about.

A baby would wreck everything.

If her resolve dissipated now, the old Laura would reappear, the responsible, organized Laura. The Laura whose dismay at her own behavior would undermine the excitement of this relationship.

Mack was her adventure and she wasn't ready to end it.

She punched the number to the clinic. During the first ring, she began to feel strange. At the second ring, vertigo struck. Apprehensive, she mistook it for nausea, but then felt an enormous pressure on her mind, a huge, unimaginable wave poised to crash upon her. She dropped the phone.

And was engulfed by sudden, overwhelming comprehension. Of death. Of life.

Space ceased to exist. Energy was compressed, yet all-encompassing. There was time without space, paradoxically static and fluid, stretching moments into eons into nanoseconds. The understanding of another dimension that contradicted everything came instantly to Laura. Immersed in knowledge, she no longer had a point of view. She felt her sense of self absorbed into entirety.

She was no longer Laura.

Forces in harmony sang, colors became panoramic fields describing energy. Images of the only dimension she'd known showed space riddled by endless exchanges between matter and energy in finite velocity. The newly sensed, and limited, time/energy dimension lusted for vastness.

The entire history of all life on earth, the source of life, the meaning, all were perfectly clear.

The source was even now, this moment, poised to . . . something . . .

Space reasserted itself. Laura felt as though she had been dropped, a physical sensation that lurched through her stomach as she felt herself once again contained, constrained by flesh and bone.

Nausea. Carpet below. A dreamlike fade.

Suddenly, briefly, a flash of something different. A bleak darkness. Unimaginable dread.

Then it was gone. That smothering blackness, the stomach-pitting dread, had nothing to do with the feelings and knowledge she'd first felt, understood. She shuddered with distaste before a resurgence of euphoria swept over her. A maelstrom of images and ideas raged through her and she fought to remember, groping for the clarity she'd had only moments before. She didn't want to lose any of it.

The meaning. It was all there.

She thought she felt a vague movement in her womb. Movement? Determined not to be distracted, she ignored it and plunged back into memory, wrapping remnants of ecstatic knowledge around her.

All too soon, the brightly colored diorama faded. She lay, exhausted, on the floor of her familiar apartment. *I have to remember, life is . . . to think we never really knew. All the religions and philosophies. Did anyone ever guess? I've got to remember more, there's more and I'm not remembering. Think, think, THINK.*

Emotionally drained, she absently rubbed her stomach as she tried to refocus her thoughts. Round and round her hand went, trying to soothe the tiny fetus with all she had seen.

CHAPTER 3

Nothing moved on the wreckage-strewn Golden Gate Bridge. For three long minutes, those who'd survived the collisions lay unconscious, ecstatically basking in exploding visions.

John Thomas regained consciousness in strobing flashes: Everythingness, nothingness. Vague euphoria. Everythingness. Singularity. John Thomas.

Reality returned abruptly: smoke, burnt rubber, oil, and blood; idling engines, stuck car horns, Lucas's voice, and a low humming he didn't recognize; twisted car interior strewn with CDs, fast-food garbage, and contents of the glove compartment; leather upholstery oddly pressed into his side, the seat belt bruising his lap and shoulder.

His head hurt, his eyes stung. But there was a leftover bit of dreamy fog, something exquisite, exciting, good. It slipped away when he tried to focus, and panic, sadness, filled the emptying recesses. He squeezed his eyes shut. What was the picture inside that whiteness that kept sending such night-before-Christmas feelings? The best dream he'd ever had and now he couldn't remember it!

"What happened?" Lucas asked loudly, excited. "My side hurts. I can't get my seat belt off." He tugged John Thomas's arm. "What's wrong with you and Dad? You don't answer and I need help. Get my seat belt off, John Thomas, now, now, now!"

John Thomas looked at Lucas—his voice, his hand plucking at his sleeve—there, but somehow, not real. Like a TV turned up too loud. Lucas.

Lucas frightened John Thomas. He'd been wanting to say something about this to his father. But what could he say? The things he felt about his brother didn't seem to have words.

His head hurt and it was hard to think. Part of him knew that something was terribly wrong, but most of him was wrapped in the memory of wonderful feelings. If only he could remember where they came from, the story that strung them together.

"John Thomas, stop pretending you don't hear me," Lucas demanded. He tried to wriggle out of his seat belt to see out the windows. All but the front passenger-side window, facing the parking lot, were shattered opaque, yet intact.

"I can't see anything, John Thomas. Dad. John

Thomas won't help me. Dad!"

John Thomas tried to focus on the spot where his father's head and shoulders should be. His father wasn't there. Where was he? Fear jolted him.

They'd had a very bad accident. Was something wrong with his father? John Thomas fumbled with his seat belt, forgetting that he'd been trying to remember something, ignoring Lucas, the pain in his head, needing only to see his father, to know he was there and he was all right.

He grabbed the front seat, heaved himself up, and saw his father, body contorted on the floor beneath the dash, head turned at an impossible angle, eyes staring at him.

John Thomas stopped breathing. His pulse thrummed his eardrums. He fastened his gaze on his father's trembling lips.

"Watch out," Craig Thomas croaked.

John Thomas leaned farther over the seat, straining to hear.

Using his last breath of life, Craig whispered, "Watch out . . . for . . . Lucas."

"Dad?" John Thomas stared, stunned. Lifeless eyes stared back at him.

Lucas screamed. John Thomas jerked upward, his head banged the ceiling, and he fell back into his seat. His screaming brother's furious eyes were fixed on him.

"John Thomas, get me out NOW."

John Thomas leaned over Lucas and pushed the belt release button. Nothing happened. He pulled at the belt by force. Still nothing. Within moments, he'd worked himself into a frenzy of pulling, pushing, and yanking.

"OW! John Thomas, that hurts! Dad, John Thomas is hurting me!"

"Shut up," John Thomas's voice cracked as he pushed words past the pain swelling his throat. "Dad's dead. He's dead, he's dead!"

His father's last words had been to take care of his brother, to watch out for him, and instead, he found himself wishing his brother dead.

Abruptly, the seat belt released.

"Finally," Lucas crowed.

John Thomas blinked at Lucas. Didn't Lucas get it? Dad was dead.

Dad's dead.

John Thomas tried to stop crying, and wiped his face with his shirt. He pictured his familiar room, shutting the door, going to bed. He felt sicker than he'd ever imagined.

"Get this open, John Thomas. It's stuck." Lucas pressed his small frame against the door.

John Thomas obeyed, pushing the door with short, hard thrusts. The door groaned open just enough for them to squeeze out. Lucas went first and John Thomas, thinking of traffic, grabbed Lucas's hand as he slid out behind him.

The two small boys stood by the car, hands clasped. John Thomas looked at the chaotic scene spread about them. On both the freeway and the Golden Gate Bridge, cars and trucks were smashed, overturned, some burning. Broken, bloody bodies sprawled within the twisted metal.

Horror overwhelmed him. He stared, breathing shallowly, until his head swam from lack of oxygen. Stumbling back, he slumped against the car.

"John Thomas." Lucas yanked his brother's hand.

"Shhh. Just a minute, Lucas, wait."

Lucas shrugged and returned his attention to the gruesome scene. He wished John Thomas would stop holding his hand so tightly. He wanted to go see that arm lying under the tire of the big truck across from them.

Lucas hadn't lost consciousness. For him, there'd been no fallen barrier, no infusion of knowledge, no understanding, no euphoria. He knew only that something had rocked the world and left chaos in its wake.

And it was thrilling.

Impatiently, he tugged again at his brother's hand.

John Thomas had no idea what they should do. Death seemed everywhere. Was everyone in the world dead?

A scream came to his throat but before it escaped, sudden elation spun his mind. The feeling of that dream he couldn't remember flooded over him again. Gratefully, he plunged into it, grasping at fragments of hope within it. The world of pain and loss receded and John Thomas was able to travel far beyond the reality through which he moved.

Holding tightly to Lucas's hand, he began their long trek home over the bridge, walking, crawling, and climbing through the wreckage-strewn roadway suspended high over the waters of the Golden Gate.

CHAPTER 4

TWENTY-THREE-YEAR-OLD ELI MALCOLM WAS TERRIfied of death.

Death. Dark emptiness.

The inevitability of his own death, the maddening paradox of being, then not being, often filled him with an unbearable ache. He would be there, then just . . . gone, the world spinning on without him.

He no longer remembered the explosion of insight. He no longer even felt he'd forgotten something.

He just knew he'd seen too much death in the past twelve hours.

It was late. He was exhausted. For hours, he'd been driving around the Presidio, trying to find a way out of it and into S.F. proper. The decommissioned army base had only three or four exits and he hadn't been able to get near any of them, there were so many accidents. The few cars he'd approached on foot had been either empty of people or full of horrible death. As darkness approached, the thought that more chaos waited outside the Presidio repelled him.

He stopped and switched off the engine. Enough was enough.

He sat in the darkness and listened to the light rainfall that had begun minutes before.

The sound increased the eerie feeling of isolation. If he weren't so tired, he thought, maybe he could figure out what had happened. He'd regained consciousness at the tollbooth of the bridge. He remembered seeing the unbelievable destruction all around him. He vaguely remembered holding his miniature tape recorder to his mouth and babbling into it. Since then, driving in circles, everything had become more confusing.

He felt lonely and scared now, but he'd felt something else, earlier: an unusual aloofness, as though he hadn't cared about all the dead people. Remnants of that bizarre detachment added confusion to his fear.

Maybe, he thought, as exhaustion drew him toward sleep, all his grief had just gotten used up in the two months since his grandmother had died. On a wave of familiar sadness, he drifted to sleep.

He woke to a face at his window.

"Hey," the man said. A perfect smile accompanied the greeting.

Disoriented, Eli smiled back at the handsome face;

green eyes with a slight upward tilt, a nose drawn with an artist's pencil, a fine mouth, a strong chin, and smooth bronze skin. The man was obviously of mixed race, with tight curls of an oaky mocha color.

Eli opened his door, stepped out into the morning, and offered his hand, which was taken in a firm clasp.

"Eli."

"Josiah."

The intersection before them held four empty cars and a truck, hopelessly entangled. The face of the truck driver was visible, its gray-white color unearthly. Eli averted his eyes. "What the hell happened everywhere?"

Josiah shrugged. "I was hoping you could tell *me.* Last thing I remember, I hit a tree." He rubbed the side of his head, where a headache was slowly blossoming. "I woke up maybe ten minutes ago and you're the first person I've seen. The first live one, anyway." He looked past the collision, at another wreck down the street.

"I don't know what happened," Eli said, suddenly aware of the eerie silence. It was so quiet they might well have been standing in a mountain meadow.

The steady rain of the night had ceased. The street onto which he'd been unable to turn was bordered by a guardrail, beyond which was a view to the northeast. Josiah walked to the guardrail.

"It couldn't have been an earthquake," Eli said, following him. "I drove around for hours yesterday and didn't see any damage to streets or houses."

At the rail, they gazed down the grassy slope it bordered, then out at the winding streets. In the distance, edging the bay, lay the main thoroughfare of the Marina District. The long strip of crushed and piled automobiles glittered under the brightening sun.

Eli frowned. "I was at the bridge tollbooth, about to pay. I must have blacked out or something, I don't really know. Jesus, maybe everyone blacked out at the same time; that would explain some of this. But how? Why?"

Josiah shrugged. "Maybe terrorists hit us with some kind of nerve drug. Maybe a government experiment went wrong."

Eli glanced quickly at Josiah. He hated conspiracy theories and, by extension, conspiracy theorists, but he instinctively liked Josiah.

He stared at the boulevard of smashed vehicles in the distance.

"Think we can find a clear street out of here?"

"There's only three or four ways out of this place and my guess is they're all jammed. Walking will be quicker. Once we get to the city streets, we'll get a car."

"You mean, steal a car?"

"Not if the owner's alive. Something tells me there's a lot of free used cars out there."

Eli squatted, rested his arms on the guardrail, and gazed out over the bay to the Golden Gate Bridge, that graceful structure that served such a useful purpose. He stared at it as if its familiarity could somehow erase the jarring strangeness of the day.

He saw something drop from midspan of the bridge. He blinked, then tracked the form as it plunged to the ocean.

With a wordless sound, he pointed at the bridge.

Josiah turned and they watched as two more forms dropped, flailing for what seemed a long time, until they smashed into the cold water below.

"Fuck me," Josiah exclaimed.

"What the—" Eli said.

"Come on," Josiah nudged him. "Let's get out of here."

"I don't get this. I don't get it." Hearing the tremor in his own voice, Eli clamped his lips shut, hard.

"I know, man," Josiah said. "Let's go."

Eli nodded. He and a stranger had just inexorably linked their futures.

Josiah stepped over the guardrail, but Eli asked him to wait. Darting back to his car, he reached in and grabbed the small tape recorder off the passenger seat. It was his last link to his grandmother.

He didn't know how many tapes he'd made for his grandmother during the last months of her life, filling microcassettes with banal chatter and amusing anecdotes. As soon as one tape was full, he'd mail it to the nursing home and begin another. The tapes filled the gaps between his weekly visits and gave continuity to the time they had together. After she'd died, he'd found himself unable to break the habit of speaking to her. He began thinking of the recordings as keeping an oral journal and was unaware of how much it had helped him through his period of mourning.

Grabbing a packet of miniature blank tapes and a new pack of triple-A batteries from the glove box, he jogged back to Josiah.

They half walked, half slid down the wet, grassy slope, then crossed the street at the bottom. Josiah, a pace or two ahead of Eli, moved effortlessly.

"Hey, Josiah."

"Yo."

Eli hesitated, then admitted, "I'm scared shitless."

"Me, too."

Oddly, knowing that Josiah was also frightened comforted Eli. "I felt this really weird detachment, yesterday," he ventured. "Did you feel that way?"

"Maybe it's a kind of shock," said Josiah, evading admission. "All this is just too much to take in." The truth was, detachment from emotion was part of Josiah's life, a lesson learned in his early years on the streets. A gang member from the age of nine, he'd quickly learned to hide emotions, to ignore pain, and to understand that his survival depended upon appearing fearless. He relied only on himself. There had been no one else.

They crossed a patch of soft, loamy soil between

pine trees. Another street lay ahead of them and, beyond that, more urban forest. Eli wished the pain behind his forehead would go away, but said nothing as he tried to match the rhythm of Josiah's boots.

He bumped into Josiah, who'd abruptly stopped.

Josiah, one eyebrow raised, said, "I've been thinking we ought to find some kind of tow truck. What we can't ram out of our way, we can tow aside."

"Sounds good." Eli looked curiously at his new friend.

"What's your mix, Josiah?"

Josiah grinned. "Black, white, and yellow. I figure that makes me peachy. You?"

"Vanilla and white. Very bland."

"Works for you," Josiah's grin widened.

Eli waved a dismissive hand. "What do you do?" he asked. "I mean—before today?"

Josiah hesitated, then said, "This and that." He bit gently on his lower lip as he squinted at Eli.

As the silence lengthened, Eli realized he'd have to give a little, first.

"My grandmother raised me from a baby after my parents died." He told Josiah about how close he'd been to his grandmother and how hard her recent death had been on him. "What about you?"

Josiah stared at a patch of blue sky speared by treetops. "CeeCee—my mother—was a junkie," he finally said.

And then he told his story.

Eli listened, concealing his wonder, biting back his questions, and began to understand what had led to Josiah's obvious air of self-reliance.

Later that night, Josiah walked calmly into a Clement Street Bank of America branch and robbed the abandoned place of four hundred thousand dollars, while Eli watched.

CHAPTER 5

DAY 2

HURRYING TO HIS SEAT BEHIND THE ANCHOR DESK, James Walsh scanned the sheet of paper Phil had thrust at him. As he read, he thought, numbly, *It's all a bad joke,* but knew it wasn't. Boston was in shambles. Death, fires, chaos. No joke. Dropping the paper onto the news desk, he cracked his knuckles. Amy hated that sound. But Amy was dead.

"Ready?" asked Phil over the sound system.

James Walsh took a deep breath, nodded.

There were three of them in the studio today; yesterday, there had been twenty. Phil was in the production booth and Carol was checking Camera One, in front of him. She held up three fingers, two, one, then pointed.

He began reading, and for the first time in twenty years, did not look at the camera.

"At 12:01 a.m., President Clayton Caldwell issued a declaration of martial law. All thoroughfares and transportation depots are now under federal jurisdiction. Every highway, freeway, street, and back road, all railway systems—tracks and stations—including subways, and all airports, harbors, and ports are now under martial law.

"Anyone obstructing or damaging any of these facilities will face federal arrest.

"Separately, President Caldwell has declared all power plants—nuclear, hydroelectric, wind, and solar—to be under federal jurisdiction. Secretary of Defense Joseph Dwight has stated, 'Anyone found tampering with such will be shot.'

"I'm James Walsh and this is WNN in Boston. Stay tuned for updates."

"We're clear," came Phil's monotone.

James Walsh's shoulders slumped. He dropped the news sheet onto the desk, folded his arms atop it, and lay his head down on his arms. He closed his eyes.

Laura woke suddenly, yesterday's experience hurtling into her mind.

She smiled. Blinking at the sunlight filtering through the gauze curtains of her bedroom window, she shifted her legs within the pocket of warmth beneath her comforter. She felt so good. Snuggling into the warmth, she smiled wider.

Everyone had experienced it. She knew this with certainty. How different the world would be today. Joy bubbled through her and she laughed. Then laughed again at the sound of her laughter.

Energized, she tossed aside her blanket and swung her feet to the floor. Still dressed in yesterday's jeans and sweater, she congratulated herself on having at least removed her shoes before tumbling into bed.

A muffled shout sounded outside her window. And another.

Marveling that anyone could be doing anything on this glorious morning, other than basking in the afterglow of life-knowledge, she padded over to the window, pulled aside the gauzy curtains, and peered up the sloped street from her second-story window. Sudden alarm squeezed her muscles and replaced the joy.

Three-quarters of the way up the block, a small Ford, driverless, was inching down the hill. In front of it, hands pressed on the grill, a slight woman braced against its motion, her body angled and feet slowly backstepping. For an instant, Laura watched the woman lose ground. Her feet backpedaled faster, and Laura heard another muffled shout.

Spinning around, Laura jammed her feet into her loafers and ran out of her apartment. Hurrying down the carpeted steps, she dashed through the lower lobby, flung open the heavy front door, and ran uphill toward the rolling car. The woman was losing ground quickly now, and it seemed any second she'd trip and be run over.

"Let go," Laura shouted as she ran. "Get out of the way!"

Just as she reached the woman's side, slapped her own hands against the car and leaned her body weight against it, she saw why the woman fought the losing battle. The car was not empty. Through the glare on the windshield, Laura saw a small child behind the wheel.

Adrenaline surged. She bent her knees and pushed as hard as she could. Her loafers slipped, then regained traction. The hill was too steep. The old Ford rolled inexorably forward. Frantically, she considered kicking off her shoes, but there was no time between each backward step. She heard the woman's breath rasping next to her.

Faster, faster. Now almost running backward. The car angled to her left. Laura glanced over her shoulder. They were headed straight for a parked car.

"Watch out!" she shouted. She let go, dove to the right, and broke her fall with her hands. Her palms skidded on the blacktop and she landed on her hip and forearm. Jerking to one side, she curled over in an instinctive cringe away from the crashing vehicle.

She heard crunching metal and glass, a yell of pain, and a string of foul language. Twisting around, she saw the woman on the hood of the Ford, one leg trapped between it and the parked car.

"My God." Laura scrambled to her feet. The

passenger door opened and the young child tumbled out. A blurred impression of brown hair, dark jacket, and jeans was all she got as the child fled up the hill.

"Get back here, you little shit!" the woman yelled.

Laura ran to her, expecting to see her badly hurt, and was relieved to see not pain but anger in the woman's face. The Ford had hit the parked car at an angle and her booted foot was wedged between the bumpers.

"If I ever catch that little—" The woman broke off and looked at Laura. "He's not your kid, is he?"

Laura shook her head. "Are you all right?" she asked. The woman was petite, about thirty years old, with short, dark-red curls and pale skin.

"Except for the foot, yeah, I'm all right." She tried to pull it free, and flinched. "Shit! I think my ankle's broken. You happen to be a doctor?"

"No, sorry," Laura said. "Should I try to pull it out?"

"Yes! I can't even sit."

Laura tried to gently wiggle the boot free. The woman grunted but told her to keep trying. Laura grasped the top of the boot with one hand and the toe with the other.

"Hold on," she said, and yanked, ignoring the yell, then yanked again, successfully.

"Holy shit!" the woman cried. She blew out a breath. "Thanks, honey." Wincing, she sat on the hood. "My name's Kate."

"I'm Laura. Laura Morgan."

Easing herself off the car, Kate timorously set her foot on the ground, grimaced, and leaned back against the car. "I'm screwed," she said.

Laura pointed across the street. "I live right over there. Do you want me to call an ambulance?"

"You're kidding, right?"

She probably doesn't have insurance, Laura thought. "Is there someone else you'd like me to call? You obviously can't walk."

"Honey, where've you been?" Kate's quizzical look matched her tone.

Laura wasn't sure how to answer. The question didn't make sense. She saw Kate's pale skin become suddenly paler, her few freckles standing out.

Laura grabbed her arm. "Are you all right?"

"I—sure, yeah. Just—kinda dizzy. Just a little. All of a sudden."

Laura put an arm around her. "You may be more seriously hurt than you think. You really should get to the hospital."

"Don't you know what's going on around here?" asked Kate. "In the city? Maybe the whole world?"

Laura was relieved. *That* was what Kate was talking about; yesterday's incredible, life-changing experience. The nation must be taking a holiday.

Laura grinned, but before she could say anything,

Kate said, "I'll tell you what, kiddo, if you want to help me on over to your place and invite me in, I wouldn't refuse. I've been up all night." She rubbed one temple. "Headache, too."

Laura tightened her arm around Kate's back and took a step forward, but Kate didn't step with her.

"Just a sec," Kate said. "I really feel woozy. Must be all the smoke."

Smoke? Laura looked up. For the first time she noticed the haze. There was a fire somewhere. She glanced along the street. Funny how deserted it was, she thought. She lived in a busy neighborhood, with several shops around the corner and three or four small restaurants just two blocks over. Odd. Not one pedestrian or moving car.

Two blocks away, a tangle of cars clogged the intersection. An accident? People always gathered at an accident. But, no, there weren't any spectators. And she began to notice other things, like a car on the sidewalk, another smashed into a pole. And lines were down everywhere.

In the unnatural silence of the morning Laura heard only Kate's breathing and her own. No sirens, no voices. And her block was empty.

"Kate," she asked, tentatively, "what's going on?"

Lucas sprinted the four blocks home. Gasping for air, he slammed the front door behind him. That had been close. The red-haired lady almost caught him. And she'd messed up his fun. He could have steered that car down the hill if she'd stayed out of the way.

No sounds coming from upstairs. John Thomas was probably still sleeping. Lucas smiled, then went into the kitchen to find something to eat. He hoped John Thomas slept for a long time. With his father dead, and John Thomas sleeping, he could do anything. This new freedom felt better than anything he'd ever known.

He'd just have to stay away from grown-ups.

Still smiling, he poured cereal into a bowl.

CHAPTER 6

PARNASSUS AVENUE, BORDERING THE HOSPITAL, teemed with people. Laura joined the crowd cramming through the main entrance into the lobby. Kate needed crutches, and Laura needed answers. So she'd walked to the hospital.

Surely, she thought, all that Kate had told her before nodding off couldn't be right. How could no one remember what had happened?

Laura vividly remembered. Not everything, but a great deal. She was bothered by a few gaps, a nagging feeling that something important was missing. Yet, everything she did remember seemed so complete. It explained everything.

Kate said she'd fainted or something, fallen and hit her head. That would account for her memory loss, Laura thought. But Kate also said that everyone she'd talked to had blacked out. Blacked out. The words felt wrong to Laura. They accounted only for unconsciousness, not for what had happened during it. Remembering her own immersion into knowledge, Laura could understand how no one had maintained consciousness, but to think that everyone had forgotten what they'd experienced during those minutes . . .

Impossible.

Voices, groans, and shouts filled the air. Considering all the wrecks she'd skirted on her walk here, Laura wasn't surprised. But, looking around the crowded lobby, she only saw faces twisted in fear. High voices verging on panic rose like steam through the heat of the mob. Crushed on all sides, she stifled her urge to bolt from the raw emotion rippling through the crowd. *Kate was right,* she thought uneasily. These people really didn't know what had happened during the . . . blackout.

And their fear was a growing contagion.

As Laura edged through the thicket of bodies, she quickly realized that the snatches of misinformation dominating the crowd were more dangerous than their fear of the unknown. One man ranted about mass hypnosis. Another group argued bioterrorism versus chemical warfare. Others shouted warnings of the Apocalypse. The noise was deafening.

Finding crutches seemed less and less likely. Chairs lined the walls, all occupied, and people stood two or three deep in front of them. Gurneys held two or three seated patients. No one was at Admitting, and she saw only two white-coated figures moving among the injured.

She hesitated, unsure whether to approach one of the overwhelmed medics with her request. Rumors of power outages floated through the rage of pessimism. Everyone complained of headaches.

Laura took a side corridor, hoping that she'd find crutches somewhere. A woman's gruff voice could be heard above others. "These headaches!" she yelled. "I'm telling you, they sprayed us with something. We're all gonna die!"

Laura turned into another long corridor, lined with stretchers bearing bodies. Some of the people were dead, though no sheets covered their faces. Behind her, a lone blue-coated figure bent over one of the living. Unnoticed, she ducked into a stairwell and shut the heavy door behind her, relieved at the sudden silence.

Taking the stairs at a steady pace, she heard only the echo of the schussing of her footsteps on the cement stairs. *All those complaints about headaches. It can't just be coincidence.* She didn't have a headache.

She was glad she hadn't said anything to Kate about what she knew; Kate would have dismissed it as another of the "half-baked theories" she'd railed against. *I'll tell her later, when we know each other better.* They'd agreed, before the painkillers she'd given Kate had wooed her to sleep, that she would stay with Laura. Her own apartment was clear across town, and she didn't even have a cat to miss her.

At the third floor, winded, Laura stepped into an empty corridor. The door shut behind her, clicking loudly in the silence.

"Is somebody there?" A voice drifted through the empty hall. "Hello?"

Another voice came from farther down the hall. "Nurse? Nurse?"

Laura moved quickly from one open door to another.

The first three rooms were empty, beds unmade. The fourth was occupied by an elderly woman who lay propped against pillows. A blanket, folded at her waist, stretched taut over the rest of her long frame. Her feet peaked the blanket at the bottom of the bed. She wore a pink quilted bed jacket, its satin ribbon neatly bowtied at her neck.

"I'm so glad you came," she said in a surprisingly strong voice. "I'm ready to go and would appreciate your assistance."

Laura didn't know how to respond. She needed to find crutches and get back to Kate. She'd left her apartment hours ago, and Kate must now be awake and in pain. She hadn't had the foresight to leave pills on the coffee table with a cup of water.

Pressed between urgency and decency, she paused. Despite her age, the woman appeared calm and capable.

Maybe she remembered.

Laura blurted, "Do you have a headache?"

"I'm seventy-four years old," said the woman, her voice firm, words carefully enunciated. "I've suffered a stroke, a minor stroke, mind you, but a stroke nonetheless. I've been through the Great War, the Great Depression, and more natural disasters than is prudent for a world to withstand. I've lost my husband, my children, my grandchild, my sisters, and my brother over the years. Apparently, another disaster has struck. My headache is the least of my concerns. I am ready to go, do you understand?"

"You want to die?" stammered Laura. "I can't do that!"

Without warning, nausea blossomed through her. It hit so suddenly, she sucked air in gulps. She grasped the doorway, her skin feeling simultaneously hot and cold, numb and itchy. The conflicting sensations passed and left her hands trembling.

The woman stared impassively at her.

"Perhaps," she then said, "as little as two days ago, I might have felt remorse for having taxed your delicate sensibilities with my request, although I must say, your reaction is a tad extreme. However—and I apologize for my curtness—I have no patience left. Please send someone else in here."

"I'm sorry, I can't. I'd still be responsible."

The woman turned her face aside and spoke to the

wall. "Then kindly leave my room."

"I can't do that, either."

"Good heavens." The woman looked at her. "Has it become your purpose in life to torment me?"

Laura knew she had only one option. "I think I should take you home with me."

The woman huffed something like *pshaw.* "I don't know you. Nor"—she frowned—"do I wish to."

"I'm Laura Morgan. I live a few blocks away and I came here to find some crutches for—my friend."

The old woman assessed Laura. After some moments, she said, "Mrs. Catherine Swithenburne."

"Mrs. Swithenburne," Laura said, sinking into a chair, "would you at least let me try to explain what's going on?"

Catherine lay against her pillows throughout Laura's summary of the chaotic hospital and the city beyond. Never averting her gaze, her silence continued for some moments after Laura completed the story.

"That accounts for the racket that kept me awake, and the neglect I've suffered. However, it does not explain why I should go home with you. I have absolutely no desire to be amongst a gaggle of mismatched misfits. I will die here."

"But, we can help you. We can . . ."

Catherine's voice was sharply edged with something new. "My family was taken from me, one by one.

Tragedy has only three possible effects on one's life; it either shakes one's faith, strengthens one's faith, or drives one mad. I consider myself a sane atheist."

Stubborn resolve brought Laura to her feet. "Mrs. Swithenburne, I'm going to go find a wheelchair for you and crutches for my friend. Then I'm taking you out of here." Laura moved swiftly.

"You will do nothing of the kind, young woman!" Catherine cried. "Miss Morgan."

Laura came back to the doorway.

Catherine sniffed, chin high. "If you must do this, please do not forget my medication. Since my survival has become imperative to your conscience, know that medications are imperative to my survival. Also, find something for this dreadful headache."

Laura smiled, and went scavenging at the vacant nurses' station.

It wasn't easy to maneuver the wheelchair through the jumble of people and cars in front of the hospital. Catherine Swithenburne sat erect, silent, swathed in hospital blankets, clutching her old valise on her lap. A pair of crutches and a cane lay at her side, their rubber-tipped ends sharing the footrest.

Laura had found two men in the lobby who helped

get Catherine down three flights of stairs and had left them with the suggestion that they search other floors for patients. Gripping the wheelchair handles, walking as quickly as she could, she felt relieved to be leaving the tumult behind.

Her vision narrowed to the twisting asphalt before her, bounded by wrecks on either side. She was aware of Catherine's gray-haired head beneath her, turning from side to side. As the sounds from the hospital became muffled with distance, they moved through the chaos and carnage.

Catherine spoke. "Parts of the city are burning."

Laura also smelled the acrid smoke.

"I imagine there is no way of knowing how extensive the power outage is."

"My gas stove isn't working, either, but I have running water."

"Do you have candles?"

"A few."

"Provisions? There are bound to be food shortages in the coming weeks."

"I'll have to stock up. There's a market not too far from my place. I'll go after I get you home."

"Looters may have already taken everything. It's getting late," said Catherine. "The streets will be dark. Will there be someone to help you?"

"There's only me and Kate," she answered.

"I assume Kate is the person requiring the crutches?"

Laura smiled involuntarily. "Yes."

It was only then that Laura began to realize that survival was now the standard for existence. Real survival, requiring food, water, and shelter, not the survival to which she had been accustomed, the kind that required money, education, and the pursuit of luxuries. Meanwhile, the new understanding she'd gained pulsed within her. She was bursting with it and had no one with whom to share her excitement. Surely someone else remembered.

"We're going to need a man," Catherine declared. "And weapons. Better get the weapons before you get the man, in the event he proves himself ill-chosen."

Laura thought of the gun her father insisted she take with her when she moved from their ranch to the city. Her father was dead now, along with her mother and older brother, their deaths almost instantaneous with the blackout. Somehow, their passing had been a part of what she'd experienced, and mourning was not necessary, though she couldn't help feeling sad about not seeing them again. She had only her younger brother, Conrad, now, but he was in Munich, at the Oktoberfest. She wondered how Conrad would ever manage to get home. Maybe he remembered the new things, as she did.

"I have a gun," she told Catherine.

"Splendid. Now we need a man."

Laura smiled. *I think I'll wait for Kate on this one.* It was strange how close she felt to Kate, after only a couple of hours of conversation. Maybe it was because Kate was maddeningly straightforward. The way she'd taken over Laura's sofa as though it were her own, chattering despite the pain of her ankle. Her brash jokes and strong opinions. Her agreement to stay with Laura. She saw no point in returning to her empty apartment, to be alone in a world "gone crazy," as she put it.

Getting Catherine up the long flight of stairs proved to be awkward but manageable. The stroke that had debilitated Catherine's right side had not affected her remarkable strength and, with Laura supporting her, they were able to slowly climb the steps.

Kate was awake and Laura told her that Mrs. Swithenburne would be staying with them, then told Catherine that Kate had been one of the Golden Gate Park gardeners. Given how briefly she'd known them, she had little else to offer as introductions. Settling Catherine into the armchair, she went back down for the wheelchair, crutches, and cane. Laura then wrapped Kate's foot with an Ace bandage she'd pilfered from the hospital.

"So, you've saddled yourself with two crippled Kates," Kate said.

"I'm not sure that Mrs. Swithenburne *is* a Kate." Laura glanced at Catherine.

"To my friends, most of whom have passed on, I

am Catherine." She removed several bottles of medication from her valise and meticulously placed them on the table at her side.

Laura nodded, unsure how to address her. "I'll see how our food's holding out."

The available food was not sufficient for three people for any extended time, but Laura found several candles, which she set around the living room. Darkness blackened the windows and rain gusted against the glass. Laura drew the drapes and, together, they ate sandwiches, washed down with water.

There were four apartments in her building, built in the forties. Each was equipped with steam-heat radiators and working fireplaces. After their meal, Laura used a little firewood for additional warmth and extra light.

They all sat quietly, wrapped in blankets and afghans. Kate lay on the couch, eyes closed, and Catherine sat in the armchair, feet on an ottoman. Laura sat cross-legged near the fire, staring at the flames.

There was so much to think about. Things she'd seen today. Disappointment at knowing that Kate and Mrs. Swithenburne had no memory of the things that had been revealed during the blackout. She wondered if that would change, once their headaches went away. Maybe the pain was blocking memory paths. Ibuprofen hadn't helped.

Somewhere nearby, horrid snarls of fighting dogs

interrupted her thoughts.

"I hate that sound," she said, trying not to imagine the fate of the loser.

"We'll be hearing more of that in days to come," said Catherine. "Cities full of domestic animals gone wild. I've seen such things with my husband, during travels to Third World countries."

Then came a series of popping sounds, punctuated by yelps.

"Idiots!" Catherine cried, thumping a fist on the arm of her chair.

Kate, startled, rose on one elbow. "What's going on?"

"They are shooting the dogs." Catherine's voice was grim. "Fools. Dead bodies litter the streets. Who is going to dispose of them all? Nature's scavengers should devour all they can. Soon, putrefaction will bring unbearable stench and disease."

Laura blanched. Swallowing hard, she grabbed a candle and fled to the bathroom. Leaning against the sink, she placed a hand on her stomach. It seemed as though every time she confronted thoughts of death, the tiny life inside her made itself known.

She knelt at the toilet and let her nausea overtake her.

CHAPTER 7

ELI LANDED WITH A GRUNT, BREATH KNOCKED FROM his lungs.

Flat on his back, he couldn't move. He gasped, sucked in a lungful of pain. He heard fists on flesh, the clatter of something, the thump of a body near him.

He had to get up, help Josiah. Sparkling pinpoints danced across his vision. He propped himself on his trembling arm and blinked. So dark out. Something vertical next to him. Legs, in jeans. Dull noises, shouts. His blurry vision traveled up the legs. Who? A fist curled around . . . a gun.

"NNNOOOOO!" The word exploded from him. With all his weight, he flung his arms around the legs, and lunged. He heard the knee next to his ear snap, heard a blast. *Not Josiah. Please—* Still down, he slammed his fist into the groin of the person with the gun.

Josiah's booted foot flashed by, slamming into the

downed man's head, which snapped sideways, gruesomely disfigured. Then, silence.

Eli sat up and pressed his hand against his head. Even with new bruises and pains, his headache still pounded.

"Eli, you all right, man?" Josiah asked. He squatted to look in Eli's face.

"Are they gone?"

Josiah nodded. "Yeah, they took off." He glanced at the body next to them. "This one, he's as gone as they get." He surveyed the dark street. "Can you get up? We need to move."

With Josiah's help, Eli shakily rose.

"My first fight," he said.

"I figured," said Josiah, with a gentle punch to Eli's upper arm. "You done good, man."

Eli looked at the broken plate glass of the storefront where they stood. The three men who'd jumped them had come out of there. Probably looting, just like Josiah and him. Like everyone.

"Is the kid okay?"

Josiah shrugged and Eli limped over to the teenager sitting in the tangle of his bicycle.

"You okay?"

"Yeah, I think so."

Eli asked a few questions, just enough to learn that the boy, who'd cycled by at just the wrong moment, was alone and scared.

Eli turned to Josiah. "Alex needs to come home with us."

Josiah looked hard at Eli, shook his head, then sighed. "Let's go," he said, picking up the gun.

CHAPTER 8

JOHN THOMAS HAD NEVER KNOWN SUCH SADNESS. HE fought it, was overwhelmed by it. He lay in his bed and stared at the mobile of the solar system above his head: the sun, surrounded by all nine planets. He focused on the earth and tried not to hear Lucas rummaging through the cabinets in the kitchen beneath him.

A plate clattering onto the tile counter, the jangle of the silverware drawer opening. The refrigerator door—bottles clinking dully in its shelves—thudding shut. He sat up, feeling dizzy. His stomach felt empty. He couldn't remember the last time he'd eaten. He didn't know how long he'd lain in his bed, only that time had passed, that he had slept, woken, slept; he felt sick and miserable awake, and nightmarish asleep.

Light-headed, he pushed his blankets aside and slowly put his feet on the floor. He had his shoes on. And he was wearing jeans. He walked to the bathroom on shaky legs, thirst filling his mind. He bent to the faucet. Water had never tasted so good.

Removing his clothing, he walked to the closet. Sounds from below had ceased. John Thomas selected clean clothes. He hated being dirty. He would have to change the sheets. He had often helped his father change bedding. A memory of his father, tossing one end of a sheet to him as they both hovered over his bed, caused tears to well. He squeezed his eyes shut. He would not think about his father now, he would not.

Freshly washed, dressed, and with brushed teeth, John Thomas descended the stairs, gripping the banister tightly. Familiar sights of his home: the throw rug in the foyer, the coat tree by the door, the photos on the walls. Thoughts without words. He paused in the kitchen doorway. Lucas sat in his usual chair, eating from a bowl obscured by clutter on the table: cereal boxes, dirty dishes, ketchup. The mess extended throughout the kitchen, plates lumped with congealed scraps, dirty glasses, gaping boxes, empty cans. Only the sink was clear.

"About time, John Thomas," Lucas complained. "We hafta go to the store and there's no TV and there's no hot water and the flashlight stopped working. And you just kept sleeping and I almost got lost when I tried to find the store. We're out of Fruit Loops, John Thomas, and I hate this stuff." He smacked a cereal box in front of him with his spoon, arcing droplets of milk through the air.

John Thomas took two slices of bread from a loaf on the counter, put them in the toaster, and pushed the lever down. He stared into the slots, waiting for the red glow.

"It doesn't work," Lucas said through a full mouth. "Nothing works, haven't you been listening to me? You need to call the 'lectric man, except the phone doesn't work either. He needs to fix the TV, too, I been missing things. It's not fair, John Thomas, it's very, very bad. You should get mad at him."

John Thomas popped the cold bread out of the toaster, put the pieces together, took a bite, then another. He was so hungry.

"It's not his fault, Lucas," he said, emulating his father. His father had always explained everything.

Lucas frowned mutinously. "Well, *somebody* broke it. Then it gets night and there's nothing to do. I don't like it. We need TV and lights and Fruit Loops, John Thomas."

Lucas thought about telling John Thomas about his nightly adventures into the chaotic streets but decided against it. John Thomas might not let him do it and then there would be *nothing* to do. Even his nighttime prowling had become less interesting. Grown-ups were clearing things away, and there weren't nearly as many dead people so it was harder to find and watch the dogs feast.

"Oh! John Thomas, let's go back to the bridge." Lucas had been wanting to explore the carnage he remembered but knew he couldn't find his own way back there. Although he didn't expect John Thomas to agree, he hoped for it. So many things were different, now. Maybe even John Thomas.

John Thomas chewed his dry bread and swallowed. He looked through the cupboard for a clean glass but couldn't find one, so he picked the least offensive glass off the counter, rinsed it, filled it with cold water, and drank.

Lucas was still waiting.

"The bridge is too far away," John Thomas said. He could remember little of their journey afoot across the Golden Gate. Most memories were obscure; a twist of dented metal, a bumper he'd grasped for leverage, a tire he'd used for a boost, a broken window crunching beneath his foot. But one image overwhelmed all others: his father, under the dashboard, neck twisted, eyes sightless.

Dark pain congealed around his heart. His eyes lost focus and he flinched at a sudden tug on his hand, jerking it away and staring, startled, at Lucas.

"Let's go," Lucas said.

"I told you, it's too far."

"No, to the store. I finished the milk. Let's go to the store and then let's find the TV man."

John Thomas unhooked their jackets from the coat tree. He helped Lucas put his on, then donned his own and slipped the house key chain around his neck. They stepped out into a cold drizzle.

He needed to find someone to help them, to take

care of Lucas, and to help him—John Thomas—understand what was happening. A grown-up would know. Mrs. Johnson, up the street, maybe. She would wrap him in her plump arms after he told her what had happened to his father. She would call him "honey." Blinking back tears, he hurried down to the sidewalk, Lucas in tow. They would go to Mrs. Johnson's house. He could already almost feel her cushiony safety.

Cars had jumped a curb and were entangled against a brick building, obstructing the sidewalk. John Thomas focused on Mrs. Johnson's house, a three-storied structure of white stucco overlaid by geometric designs in dark timber. Once there, he stepped onto the stoop, pulling Lucas along with him.

"John Thomas? Is this where the TV man lives?"

"Shh. No. Mrs. Johnson lives here." John Thomas rang the bell, then peered through one of the beveled glass windows bracketing the door. A gathered lace curtain hung against the window inside, preventing him from seeing anything other than vague shadows.

"Does she have Fruit Loops? Is that why we're here?"

Ignoring Lucas, John Thomas rapped his knuckles against the window. Maybe the doorbell didn't work. Maybe she'd gone out, or maybe she was in her backyard, with her flowers and fruit trees. John Thomas walked to the side of the house where a high wooden gate barred entry to a walkway leading to the back of the house. Lucas followed.

The gate opened with a latch, but John Thomas felt suddenly uneasy and glanced behind him into the eerie fog. Nervously wiping beads of drizzle off his cheek, he depressed the latch and pushed the gate wide enough for the two of them to slip through. The rattle of the latch falling into place behind them sounded unnaturally loud.

As they walked single file along the narrow walkway between the house and the high wooden fence, John Thomas was assaulted by a terrible, unfamiliar odor. He cupped his hand over his nose in disgust.

"She must be dead, too, John Thomas," Lucas said matter-of-factly, recognizing the odor from his nightly prowling.

Startled by his loud voice, John Thomas whirled around. "Hush up, Lucas," he whispered harshly. "You don't know what you're talking about."

Lucas smiled, happy to discover he knew something that John Thomas didn't. He liked to surprise—no, to shock. When John Thomas had come down the stairs this morning, Lucas had told him all kinds of new things, but John Thomas hadn't reacted at all. But this reaction. Oh, boy, this reaction was more like it!

"I do too know," he trumpeted. "She's dead. Lots of people are dead."

John Thomas hurried along the walkway. The smell was making him feel sick again. He finally reached the end of the house, and the garden spread out before him, nothing like he remembered it. The fruit trees stood bare of leaves, the rose bushes held no blooms. The central fountain was empty of surrounding flowers. Only bordering camellia bushes and a profusion of calla lilies in one corner provided greenery.

Mrs. Johnson lay sprawled on the hard ground near the calla lilies, her body hideously bloated and distorted.

Lucas hurried in front of John Thomas so he wouldn't miss his expression. "I told you, John Thomas. I was right. I told you she was dead, and she is."

John Thomas shoved his hand hard against mouth and nose.

"Shut up!" he shouted, his voice muffled by his hand. "Shut up, shut up, SHUT UP." He almost smacked Lucas. And why shouldn't he? There was no one to stop him now, no one to say, *"Don't ever, ever hit your brother again."*

Trembling, John Thomas turned from Lucas and ran to the back door, pushed it open, bolted through the kitchen and the long hallway, into the foyer, and to the front door. Gasping for air, hands on his knees, his small back rounded, the weight of his thoughts crashed down on him.

What should he do now? Was everyone dead? Were only he and Lucas left? Hot tears swam in his eyes and he collapsed onto the floor. Huddling against the front door, he cried with choking awful noises, his body rocking furiously in time with his sobs.

Then he heard the music. It came in choppy notes. He gulped himself into silence, straining to hear. Yes, it was music, music coming through the door. People. He scrambled to his feet, grasped the brass doorknob, and fumbled with the deadbolt. A click. A turn.

A small body squirmed forcefully between him and the door.

"No, John Thomas, don't," Lucas said in a loud whisper. "They're bad people, *very* bad people. I saw them before, they're taking kids away, John Thomas, *all* of them. They're going into houses and taking kids," Lucas whispered as fast as he could, desperate to keep his brother from opening the door.

It was true, Lucas had seen those grown-ups before, and he'd hidden from them. From hiding, he'd watched them go into two houses and come out with frightened children.

Lucas didn't want to be taken from his house, from his newfound freedom. He was determined to keep John Thomas from letting the grown-ups in. They would wreck everything, make him do things he didn't want to do, watch him all the time.

Lucas leaned into John Thomas's face. "They're probably *eating* the kids, John Thomas, *cooking* them and *eating* them."

John Thomas blinked numbly at Lucas, unsure if he'd heard right. Overwhelmed by grief and loneliness, he felt dazed. His head hurt and his nose was stuffed.

Lucas looked at John Thomas's tear-smeared face. He needed to see shock and surprise. So he embellished his story. "They were crying, John Thomas, and the people told them to shut up and they shook 'em and shook 'em and took 'em away." Lies came easily to Lucas, and, focused on keeping John Thomas from opening that door, the story became his reality. "They're very, *very* bad people."

John Thomas stared at his brother. Could it really be true?

"*Don't ever go* anywhere *with an adult you don't know, John Thomas.*" His father's warning, repeated often, boomed through him. He could almost hear his father's voice. *"There are bad people out there, John Thomas, bad people who do terrible things to little boys. Promise me that you will never go anywhere with a stranger."*

The music filtered through the door. The people out there playing the music were strangers, maybe the very strangers his father had warned him about.

He remembered asking his father what the terrible things were that such people did to little boys, and his father, who'd answered every question, hadn't answered that one. He'd wondered what could possibly be so bad that his father wouldn't talk about it.

Now he knew. Horror cramped his stomach. *They eat children.*

The music was passing right outside the door now,

the notes a caricature of melody, a trap, like candy, or a request for help. It was the music of children-eaters.

Lucas, satisfied with John Thomas's shock, hissed, "We gotta hide." He turned and ran to the stairs.

John Thomas watched Lucas pound up the stairs. The terrifying music, so loud. With a sudden jerk, he ran after his brother.

Three flights of stairs left them breathless. Lucas plunked down on the last step and watched his brother clamber up to stand, gasping, over him. The attic ceiling sloped steeply. A short hallway had a door on either side. Before them, a curtained, mullioned window framed the sky, three stories above the street.

John Thomas didn't think his heart could pound any harder. The street below, so empty ten minutes earlier, was suddenly loud with noise. Engine sounds. Voices. The terrible music.

"It's *them*," Lucas said. He scrabbled on hands and knees and peeked out from one lifted corner of curtain.

John Thomas dropped to the floor. Terror freezing his insides, he couldn't sound a warning, *Get away from the window.* They'd see him and come into the house.

His fear was so huge, so real, his still-fresh grief and loneliness so raw and overwhelming, that it was harder to have faith in the old reality than it was to tumble headlong into nightmarish possibilities.

He forced himself to crawl over to Lucas, to reach

up and grab the back of his shirt and yank him down.

Lucas fell hard, twisted around, and punched out with a small fist. It landed on John Thomas's thigh.

"They won't see me," Lucas spat.

He persuaded John Thomas that they should keep an eye on the enemy, so, together, they very cautiously peeked out.

It looked like something from a horror movie. Frenzied people, faces covered with masks, scarves, bandannas, sprinted into houses, and came out with arms full of things they stuffed into cars. Then it shifted, from robbing and looting to dark insanity.

Some dragged bodies out and threw them in a pile in the middle of the street. Others doused the pile with liquid and threw lit matches onto the heap. Flames exploded upward. Neither brother could tear his eyes from the insatiable flames.

The bodies writhed in the heat: a shifting leg, a curling arm, a jerking head. Terrified, John Thomas mistook the movements, thinking the people alive as he watched the malevolent flames leap in gaseous colors, shriveling clothes, igniting hair, blistering and blackening skin.

Was this how they cooked children? Moaning, he backed away from the window.

Then came the sound of banging on the front door.

John Thomas grabbed Lucas and darted into a storage room on the left of the short hallway. Yanking open a closet door, he shoved Lucas before him until they were both deep into a dark corner behind stacked boxes and hanging coats smelling of mothballs.

John Thomas's heart raced. He was now convinced that his brother was right and that his earlier warning had saved them from those very strangers his father had warned him against. A searing ache of longing shot through him and he wished with all his might for his father's return, for an end to the terror, the aloneness.

He heard voices in the house. Faint at first, but getting louder, closer. Then heavy footsteps on the nearby flight of stairs. The door to the room crashed open. He held his breath. Any second now, the door to the closet would be flung open, their hiding place revealed. But the heavy tread receded, the stairs creaked, fainter now. The slam of the front door.

Breathing hard, too scared to move, he strained to hear.

The smell of mothballs was strong. Darkness, odor, and only two sounds, his own and Lucas's breathing. Lucas's small body pressing against him, the only familiarity left, mingled with tentative quivers of relief. His brother's actions, keeping him from opening the front door, blended with his father's warnings, his father's essence of loving protection. For the first time in a long time, he felt stirrings of affection toward Lucas.

Warmth for his brother began to fill the cold black hole in the very center of him. His mind, unwilling to endorse a brother both good and bad, aligned itself with the more comforting idea of the good brother whom his father had loved. And as his mind retreated from the edge of a chasm of which he was only dimly aware, distancing itself from the dread that had once proscribed his relationship to Lucas, he felt only welcome relief.

Watch out for Lucas, his father had said. John Thomas could still hear his voice as he'd uttered those last words. New purpose and strength flowed through him. He would protect Lucas, just like his father had told him to do.

In the tight darkness, he grabbed Lucas in a fierce hug.

And that contact gave John Thomas a taste of what he'd craved. Desperate for the comfort of being protected by someone older and bigger, he felt comforted holding someone younger, smaller.

He imagined his father's approval and it seemed almost as though his father sat beside him, smiling at him. Proud of him.

Lucas suffered the hug in silence. As long as John Thomas hugged him, he wouldn't be leaving the closet and letting the grown-ups in. His ear, squashed against his brother's chest, filled with the erratic beat of John Thomas's heart.

It was wearying, this deep restructuring that went on inside John Thomas. His traumatized brain, reacting in defense, began to relax. Though he tried to keep his muscles poised and his ears alert, his heart rate and adrenal system slowed.

And while John Thomas waited in the darkness for the danger to pass, Lucas, crushed into a tiny space beside him, sat patiently, every sense keen.

Without warning, the headache that for days had throbbed behind John Thomas's eyes suddenly coalesced into a spear of bright pain. He cried out, covered his eyes, and slumped against Lucas as the pain exploded.

CHAPTER 9

ELI PARKED THE TRUCK FACING MARKET STREET and set the brake. They had to cross Market to get to the warehouse and it didn't look like that was going to be easy.

Reaching for the mask that would help filter out dust and odors, he looked at the chaos ahead. Market Street, deep in the downtown section of the city, had always been snarled in traffic. But it now looked more like a war zone with its burned-out buildings and gas-line explosions.

No doubt other routes to the warehouse were as bad. He set his mask in place and nodded to Josiah.

Josiah was ready. They both stepped out into a street filled with the twisted debris of cars, glass, and blackened building rubble. Decaying bodies sprawled amongst the wreckage, limbs poking from every niche. And rats. Everywhere.

The new addition, Alex, scrambled out of the backseat as he adjusted his mask, then jammed his cap on. He'd considered walking away but knew he was lucky to have hooked up with Eli and Josiah. He felt safe with them. People were acting weird, like they'd been bitten by some shit-crazed bug.

Two boxes, one packed with surgical gloves, the other with heavy work gloves, were in the bed of the pickup. The three of them struggled with the tight surgical gloves, then pulled work gloves on over them.

A group of people a block to their left were already at work near a large burn pile. Two men heaved a corpse atop the pile. Eli looked away. After two days of rain, followed by two days of sunshine, the stink of decomposing bodies was overwhelming, even through the mask.

Many misshapen corpses weren't whole, their discolored, shriveled flesh gnawed by scavenging animals. There was no place where his gaze didn't fall on rotting flesh hanging from splintered bone. The maggots were the worst; fat, burrowing. A gag constricted his throat as he asked Josiah where they should begin.

"That blue truck," Josiah said. "If we can crank it over behind that bus, we can probably move those compacts. They look locked together." He moved to the front of their truck, unlatched the winch, and took the hook to the blue truck, cable unraveling behind him.

Alex impatiently watched Josiah kneel and grope

beneath the wrecked vehicle for a place to hook the winch. "Hey, Eli," he finally said, "two-man job, huh? I'll be back."

Eli nodded and watched Alex saunter toward the other group. Poor kid, he thought. When they'd taken Alex home that night the men attacked them, Alex had aroused Eli's sympathies.

He was a runaway from New Jersey but hadn't yet told Eli his reasons for leaving home. He had no way of knowing if his parents had survived, or if he'd ever manage to get back home.

Eli wondered again why Josiah wasn't curious about what had prompted Alex to leave home at seventeen. Josiah seemed to be indifferent to Alex. Not that Alex seemed to notice. He'd taken a real liking to Josiah and was constantly asking his opinion, although that wasn't unusual; Josiah looked like a man with answers. He had that air about him.

In his heavy work boots, one of the perks of a city full of abandoned stores, Eli glanced down the street after carefully picking his way over the rubble to Josiah.

Several burn piles, hidden by wreckage but distinguishable by their smoke, smoldered in the distance. People poked among the rubble, dodged around wrecks, or disappeared into, and appeared out of, the businesses that lined Market. Chaotic noise, voices, shouts, rumbling engines, the screech of metal, and the crunch of glass filled the air.

Just as he reached Josiah, he heard a high-pitched roar as three military jets came in low from the east, flying in formation, and passed like thunder. Along the street, faces turned upward and followed the wake of the formation. Some cheered, others yelled in outrage.

Most of the people Eli had talked to thought the government was involved with the disaster; had either instigated it or been unsuccessful in averting it. As always, people assumed the government knew more than it was saying.

A block away, a man raised his arms and shouted for attention, then began a loud singsong sermon. A few people drifted his way, including Alex.

"I wonder what it looks like from up there," Josiah said. He searched the sky.

Eli squatted next to him. "Pretty bad," he ventured, "but not as bad as it looks and smells from the ground."

Josiah showed Eli the problem he was having. The locking lip had skewed itself out from under the tip of the hook and was now useless. There was nothing to keep the hook from slipping. Under the tremendous force of both the winch and the truck, a suddenly released hook could be disastrous.

Josiah watched Eli examine the hook. He held it close to his face, looking down his nose at it. He looked cross-eyed, and Josiah laughed. It reminded him of Bob. His laugh subsided into a bemused smile. He hadn't thought of Bob in years.

"What's so funny?" grinned Eli.

Yeah, Josiah thought. *Just like Bob.* He'd always been ready to join in, too. And had always known, like Eli, that Josiah wasn't laughing at *him.* He considered telling Eli about Bob, an old, yellow Big Bird doll that he'd bought from a thrift shop when he was nine years old. After his mother had OD'ed. But how to describe what Bob had meant to him, a nine-year-old gangbanger?

He was about to start, knowing Eli would try to understand, even if he didn't tell it right, when the pressure of the headache he'd had for days abruptly blossomed into knife-sharp pain. One look told him Eli was experiencing the same thing.

They both raised their hands to their temples. Josiah saw other people crumple to the ground clutching their heads. He saw terror in Eli's eyes.

Nerves on edge, Laura inched the Bronco onto Market Street. Moments before, the truck she'd been following had turned a corner, taillights flashing. The unknown driver had had no qualms about creating a path through the mess; wrecks had shuddered and rocked aside as the truck crashed its way through, with Laura driving in its wake. Now left to make her own way through the wreckage, she nervously adjusted the bandanna covering her nose and mouth.

Easing the Bronco ahead, she tapped the fender of a car in front of her, a bloated arm dangling from its window. She'd have to ride the sidewalk to avoid the next obstruction.

Broken bodies lay on a sidewalk stained dark with blood. *I can't drive over them.* If Catherine were here to see this, she'd stop demanding that she get to a warehouse before it was emptied.

"Don't forget these, Laura," Catherine had said, handing her both the gun and a shopping list. A shopping list.

Just a few more measly blocks. They're dead, just go. Turn that corner and you're there. She tightened her grip on the wheel.

The Bronco shot forward as she jumped the curb and rode a path littered with flesh and bones. A last lurch, and she was rolling on a clear stretch of sidewalk. She stopped, her foot shaking uncontrollably on the brake.

She leaned against the steering wheel and tried to judge whether a broken lamppost's angle left enough room for her to squeeze the Bronco between it and the building. To her left, cars blocked the street. Her small car would have made it, but she was unfamiliar with the abandoned Bronco she'd appropriated an hour ago.

"You won't be able to fit enough into your car," Catherine

had decided. "You'll have to find a larger vehicle."

"Yeah, Laura," Kate had drawled from the couch.

"No time for levity, Kate," Catherine reprimanded. "Our survival depends on what we can collect in the next few days. People are supplying themselves and fleeing the city. We must do the same, before disease comes."

"What's with the *we* shit?" Kate had retorted. "Laura's doing everything."

"I am aware of that," Catherine said icily, turning immediately to Laura. "Don't hesitate to use the gun." Then she'd gently patted Laura's hand, startling a smile from her.

Laura eased off the brake and edged the Bronco forward, steering close to the building beside her. When the hood moved under the lamppost, she stopped, set the emergency brake, and jumped out to gauge the distance between the Bronco's roof and the lamppost. There were inches to spare, she decided, nervously aware of the Bronco's coughing idle. Hurrying back to hit the accelerator and keep the engine going, she was too late. With a protracted belch, the engine died.

She struck the hood in frustration. This was the third time in an hour it had died.

Then, to her left, across the street, three young men, their arms filled, emerged from a building and disappeared among the jumbled destruction. There was other scattered activity on the street. Distant voices called out to each other in efforts to push wrecks aside. Scarves, handkerchiefs, masks, or mufflers covered every face she saw, giving all the appearance of refugees.

She was about to get back into the Bronco when all noise suddenly ceased.

Clusters of people, active and noisy an instant before, grew still. Everywhere she looked, people clutched their heads and slowly collapsed to the ground.

What's wrong with everybody? She pulled herself into the driver's seat, shut the door, and watched the stricken people. Catherine's prophecies of disease and plague came fearfully to mind.

A wail rose thinly, strengthened, became an unbroken scream. Other voices combined in an agony of sound that pierced the air. She clapped her hands to her ears but could not shut out the shrieks of despair. Staring at the wretched people, she feared everyone had gone mad.

A gaunt man startled her as he emerged unsteadily from behind a smashed bus, not ten paces from her.

Her breath caught as she stared into his eyes. She'd never seen such bleak anguish. It carried an energy of its own, emotion on the verge of detonation. He screamed from his eyes with a sucking silence more powerful than any voice.

Compassion beseeched her to do something about his terrible despair. Instead, she froze as he raised a gun, aimed at her.

Eli moaned as the unbearable pressure in his head increased. Pain stabbed his eyes, his temples. Certain of imminent death, he squeezed his eyes shut. Any second, the throbbing vessels in his head would burst.

Then it was gone, so quickly and completely that his body jerked. He felt wonder, relief, then something else was in him. Something huge. Black. Terrifying. He sagged, shrinking from inside. Tears swam in his eyes.

Filled with fear and a despair too large to comprehend, he turned to Josiah, forcing words past trembling lips. "It—it's like the end of the world, Josiah. Is it—?" His throat constricted, heart seared by desolation. A chasm of lonely sadness suddenly opened beneath his feet.

"Hold on, Eli, hold on," Josiah managed to utter past his own swelling despair. He didn't know what was happening, only knew they must survive.

"What IS this?" Eli whispered, his face twisted by anguish. "What's happening?"

And then the darkness Josiah fought engulfed him. Desolation. Primordial loneliness so fierce, he nearly cried out under its weight. He lost focus on Eli as he braced himself against the hopelessness devouring him, sucking him downward. Fighting to regain control, he tried, as he often had, to will himself not to feel.

How, he wondered, had he fallen, so quickly, so completely, into this gluey darkness? How? He attached himself to the question like a shipwrecked man clings to a scrap. How had this blackness hidden within him, so concealed, yet so overpowering? How? He repeated it like a mantra, until the horrid blackness dwindled to a vanishing point.

He was shaken. Nothing in life had prepared him for this. His self was the one strength he had never questioned.

His self had withstood brutality, poverty, betrayal, and emotional wounds inflicted by his loving/hating mother. Having withstood all that without self-doubt, he'd thought himself inviolable. He had faced his own mortality so often, he'd come to accept it as just as real as being. He accepted his life. He accepted his mortality.

It had never occurred to him that something else might lie between the two.

He stared at his hands, their stillness belying the struggle he'd just endured: to keep his soul from being torn from his body even as he still inhabited it. Breathing raggedly, he juggled the paradox. How could he exist without that which defined him?

The answer jarred him with its simplicity: Madness. A state of insanity.

Relieved to be intact, he was yet numbed by the glimpse of his own madness.

He became aware of Eli, sitting so quietly near him,

pale, his skin stretched over the bones of his face, his eyes shuttered by bruised lids. *He's still there.* In that darkness. Carefully, he took Eli's hands in his own.

"Hold on, Eli, hold on." Tightening his grip on Eli's hands, he felt helpless. He rubbed Eli's hands. "Hold on, hold on, hold on."

"Holding," Eli's voice finally came, barely audible. "Holding." Fingers twitching in Josiah's grip, Eli's eyelids fluttered, the lifeline of Josiah's voice guiding him out of the murk. Trembling, he leaned into his new friend.

Down the block, Alex lay in agony. Curled around himself on the cold street, he wanted to die, to feel nothing ever again, if that meant being free of the anguish.

And then a warm hand clutched his shoulder, warm breath filled his ear.

"Rise, boy, rise up," a voice demanded. "We got to fight, boy," the preacher hissed, "for Satan has unleashed his demons upon the world."

CHAPTER 10

Laura barely had time to recognize the gun aimed at her.

The next instant, the gaunt man with the eyes full of torment placed the muzzle against his own temple.

Laura's breath caught in her throat, relief and fear trapped between heartbeats.

He squeezed the trigger, a tiny motion, just before his head burst outward and his body slumped to the ground, his death painting her world.

She pressed a hand over her mouth to keep from screaming, certain that someone would now break free of the pall that had befallen them and rush to investigate. But people remained huddled in the chaotic debris, an inversion layer of despair and depression trapping them, thick, unmoving, its weight increasing every moment.

Shaking, desperate for escape, Laura started the engine, barely hearing it wheeze before it caught. She floored the Bronco, surged under the angled post, and fishtailed onto a four-lane thoroughfare. She wheeled around smashed cars, the wide street bordered by two-story buildings, reasonably free of rubble.

She almost drove past the warehouse. The entrance bays flashed by on her right, and she hit the brakes hard, tires screeching as she rocked to a stop. After backing up, she nosed the Bronco into the dim street-level garage. Close to the ramp walkway, she killed the engine with a shaky breath. What had just happened to everyone?

Everyone except me. Her hand went to her stomach, began the familiar, soothing circular motion and, for the first time in weeks, she realized she wasn't nauseous.

She got out of the Bronco and hurried up the walkway, where she saw that the open bay doors in the front of the building did little to light the interior. She stepped into the warehouse, but before her eyes adjusted to the dimness, she realized she wasn't alone. Several shadowy figures moved in the semi-darkness.

She grabbed a shopping cart and moved through the gloom as new anxiety struck. No one spoke. There was only the sound of shuffling footsteps, the thud of boxes, the rattle of things dropping into carts. And crying.

She was frightened by the despair of these people. *Words cannot describe this,* their features said, *do not come at us with pitiful words.*

Like the man who'd shot himself.

Laura quickened her pace, feeling vulnerable in the gloom. Something was almost recognizable about them. A memory she couldn't quite grasp. Then a woman, standing motionless by the cereal shelves, seized her arm. Laura cried out and yanked herself free as she whirled to face the woman. And saw bottomless emptiness in her eyes. Laura's breath caught and she fled. The woman didn't move.

Laura was terrified. She wanted to abandon her cart and run, speed home to Catherine and Kate, and never leave again.

Instead, she forced herself to move through the echoing aisles, snatching items from ransacked shelves. Tossing packs of batteries into her cart, she realized she'd have to tell Kate and Catherine what she knew. They might not believe her, but she had to try to close the gap between what she knew and what others were experiencing.

Avoiding the ghostly shapes of people, she loaded her cart with flashlights and camping supplies, tools, canned foods, and powdered milk. Her heart pounded. She heaved two fifty-pound sacks of rice onto the lower rack of her cart. She threw in boxes of bandages, packages of soap, bottles of medicine and vitamins, and hurried away as someone entered her aisle. She loaded in bags of dried beans and flour, cans of coffee, and sacks of sugar and potatoes, while nervously keeping her distance from others.

For the first time in days, she thought of Mack.

How much safer she'd feel if he were with her now. A fight broke out somewhere deep in the echoing dimness, a sudden flurry of shouts and smacking flesh.

She leaned hard against the weighted cart and hurried to the exit.

At the Bronco, she flung everything inside. Winded, she pulled herself in behind the wheel and turned the key.

Nothing. No engine sounds. Not even a whir. Just a faint click when the key turned.

Biting back her frustration, she yanked the hood release and leaped out of the car. It took both hands to raise the hood. Perplexed, she began jiggling hoses and wires.

"Problem?" A voice asked.

Laura gasped and shot upright. A slim, brown-haired young man stood a couple of feet away, on the passenger side of the Bronco, looking at her expectantly.

"Need some help?" he asked with a smile.

Normally, she wouldn't have thought twice about accepting such an offer. But circumstances had left her unable to judge motives.

Without another thought, she plunged her hand into her jacket pocket and withdrew her gun.

"Hey," he said, raising empty hands in alarm. "Hold it, I just wanted to help."

"I told you," said a voice from the driver's side of the Bronco.

Laura cried out, stumbled back a step, and swung

her gun to the other side. The second stranger was taller. He leaned easily against the car parked next to the Bronco, his arms folded loosely. He wasn't looking at Laura, though.

"What'd I tell you, Eli?" he said, then looked at Laura with a smile.

"I know, I know," the one named Eli replied. "But—"

"But nothing, man. You're gonna get us both blown away." Before Laura could respond, Josiah said, "Can't you see she's still scared?" His eyes were clear, water green. "You want us to leave," he offered gently, "then you just say so. No need to shoot our balls off."

"Jesus, Josiah," Eli said.

"What?" Josiah laughed. "You think she doesn't know that just pointing her piece that direction is making me sweat?"

Laura then realized the gun had sagged in her hand and was now pointed at his crotch. Despite herself, she nervously smiled at him, lowering the gun to her side. After introductions and talk about the Bronco's failure to start, she felt herself relaxing. They were behaving quite normally.

"Do you know what just happened to everyone?" she asked.

Eli shook his head. "No," he said. "But I swear I thought I was going to die."

Josiah moved to the front of the Bronco and leaned

over the engine. "If hell exists," he said, unclipping the distributor cap, "that had to be it."

Laura watched him explore beneath the hood. She asked carefully, "And if hell doesn't exist?"

Josiah ducked out from beneath the hood and met her gaze. He was good-looking. Very. Flustered, she looked at Eli, who was peering at the engine.

"If hell didn't exist before," Josiah responded in a soft voice, "maybe it does now."

The Bronco was indeed dead. Eli and Josiah offered to take Laura home and, hesitatingly, she accepted. Their truck was loaded with their own supplies, yet they managed to pack Laura's things in, piling the overflow into the back of the crew cab. The three squeezed into the front seat, Laura in the middle.

Crossing Market Street, Josiah stopped and Eli jumped out.

"Back in a minute," said Eli.

"What's he doing?" Laura asked as she watched Eli skirting wreckage. He appeared to be heading for a group of people halfway down the block. Aware that she was pressed close to Josiah, though Eli's seat was now empty, she carefully shifted herself, opening a gap between them.

"This kid we've got with us, Alex," he said. "Eli's rounding him up."

However, Alex, it seemed, wasn't ready to go.

Reverend Perry, who had helped him during the painful blackout, was preaching his heart out, and what he preached was fascinating Alex.

When Eli placed a hand on Alex's shoulder, Alex said, "Go on without me, man. I'll catch you later."

Josiah and Eli helped Laura unload her supplies from the truck. During their first trip up to the apartment, Laura did introductions. During unloading, Kate's and Catherine's duties were to stay out of the way.

Eli, Laura, and Josiah coordinated themselves so that one of them was always by the truck, guarding it. The street, however, remained empty. When the last of Laura's provisions were up and the five of them were in the apartment, Josiah stayed by the window so he could see the truck, still full of his and Eli's supplies.

Catherine sat in the armchair. She'd asked Laura for her gun and now sat with it in her lap. She'd never stopped watching Eli and Josiah while they were in the room.

Kate offered to fix sandwiches, but Josiah and Eli declined.

"We should get going," Eli said, "get our stuff home."

Josiah's survey of the room stopped at Catherine. She stared unwaveringly at him, her head high, saying nothing. He nodded, acknowledging her attention and the suspicion that prompted it. Her eyes narrowed. He turned to Laura and gestured at the room.

"Looks like you're packing. Are you leaving the city or just the apartment?" he said.

Catherine spoke directly to him for the first time. "I imagine a great many people are evacuating the city. Have you similar plans?"

"Yes, we do," Josiah answered.

"What'd Laura do, shanghai you guys?" Kate asked. "She has a reputation for that, you know."

"I do not," Laura laughed, then added, "Although I did nearly shoot them."

"No shit?" Kate looked at Laura, then at Eli and Josiah. "What happened?"

"It was my fault," Eli said. "I sort of scared her."

Josiah turned again from the window. "It happened after that weird thing hit." He moved toward the door. "Eli, we'd better go."

"Wait a minute," Kate said. "Weird thing? You mean that—that horrible—" she grabbed two handfuls of red curls, shook her head and groaned.

Eli grimaced. "That's the one."

"Then everyone felt it?" Catherine asked faintly. "Kate and I were quite . . . Rather a nerve-wracking experience."

"Nerve-wracking?" Kate rolled her eyes. "Shit, Catherine, it kicked my ass through my head. Some headache cure."

Everyone agreed.

Laura looked at Kate, then the others. No more headaches? she wondered. Then the headaches hadn't been blocking the knowledge. If they had, and everyone now knew what she knew, they wouldn't have been able to contain the joy. There was no more reason to wait before telling Kate and Catherine what she knew, no hope that the knowledge would revisit them.

Laura wondered how they would take it. It would probably be impossible to convince them that it was real, but that was no reason to change her mind about telling them. As soon as Eli and Josiah left, she'd tell them everything she remembered.

"Sound good to you, Laura?" Kate said.

Laura's head jerked up. "What?"

Kate laughed. "Pay attention, honey, there's something new every minute. I just asked the guys if they wanted to caravan out of the city with us. Safety in numbers and all."

Laura looked at Catherine, whose caution of the men hadn't escaped her. Kate followed her glance.

"Oh, for chrissakes," said Kate, "Catherine probably wants their resumes."

"No need to decide right now," Josiah said. He reached past Laura for the doorknob. "We checked out the Golden Gate Bridge yesterday and it's still a huge mess."

"We've heard the southern routes are even worse," Eli offered, "and the East Bay's a nightmare. A lot of people are walking out, maybe figuring they'll get a car once they're past the worst of it."

Laura stepped away from the door as Josiah opened it. He said, "We'd rather get as many supplies together as we can before we leave. Who knows what's left out there."

They all agreed to meet again in two days, then the two men left.

There was a moment of silence before Catherine thumped her cane on the floor. "I think it's a splendid idea," she said. "What do you think, Laura?"

"I—" Laura began.

"Jeez, Catherine," Kate interrupted. "You coulda said so while they were still here, you know."

Laura took a deep breath. It was time.

"I know what happened during the blackout," she said. "I know what it was."

CHAPTER 11

Catherine and Kate stared at Laura. Curiosity flickered in Catherine's eyes. Kate became guarded.

And I haven't even started, Laura thought.

It doesn't matter if they believe you, she told herself. *At least you can stop feeling like you're keeping the biggest secret ever.* Maybe it would trigger their own memories.

"I can't explain all of it; there are some gaps in my memory, but I do remember a lot of it and it was . . . beyond wonderful. The blackout was . . ."

"What?" said Catherine.

"It was knowledge," said Laura triumphantly.

Having begun, she couldn't talk fast enough. "Knowledge of everything, of life after death. It exists, we're all there, we're everywhere, on that side and on this, in the trees and grass, we're in ponds and oceans and dirt, in bacteria and animals and—all of life—it's all us." She ignored the sidelong glances.

"We're it," she continued. "We're the creators. We made this earth—I mean, not the minerals and gasses that formed it, but everything that came after, everything organic." She described the *being* which she—and everyone else—had experienced. The oddness of time/energy without space.

"The—the *huge* effort that went into creating life—indescribable. The *pushing* it took to cross the barrier into this other dimension . . . I can't explain it right. We learned to push our energy into this space, into form, and it was incredible. Just single cells, at first. Years, eons, of firsts. But we learned—and, and since then, building has consumed us. We're the directors of evolution, it's *Us*—the soul Us, *Our* plans, *Our* designs, that have gotten us from algae to human." She drew a deep breath, her eyes glowing.

"There are no missing links," she said. "Every single life-form is a link."

It was the first time she'd put it into words and, instead of doubt, she found certainty. It was as she said, and she knew it.

Catherine's face was inscrutable, but Kate's skepticism was obvious.

"It's all right, Kate, I didn't think you'd believe me," she said, quietly.

"Laura, it's not that I don't believe you."

Laura smiled. "It's okay, really. I just wish you

remembered—that somebody, other than myself, remembered it."

"I must admit, it's interesting," Catherine said. "Appealing, even, to think that we are responsible for our own lives, in the greater sense, and that death is not an end. However," she smiled gently at Laura, "I was never one for fantasies, not, mind you, that I am saying flatly that your epiphanous experience is fantasy. The deficit of being irreligious is that I have no religious entitlements."

"Someday, Catherine," Kate drawled, "I'm gonna have to teach you how to talk normal."

"This is not about religion," said Laura. "Not at all."

"Let's assume, Laura," Catherine resumed, "that everything you have said is true. You are suggesting that a disembodied *We* are the creators of physical life; and that *We,* in turn, caused what we have come to call the blackout. To what purpose?"

"I'm not positive," Laura answered, "but I think maybe just to connect us with *Us*. So that we know."

Catherine frowned. "It seems to me a contradiction that, having worked so hard to create ourselves, *We* would cause an event that has wrought such havoc. The count of dead must be in the millions, if not billions."

"Maybe," Kate suggested, "it was some kind of population control. Earth is overpopulated and if we just keep coming back, then what's the diff?"

"No," Laura frowned. "That doesn't feel right. Life

is," she groped for the right word, "sacred to *Us*. *We* wouldn't do that."

"Honey," Kate retorted, "we've been slaughtering life since Day One. Christians to the lions, Jews to the ovens, hell, even babies to the gods."

"That's different," said Laura. "It's our earth selves that are doing all those things, not *Us*."

"Great," Kate rejoined. "We're screw-ups in the afterlife, too."

Catherine shifted. "Laura, dear," she said. "I hate being a bother, but could you please help me to the powder room?"

"Uh-oh, Laura. You're gonna get it now," remarked Kate.

"Don't be crass, Kate," Catherine said over her shoulder.

"Me? Crass? No way. What's crass mean?"

Catherine shut the bathroom door. It was just as well that she'd ended the discussion. Obviously, Laura didn't think she was offering a theory, but a Truth. One shouldn't add fuel to such a fire, not even a twig. Poor Laura.

That night, Laura lay in her sleeping bag by the dying fire, listening to Kate's breathing, reviewing their conversation. She struggled now to remember a word Catherine had used. A "something" experience, she'd said. Epiphanous. Yes. Epiphanous experience.

Epiphany. The word fit well the exalting revelations that had burst upon her. She hunched deeper into her sleeping bag, feeling a small spot of warmth on the small of her back from the dying fire.

Even if Kate and Catherine didn't believe her, she reflected drowsily, they had tried to understand. And neither of them had made her feel foolish. Warmed by the friendship this implied, Laura drifted off.

CHAPTER 12

James Walsh cupped a handful of vitamins and ibuprofen into his mouth and gulped them down with tepid water. He tossed the paper cup atop the trash can overflowing with empty beer and vodka bottles. He'd needed the vodka last night, even if he didn't usually drink.

The mirror in the men's washroom indicated his eyes weren't bloodshot. Not that anyone watching the news would care. Was anyone even watching? He had no idea. He hadn't been outside in four days. Neither had Carol. Phil had brought in food and booze.

They were due to broadcast in five minutes, as soon as Carol finished printing out the latest from D.C.

At least he wasn't shaking anymore. The first two days after whatever the hell had happened, he'd felt like his muscles were going to burst through his skin.

He stuck his right hand out and held his breath. Okay. Steady.

"Hey, James." Phil's voice came through the door. "Atlanta's standing by. Let's go."

"Right," he called. He left the washroom and hurried down the corridor into the studio. Carol, standing by the camera, handed him the news sheets.

James waited behind the anchor desk and watched her count down to the point.

"President Caldwell today announced that a team of scientists has been assembled to determine whether the blackout was caused by a biological pathogen. The president stated that, although it is too early to speculate on the possibility that a bioweapon was used, he was taking no possibility from the table.

"Ten teams of professionals have been gathered. In addition to forensic pathologists, the groups include physicists, geologists, biochemists, etiologists, toxicologists, meteorologists, astrophysicists, military strategists, and engineers. Churches have demanded the involvement of theologians. There has been no word as to whether the pope will be asked to participate.

"Several more countries have been added to the list of those that have contacted the network set up by the U.N. Among these are Panama, Greece, Iceland, Israel, and New Zealand. There is still no word from China.

"We now go to WNN's Manny Milowicz, at the Centers for Disease Control, Atlanta, for announcements on preventative measures people should be taking."

John Thomas crouched behind a bush and peered out at the small group of people slowly passing. They were led by a man pedaling an old-fashioned ice cream wagon, its child-beckoning tune filling the air. The music filled John Thomas with dread.

He made himself as small as he could and thought about food. He was so hungry.

He'd already sneaked into most of the empty houses on this block looking for food, any kind of food. But people were stealing everything. If he didn't find something here today, he'd have to go to the next block, or even the next one after that. What if he got lost? What if Lucas got tired of waiting for him and he . . . He held his breath as the group passed. He couldn't remember what it was like not to be scared all the time.

Seeing the bad people reach the end of the block and turn the corner, he eased himself out of his crouched position and waited for the music to fade completely.

Satisfied with the silence, he darted quickly along the side of the house and squirmed through a gap between two broken boards in a fence, then paused in the backyard, a tangled expanse of evergreens and spreading trees. He quickly followed an overgrown walkway to the back door.

The kitchen had been ransacked, its drawers and cabinets open. But John Thomas was elated; whoever had gone through this house had missed things. Already, he saw some cans in the dim recesses of an open cabinet. He boosted himself onto the counter, grabbed a shelf for balance, and removed five cans, one at a time, hesitating only briefly when he saw that they were dog food. Moving along on his knees, he went through all the cabinets, taking everything he could find. He giggled with delight when he opened a canister and found it full of spaghetti, the raw lengths packed together. John Thomas could hardly wait to surprise Lucas, who loved spaghetti.

When he was done, he stood at the counter gazing at his prizes. He'd gathered some things, such as baking soda and cornmeal, that were unfamiliar to him. His best finds were the spaghetti and a bag of sprouting potatoes.

A snuffling sounded behind him.

With a gasp, he whirled. A dog stood in the doorway, golden head lowered. Brown eyes, edged beneath by white crescents, gazed up at John Thomas, who froze. He had no experience with dogs. He risked a glance at the back door, then riveted his attention back on the dog, afraid it would lunge at him.

The dog moved forward one hesitant step, floppy ears pressed tightly back. Then another. Just as John Thomas braced himself to dash to the door, it slowly lay down and rolled to its side, head tucking in with a small whine. John Thomas relaxed when he saw the dog's tail, its tip quivering in tiny wags.

"Poor little puppy," he crooned as he approached it. His fear gone, he saw now how thin the dog was beneath its silky fur, even though its stomach was terribly distended. Tenderly, he touched the soft ears, the fluffy neck, and smiled as a warm tongue tentatively licked his hand. Something tugged his mind. The image, one of a golden dog being struck by a car, a dog similar to this one, faded before he could grasp it.

The memory it would have evoked, linked to Lucas before, sank back into its dark depths.

CHAPTER 13

"Look to your souls, sinners, look into your hearts and cast out the evil that is Satan's mark. He has poured his evil upon us. Six days ago, we all felt the fire of that evil as it filled our world and seared our souls. The Devil was recruiting, brothers and sisters, the battle has been joined. Armageddon is upon us. Join the army of the Lord. We must all choose the side of good, or evil will choose us. Now, let us pray . . ."

Fifteen of Reverend Perry's followers fell to their knees in the crowded studio, heads bowed. Fourteen of them prayed in fear, groping for the right words so God would know they were good, worthy, wholly at His disposal. The fifteenth prayed that the decrepit generator he'd set up for the reverend's broadcast wouldn't fail. The reverend's message had to get out.

If it didn't, and Armageddon swept across the nation, without all the good Christians out there knowing about it, it would be his fault. He clasped his hands with bruising force and prayed for the generator as he listened to the reverend's exhortations.

"Back off, man," Josiah thundered.

Startled, Eli jerked his head around the open hood of the truck. He'd never heard anger in Josiah's voice; violence loomed. Through the dusky evening light, he saw Josiah and Alex, facing off at the tailgate.

"What the hell's wrong with you, man?" Alex challenged. "All I said was maybe we should rethink this leaving shit."

Josiah turned away from Alex, shut the tailgate. "No one's forcing you to come," he said, his suddenly low tone more menacing than his shout.

Eli cleared his throat. "Alex, you heard the broadcast. California is a dead state; no power anytime soon." He shrugged. "No point in staying here."

Josiah walked angrily toward the garage. "Save your breath, Eli," he said. "The kid's been suckered by that preacher."

Alex, shoulders slumped in surrender, said, "Shit, Josiah." But Josiah was gone. Frustrated, Alex turned to Eli.

"It'll be okay," Eli reassured him.

"He hasn't even listened to the guy," Alex complained.

"How's he know the reverend's not right?"

"It doesn't matter," Eli said, sharply. "He decides for himself. You heard him; nobody's forcing you to come with us."

Eli couldn't help feeling sorry for Alex. The kid was confused, scared. Listening to Reverend Perry's diatribes about Armageddon, about the battle against evil, had triggered something in Alex. Everyone was looking for someone to tell them what had happened to the world. The preacher had managed to get on the air, and Alex stayed glued to the broadcasts. Station ATL, Preacher Perry called it. Army of the Lord.

Eli said, "If you think the preacher can get people organized and get stuff back on line, stay. But we're leaving in the morning." Eli felt the cold breeze stiffen in the growing dusk. He went to the garage, where Josiah was moving boxes so there'd be enough room to pull the truck in.

During the evening meal, Josiah behaved as if nothing had happened. Encouraged, Alex casually mentioned their upcoming trip. He offered to drive the second vehicle, a Cherokee Chief they'd found two days ago.

Josiah nodded. "Remember to watch the oil gauge."

A little later, Alex asked, "It's okay if I listen to Reverend Perry on the radio, isn't it?"

Eli looked at Josiah and rolled his eyes. The kid was a glutton for punishment.

Josiah set his plate aside. "You listen to people like Preacher Perry," he said to Alex, "and pretty soon you can just stop thinking for yourself."

Josiah thought of his mother's illiteracy and his own struggle to teach himself to read, to think clearly, to see the world for what it was and not for what he wished it to be. Part of Josiah's problem with Alex came from knowing that Alex was from a well-to-do family but dropped out of high school to experience "real life." The futility of that bad choice angered Josiah, knowing the "real life" he himself had experienced, on streets he hadn't chosen.

He had every intention of surviving in this new world and of helping Eli survive it, too. Alex? Alex could make his own bed.

CHAPTER 14

LOW CLOUDS FILTERED THE DAWN, CHILLING THE GRAY morning. Laura staggered down the stairs with another box and placed it on the curb near Kate. Breathing hard, she leaned against the Chevy she'd taken from a garage next door. Exhausted from all her trips up and down the stairs, she'd stopped wondering where the neighbors were. Still with dozens of trips to make, she grabbed a large sack of rice from the sidewalk.

"There's hardly room left for this," she grumbled to Kate, who hobbled closer and peered through a tinted window. The back of the Suburban was jammed. Even the floorboards were covered by an assortment of last-minute additions.

"Just toss it in," Kate said. "I'll find a spot."

As Laura heaved the sack through the door, Kate cried out, "That's him!"

Laura looked up the street in time to see a small figure

vanish from sight. "Who?" she said, but Kate was already hobbling up the hill as fast as her crutches would allow.

"Kate!" Laura called. Catherine stood at the open rear doors of the Suburban, shaking her head. Laura took the gun from her jacket pocket, gave it to Catherine, and ran after Kate.

"It's the kid I saw in the car," called Kate. "He's the reason I'm on these damn sticks."

"I know, but—"

"Hey, kid," Kate yelled. "Stop! You little shit."

"Kate! Watch it!" Laura jumped to the side, barely avoiding being smacked by a flailing crutch.

A block later, they rounded another corner just in time to see the boy disappear into a house up the street.

"Hah," Kate wheezed. "Gotcha."

As they neared the house, Laura said, "You're going to tell his parents? What's the point?"

"Laura, I've had nightmares about that kid. He can't be more than five, who knows what the hell else he's doing? He's out on the street all by himself." Kate was angry.

"Wait a minute." Laura put a hand on Kate's arm. They stared up at the shuttered windows. "What if his parents are dead? And he's there all alone—scared. It's been two weeks. If he's been alone . . ."

"All the more reason." Kate moved a crutch.

"Wait. We don't want to scare him more."

"We don't want him sneaking out the back, either. Come on." Kate put both crutches into one hand, grabbed the banister, and hobbled up. Laura followed her, ready if Kate stumbled. They reached the door. Kate rapped her knuckles on it, put her ear to the wood, and knocked again, louder.

Laura put her head close to the door. "I think I heard something," she whispered.

Kate nodded. She'd heard it, too, a distant, furtive sound.

"Wanna bet there's no adults in this house?" Kate put her hand on the doorknob and turned it. It was unlocked. They looked at each other, nodded, and Kate swung it open.

Laura followed Kate into a large foyer that fronted a wide, carpeted staircase. To their right was a high-ceilinged living room, to their left, a kitchen. She could see a chair and part of a table, the rest hidden by the doorway.

"Hello!" Kate called out. "Come out, come out, wherever you are. Olly, olly, oxen-free-oh." Then she whispered, "How about you check upstairs while I look down here?"

"Don't leave the door, he might bolt. Wait here while I see about a back door." Laura hurried away.

John Thomas barely breathed. Pressed into the farthest corner of the hall closet beneath the staircase, he listened as the two strangers discussed their strategy for finding Lucas. He wished he'd grabbed Lucas as soon as he'd dashed in the door, yelling that people were after him. Lucas had pounded upstairs, shouting "Hide! Hide!"

John Thomas had run up the stairs after Lucas, but as he neared the top he'd realized the front door was unlocked. Stifling his fear, he'd hurried back down. He'd almost reached the door when loud knocking had frozen him. Afraid to take his eyes from the door, he'd tiptoed backward, along the staircase, until he'd felt the knob of the closet door. Darting in, he'd shut the door and buried himself in the corner.

The children-eaters entered the house.

John Thomas's scalp prickled in terror. He'd been so careful these past weeks to keep them both safe. The dog, Reina, too. He hoped she'd stay quiet, not come scratching at the back door. He couldn't bear the thought of her being hurt.

Reina soothed something inside him, a jagged harshness he carried with him through the painful days, the constant worry over keeping her and Lucas safe and fed. He'd named her Reina because it meant "queen." At first, he'd worried about food for her, but, in many of the houses he looted, pet food was all that was left.

He wished Reina was with him now, pressed against him in the dark corner. And hoped that Lucas was well-hidden. His world had shrunk to himself, Lucas, and Reina. Now, even that tiny world had been violated by outsiders.

Children-eaters.

His heart thumped. Eyes squeezed shut, he hoped the bad people would go away.

The door swung open. He held his breath, too frightened to cry.

Kate nearly shut the door, but something caught her eye. A tiny movement of a shoe. Now she could see a child, partly obscured by a hanging garment.

"Come on out, kiddo. The jig is up." Kate reached in to press aside the overcoats.

A moan of terror came from John Thomas's small body. His heart felt ready to burst, and he was unaware of the warm urine soaking his pants. He felt nothing but paralyzing panic.

Kate caught her breath at the sound of his moan. This was no longer a game. She knelt, ignoring the pain in her foot.

"Hey, little guy, it's all right," she crooned gently. The child sobbed. "Come on, honey, come on out and let me help you. It's all right, honey, really it is."

John Thomas flung up his head, stunned. *Honey.* Such

a good word. Honey. That was him, he was Honey. An eternity of repressed tears flooded his eyes.

"Come on, honey, come on out." Kate held herself still, fighting the impulse to just reach in. The boy shifted onto his hands and knees and began crawling toward her. She saw his wild eyes shimmering with tears and a mixture of fear and hope. This was not the child she had faced through the windshield of the car. She placed gentle arms around him and drew him onto her lap.

Emotions gave way as he crawled into her lap. With sudden ferocious strength, he gripped her to him, his small fingers pinching her arms, his head pressed against her breast, his sobs shivering through her.

Kate laid her cheek against his soft hair. Tears burned her eyes as she rocked him.

Catherine, pistol in one hand, cane in the other, stood erect by the Suburban and watched their approach. Kate and Laura had not only two children in tow but a dog as well, and were laden with duffel bags and backpacks.

"This wasn't quite what I had in mind when I asked you to find a man or two."

Laura laughed. "What can I say, Catherine? They stole our hearts." Stepping close to Catherine's ear, she whispered, "Orphaned."

Catherine murmured, "And now shanghaied."

"Kate's doing, this time," Laura said, swinging a duffel bag into the back of the Chevy.

Kate grinned. "That's Lucas, and this is John." John Thomas tugged on her hand. She bent to his whisper. "Oh—sorry. This is John *Thomas*," she corrected. She had both crutches in one hand and John Thomas's hand in the other. Reina paced around them both, to the limits of her leash. Dropping the crutches, Kate began shrugging off the backpack stuffed with the boys' clothing and found that John Thomas would not release her hand. She was about to shake him free until she saw the panic in his eyes. "Come on, kiddo," she said, "let's help Laura pack this stuff into the car."

"Just leave the rice on the seat," Kate suggested to Laura, looking past her into the car. "Lucas can sit on it. The sack's soft enough and it'll boost him up to the window."

Catherine peered in at the tightly woven sack. "Cover it with plastic and a blanket," she said. "I prefer my rice without child flatulence."

Kate turned to Lucas. "Hear that, kiddo? Don't fart on the rice."

John Thomas giggled and pressed himself even closer to Kate. The added pressure put too much weight on her injured foot. "Ow, shit." She glanced at John Thomas and could have kicked herself. Sudden worry clouded his eyes and his chin quivered.

Kate dropped to one knee and gathered him to her. The child attached himself to everything she said. This wasn't going to be easy.

Hearing a car, Laura recognized Josiah's and Eli's truck coming around the corner below. A Cherokee Chief followed and, as the two vehicles parked behind the Suburban, she saw both were heavily loaded.

Greetings and introductions of Alex overlapped.

Laura glanced repeatedly at Alex. Something in his lanky awkwardness and shaggy hair reminded her of her younger brother, Conrad. She imagined poor Conrad, stuck in a foreign country, and wondered if she would ever see him again.

Then Josiah was beside her, smiling, his smoothly planed face capturing her attention. "A yen for your thoughts," he said.

She grinned, then the double meaning struck her. Was he flirting with her, or was she being stupid? She said, "Could you pay up if I told you?"

"Yup."

Laura laughed. "In yen?"

Grinning, he drew a coin from his pocket and held it out on his flat palm. She looked closer.

"I don't believe it," she said. "It really is a yen." She touched it and, in doing so, was abruptly aware of her fingers brushing his skin.

Kate called, "Time to hit the road, people."

Josiah and Eli took the lead, with the Suburban and then the Cherokee following behind. The route had been planned. North, over the partially cleared Golden Gate Bridge, along Highway 101 to Ukiah, then inland on Highway 20, avoiding the worst of the urban growth east of the city, nearly a solid sprawl from San Francisco to Sacramento. They would rejoin Highway 80 at some point past Sacramento, where they hoped to get more information.

It took them an hour to reach San Rafael, normally a fifteen-minute drive. Although a makeshift lane had been bulldozed through the debris, its path twisted through four lanes of dense destruction.

Driving slowly, Laura looked at Kate and the boys in her rearview mirror, crammed in among the supplies.

Despite their slow progress, Laura maintained a safe distance from the truck in front of them. She began worrying about their fuel supply, then realized her worries were groundless; the highways were littered with the tanks of crashed and abandoned cars.

She slammed on her brakes as a small black shape darted in front of the Chevy. "What was that?" she exclaimed.

"Who cares?" said Kate. "We got miles to go and we're only in San Rafael. Get on the mike and tell Eli he drives like an old woman."

"I believe it was a cat," Catherine said, sitting next to Laura. "Although it might have been a large rat."

"Cats an' rats an' elephants," Lucas sang loudly and tunelessly, then, straining forward against his seat belt, said, "Maybe it was a small elephant. There's lots of small elephants around here, I've seen 'em. Do you think it was a small elephant?"

John Thomas laughed. He sat between Lucas and Kate in the backseat, with Reina behind him, atop boxes in the crammed cargo area. As though John Thomas's laugh were a signal, she poked her muzzle at the back of his head and he reached a hand up to her.

"There aren't no elephants in America, Lucas, except for in zoos and circuses."

"Let's go to the zoo." Lucas bounced with excitement.

"My God," said Laura, "the zoo. Those poor animals."

"I must confess, I hadn't had a thought for them, myself," Catherine sniffed.

"Maybe someone put them out of their misery," Kate offered. Noticing John Thomas's sudden deflation, she nudged him. "Hey, cheer up, honey, we got Reina, don't we? Good rescue job, by the way. She's one fat, happy dog."

"She's not fat, she's pregnant," Laura said.

The sad fate of zoo animals overshadowed, John Thomas squealed. "Puppies? Cool."

Kate rolled her eyes. "Cool, huh? Just wait 'til you have to take care of them."

"How many do you think she'll have, Katie?" John

Thomas squirmed with excitement and looked at Reina with glowing eyes.

Laura smiled and wondered if he'd be as excited to hear about her own pregnancy. She hadn't said anything yet to anyone about her baby. But she worried about such things as finding a hospital when her time came. Or even a doctor. She remembered well the chaotic scene at the hospital. Would things be back to normal by the time her baby was born?

For the first time since the blackout had changed her entire outlook, she remembered that she'd been planning to abort, because she'd wanted Mack, and a baby would have complicated things. She could not now imagine trading this baby for anything. She could barely remember what had made her so willing to do just about anything for Mack.

Thank God he was on another continent, she thought. He probably wouldn't have stayed with her anyhow. The baby was hers. Hers.

PART II

CHAPTER 15

THE BLEAK DESPAIR THAT STRUCK EVERYONE ON THE third day following the blackout had destroyed many people, and changed many others.

Mack Silby had changed. Forever.

The sucking darkness had filled his mind, extinguished every thought, obscured every emotion, and then formed a funnel through which everything that was him fled, screaming. When he was emptied, a whisper, soft and cool as silk, slid the last of his empathy from him. Then the darkness dissipated, was gone. And so was Mack.

He sat up and wondered what had happened. First, he noticed his headache was gone. Second, he realized the crowded Munich airport, moments ago stricken silent, was now noisy with the voices of hundreds of people speaking dozens of languages, thankful for their miraculous release from black despair. The murmur grew to a clamor.

Annoyed, he shifted in the plastic chair. People. A woman bumped his legs and he glared at her. Stubble on his chin itched and his annoyance grew. He needed a shave. Jumping to his feet, he looked for a restroom.

For three days, travelers had been jamming the airport, desperate to get home. The airport was packed with people awaiting flights, as exhausted personnel used the one runway left operative after the blackout. There'd been horrific collisions directly overhead as well as on the runways when the blackout hit, and debris from the explosions and crashes still littered all but one runway.

Mack cursed when he couldn't see a restroom sign.

A bubble of pure rage rose in him, exploded, and flooded him with fury that coursed through him. In the first instant, he felt a vague suggestion of pain, but that was quickly subsumed in something vast, on the very edge of fear. Then, with a tumbling drop in the pit of his stomach, he exploded past all known sensation. Nerve-endings buzzed.

He was heat, ice, raw power. His eyes glittered. His nostrils flared like an animal smelling blood.

Twelve-year-old Mohammed Al-Kujbahan was barely aware of Mack standing next to him. He sat, hunched over by the terrifying desolation from which he'd just emerged. He prayed over and over. *Praise Allah, the One and Only God, Allah is His name.* Allah had saved him from the darkness. He had pulled His miserable servant into the light.

He looked up and saw Mack's icy eyes staring down at him.

"Mack?" he ventured, uncertainly. Why was Mack looking at him like that? Then someone bumped into Mack, hard enough to make him almost lose his balance. A snarl of rage twisted Mack's face. He grabbed the stranger, fingers digging into his arms like talons.

Panic in his eyes, the paunchy, middle-aged man froze in Mack's grip.

Mack's rage had no plan or thought. Violent images filled his mind.

"Sorry, sorry," the man stammered. "I didn't mean to, I—someone pushed, I—"

Aware of others turning toward them in curiosity and apprehension, Mack pushed his fury down and fought for composure. He smiled.

"No problem," he said, and released the man. Glancing at the onlookers, he shrugged.

Mack was still irritated. *Stupid people,* he thought. First they're scared there'll be a fight, then they're disappointed when there isn't. Maybe he should pick a fight, scare the shit out of them. His restlessness grew to an itch. He knew it had something to do with the new feelings that wanted out. Controlling them wasn't easy. Harder yet, keeping a grasp on the fact that he should.

Disoriented by this new balancing act he felt

somehow bound to perform, he glanced around for distraction. He spotted a young man slouched against a pillar. He'd noticed him before. What was it about him? Something familiar.

Mack wove through the crowd, toward the slouched figure. The young man looked up, looked right at him. *Goddamn. Looks just like her,* thought Mack. Laura's younger brother, whom she'd often mentioned, whose photograph sat on Laura's dresser. They had the same honey-tinted hair, brown eyes, red cheeks.

Hiding his surprise, Mack struck up a conversation with the young man. An expert at small talk, at conjuring a veil of camaraderie, within minutes Mack had Conrad at ease.

"Name's Mack," he said, inviting Conrad to follow him to where Mohammed was saving his seat.

"Conrad Morgan," said Conrad.

It was impossible to move through the crowd without being jostled. Mack felt a new surge tightening his stomach, heating his limbs, but he managed to stem the eruption.

It felt dangerous. And exciting.

Whatever *it* was begged to be savored. Predatory impulses swirled through him. He was thinking, feeling differently. And he liked it.

Conrad asked if Mack had heard anything about the next flight to the States. He'd been waiting in the airport for two days, he said, and had heard nothing but rumors.

Mack ran a hand over his stubble. "Shouldn't be too much longer. Be glad you weren't in India when it hit, or Tunisia, like me." He yanked open the zipper of his duffel, found his shaving kit.

"I'll be back," said Mack. "Keep an eye on my stuff, would you?"

Conrad was extremely tired. For the past three days, he'd been snatching sleep as he could. He dozed in Mack's chair.

And startled awake when his arm was joggled. Turning to the squirming figure next to him, he saw a skinny, dark boy with large brown, thickly lashed eyes who grinned and bobbed his head. The turban he wore fascinated Conrad.

"Hello, hello," the boy said in clipped syllables.

"Hi. What's your name?"

"Mohammed. I em called Mohammed."

"Where's your folks, Mohammed?" asked Conrad. "This group's headed for New York. You sure you're in the right place?"

Mohammed tilted his head. "Please?" he said. He pecked his lips with tucked fingertips, "Slow, hah?"

Conrad gestured toward the crowd. "We," he said, speaking slowly, "are going in an airplane." He flattened his hand and flew it over Mohammed's head. "To America."

Mohammed brightened at the last word. "Yes,"

he said excitedly, prodding a thumb into his chest. "America. I go. I go America, yes."

"Hey, Ali Baba, you hungry?" Mack asked, appearing before them. He spoke a few guttural words and Mohammed scampered off through the crowd. Food was being rationed by tired personnel and the queues were long. Mack sat in the vacated chair.

"He's with you?" Conrad inquired.

Mack's ice-blue eyes shone in his freshly shaven, tanned face. "Yup. Like I said, I was in Tunisia when this thing hit, at the edge of the desert. Ali Baba was one of the camel boys. His sister was trampled by the herd and I never found out how his mother died. His uncle was head of the family, but he disappeared.

"I had a hell of a time getting out of there and it'd have taken me a lot longer if it wasn't for Ali Baba."

Conrad barely listened, his thoughts on getting home. "What do you suppose we'll find back in the States?"

Mack shrugged. "More of the same. Where you headed?"

"California."

Mack squinted at Conrad. It was like looking at Laura.

She should have come with him, like he'd asked. She couldn't leave her job, she'd said. He'd let it slide, but now, thinking of her refusal angered him.

Conrad stared back at Mack, his strange eyes.

"Tell you what, Conrad," Mack said, abruptly. "We

get to Kennedy, and it doesn't look good, I'll get you to California."

"How?"

"I fly small craft," Mack said, his smile hiding his thoughts. He couldn't remember why he'd wanted Laura to come with him, only that she'd refused. Conrad looked like Laura, was related to Laura, but knew nothing of Mack's relationship with her. He was intrigued by that. He couldn't make a useful connection, yet. But he would.

And then he'd use it.

Two days later, Conrad and Mohammed sat in a commuter airport in upstate New York, guarding Mack's three suitcases while Mack conferred with an old man in overalls. The small airport was virtually deserted, nothing like the chaotic mess their commercial flight from Munich had landed them in at Kennedy Airport.

Conrad glanced at Mack and saw him press something into the old man's hand. The man nodded. Mack walked back to them.

"Let's go," Mack said, lifting a suitcase.

Conrad grabbed another suitcase, leaving the third for Mohammed. "Did you buy it?" he asked.

"I sure as hell didn't rent it."

The three went out the swinging door into an unseasonably warm fall day. The sky was hazed by smoke from forest fires, as it had been throughout their entire tortuous drive upstate over demolished roads.

The plane was fueled and ready. As Conrad buckled himself into the copilot's seat, he saw the old man give a halfhearted salute and limp back to the terminal.

Conrad had never experienced a small plane. He tried to fathom the dials and gauges.

Mack started the plane and Conrad felt his first doubt. "It sounds like a Volkswagen," he commented. "Is this thing all right to fly?"

Mack maneuvered the plane onto the runway. "That's how they sound."

The small cabin filled with noise. The engine backfired and Conrad gripped his armrests with clammy hands. "Maybe this one needs a tune-up, or something," he said nervously.

As Mack accelerated down the runway, the gray strip blurred beneath the nose of the plane. Conrad was certain the tiny, shuddering aircraft wouldn't leave the ground but would, instead, rattle apart into a million pieces. He squeezed his eyes shut, felt a terrifying lurch, and they were in the air, in a steep climb.

Banking a wide turn, Mack settled into a cruising speed, scanning the sky for other aircraft. Flying was second nature to him, but now he couldn't remember why he'd liked it. He shrugged it off. Who cared what he used to like? None of it had ever felt as good as those moments at the Munich airport.

That hot exquisite ice.

The panic in that man's eyes when he'd grabbed him: *It's the fear I want,* he realized. It tugged at that new feeling, and he wanted more than anything to feel that again. He bared his teeth, not realizing it wasn't a smile anymore.

Conrad took several deep breaths. Looking at the countryside far below, he saw plumes of smoke, roads dotted with smashed vehicles. He wished he felt safer.

"What's our first stop?" he asked. He didn't see the hot look Mack shot him.

"I don't know," Mack said. "Depends on a lot of things: runways, the amount of fuel we burn. We need to land somewhere we can refuel."

Conrad looked at Mack's tanned profile, his muscular hands on the controls. What did he really know about Mack? That he dressed in a bush outfit. That he'd been in Tunisia during the blackout. That he had three suitcases he refused to leave behind.

Conrad had no experience with unknowns like Mack. All his life, he'd known everyone around him, most of them ranchers like his parents. His friendly, cheerful personality had caused everyone to like him.

He assumed Mack liked him, too.

He swiveled around and looked at Mohammed. The boy's presence said something good about Mack: he hadn't abandoned the orphan.

"Hey, Ali, whatcha think? Pretty cool, huh?" Conrad pointed out the window.

Mohammed grinned and nodded. "Cool, Conrad." He wasn't sure what "cool" meant, but Conrad said it, so it must be good. Conrad was good. Mack had become frightening.

Mohammed's attention was on the gentle curve of the horizon that he intuitively understood; the earth was a giant orb. As they flew over a small town, he strained to see people, but the ground was too distant. No matter, he thought, enjoying the spread of forests and farmland. *All of it, all of it is us.*

He wished he had the English for his new understanding. Had Conrad and Mack forgotten, like everyone he'd questioned back home had?

And now, there was this new, more recent knowledge. Did anyone else know that the terrible darkness that struck everyone two days ago still yawned before them all, just on the other side of life? That the insurmountable void barred them from rejoining their source?

Mohammed shivered. Surely Allah would fix it. Or maybe He would leave it up to them to find their own way.

Mohammed knew he had to stay alive until the way was fixed, knew he would be forever lost if he fell into that void. He wondered sadly about his little sister, Aida. Had she made it across before the cold blackness swept in?

CHAPTER 16

MACK LANDED ON THE OUTSKIRTS OF KANSAS CITY, Missouri, at a private airstrip. He'd flown low above the runway several times to determine its safety before landing. When he cut the engine, the small cabin throbbed with silence.

Jumping to the ground, Conrad stamped his feet to get his land-legs back and laughed at Mohammed, who was imitating his every move. Mack ignored them as he locked the plane and looked around. The light was fading. Across from the field was a farm, composed of a house, a barn, and several outbuildings, corrals, and fenced yards. At least four vehicles were parked between the house and barn, and the place appeared deserted; no lights, no smoke from the chimneys, no movement. He set off briskly.

Conrad and Mohammed hurried after Mack. They were going to get a car, Mack had said, and go to town for food. As they crossed the field, the aroma of the soil reminded Conrad of home.

By the time they reached the dirt road leading to the farmhouse, dusk had deepened to darkness. They approached the farmhouse and stopped in the front yard, a mere widening of the driveway.

"Looks empty to me," Conrad said.

The bare windows gave the house a desolate look, a stark collection of cold, empty rooms.

Mack moved to one of the cars parked alongside a decrepit fence. Removing a pencil-flashlight from his shirt pocket, he opened the door of the large, dusty vehicle and inspected the dash and ignition. He ducked back out and shut the door. "No keys," he said as he moved to an old truck parked in front of the car.

In the darkness, Conrad followed the narrow beam of light. "Keys? I thought you were going to hotwire it."

Mohammed plucked at his sleeve. "Conrad," he said. "Haht-wire?"

"Not now, Ali, it's too hard to explain."

"Way cool."

"None here, either," Mack said. "Why go through the trouble of hotwiring when we're likely to find keys?" He walked toward the huge, weathered barn, and the two cars parked before it.

The entrance to the barn was darker than the night. Edging around the cars, Conrad peered into the cavernous gloom. He sniffed the musty odor of old hay and motor oil.

"Maybe there's something in here, Mack." The barn seemed to swallow his voice. Something rustled faintly in its depths before black darts flew over their heads. Conrad pinned himself against the wall.

"Aieeee," Mohammed screeched. He curled into a ball on the ground. Mack nudged him with his boot and he exploded to his feet with a cry.

Mack laughed. "Lighten up, Ali Baba," he said. "It's only bats."

"Some country boy you are," Mack said to Conrad.

"I hate bats," Conrad said. "And what makes you think I'm from the country?" How could Mack know that?

Ignoring the question, Mack walked back toward the house. They hurried after him.

Conrad held the screen door as Mack pushed the back door open and flashed his light into a small mudroom. An inner door stood ajar and they saw the linoleum flooring in the room beyond. A greasy pile of rags lay just inside the second doorway and the sharp smell of gasoline filled the air.

"Hello," Mack called into the house. They listened to the silence. He stepped into the mudroom and inspected the wall just inside the door, shining the light in quick sweeps. "Bingo."

He flipped a switch and Conrad blinked in the sudden light.

"Double bingo," Mack said, reaching higher up on the wall. He removed a set of keys from a hook then stepped back out, knocking the screen door all the way back against the house, where he latched it with a dangling hook. "Whew. Those rags are potent. Don't light a match, whatever you do. See if you can find any more keys while I check these out." He trotted down the steps.

"Come on, Ali," said Conrad, and the two of them entered the house. Conrad stretched his hand around the second doorframe, seeking another switch. Mohammed stepped past him. They were both in the kitchen when he flipped on the lights.

Conrad froze, hit by sickening odors mixed with the smell of gasoline. Outlined by the glaring overhead light, a woman stood five feet from them, fair hair matted around her face, eyes open so wide that her dark irises were ringed by white. She was shapeless beneath the stained blue shift she wore. Doughy arms braced a shotgun in front of her ample chest, its barrels aimed at them.

She whispered harshly, "Come in, duckies, come in and sit down," and smiled crookedly. Waving the gun in short circles, she motioned them to the table behind her. As she stepped aside, Conrad saw two seated corpses, portions of their faces replaced by glistening red tissue mingled with crushed bone and edged by ragged flesh. He moaned, not hearing Mohammed's terror beside him. His eyes darted back to the woman.

She stared greedily at him, nodding her head, her mouth open as she breathed loudly with excitement and rasped, "Dinner guests, ducky, dinner guests. Join them, join them, the more the merrier. Mom always said the more the merrier. Didn't ya, Mom?" She grinned at the corpses, then swung her gaze quickly back to Conrad. "Mom loved to cook. But there's no more to cook, no more roasts, no more chickens, no more pork chops. No more duckies, ducky." She screeched a laugh, then jerked a hand to her mouth as she turned her head toward the yard.

She knows Mack's out there, Conrad thought, as terror overwhelmed him. Fear weakened his legs. From outside came the wheezing of an engine, with the slow rhythm of a low battery. Conrad saw the woman's eyes lose focus as she tilted her head toward the sound.

Conrad couldn't keep his eyes from the ghastly, mutilated forms at the Formica table. Insanity. The woman had shot her own parents, then propped them at the dinner table.

Outside, the engine made another slow turn, then caught, coughing and popping. *Please come inside, please, Mack.* The engine sound changed. Conrad refused to accept what he heard. The car was moving around the house, to the driveway, to the road. *NO!*

He heard a chuckle as the rumble of the car diminished.

His vision narrowed with fear. For a moment, the crazed woman appeared two-dimensional, a cutout under the harsh overhead light. He watched the glinting barrels of her shotgun.

"Well, well," the woman said, loudly. No more raspy whisper, now. The anger in her voice threatened as much as the twin-barrels. "In this house we don't have to be asked twice to sit down to a meal. SIT!" She gestured with the gun. "Your friend out there didn't have no manners. In this house, that would have earned him a missed meal." She snorted laughter. She backed to the sink, her expression sly as she waved them to the table.

A hand clutched Conrad's arm, and he yelped in terror at the unexpected touch. That sent the woman into gales of demented laughter. He looked down at Mohammed's horrified face.

The woman's laughter stopped, and she indicated with the gun for him to be seated.

He moved on shaky legs, but Mohammed again grabbed him, trying to stop him from approaching the atrocities at the bloodied table and was pulled forward with him.

Mohammed cried out and let go.

Abruptly released, Conrad stumbled against the table, the mutilated faces of the dead suddenly on level with his own. Bile seared his throat.

Straightening up, he stared at the woman, who stood at the counter. She was looking past him at Mohammed. "You too," she said to the boy.

Conrad opened his mouth. "He doesn't speak

English." His voice cracked.

"He's a foreigner?" she shrieked. "You brought a damn foreigner to my table?" Her white-ringed eyes glared at Conrad, then shifted to Mohammed. "Course he is just a boy," she remarked, almost to herself, in a voice gone freakishly gentle. "A pretty boy, too, ain't he? Why's he got that rag on his head? Is he hurt?" Her voice shifted again, crooning to Mohammed. "Come on, sugar-sweets, come to Auntie Dilly, come along now, sugar-doodle."

Cradling the gun, she moved slowly around the table. Three feet separated her from Conrad, and he held his breath. Her lips pouted, crooning endearments of insane tenderness to Mohammed.

Horrified, Mohammed stumbled backward and was now closer to the darkened interior of the house than he was to the back door.

She took two more steps toward him, wheedling, "Here sugar, sugar," in a kitten-calling voice.

Mohammed lurched toward the dark doorway. Her shot was deafening percussion as she blasted the doorway. Certain the next shot would rip through him, Mohammed stopped, anchored in terror.

Conrad's ears rang so loudly that he hardly heard the second crack. The woman's face transformed to a red smear. Her cranial contents were flung against the wall and over the counter. Her body fell onto Conrad as he frantically backpedaled. She slid to the floor, smearing blood and bits of flesh down his shirt and jeans.

Mohammed wailed but Conrad couldn't take his eyes off the newest corpse, backing away until he was against the wall. Movement at the doorway speared his attention: Mack, a black pistol in his hand, lowering it to his side.

Ears roaring, he moved toward Mack on wobbly legs. Mohammed's lips moved, but the sound was muffled, distant.

Mack's head jerked to the side.

Dazed, Conrad followed Mack's line of sight toward the inner doorway, aware of Mack's gun swinging upward. A small blond child barely registered in his mind when he heard Mack's gun go off again. The child flew back, chest exploding, as it landed somewhere in the dark room beyond.

Conrad turned away, lurched past Mack, ran through the mudroom and down the worn wooden steps. He reached an old fence, and held onto the splintered wood. Further thoughts simply would not come.

They raced down the dark, empty highway in a twenty-year-old Buick with worn suspension. An occasional snuffling came from the backseat where

Mohammed sat curled. Mack drove casually, wrist over the wheel as he explained how he'd rigged the steering and accelerator of the other car and sent it off down the road while he'd crept back around the house. Conrad listened and stared into the night, unutterably grateful to be alive.

Mack was ebullient. Conrad didn't interrupt. He was safe, hurtling through the night, miles away from horror. He pushed aside an image of the child in the doorway, chest exploding when Mack fired. Mack hadn't said anything about that killing, and Conrad didn't bring it up. Was it the crazy lady's child? They'd never know. Mack heard a noise and shot, Conrad reasoned. He couldn't have known it was a child.

Mohammed huddled in the backseat, wiping his runny nose on one sleeve. They'd gone back to the plane to change clothes before going to town. His clothes hadn't been soiled like Conrad's, but they'd reeked of that awful room. Mack had put his suitcases in the trunk of the car while he and Conrad were changing. Mohammed wished now he hadn't left his turban behind to air out. He'd never felt so alone in his life and longed for its comforting familiarity. He glared with aching eyes at the two men in the front seat. Conrad had betrayed him and Mack was evil.

Conrad had forsaken him in that butcher's lair and would have done nothing, *nothing* to stop that she-devil from attacking him. He remembered the fear he'd felt when the woman had come at him and Conrad had let her. He could have jumped on her when she had her back to him. Conrad's betrayal was so complete that Mohammed could not imagine what had led him to expect more.

Mack was even worse. Mohammed envisioned Mack's face when he'd shot the second time. The delight, the satisfaction in his eyes! Mohammed hadn't known at first whom the second bullet had pierced. He'd watched Mack raise his gun and pull the trigger. Turning, he'd seen the destroyed child. And when he'd looked back at Mack, he'd seen no remorse, only joy. Mack had known he'd killed a child, and it had made no difference. The joy of killing was all that mattered. Revulsion shuddered through Mohammed.

He thought about the last two weeks of travel, first just with Mack and then with the addition of Conrad. He'd gladly left Tunisia with Mack. His mother and sister were dead, his uncle vanished, the country in chaos. His new understanding of interconnectedness had buoyed him. All earth was his home, and whomever he met was his brother or sister. He had let himself feel, for the first time in his arduous life, like a child; carefree, dependent. But no more. His two-week childhood was over. And of what use was the knowledge that had freed him if people still turned their faces from Allah, she-devils lurked in darkness, and men like Mack and Conrad ignored the teachings of the prophet?

Except for the words of the prophet, Mohammed was alone.

They ate in a bar on the edge of town. It was crowded, noisy with laughter, a contrived pre-blackout oasis.

They took a booth, and Mack insisted on drinks before they ordered dinner. The waitress brought a pitcher of beer, two frosted glasses, and an Irish coffee, which Mack indicated she should set before Mohammed. The waitress hesitated, then shrugged and placed the coffee drink before the boy.

Conrad's sip of beer turned into gulps, and he emptied his glass before setting it down. Quickly, his legs grew heavy, and he found himself feeling light and happier. A jukebox blared country music. *This is how things should be.* Enveloped in familiarity, he thrust away recent terrors. He refilled his glass and topped Mack's.

Mack's eyes glittered as he drank, and he enjoyed the memory of the woman's face exploding. His fingers twitched around his glass. He saw again the child's blasted body flying backward into darkness.

Mohammed sat next to Conrad, his thin hands wrapped around the hot mug of whiskey-blended coffee.

A smear of cream lined his upper lip.

"Isn't liquor against his religion?" Conrad asked.

Mack shrugged. "So what?"

"So maybe he doesn't know it's in there."

"So what?" Mack refilled both their glasses. "You think we're corrupting him?" He smirked. "What is corruption, really?"

Conrad thought. "Making something good turn bad, I guess."

"And how is a little whiskey going to turn that boy bad?" Mack's light eyes shimmered. "There are too many rules. Maybe rules are okay for certain people, or for certain times. Don't swear, don't fuck, don't kill—but there's a time for all those things."

Conrad jerked at a memory of the madwoman, her shotgun, her pulped head falling toward him. He gulped his beer.

"Sometimes, killing's good, Conrad."

Aware of noise and music and color around him, Conrad knew he wouldn't be here if Mack hadn't shot the woman. He raised his glass. "Maybe you're right," he said.

As Mack gave the waitress an order for three steak dinners, Conrad turned to Mohammed. His head was bent over the coffee mug. "Hey, Ali," he said, nudging the boy, "how you doing?"

Mohammed shifted away, his eyes flat and unsmiling. He didn't care to understand whatever Conrad had said to him.

Conrad had grown fond of the boy shadowing him. Now, not only was Ali ignoring him, he was almost falling off the edge of the booth to avoid even touching him. Conrad put his hand on Mohammed's shoulder. "Hey, Ali, are you okay?"

Mohammed dipped his shoulder from beneath the hand. "Way cool," he said, flatly.

Conrad looked into Mohammed's face and realized, *Of course. The kid went through the same hell I did, no wonder he's acting goofy.* He was just a kid, what a nightmare that must have been for him.

Wanting to show his concern, Conrad tapped Mohammed's mug. "You want more coffee, Ali?"

Mohammed nodded, not looking up, so Conrad added it to the order.

Mack squinted speculatively at Mohammed. He didn't like this new, sullen attitude. Maybe he ought to just smack the look off his face.

Mohammed's face reminded him of their difficulty leaving his hot, chaotic country. Everywhere, frantic people had impeded their path. Mohammed's uncle, whose broken English had been sufficient to act as translator, had vanished, and Mack had found himself stranded, surrounded by tides of people who hadn't the slightest interest in him. During those first hours, Mohammed had attached himself to Mack, and as the gravity of being trapped in a foreign culture whose ranks had closed against him became clear, he'd found himself relying heavily on the boy. He remembered feeling—grateful?

Mack drained the last of his beer, looking over the rim of his glass at Mohammed's bent head. Grateful? He couldn't remember what gratitude felt like, only that it had caused him to keep Mohammed with him. He was realizing that he couldn't remember any of the feelings he'd had, though memories of the passing days remained intact.

Truth? He'd needed to get the hell out of there, and that dirty little Arab had only made it a little easier. *I didn't need the little shit then and I don't need him now. I don't need anybody.*

Except to kill.

The thought electrified him, surged icy heat through his veins. This was what he was all about. His fingertips tingled with power.

His eyes darted between Conrad and Mohammed. What a game he could play in the coming days. And they'd never know it. Maybe he should drop hints, see which one of them caught on first. He grinned when he saw Mohammed's eyes, flat and emotionless, turn to him.

Mack winked, not caring that Mohammed remained

impassive. No matter. Only *he* mattered, he and this delicious new thing that coursed through him.

One old thought came to mind. *When did this happen?*

He let it go.

CHAPTER 17

MONTH 2

ALONE IN THE PRODUCTION BOOTH, PHIL WINSLOW spliced the tape. The discarded segments held a great deal of excellent footage, he thought, regretfully. The whole damn thing was great. Before the blackout, it would have been pure gold. But the bosses had new guidelines for gold, and Phil wasn't about to blow his recent promotion. Hell, he'd just skyrocketed to the fucking top.

He squelched an impulse to add ten seconds of a major shoot-out at the docks. "People need reassurance, stability," the bosses instructed. "They see enough death right outside their doors. We've got to offer them a place to escape."

Bernie Campbell nicked his attention with a wave from the studio floor.

Phil held up five fingers, then a thumbs-up. Campbell nodded, turned away, and Phil watched him join Carol. Together, they bent their heads over her clipboard. Campbell put his hand on her shoulder.

Phil's lip curled. Campbell was such an ass, throwing his weight around. Before the blackout, he'd been weekend sports anchor. And he now controlled more airtime than Anderson Cooper once had.

Phil knew exactly what he wanted to isolate in the next few minutes. Almost time to go on the air, and it'd be his responsibility if they didn't make it. By some freak of luck, he'd been in the right place at the right time. The ground floor, going up.

Just follow orders, minimize graphic violence and death. But still broadcast news. Piece of cake . . . or tape.

The studio was busy, nothing like those first days after the blackout when it was only him, and Carol, and James Walsh. People had trickled back in, some to find their old jobs waiting, others unsure of what lay in store. On the sixth day, James Walsh had wandered out and never returned. Phil missed him a little. Sure, he hadn't been the same as before, but he'd still been Walsh. Not stupid-ass Bernie Campbell.

Finding the bit he wanted, he cued it, checked the clock. One last time to review the bite: a middle-aged woman wearing a gaudy dress and beaded shawl, gold hoops dangling from her ears. The bite caught her mid-sentence.

". . . they are *Shaitan*. *Shaitan*. First the blackout filled our world, now the Darkness is upon us, and the Darkness has spawned the *Shaitan*." Her piercing, mad eyes glared directly into the camera. "Fools who call themselves 'experts' say the *Shaitan* are just people who were driven mad by the second blackout. They're wrong. The *Shaitan* are *evil.* Evil, evil, evil."

It was pure poetry, possibly the signature sound bite of the decade, destined to be rebroadcast on every major station for weeks to come. And it was *his.*

"How long will it take us to get there?" Kate asked from the backseat. Donner Pass was covered in snow and Laura was driving carefully. A lone snowplow had recently cleared one of the eastbound lanes, but snow was already reclaiming the road.

"I'm not sure how far it is," Laura said.

They'd left San Francisco two weeks ago and had spent the past three days in an abandoned cabin, where they'd taken refuge from a blizzard. This morning they'd resumed their journey across the Sierras. The plan was to reach Reno before nightfall, but it was dusk and they still weren't through the pass.

Laura's hands tightened on the wheel, trying to avoid being mesmerized by oncoming snowflakes in the tunneling headlights. She focused grimly on the taillights of the Cherokee as it disappeared around a curve. Eli's and Josiah's truck was even farther ahead.

"What if Reno's deserted?" said Kate.

"It is not deserted," Catherine said firmly. She sat in the front passenger seat, hands folded in her lap. "The snowplows are evidence of that. Many people fleeing California will have found this to be the best route out of the state and Reno will be a place everyone will gather."

"You think that the one preaching station we got at the cabin is all there is? I hope Reno has some stations that are playing music and news."

"I'm sure we'll hear plenty of news in Reno," Laura interjected, in no mood to hear another of Kate's rants about preachers. "Maybe things are back to normal."

Catherine sniffed. "Things couldn't possibly be back to normal."

"Look!" John Thomas cried, his face pressed to the window. They'd rounded a curve, the truck and Cherokee already headed downhill. In the distance, the glow of Reno reflected off low clouds.

"They have electricity," exclaimed Kate. "Hot water. Showers!" She grabbed John Thomas's hand. "You ready for some fun, honey? What say you and me paint the town?"

"Yellow." John Thomas laughed, delighted. He'd never even painted a house, much less a whole town. He could imagine himself and Kate dashing down streets with buckets of paint and dripping brushes. He leaned past Kate toward his brother. "You wanna, Lucas, huh? That'd be fun, huh?"

Lucas looked back solemnly. It sounded like a lot of work. "No. You paint, John Thomas. I wanna do video games."

Laura glanced in the rearview mirror. Kate was looking out the side window, acting as if she hadn't even heard Lucas.

"I bet there's lots of video games, Lucas," Laura said. Kate's coldness toward Lucas puzzled her and she tried to pinpoint its origin. Lately, Kate barely acknowledged Lucas, lavishing all her attention on John Thomas. Laura felt sorry for Lucas and annoyed at Kate for her obvious favoritism.

Lucas, however, was not bothered at all.

He was as oblivious to Laura's thoughtfulness as he was to Kate's indifference. In Lucas's world, there was only himself and John Thomas, and between them stretched a dark, bonding conduit. John Thomas needed it for familial security; Lucas used it as a conduit for control. He was learning to bend John Thomas to his will, though John Thomas made that easy. Lucas didn't know how to manipulate the grown-ups yet, so he tried to avoid them. He modeled his behavior toward them by mimicking John Thomas.

He'd known about smiling. But he was learning that other tools seemed to be as important, like hugging, and tears. John Thomas was effective with those.

Step by arduous step, Lucas taught himself to socialize.

Unaware of his complete lack of empathy, without the ability to decipher others' emotional cues, he was unable to extrapolate one situation from another and had to learn the response to each situation by rote.

He was only five. It wasn't easy.

Reno was jammed. Burdened by an early winter, geographically isolated from other cities, it was physically linked to some of the world by tenuous wreck-strewn highways, and electronically linked by unpredictable television, radio, telephone, and Internet. From these sources came news of devastation, reconstruction, disease, and wars, national interests and decisions, presidential speeches, chat-show cacophony, and mostly inaccurate weather reports.

The world was in turmoil, its future uncertain. From their lonely outpost, Reno's residents and visitors watched and waited. Opinions became arguments. Prophets, preachers, and professors were on every corner, to give insight or to incite. The massive convention centers held twenty-four hour rallies, and casinos bulged with milling throngs, exhausted by it all. Many people carried weapons openly.

The population rose and fell with the weather. In clear weather, refugees poured in, from upper and lower regions, or over the western passes. And those who'd tired of the harsh climate and surreal frenzy fled south to escape. Their places were quickly filled.

Despite tensions of the drive, Laura's excitement grew as they neared the spill of lights that defined downtown Reno. She followed the truck and Cherokee along the freeway off-ramp and into the city, rolling slowly along noisy, crowded South Virginia Street.

After weeks of relative isolation, the tumult and glitter were both fascinating and nerve-wracking. Kate and Laura exchanged amazements and the boys squealed their excitement, but Catherine remained silent, missing nothing.

"Can you believe that?" Kate exclaimed. A banner that covered a three-story casino sign read "Play 'N Pray."

Leaving the downtown, their caravan explored neighborhoods until they found an abandoned house with a large two-car garage not far from the university campus. There they parked the truck and Cherokee in the garage, unloaded the Suburban, and locked everything up.

Everyone was eager to hear the latest news, to eat a meal that wasn't from their own supplies, and to collapse into beds they didn't have to make. Crammed into the Suburban, they returned to the heart of the city.

"The town has a primitive feeling about it," warned Catherine. "Be wary of those to whom you speak." By this time, they had learned to trust Catherine's sophisticated instincts, honed by years of world travel with her late husband.

"When the weather clears," she added, "we should move to a smaller community, where we can be more certain of our security."

As a convenience, not to mention luxury, they pulled into the gigantic parking facilities of the Peppermill, went inside the recently enlarged hotel/casino, and asked for a suite where they could rest and where Reina, their now-constant companion, could stay.

"Six hundred dollars," the gruff man with a shaved head at the front desk said. "Cash," he added emphatically.

"Jesus, that's highway robbery," said Eli.

"Take it or leave it," replied the thug-clerk, retracting the registration card.

They took it, then went to dinner at the buffet restaurant in the hotel. Food seemed plentiful, but Catherine noted the lack of fresh fruits and vegetables, and again commended Laura for the cache of vegetable seeds she'd brought home weeks ago.

"They will prove to be our salvation," she said as she cut a dainty piece of liver.

Josiah jammed steak in his mouth and grinned at Catherine. "You just can't wait to see us plowing the fields, can you?"

"With mules, too," Eli added. "No tractors for us."

"Of course," Josiah said. "The more primitive, the better."

Laura laughed. Catherine and Josiah had verbally sparred before, mostly about humanity's primitive inclinations. Catherine insisted that humans were nothing more than cavemen with remote controls, while Josiah held that intellect trumped primitive impulses. The jousting had, on several occasions, become the evening's entertainment.

Josiah asked their waitress about world conditions, but she had little to add and, in fact, contradicted several things others had told them. The only consistent information concerned Reno: its water treatment plants were maintained, hospitals open, and railway freight lines functional. While no one was sure of the origin of Reno's freight, it was certain that loose-knit groups of "posse police" acted as security for almost everything.

"You folks made a good choice, coming here to the Peppermill," the waitress assured them. "We've got the best casino posse in town, ex-Reno police officers, our own security folks. Not many *Shaitan* get past them."

"*Shaitan*?" Kate asked. She glanced around the table, meeting expressions as puzzled as her own.

"The *Shaitan*. The crazies. Just this morning, I heard on the news—" Her attention was caught by a signaling customer. Hurriedly, she added, "They're saying *Shaitan* are people gone crazy in the second blackout, but if you ask me, I think they're convicts. Everything went nuts after the first blackout, prisons, too. They won't say how many escaped."

"Why do they call them *Shaitan*?" asked Alex.

"Don't know," said the waitress. "It's just what folks always call them. Sorry, gotta go." She hurried to service another table.

Alex could barely contain his excitement after dinner; he'd been served beer without being asked for ID and had deduced he'd also be able to gamble. Everyone, except Catherine, seemed ready for fun.

"Who's ready to hit the casino?" asked Alex. His wallet was full of cash Eli had given him. Josiah and Eli had paid for the rooms, as well. Alex didn't ask where they'd gotten the money.

"Somebody carry me to the nearest slots and dump me on a stool," groaned Laura.

Kate swallowed her wine and set the glass down with a thump. "I'm in."

Eli chimed, "Me too."

Josiah grinned and nodded.

"It appears I'm the designated nanny," Catherine said, nodding at Lucas and John Thomas, both of whom had heavy eyes and flushed cheeks. Laura offered to take care of the boys, but Catherine said, "Go with the others. I hate to admit it, but I'm feeling my accumulation of years." She grasped her cane. "If you could just help get the boys into bed?"

"But, Katie," John Thomas protested. "What about the paint? You said—"

Kate hugged him to her. "Don't worry, honey, we have plenty of time. Look at you. You can hardly keep your eyes open."

"Come along boys, bedtime," Catherine said.

Lucas looked at John Thomas. "I wanna play video games."

John Thomas turned to Kate. She laughed and tousled his head. "Tomorrow, kiddo. I promise." With a quick kiss to his cheek, she held out a hand. "Come on, I'll help tuck you in."

Catherine walked away, leaning heavily on her cane. Kate followed, her arm around a sleepy John Thomas. He waved at Lucas to follow.

Lucas stared, unmoving. "John Thomas, I wanna play video games."

"Come on, Lucas." Laura smiled, holding out a hand. "We'll stop by the arcade for a quick game. But we have to hurry."

Lucas beamed at his victory and placed his hand in hers.

Twenty minutes later, Laura and Kate were sitting next to each other at a bank of video poker machines.

Kate immersed herself in the game, but Laura was distracted by the kaleidoscope of people, colors, noise, and flashing lights. She became nostalgic for the calmness of the small cabin in which they'd stayed during the blizzard.

There, she and the others had talked long into the night, sprawled before the fireplace. One particular memory of Josiah made her stomach flutter. It hadn't been much, just a look he gave her, a long look that caused her breath to catch. Just as a smile started easing across his face, she'd looked away. *You're pregnant,* she'd reminded herself. But the reminder wasn't enough to stop the flutters. It did, however, stop her from making a fool out of herself, in case what she thought she saw in his eyes was only in her imagination.

She'd told Kate about her pregnancy, and had sworn her to secrecy. She wasn't ready for everyone's questions. Or so she'd told Kate—and herself. But now she wondered if Josiah was the real reason.

She looked for Josiah, or for Eli's grin, or even Alex's shags of unruly hair. But they'd been swallowed by the crowd. Turning back to her machine, she barely registered the electronic images. Telling Kate she was going to look around, she joined the flow of people in the nearest aisle. Maybe the frenetic, barely contained, undecipherable energy of the place was causing her restlessness, she thought.

In a narrow gap between machines, a woman jostled

her. Sidestepping her, Laura was bumped again, hard from behind, and lost her balance and fell against a man in front of her. The stocky man turned just as the crowd surged against both of them. To her right, shouts erupted. Two arms flailed through a space that suddenly gaped as people backpedaled, flattening themselves against the tables and machines. A blur of male torso flung through the air to disappear below the wall of bodies. The sickening sound of fist striking flesh cracked through the pandemonium.

Laura twisted away and found herself pressed against the stocky man she'd bumped into moments before. His large hand grasped her arm, but his attention focused on the fight, his eyes lit with fire. Sounds of flesh being struck punctured the air. Like fire through dry grass, the adrenaline of violence spread through the crowd. Voices roared. A stray nudge, an inadvertent elbow from the closely packed bodies, erupted into violence.

Desperate to escape, Laura tried to free herself from the stranger's grasp, but she had no leverage. She yanked again to release herself from the painful grip. The man's eyes were suddenly on hers. Sweat dripped from his coarse eyebrows, beaded on his pored nose. His pupils dilated with fierce excitement.

Breathing roughly, he said something to her, but the noise prevented her from understanding him. His fingers tightened, his other arm crushed her to him, and he ground his erection against her.

Laura's cry was lost in the roar of the crowd. She squirmed frantically. He shifted her into a bear hug, and gripped the back of her neck, forcing her face to his.

Inches away, his eyes: in them, a sucking emptiness, dark, throbbing, powerful.

Terrified, she couldn't think, couldn't look away from his eyes, from the intense darkness that swelled behind them.

Her fear became overwhelming terror.

"It's good," he rasped. "You feel it. Feel it feel IT FEEL IT."

Suddenly, his face snapped aside; his hand dropped from her neck. She twisted free of his arm, turned to flee, and collided with another body.

Josiah!

He had removed the man's hand from her neck and still grasped the wrist. Sandwiched between them, Laura felt Josiah's energy as he stared down at the man.

"You son of a bitch," Josiah said, his tone lethal.

The fight abruptly fell into their space, and a caroming body slammed into the man. He spun and locked his arms around the neck and shoulders of the intruder, struggling to keep his feet under him while others fell against them. Roaring with glee, oblivious to stray blows, he immersed himself in the fray.

Josiah stepped between Laura and the ragged edge

of the fight. Using himself as a wedge, he shoved them both through to a clear aisle.

"Exciting stuff, these casinos," he said, drolly.

Laura stopped walking and threw her arms around him. For the first time since they'd met, she was oblivious to any undercurrents and felt only vast relief at his solidness next to her. Head pressed into his chest, she said, "I have never been so happy to see anyone in my whole entire life."

Josiah held her easily. When she finally looked at him, he smiled and almost spoke, but stopped himself.

"How about," he said after a pause, "we go have a drink?"

They followed a path to a dark bar. Laura kept her arm looped through Josiah's as they stepped aside for security guards who were hurrying to the spreading fight. Despite her intense emotions, she made several connections: the mood of the second blackout, the faces of the people in the warehouse, and the eyes of the man who'd just terrified her. All shared the same empty darkness.

She'd felt the touch of it herself, just as she'd emerged from the first blackout, but had been unable to grasp its contradiction of empty depths and powerful fullness. What was it? What did it mean?

They slipped into a corner booth at the lounge and Josiah ordered drinks. With a sinking feeling of certainty, she answered herself. What she'd experienced wasn't a fragment of these people's minds. It was real, something outside of them, something deadly. The man who'd assaulted her was lost, gone. But *it* was there.

"That must have been terrible for you," Josiah said. "Did he hurt you?"

The man's eyes. She'd never seen anything like it. "Did you see his eyes?" she blurted.

Josiah gently bit his lower lip, a familiar habit. He tried to picture the man's face, but his memory held only snatches of the man's features. He shook his head and smiled. "I was a little busy."

Laura was deep in thought. "He must be one of the *Shaitan* the waitress talked about. She said people think *Shaitan* are people who went insane during the second blackout. But I don't think that's the whole answer." She tucked a strand of hair behind her ear. "This is going to sound really crazy, and I don't know how to say it."

Josiah leaned forward. "How about this? There are dangerous people in the world. Dangerous in a way you've never come across, and these people are a real threat."

"Yes." She smiled uncertainly. "But there's more." How could she explain it? She took a tiny sip of the wine Josiah had ordered for her. "There's something new happening, something out of context to the world."

Josiah almost said, *Maybe you just haven't experienced enough of the world.*

"How do you mean?" he asked instead.

Laura felt a boundary had been crossed. There had been the blackout and now there was this new thing in the world, a dark thing that she knew was real.

She stared into Josiah's eyes. *How green they are, she thought, how clear. His soul's right there, just inside, just behind that thin, thin green lens.*

"I'm sure now that I know what I know," she said.

"That's good. Now you can tell me," Josiah said. He widened his smile to show he was kidding. He felt a strong impulse to tread gently with her.

Laura thought, *maybe now is the right time.*

"It's—I call it epiphany."

Josiah blinked. "What's called epiphany?" He'd tried to stay focused on their discussion, but somehow he'd fallen into Laura's eyes and couldn't get out.

"Epiphany," Laura began. "It's all about what happened during the three minutes that blinded the world."

Josiah said nothing, listened intently. Laura spoke rapidly, groping for words, painting images, relaying concepts. She interrupted herself, backtracked to fill in gaps, explained what it seemed she alone remembered, and talked about the second blackout. Though somehow connected, it was different, she said, something outside the context of life, outside of everything.

"The *Shaitan*—there really is something different about them," she said. "They're not escaped cons, or insane people. They're truly *other* than us. There's an entirely different force inside them."

She could hardly sit still, and she rose with her last words.

Josiah touched her hand. "Please tell me you're just going to the bathroom, after which there will be a short question-and-answer period."

"It's not that. Please come with me—Kate's alone and I'm worried she's—"

"She's what?" Kate said.

Laura turned and saw her coming toward them, Eli and Alex behind her.

"Thank God." Laura grabbed her in a hug.

"Wow," Kate said. "I love you too, honey, but we really haven't been apart that long. What's up?"

She slid into the booth while Laura hugged Eli and Alex with relief. Grinning, Eli planted a kiss on her cheek, wiggled his eyebrows like Groucho Marx, and tapped an imaginary cigar with his fingers.

"It's those *Shaitan* the waitress told us about," Laura began, after everyone was seated.

Kate caught the bartender's attention and ordered drinks all around.

Laura told them about the man in the crowd, and of her certainty that there was a new force at large in the world.

Josiah sat quietly, thinking about Laura's explanation of the blackout, of an energy-dimension, a community of what could only be called souls, though that might not be what they were, and their responsibility for the physical presence of every life-form on the planet.

Even though Josiah believed life was something greater than energy and matter, he didn't believe that anyone could possibly know what it really was. If a greater truth did exist, there never would be any proof to substantiate it.

In the final analysis, he thought, you can really have faith only in yourself.

He watched Laura's animated discussion with the others. Obviously, something had happened to Laura during the blackout. But if the knowledge she described had come to every being on earth, why did only she remember it?

Kate noticed the intensity with which Josiah's eyes followed Laura's lips. "Well, sunshine." She nudged him. "Where are you at on all this dark stuff?"

"Sorry, I was thinking about something else," he said.

Kate turned to Laura. "Are you talking the real Bible kind of evil Devil shit?"

Laura barely heard her, engrossed in threading connections. "What if *Shaitan* aren't just filled with an outside force, but only have that force in them now? If they're empty of life, that means they're filled with something entirely different. Because," she concluded, "when life leaves bodies, it's called death. And these people are not dead."

"Huh?" Kate squinted at her.

"That's it," Laura muttered to herself. "It's not just that something else is in them. It's actually replaced them. The *Shaitan* don't have what we've always called *souls*."

Alex said. "Is that, like, even possible?" Confusion crossed his features. "No. Impossible," he said defiantly. "Our souls are in God's keeping. He can't *lose* them."

"Read your Bible," Kate needled him. "Stealing souls is the Devil's pastime."

Alex thought of Reverend Perry's warnings of Armageddon, his certainty that the second blackout had flooded the world with evil and that some big final battle was at hand. Was that what he meant? Satan had stolen people's souls and filled their bodies with evil? He sprang to his feet and slammed his empty beer glass on the table.

"Enough of this shit. Nobody's taking my soul," he declared, listening to the casino noises. With a choppy wave, he stomped off.

"What's chewing his shorts?" said Kate.

"Preacher Perry's hooks," replied Josiah. "You know, Laura, I remember thinking after the second blackout that it felt like something was trying to tear an essential piece out of me."

Kate frowned. "Now *you're* talking souls? I thought you weren't religious, Josiah."

"I'm not. This wasn't a religious experience. Who knows?"

"I sure as hell don't," Eli muttered. He slid out of the booth. "I'll go find Alex."

With an edge of sarcasm she tried to disguise, Kate said flippantly, "Laura knows. Go ahead, Laura, tell Josiah about your *epiphany*."

"I already told him."

"Yeah?" Kate turned to Josiah. "So, what do you think?"

"Interesting."

"Interesting." Kate snorted. "*Bugs* are interesting. Laura knows I don't believe that shit. But I know *she* believes it. And now that she's thrown in all this evil crap . . . hell, sounds like religion to me." She rose, chugged the rest of her beer, then set the bottle down hard. "Let the party begin."

Laura started to protest but suddenly felt drained.

CHAPTER 18

JOHN THOMAS WAS THE FIRST TO AWAKEN, AS USUAL. His arm draped over the side of the bed to feel Reina. The room was so dark, he thought it must still be nighttime. Heat from Lucas's body made it warm under the covers. Sometimes, Lucas got so hot that John Thomas scooted to the edge of the bed, seeking coolness. He tried to put off his new morning ritual a few more minutes. But it was no use, he had to check.

Easing himself out of bed, he padded into the next room. Yes, there was Katie. He stood quietly and listened to her deep exhalations, and the knot in his stomach eased.

It snowed that day. By the time the group seated themselves for breakfast, the Nevada blizzard had shifted, pounding icy flakes against the windows of the hotel restaurant.

Catherine spread jam on her toast and glanced around the table. "Did anyone win a fortune last night?" She received headshakes and mumbles. "Did anyone gamble themselves into the poorhouse?" Another series of headshakes and mumbles. Catherine smiled, bit her toast, then said, "All those with hangovers, say 'aye.'"

The chorus of loud ayes caused Kate to flinch. She sipped her coffee. A muffin sat, untouched, on her plate.

"Actually, I broke even," Alex said. He leaned his forehead into the palms of his hands and closed his eyes. "But I don't think I'll ever drink again."

Eli laughed and dunked toast into his eggs. "Eat something, you'll feel better."

Alex peeked at Eli's plate of runny eggs. "I might never eat again, either."

Eli mixed his hash browns into his eggs then squirted ketchup onto the mess.

Lucas's spoon poised over his bowl of Cheerios, his attention riveted on Eli's plate. He loved ketchup but had never seen it used on eggs. "I want some of that, John Thomas," he said. Milk dribbled from his spoon onto the tablecloth.

"Mind your spoon, Lucas," Catherine said.

Lucas resumed eating. "I'm still hungry," he said through a mouthful of cereal, "and I want stuff like Eli's."

"Maybe after you finish," John Thomas said, looking to Kate for permission.

Kate shrugged. "Why not?" She watched snow blowing past the window. "It doesn't look like we'll be going anywhere real soon, anyhow."

"I think I'll check out the sermon over at the Play 'N Pray," Alex mumbled. "I ran into a guy last night who said the new preacher they've got really knows his shit. Hey, what if it's Reverend Perry? That'd be awesome."

"Why bother?" Kate asked Alex. "Can't you just pray in your room?"

Laura glanced up from her pancakes. When they'd been in the small cabin and Alex's interest in religion had become obvious, Kate had often baited him. It seemed she hadn't had enough.

"I could pray right here at the table, if I knew what the hell I was doing," said Alex, peevishly. "I'm just starting to learn this shit. You know, maybe you could learn something, too."

"I've done my church time, fifteen years' worth," said Kate.

"Out on parole?" Eli grinned.

Kate flicked a ball of muffin crumbs across the table at him.

"Watch out," Eli said, "she's armed with muffin and a mood."

Josiah met Laura's eyes and smiled. Their gazes

locked in a way that was not lost on Kate.

"You're getting religion now, too, huh Josiah?" Kate challenged.

Josiah lifted his eyebrows. "Come again?"

"All that talk about souls last night," Kate said, "I was just wondering if you got religion."

"It's not a disease, you know," Alex blurted.

"Did I say it was?" Kate shot back.

"It's how you sounded."

Kate laughed merrily, invoking one of her signature mood changes. "Aw, what do I know, honey? Hell, say a prayer for me while you're there."

Laura realized she'd been holding her breath, and quietly let it out.

Kate pushed her coffee to one side. "I think it's time for a little hair of the dog. Who's for a Bloody Mary?"

"Not me." Laura reached for her juice. She still felt guilty about the one glass of wine she'd had the previous evening.

"How about it, Alex?" Kate smiled conspiratorially, all traces of aggression gone. "Is your head still doing a number on you?"

Alex looked tempted but uncertain. How long would Kate's friendliness last?

"Oh, come on," Kate said, "I don't want to drink alone this early in the morning." She coaxed with a smile, "Come on, I'll be your best friend."

Alex succumbed and they left. Eli, deciding to tag along, jumped up and followed.

Laura looked at Josiah, engaging Catherine in one of their many debates. It seemed her attention invariably drifted to Josiah. She looked at his profile, and his hands. He had beautiful hands, strong, long-fingered. She watched his lips as he spoke to Catherine and recalled a special moment from the night before: Seeing the clear, green depths of his eyes. The sensation of his most intimate self pooled within them, awaiting her . . .

What's the matter with me? she wondered. *I'm in love with him. Oh, my God, I am. I'm in love with him.* It happened just like that.

She bowed her head, flustered. She'd often heard that when you fell in love, you just knew it. But no one ever told her you'd know it so suddenly. Had it been love the first time she'd seen him, when she'd held a gun on him? Or when he'd pulled the yen from his pocket and her fingers had grazed his hand?

She loved Josiah. She was pregnant with Mack's baby.

Grabbing her glass of juice, she held it tightly to still the trembling in her hands. Like the needle of a compass, her eyes turned to Josiah. As awkward as she felt, she was more greedy for the sight of him than any desire she'd ever felt.

CHAPTER 19

RENO, DAY 3

IT WAS ALMOST AS THOUGH RENO EXISTED IN A VOID, thought Catherine. She switched off the television and grimly sat back in her chair. She hadn't found a single national newscast, just local news and panel discussions. And the frequent replay of a woman dressed like a gypsy fortune-teller speaking of the "*Shaitan*," spawned out of the darkness.

Catherine decided they needed to leave this hotel immediately. Decomposing bodies were sprawled across the nation, and death bred diseases. There had been no plague in Reno yet; most likely it had been delayed by the intense cold. The city reeked of danger. Too many of the people who crowded the town were transient and might easily have contracted something along the way.

Agitated, Catherine took a pill from her pillbox on the table beside her and swallowed it dry. She'd warned her companions of diseases since the first day at Laura's home. With her husband, she'd seen the plagues of Africa and India.

As soon as one of them came through the door, she would demand they leave.

Immediately.

With more storms predicted, they decided to settle into the house they'd found the first night in Reno. The vehicles they'd parked in its garage had remained unvandalized, a good sign.

Laura set the can of disinfectant aside and sat back on her heels. They were cleaning the house from top to bottom. She was glad to keep busy, to allow time to become accustomed to the idea of loving Josiah. Yet, sadly, she could not see Josiah loving her. She was pregnant.

Sighing, she scrubbed every surface Catherine had decreed must be sanitized.

Kate had reluctantly agreed to leave the hotel but insisted that Catherine not try to imprison them in the house. "We were already cooped up in the mountains, for chrissakes," she'd said. "We'll be careful—wash our hands every time we pee and not let anyone breathe on us and shit."

Reno was both settled and unsettled, thought Laura. Midtown activity was frenzied, yet the outlying districts were deserted. The town had power—heat, water, and electricity—casinos, markets, gas stations, and restaurants flourished. Yet most of its inhabitants had fled, and most of those who came in from outlying regions stayed only a short time before continuing south or east.

Catherine said the town's economy had been based on the entertainment industry and that most of the people who'd lived in town had migrated there for the work. From this, Catherine deduced that survivors of the blackout, whose jobs had been dependent on vacationers, had no reason to stay because only three of the major hotel/casinos were in full operation. The rest of those working in what was once a booming economy, those in construction, or who'd worked at the throngs of shopping centers and stores, or in support services, no longer had means of income.

A migrant population based on a migrating population.

Who knew how long power would continue to be provided, or how reliable food and other goods would be? Nevada's harsh desert environment, its soil rich in minerals but almost impossible to farm, and its extreme weather, did not lend itself to self-sufficiency.

Outlying areas could provide local beef, as long as the wild forage held out.

They were lucky that the house they'd found had truly been deserted. Or, as Kate had put it, "No rotting bodies, thank God."

Laura surveyed the large living room. She'd removed

all the knickknacks—easier than disinfecting them—and packed them into boxes, ready to be moved to the garage. Out the large picture window, the patchy blue sky predicted storm clouds to follow.

According to the local news station, many of the satellite downlinks were not functioning. In the odd mixture of news and rumor that had become the staple of TV, they learned that a cult, calling themselves Alienists, believed the government was clandestinely involved in a galactic war.

Laura had watched Alienists involved in a shouting match with a Fundamentalist sect, in the heart of downtown. Taunts had degenerated into a brawl, and a red-faced man screamed into the camera something about blaspheming against God while brandishing what looked like a musket.

"Hey, Laura." Kate appeared in the doorway, rubber-gloved hands hanging at her sides. "Break time?"

Laura brushed back a shock of honey-colored hair. "Sounds good. This room's done, how's the rest of the house?"

Kate stripped off her gloves. "Done, except for the guys, still working on the bathrooms." She dropped the gloves on a box at her feet. "Catherine's having tea in the kitchen. What a slave driver!"

"Well," Laura said, "it won't hurt to be clean."

They walked down the short hallway to the kitchen.

"Where are the kids?" Laura asked Catherine.

"In the back bedroom," Catherine answered. "Apparently, two viewings of some dinosaur epic weren't enough. When I checked, they were restarting the disk."

"Maybe I'll take John Thomas to the park," Kate said. "He must have seen that thing a gajillion times by now." Laura removed items from the refrigerator, and Kate rummaged cupboards for a snack.

"What about Lucas?" Laura asked.

"He'll probably tag along, as usual." Kate found a soda and joined Catherine and Laura at the table.

"Kate," Catherine said, "the favoritism you show John Thomas isn't lost upon Lucas."

Kate shrugged. "I know you both think I'm a real bitch for ignoring Lucas, but the kid gives me the creeps. And I don't think he gives a shit if I pay attention to him or not."

"That's ridiculous," said Laura.

Kate bit into a piece of cheese. "No, it's not. I don't think he gives a shit about you both, either."

Laura didn't know how to respond. That Kate ignored Lucas was one thing, but intensely disliking him was another.

"I am curious," said Catherine. "What led you to form such a strong opinion of him?"

Kate shrugged. "Gut feel."

"I see. And just what is it that your—gut—feels?"

Kate shrugged, annoyed.

Laura put her hand on Kate's. "Maybe you haven't

really given him a chance to like you. We've all been so busy working out our own problems, none of us have given him the attention a five-year-old needs."

"Uh-uh," Kate said. She picked up her soda. "Remember that day we found the kids? And John Thomas had peed all over himself because he'd been so scared?"

Laura nodded.

"Well, when you went upstairs to pack their stuff, Lucas grabbed one of John Thomas's hands and pulled on him. John Thomas was still hanging on to me, so I told Lucas to let him be, just give him a minute and he'd be okay, and Lucas said, 'No, John Thomas has to stop crying, it's stupid.' I said, no, it wasn't stupid, his brother felt bad, but Lucas acted like I hadn't even said anything and he kept pulling John Thomas. I finally had to grab his wrist and shake him off."

"Maybe he was just jealous," Laura said. "You were cuddling John Thomas."

"Another time," Kate went on, "I went to check on them about ten minutes after we'd put them to bed. I could hear John Thomas crying, and Lucas asking him what their dad had looked like, dead. John Thomas was crying, and the little jerk was mad at him for not answering.

"And don't forget when he practically ran me over. He still won't tell me what the fuck he was doing trying to drive a car. Hasn't apologized, either."

Laura opened her mouth but Kate rushed on. "And

then, one day at that cabin, me and John Thomas were trying to get a snowman started when I noticed Lucas out by that shed in the clump of trees. He was stooped down and whacking this stick down in the doorway, whacking and whacking, over and over. I called to him but he just kept whacking, so I went over to him, and— Jesus." Her face twisted in disgust.

"It was a tiny little field mouse and he was whacking it. It was still alive! It was disgusting. I grabbed him and I don't even remember what I yelled. He looked at me all surprised . . . mad . . . and then all of a sudden he's smiling—smiling—and asking me if I like mice." Kate snatched up her soda and took a long swallow.

Laura shook her head in dismay. Catherine stared intently at Kate.

"He's creepy," said Kate. "I can't keep him from hanging around John Thomas, but I'll be damned if I'll encourage him."

"This is not good," Catherine said quietly. "Why didn't you tell us about this when it happened?"

"I didn't want to leave John Thomas out there alone with Goddamn Damien. When we got back to the house, I didn't feel like talking about it. I thought I'd mention it later." She shrugged. "It's later."

"I now understand," Catherine said, "why you are put off by the child."

"Put off." Kate snorted, then suddenly grinned. "I

love that about you, Catherine—you're soooo civilized."

"Humph. Frankly, I would not have guessed civilized expression to be high on your list of priorities. We seem to have a serious problem and, much as I hate to admit it, I, too, have had bad feelings toward the child. Until now, I assumed it was my lack of patience."

Laura tried to understand this new aspect of Lucas. She'd read enough magazine profiles of criminals who committed gruesome crimes to know they were often called sociopaths. The childhoods of such people included, as a common thread, mistreatment of small animals.

A thought struck her. Maybe Lucas hadn't survived the second blackout.

Lucas appeared in the doorway. Her heart jumped. How long had he been standing there? She chided herself for leaping to conclusions. Of course Lucas hadn't lost his "soul." She'd looked into his eyes enough that there was no possible way she could have missed the paralyzing black emptiness.

Kate turned and said, "So, you guys had enough of *Jurassic Park*?"

Kate's normal tone of voice was unnerving, after her bleak disclosure. How, Laura asked herself, could they determine if Lucas was . . . mentally deficient—she shied away from the term "sociopathic"—or if he'd just been traumatized by events of the past weeks?

She could ask John Thomas. Was he too young to

have noticed changes in Lucas? To know whether Lucas had acted strangely before?

"I'm bored," Lucas said, to no one in particular.

"Go get your brother," Kate said, sliding back her chair.

That evening, as Laura helped Kate put the children to bed, she was aware of every word and gesture she made to Lucas. She felt awkward and stilted, and admired Kate's ease. What had before appeared to be Kate's inattention, her habit of not looking at Lucas even when she spoke to him, her offhand manner with him, now seemed a monumental achievement of normalcy. She struggled to imitate Kate's casual gestures but couldn't overcome her hesitation to touch him.

Kate's worked on dealing with him and now it's just a habit, thought Laura. She hurried from the room, leaving Kate to flip off the light switch and say a final good night to John Thomas.

CHAPTER 20

LAURA BOLTED UPRIGHT, SHRINKING FROM THE TOUCH that had jolted her from sleep.

"Laura," John Thomas whispered in the darkness.

"John Thomas." She blinked at his vague shape next to her bed, her heart still thundering. "You scared me. What is it? What's wrong?"

"Something's wrong with Reina. Please come, Laura." John Thomas pulled her arm anxiously.

Laura pushed her blankets aside, kicked her feet free of them, and swung her legs over the edge of the bed. "Where's Kate?" she whispered. The bedside clock glowed 5:18. The dim outlines of the two other beds in the room, the humped shapes in them, were difficult to see.

"She won't wake up. Reina's crying something awful. She's hurting, Laura, hurry, come on."

"Okay, I'm coming." Laura padded behind John Thomas, his small hand tugging hers. They passed from the carpeted hallway into the kitchen and Laura gasped as her bare feet met icy linoleum. Flipping on the light, she followed John Thomas through the kitchen and into the small den where he and Lucas slept.

The den was brightly lit. Reina lay on her blanket in the far corner next to the TV, whimpering, and Lucas squatted near her. Reina suddenly yowled, her head and neck stiffened upward, her back legs flexed. Lucas's head tilted to one side, his attention fixed on Reina's rear. Just as Laura knelt beside him, Reina's tail lifted at the croup and a small, glistening shape slid out onto the blanket.

"That's two," Lucas piped. "See there?" He reached toward another small shape, almost hidden under Reina's leg. Laura grabbed his hand before he nudged it.

"Don't touch, Lucas."

Without looking at Laura, Lucas asked, "How many more are coming?"

"I don't know." Laura felt John Thomas's hand on her shoulder.

"Why's she crying, Laura?" he asked, his voice choked with tears.

Laura reassuringly squeezed his hand. "It's hard work to get these puppies out, but she's okay, John Thomas." Reina grunted onto her front elbows, twisting her head along her side to lap at the puppies, first one, then the other, lifting her leg out of the way as she licked them with long strokes.

"EEEYuuu! They're slimy," Lucas exclaimed, moving closer.

Laura rose and pulled Lucas with her. "Come on, boys," she said. "Reina will be fine. We're just distracting her."

John Thomas slipped his small, cold hand into Laura's. "Katie said she's young and this's probably her first litter, so how can she know what to do?"

Laura drew both boys toward the kitchen, then stopped in the doorway and looked back at Reina. "It's instinct. Something inside her makes her know what to do. Really, John Thomas." She smiled at him. "She's doing just fine."

She settled the boys at the kitchen table and went back to her room for her robe and slippers, flipping on the thermostat in the hallway as she went. Reentering the kitchen, she saw both boys twisted around in their seats to watch Reina. Laura shut the door to the den then switched on the small TV on the kitchen counter. Cartoons. Perfect.

"Okay," she said, "what'll it be? Cereal and toast?" She glanced at the dark window. "I'll bet you've never had breakfast this early."

As she prepared the boys' breakfasts, and tea for herself, she wished Josiah were awake. For an entire week, she had loved him. She tried to define what it was that made her so certain. *What is it? Why Josiah, why not Eli? Eli's nice, he's cute, he's comfortable to be around.* Or why not Mack, the father of her unborn child?

She settled herself at the table with the boys and her tea and thought back to the day she'd met Josiah and Eli. Her first impressions in their initial, frightening meeting had been that Eli was younger than twenty-three, more a teenager, somewhat nondescript.

She saw Eli differently now. More mature than his years, he was thoughtful, sincere, and very funny. Hardly nondescript.

She tried to remember first impressions of Josiah, but, unexpectedly, Kate loomed large in her mind. Kate, sitting on the hood of the car, arms braced behind her, one leg dangling, caught between the smashed cars. Dark red, curly hair, slim and small. She seemed to be what might be called a "complete" person, in control, even though the situation was not. There was Kate, grinning at her through her pain, flippant, defiant.

Now Laura knew Kate was spontaneous rather than practical, experienced rather than knowledgeable. Her emotional energy, instead of her reason, led her actions.

She was not always predictable. When angered, Kate stopped thinking about what others thought or felt. Overall, her kindness ran deeper than her thoughtlessness, unless she'd been hurt. Then she shot from the hip, and the battle, for her, was over.

Kate's unpredictable vengefulness had surprised Laura, but she'd come to accept the unexpected flurries and had learned to ignore them. Kate was what she felt. And feelings changed.

Laura's mind ventured next to her first meeting with Catherine, of coming upon the older woman, lying propped in her hospital bed, her gaze steady, her tone supercilious, domineering, demanding. Old-fashioned. Laura smiled. Catherine was few of those things. Not domineering, she was disciplined and pragmatic, the most practical of them all. And her clothing was the only old-fashioned thing about her. She was educated, organized, and perceptive. The only dismissive thing about her was her impatience with muddled thinking, and the only demands she made were for clarity.

Which brought Alex to mind, but thoughts of Josiah overrode him.

Josiah. Lounging casually against a car in the warehouse parking lot. Gentle. Confident. Reassuring. Intelligent. Her first impressions. And now?

The same.

There were no first and second Josiahs, Laura realized. When she visualized the moment of their first encounter, he was the same Josiah she now knew.

It's like all those people who say they felt like they'd known the other person forever. First impressions are exactly who that person is. They know them. Their impressions don't change, they just fill out, get colored in.

"Laura, maybe we should check on Reina," John

Thomas said. "She's awful quiet."

Laura ruffled John Thomas's hair. "First you're worried she's noisy, then you're worried she's quiet? Maybe we should teach her to sing, so you can stop worrying."

John Thomas giggled but his glance darted to the door.

"Come on. We'll peek in on her," Laura said softly.

John Thomas was at the door before Laura finished speaking. Lucas, engrossed in a Road Runner cartoon, methodically spooned cereal into his mouth. Maybe he'd lost interest in Reina, Laura hoped. Lucas. A new unknown. She walked into the den with John Thomas, and they knelt near Reina's blanket.

The dog greeted them with quivering tail, her silky ears pinned back in affectionate submission. While John Thomas gently scratched around her ears, Laura counted. Four puppies were clearly visible, two snuggled against Reina's stomach and two more lying farther out. Laura saw a fifth puppy partially obscured between Reina's back legs and only then realized the two outer pups weren't moving. She looked closer, trying to find a flutter of breathing, and saw that one was still partially encased in its glistening sac.

She caught her breath and wondered if she could coax the tiny bodies into life. With gentle fingers, she massaged one of the small bodies, simulating the motions of a mother dog's stroking tongue.

"John Thomas, go wet a kitchen towel with warm

water, please."

"What's wrong?" Worry and fear filled his features.

"Hurry, honey. Maybe nothing, but I need that towel."

Laura turned back to the puppies. A rush of water in the sink mingled with the "Meep, meep" of the Roadrunner evading another Acme booby trap.

Reina's ears perked as she watched John Thomas through the open doorway. Laura gently scooped up a neglected puppy, cupped it in her hand, and moved it under Reina's nose. "Come on, Reina, clean it up, girl, come on." Reina's tail wagged once, but her attention remained on John Thomas. "Come on, Reina." Laura nudged the puppy under Reina's muzzle. "John Thomas isn't going anywhere."

Reina turned briefly to Laura, her head tilting to John Thomas's name, then turned back to keep sight of her adored one. Laura replaced the small, still form onto the blanket next to the one she'd been stroking.

John Thomas brought the towel and squatted by Reina, stroking her while he stared at the small shapes on the blanket. "Are the puppies okay?"

"I don't know, John Thomas," Laura admitted. She used the towel to wipe the puppies from nose to tail with delicate strokes. "Sometimes they need a little help, but sometimes they don't make it."

"Why isn't Reina helping them?"

Laura continued to stroke with the hand towel.

"She's giving her attention to the others." Reina twisted to lick the two mewling pups cuddled into her side, tiny grunts greeting her lapping tongue. As she shifted herself to better reach them, her hind leg rose and uncovered the fifth puppy. Laura's breath caught at the sight of the grossly malformed shape. She quickly bent forward to hide it from John Thomas. "Go get Kate, okay?"

Fortunately, he hadn't seen the fifth puppy. "I tried to wake her before, but she's sleeping real hard."

"Try again, please," she said.

John Thomas trotted from the room. Easing out of her cramped position, Laura looked for something to wrap the deformed puppy in. Nothing handy. She'd have to use the wet towel in her hand. With a grimace, she pulled the misshapen pup from between Reina's legs, using the towel to grasp it. She began to roll it in the towel, then stopped with a gasp. It was breathing. *Oh God, now what?*

"What are you doing?" Lucas said, startling her so badly that she jerked and bumped into him as he looked over her shoulder.

Lucas stared at the small pulsing form on the towel, its back oddly twisted, with two stunted, flipperlike forelegs, and a fused lump of cartilage and flesh for its rear legs. The lower jaw was so abbreviated, the roof of its mouth was exposed. But it was breathing.

"He looks weird," Lucas commented just before

Laura folded the towel over it. "Where's his feet?"

"Lucas, go back to the kitchen. I need to help Reina now."

"You said she didn't need help. You said—"

"Lucas, go," Laura said sharply.

Before he'd taken a step, John Thomas was back, a sleepy Kate in tow, in pajamas and bare feet, red curls flattened around her pale face. She yawned and stretched.

"What's going on?" she asked. "God, my head. I didn't get in 'til two. What time is it?"

"Kate," Laura said, trying to indicate that the children should be kept at bay. "Could you get the boys a piece of cake and see what other cartoons are on?"

"Yeah, cake." Lucas ran to the kitchen and yanked open the refrigerator.

"Cake?" Kate asked, ignoring Lucas. "You woke me to serve cake?"

"It's morning, Katie." John Thomas giggled. "Early, early morning."

Laura stared a steady signal at Kate. "And it's a special morning, one we should celebrate with cake. So, why don't you get them some, Kate, and then come right back."

Kate frowned a question at Laura, then smiled at John Thomas. "Right. Cake it is, kiddo."

When she returned, Daffy Duck was whooping insanely in the kitchen.

"What's going on?" she asked, kneeling next to Laura.

Laura uncovered the live malformed puppy. "Holy shit," Kate breathed, then noticed the two still forms nearby. "Oh, wow, I hate funerals."

"How do you feel about euthanasia?" Laura whispered.

"I agree with Dr. Kerouac."

"Kevorkian."

"Whatever."

Laura grimaced. "How do we do it?" They stared at the grotesque, palpitating form.

"Maybe it'll just stop breathing."

"What if it doesn't? Reina won't have anything to do with it and it'll starve."

"Look at its mouth," Kate said, pointing. "It'll starve whether she tries or not. Jesus. Have you ever seen anything like—?"

"Shhh." Laura glanced over her shoulder, but the doorway was clear.

"We could drown it," Kate whispered.

"I don't think I could hold it under."

"Me either. Maybe we should get Catherine. Bet she'd do it."

Laura nudged her in admonishment. "Maybe we could smother it," she said, looking at the throw pillows on a loveseat against the wall. "Close the door. I'll get the pillow."

Kate locked the door, then rejoined her.

Kate whispered, "Maybe one of the guys . . ."

"Why should they have to do it?"

"Well, why should we?"

"Because we're here. Let's get this over with." Laura held the pillow aloft.

Kate grabbed her arm. "Maybe the pillow's not such a good idea. What if we end up squishing it to death?"

"Jesus, Kate."

"Look. I think it's dying." Kate leaned closer.

Irregular breaths shuddered through the tiny body as it gasped for air in fishlike gulps. The two women breathed in concert with the pup and held their breaths during the long intervals of stillness.

Finally, Kate released a loud sigh. "It's over." She nudged Laura. "Breathe, honey. I don't want to bury you, too."

CHAPTER 21

KATE WANDERED INTO THE LIVING ROOM, AT ODDS with the world. During the week since Reina's puppies had been born, the city had been battered by serial snowstorms. Housebound, Kate felt oppressed. Eli, on the couch, his stocking-clad feet resting on the coffee table, ignored her and watched TV.

Kate rested her forehead on the cool windowpane and looked out at a world blurred by endless snowflakes.

"Where is everybody?" she asked.

"Laura took the kids to the play-gym, Alex's at some church meeting, and Josiah went for a walk. Catherine's around, somewhere," Eli answered without taking his attention from the screen.

Heaving a sigh, Kate moved to the couch and flopped down in the corner opposite Eli. Tired of being inside, she contrarily didn't feel like going out.

"What's with all these talk shows and panels?" she finally

said. “All they ever talk about anymore is religion. I’m sick of it. Change the channel.”

“It’s all that’s on, unless you want to see cartoons or news.” He upped the volume with the remote and pointed at the screen. “See that guy? He’s a Jesuit priest. He heads the discussions on this show—it’s local. They’re televised live from that convention center over on Kietzke. It can be sort of interesting, all these different religions ragging on each other. He’s got the honcho rabbi and some evangelical preacher today. And a Buddhist monk. Look at that guy, he—”

“Eli, ask me if I give a shit,” Kate said, annoyed.

Catherine entered the living room, her cane thumping the rug, and carefully lowered herself into her favorite armchair. “Ah. The Father Bullard Show. What’s today’s topic?”

Kate blew a raspberry while Eli answered, “Conversions. People are joining in droves—churches, temples, chapels—you name it. There’s a new type, too, people who are joining a whole bunch of faiths at the same time.”

“Really,” Catherine said.

“Really,” Kate mimicked, then laughed and abandoned her moodiness. “So,” she said to Catherine, “does it surprise you?”

“Does what, dear?”

“This cross-faith membership drive.”

“It’s not a drive, Kate,” Eli interjected. “I said they

were joining in droves."

Kate waved an arm. "Whatever."

"We can be irreverent at home, Kate," Catherine warned, "but please promise me you'll temper your comments outside this house."

Kate grunted. They fell silent at the sound of the Jesuit's voice.

"Faith," said the priest. "What a beautiful word! A word that denies doubt and defies inquiry."

"How handy," quipped Eli.

"Perhaps it is true," continued the Jesuit, "that all thought exists in an infinite receptacle, alongside all the thoughts that came before and all those that have yet to come, a place from which we pluck ideas and shape them into our own notions." He turned to the evangelical preacher. "What do you think, Reverend Perry?"

"That's the guy from San Francisco." Eli sat up. "I wonder if Alex knows he's in town."

"—nothing but hogwash," Reverend Perry was saying. "You got faith on the one hand, Father Bullard, but on the other hand, what you've got is evil. Pluck one of those thoughts out, some thought that most people have had, something like, oh—'I think we'll have chicken tonight.'" Laughter tittered through the audience. "And try to justify the real existence of that puny notion. Hogwash. That thought didn't come from no giant pot. That thought came from a person who knows he likes chicken. Chicken for the body, like prayer for the soul."

Ripples of laughter came from the audience, along with a collective "Amen."

Reverend Perry nodded to the audience, then leaned into the table and stared at Father Bullard. "You are right to speak of a receptacle," he said, "only it's not a receptacle of thoughts, it's a cauldron of evil. That evil is real, that evil is the souls of sinners Satan eats every day. And four weeks ago last Tuesday, Satan upended that cauldron and poured his filth on mankind. And there are those among us who weren't prepared.

"Satan has unleashed demons and we need to join the war, fight so we can join God's kingdom. Hallelujah!" He turned to the audience. "Time has come for the Lord to walk among us again, to bring His peace to the world, and we cannot abandon Him." His voice thundered, "Stand by the Lord and banish Satan, and we will dwell in His house forever!"

The audience erupted. TV cameras panned the crowd, showing arms raised, faces in surrender, people shouting, writhing, humanity ready to be enveloped, as it had for millennia, in the promise of safety.

A commercial interrupted. A cartoon figure scurried among real cars, jamming a length of garden hose from one gas tank into another, its cheeks bulging in useless efforts to siphon. A voice-over chided the frenzied cartoon, telling it about Syphoze, the new product guaranteed to penetrate the anti-siphoning devices found in most cars.

Eli pushed the remote's mute button and, in the sudden silence, said, "If ever there was a time for people to believe bullshit, this is it."

"Aw, hell," said Kate uneasily. "Brimstone-breathers have been around forever."

Catherine, brow furrowed, said, one syllable at a time, "I believe we should leave this town as soon as possible."

"If we let every jerk like that preacher chase us off," Kate protested, "we'll be running forever, Catherine. This place's got everything we need—electricity, running water, gas, food, things to do . . ."

"I don't know, Kate," Eli began.

"Well, I do," Kate interrupted. She glowered at them. "I'm not going anywhere."

CHAPTER 22

John Thomas walked along the edge of the side-walk where the snow lay in thick drifts. He stomped hard, making deep impressions, then looked over his shoulder at his trail. Someday, he'd make footprints as big as Josiah's. John Thomas giggled as he continued tromping. He couldn't imagine himself grown up, only as he was now but with Josiah's big feet.

"What's funny, John Thomas?" Lucas asked. He walked on the sidewalk's mashed path, holding Laura's hand and hanging back against her steady pull.

"Big feet," John Thomas said, abandoning the game. They were almost home.

Lucas laughed loudly but wondered why big feet were funny. He filed it among other things he'd been told were funny but didn't know why. He had small feet, so nobody would laugh at him. Lucas hated to be laughed at.

Tromping through the cold, Laura felt only Lucas's small, mittened hand in her own. She'd tried to behave normally around him, but her apprehension had grown. She'd questioned John Thomas, careful not to reveal her uncertainty, but learned nothing. It was as if John Thomas didn't remember Lucas in his life before. He took a long time to frame answers and never mentioned Lucas in them.

It was always the same. He'd hesitate, and then he'd talk about all sorts of things but never about Lucas.

It was cold. Josiah hunched into his jacket and burrowed his fists in the pockets. A block ahead of him, three people were receding into the gray-white. He watched as John Thomas stomped through drifts of snow and Lucas dragged against Laura's arm, then turned from the sight and crossed the street in the opposite direction, toward downtown.

Cars passed, tire chains crunching snow with a slapping rhythm. A man emerged from a doorway down the block and walked toward him. Josiah averted his eyes until the instant they passed each other. In that moment, he glanced up and looked steadily at the man, who gave a brief nod and flicked his eyes forward.

Josiah looked at the eyes of every person he encountered on his frequent, solitary walks, searching for the presence Laura had described. Had it been hidden in the furtive glance of the woman he'd passed the other day, or the man who'd refused to meet his gaze? Maybe he'd never see it, because Laura had just experienced a meanness only she'd never encountered before. Not something new to the world, just new to her.

The brooding, gray day matched his mood. He struggled against wishing for the world that no longer existed. A fresh peach. A new movie. A predictable tomorrow.

He wanted things with Laura, without baggage.

She wasn't crazy, so what difference did it make what she believed? Why was he trying so hard to prove her right? Somehow, she'd pushed him off center, off that sweet spot he'd found the secret to maintaining: acceptance.

He'd accepted the blackout, the changed world, just as he accepted his own life; things happened. You accepted change, because change became life.

Realizing that had allowed him to stay centered throughout his childhood, those long periods of being locked in the bedroom of their squalid apartment while his mother whored for drugs, endless hours waiting in line with her for a welfare check or a dose of methadone. Always waiting. For a pimp. For a john. For a dealer.

He wasn't sent to school. He wasn't allowed outside the apartment without her.

His world was filled with damaged adults, people

who used drugs, people who used people, people whose dreams were limited by their cravings. He learned to set himself aside, a small, sad chameleon, to blend into the background by being whatever was expected. Those expectations changed moment by moment as drugs destroyed the people who regulated his life.

His gentleness, having found no form of expression, burrowed deep within him and became spiked with defensive cynicism. He spent as much time as he could alone, in his shabby room with his small old black-and-white TV. Rabbit ears received only one station, which played old movies and sit-com reruns.

One night, when he was about seven, he was watching *The Three Stooges* with the volume turned up as loud as it would go. It still didn't drown out the crashing and shouts beyond the rickety door.

The screaming, slapping, and punching that night ended with his mother in the emergency room with a broken jaw and dislocated shoulder. As he sat next to her in the crowded waiting room, he clutched the little TV on his lap. His thin arms ached with the effort of holding it, but he'd feared having it stolen. Their front door had been demolished.

His mother went from the emergency room into the arms of Jesus, and the next two years were filled with threats of hellfire, crushing expressions of love, and demands of duty. His mother made him listen while she "read" the Bible aloud. Functionally illiterate, she'd move her finger along the page as she repeated the stories she'd heard at the ghetto mission. Josiah would frown with concentration as he tried to match the black squiggles on the page to the sound, trying to understand which symbols matched which words.

Just when Josiah would think that "Behold!" was linked to a specific group of marks, "Behold!" became an entirely different group of symbols beneath his mother's nail-bitten fingertip.

"Show me how to read, CeeCee," he once demanded, caught up in enthusiasm. A stinging slap was followed by, "Don't you order your mother around, boy!" Her fierceness prevented him from repeating the request again. Two years later, he discovered *Sesame Street* on his fuzzy black-and-white, and with it, the revelation that groups of squiggles could be broken down into individual marks, each with its own sound. To Josiah, this was more a miracle than any his mother had read from the Book.

When Josiah was nine, his mother fell from grace, back into addiction. Within a month, she was dead, in an alley, from an overdose of bad heroin.

"Anyone know her?" asked the policeman, but no one in the gathering of ragged spectators answered, so the gaunt filthy body was unceremoniously tagged and bagged. Josiah, squeezed behind trash and garbage cans, watched the departure of his mother, as red and blue flashes of the police cars bounced from pitiful walls. Silently, he answered the policeman's question: *She's CeeCee.* CeeCee Jackson. Never Cecilia, never Mama, Mother, or Mom. Just CeeCee.

That night, he returned to the cold, dark apartment, stretched out on the lumpy couch, and lay wide-eyed until dawn broke through the bare, dirty windows. He brought his television into the living room and tuned through the numbers, fiddling with the rabbit ears until he found a picture. It was PBS, a station he'd never before received.

At nine o'clock, Josiah watched *Sesame Street*, featuring the letter C.

He didn't know the symbol, but the sound was as familiar to him as his own name. *Cee. CeeCee.* A miracle had happened.

During the following months, in a condemned building with pirated electricity, *Sesame Street* became his school, the characters his classmates, its music the lullabies he'd never heard.

To survive the streets without the protection of CeeCee and her network of whores and addicts, he joined a gang and submitted to the ritual kicking-in initiation, pushing the pain to the farthest reaches of his mind.

He lived alone, raising himself in the same rundown tenement in which his mother had given birth to him, and paid for food with money from the gang's burglaries and drug deals. He became expert at separating his thoughts from his actions.

Bob helped him survive those years. Bob, the Big Bird doll who sat on the couch in the smelly apartment, his goofy happy face staring at him. Always at him.

Three weeks after his mother had died and had been replaced by the equally unapproachable, but friendlier, *Sesame Street*, he'd found Bob in a thrift store. He'd even paid for the small fuzzy yellow doll, instead of stealing him. He hid Bob in his ripped jacket until he was home.

Josiah was a tough guy with a doll, but he resolved the contradiction by naming him Bob. Dolls were girls and Bob was a guy.

Bob was the first word he'd ever created with his new understanding of letters. He found it amazingly simple. Big Bird's initials separated by a vowel. Within moments of being named, Bob ceased being a doll and became his confidante and partner.

When he was twelve, the tenement he called home burned down. By then, he'd stopped watching *Sesame Street*, but Bob was still a big part of his private life. He'd known that the stuffed doll was inanimate, silent, but in his lonely heart and imagination, Bob had been a source of comfort and conversation. The morning the fire started, Josiah had been gone. By the time he returned home, the entire building was engulfed in flames and the firemen were trying to save the buildings on either side of it.

Oblivious to the noise and chaos on the street, Josiah stared upward in disbelief. In his mind's eye, he could see the flames lapping Bob's yellow fuzz, his silly friendly face disbelieving the fire licking at his beak.

He cried as he watched the building burn, aching with a crushing grief he'd never felt before. He didn't have a single tarnished memory of Bob in the three years they'd shared, not one moment that had been bruised, as had all the moments with other people in his life.

He'd watched the flames, knowing Bob was dying. It had been unbearable.

Trudging down a snow-covered Reno sidewalk, amidst an increasing flow of pedestrians, Josiah passed pawnshops and souvenir stores, most shut down long ago.

On one plywood-boarded storefront splashed with graffiti, large red letters were sprayed over previous graffiti: JOIN THE BROTHERHOOD. It was a slogan he'd been seeing more and more often on his daily walks. He realized he didn't want to be here.

Turning to retrace his steps, he confronted a crowd surging around the corner toward him. He ducked into a doorway and watched.

Many of the people held signs and chanted a slogan. The crowd spilled into the street as more and more people flowed around the corner. Cars slowed, horns blared, and vehicles tried to inch through the mob but came to a halt as traffic backed up behind them. The mob coursed around and between the cars.

Most of the signs read: "BROTHERHOOD NOW," "JOIN TOGETHER," and "WALK WITH JESUS." He saw one sign that caused him to step back farther into the shadows of the doorway. Badly hand-lettered in red on a black background, its first words were written in large letters, with each subsequent word getting smaller to accommodate the entire message: "KILL THE SHAITAN. SATAN IS LOOSE. ALL EVIL MUST DIE. KILL THE EVIL!"

Josiah peered around the doorway. Yet more people were pouring onto the street. Now they were coming from the other cross street as well, with more signs declaring war on *Shaitan*, on evil. Josiah breathed deeply. There was going to be trouble.

A white sedan directly across from him was blocked by traffic and the mob. Josiah looked at the couple inside. The driver appeared angry, the woman beside him scared.

A man leaped onto the hood of their car. The driver's face contorted, ready for confrontation. The man on the hood leaped to the roof of the car and brought a bullhorn up to his mouth. A river of people parted around the car. The red-faced driver leaped out, his passenger's hand clutching his arm, trying to restrain him. She lay across the seat, straining to pull him back in.

Her movements were frantic, her pleas drowned out by the crowd and the shouts of the man on the car's roof.

The man with the bullhorn shouted, "He walks! He's been seen! He is among us, He has come and we are with Him!"

The crowd roared as it became one ferocious mind. Signs were waved fanatically to confirm the messages they carried.

Then Josiah saw Alex.

Capless, his sandy hair blowing in strands across his eyes, his freckles stark on his white face, Alex was part of the crowd near the sedan. He, too, held a sign and shouted, his attention focused on the man with the bullhorn, his expression as avid as those around him.

Josiah's gaze moved from Alex to the driver of the car, who was now grabbing the ankle of the man standing on its roof.

The startled speaker looked down, kicked out viciously, screamed with rage, then swung the bullhorn down toward the head of the driver. The driver ducked but held on. With both hands clamped on the ankle, the driver heaved back, toppling the speaker, who crashed onto the roof of the car. The mob surged and the driver disappeared beneath hunched backs, pummeling fists, and kicking feet.

Through the shouting, Josiah could hear the woman passenger scream as she struggled out of the car and lurched against the crowd assaulting the man. A hand snagged a fistful of her hair and yanked her head back with terrifying ferocity.

Other people scrambled onto the car from its other side. Alex was one of them.

Josiah saw Alex's face, but it no longer shared the excitement of others. He was screaming, "No. No. No," while the crowd chanted, *"Shaitan. Shaitan. Shaitan."*

Get out of there, you idiot, Josiah thought, trying to will Alex to see him, to pay heed to his gesture, his get-your-ass-the-hell-over-here wave.

Alex was intent on the woman who was about to be caught in the bloodlust. Josiah saw Alex's face fill with fear as he realized what was about to happen. Alex tried to back away, but bodies pressed forward. Shoving and squirming against the madness, he found himself surrounded by the people who'd heard only the cry, *"Shaitan!"*

Alex, in trying to escape, suddenly became the *Shaitan*.

They attacked him. With rage.

There was no possibility of aiding Alex. It would be suicide to battle the zealous crowd. A narrow path of escape opened for Josiah, and he wanted nothing more than to get away from the uncontrolled insanity.

But he had to be certain, for Eli's sake.

Unblinking, he watched. With a roar of triumph,

the crowd hoisted a limp form above their heads. It was Alex, broken and bloodied, head dangling.

Josiah tucked his chin into the warmth of his jacket collar, stepped from the doorway, and slid away. A distant siren ululated. Josiah walked faster, beyond the edges of the crowd, down a street of stragglers, until sidewalks were empty.

The new world was a dangerous place.

And Josiah knew it would only get worse. Even if someone now answered all questions about the blackout, it was too late. People had taken ownership of their own reasons. And they were terrified of each other, of any challenges to the shadows chinking their own ignorance or innocence. Their fear left no room for anything else.

Snow crunched beneath his boots. The bleak harshness of the unforgiving world was no longer confined to the streets of his youth. This entire city was in its grip. And he knew of no reason why the rest of the country would be any different. *The whole fucking world.* What had begun with the blackout had become a terrible darkness that dimmed all reason. The world gone dark with fear.

Josiah forced himself to breathe deeply. Just as he had refused to become the person his childhood dictated, he now refused to let fear immobilize him. He and Eli would survive this new world. And, he found himself promising, Laura would too.

It was bitterly cold. The wind picked up, creating

eddies of tiny snowflakes. There was a coffee shop on the next corner. Even at ten bucks a cup, it was worth it, Josiah decided. Juan Valdez just wasn't shipping any more. He opened the door and stepped into a wall of warmth.

Sitting at the counter with a cup of hot, fragrant coffee, he thought about the unexpected promise he'd just made to himself to protect Laura. Lately, thoughts of Laura had become more insistent. He wanted her. His urges were familiar, but the caution she aroused in him was new. Remembering how they'd met, he felt again the inexplicable energy that had flowed between them. Had it just been the bizarre circumstances? Or was there something special about her?

It was strange, having people become important to him.

First Eli, now Laura.

Eli was his best friend. Josiah felt embarrassment at the thought. It was childish, he told himself, but it was true. He'd never had a friend like Eli, hadn't known that such friendships existed, had never made a real connection with anyone. There was Bob, but Bob hadn't been real and Josiah had always known that.

The connection he'd felt upon first meeting Eli had become immutable, and Josiah's acceptance of this new and powerful friendship now defined him in ways he still didn't fully understand.

Josiah tried to catch the waitress's eye to signal a refill. But one glance at the hands of the man who'd taken the stool next to him, and Josiah forgot about coffee; the hands were pocked with scabs that outgrew the filthy bandages that tried to hide them. Infection yellowed the edges of the rags. Josiah's eyes flicked to the man's profile. There were no marks on his face, but the scalloped swell of another suppuration poked from where his collar pressed against his fleshy neck.

Anger surged through Josiah as he slid off his stool and stepped away from the man. "Yo, mister," he said as he moved. The man gave him an unconcerned glance. "You have no business being out," Josiah said.

"Fuck you, asshole," the man growled. He locked gazes with Josiah, his eyes filled with an awfulness that caught Josiah's breath.

These were the eyes Laura had described. Breath trapped in his throat, Josiah couldn't look away. The man's pupils became darker, fiercer, sucking Josiah into their bottomless black chasm. Their indescribable emptiness was real, viscerally terrifying. An unfamiliar dread struck Josiah and he wrenched his gaze away.

"Rot away, fuckhead," said Josiah, thrusting open the door of the cafe. He stepped out and drew in a frigid lungful of air. Fear of the man's possible contagion wasn't nearly as crippling as the memory of what was in his eyes. Josiah shuddered, knowing it wasn't just the cold sending shivers through him. The *Shaitan* were real. Laura was right.

It was late when he finally stepped into the house, removed his jacket, and hung it on the coat tree. Catherine was in her recliner, Eli and Kate were on the couch, and Laura sat cross-legged on the floor near the blaze in the fireplace.

He crossed the room and lowered himself to the carpet next to Laura, letting his knee nudge comfortably against hers. He'd come to several decisions during the walk home. One was that he would pursue what he felt toward Laura, not wait until he figured it out.

"We were talking about Lucas," Eli said.

Josiah nodded somberly. "We've got to get out of here."

Eli cocked his head to one side. "We do? Where to?"

"I don't know yet," he answered, "but definitely out of Reno."

"Hear, hear," Catherine said.

"Why?" Kate demanded.

"A couple of reasons." He cast Eli a concerned glance. "Look, there's no easy way to say this. Alex is dead."

There were gasps of shock and a staccato outburst of questions. Josiah described the mob scene downtown. Kate grabbed one of Eli's hands. When Josiah finished his narration, everyone expressed horror and disbelief about Alex's death.

"I can understand," Catherine finally said, heavily, to Josiah, "why, having seen such madness, you believe we should leave this place. I concur." She drew a steadying breath and added, "You said you had more than one reason. What is the other?"

Josiah nodded. "You were right to be worried about diseases. I just ran into this guy who had open sores and didn't give a damn about contagion. There are probably more like him." He looked at Laura, then away. He decided to tell her later about the man's eyes.

"There'll be diseases no matter where we go," Kate said. She really didn't want to leave Reno and resented having to defend her position again. "At least here there's hospitals and food and water. We know this city's going to make sure the water stays uncontaminated. And there are more patrols every day."

Josiah shook his head. "Patrols don't matter. Maybe the guy I saw wasn't contagious. That doesn't matter, either. The real problem is the people like him out there. There's something wrong with those . . . people."

"Are you talking about *Shaitan*?" asked Kate. "The shit Laura thinks?"

He hadn't wanted to say "*Shaitan*." He'd seen a frightened mob inflamed beyond reason by that word.

He considered confirming Laura's certainty that a new kind of person walked among them. He now believed the same thing. He'd seen the man's eyes. The raw emptiness in them was something he'd never seen before, and he'd faced tough people during his life. Tough—mean—in the way of certain predators that killed just to kill. This new thing was worse.

His voice lowered ominously, he said, "Call them *Shaitan*, call them whatever you want. There's something unreasonable and dangerous out there. I think the best way to deal with it, to *survive*, is to get the fuck away from them."

Josiah's soft, deadly tone aroused fear in Laura. She glanced at him, sitting so close to her that their knees touched.

"You saw it, didn't you?" she said.

She searched the clear green depths of his eyes. "You did. You saw it." *He believes me.* She finally had an ally.

"What're you talking about?" Eli asked. "What did you see, Josiah?"

"Goddamn it," Kate interjected, "If you say you saw Satan, I swear I'm leaving all of you."

"Josiah," Catherine said, "are you confirming this notion of Laura's?"

"I did see something," he answered reluctantly. He'd wanted to talk to Laura about it, first. Alone. "I saw it in the eyes of the man I was just talking about, and it must be the same thing Laura saw in the casino. There is definitely something new in the world, and I don't have the words to describe or explain it."

Catherine, her face expressionless, nodded decisively. "We'll go back to California."

Kate turned to her. "California? Back over that damn pass? Why?"

"Because there we can find a place with a mild climate

and good soil. Because the state is still off the grid and more people are fleeing it than staying. Because now it sounds as though isolation is far preferable to community living."

"She's right," Josiah said.

"But it'll be hell trying to get back over the mountains," Kate protested. "With all the storms we've been having . . ."

"It's still our best option," Josiah said. "Most people are heading southeast. This weather's got to break soon and when it does, there'll be another group coming over the mountain. One way or another, the passes will be cleared, at least for a while."

Kate jumped to her feet. "This is stupid. We should just stay here. Things will settle down, get better. And there's people here, and stuff to do. You guys are just being paranoid. For chrissakes—"

Laura grabbed Kate's hand. "It's dangerous here. I've seen it. Josiah's seen it."

Kate wrenched her hand from Laura's. "No. You, of all people, Laura—you're the one who should be trying to stay here. You're the one who's going to need a hospital—"

"Kate," Laura warned.

"What's this?" Catherine said. "Laura?"

Kate whirled to Catherine. "She's pregnant. She's going to need a doctor."

Everyone stared at Laura. Furious, Laura glared at Kate.

For a moment, Kate glared back defiantly, then became abruptly contrite. "I'm sorry, I'm sorry, I'm sorry, Laura, but shit, you had to tell them sometime. They're ready to move somewhere with no doctors, or hospitals, or—or anything . . ."

"We must go," said Catherine with a ferocity new to her. "You are sadly mistaken if you believe Laura, in her condition, should remain in this town, much less give birth in one of its hospitals."

"But—" Kate sputtered.

Catherine ignored her. "Josiah? Eli? Speak."

Laura couldn't bring herself to look at Josiah.

"It'll be okay," he said softly, then, to Catherine, "I say go."

Eli nodded. "We go."

"Laura?" Catherine prodded.

Laura turned hesitantly to Kate, her anger gone. "What do you say, Kate, all for one and one for all?"

Kate, deflated, mustered a shrug. "Yeah, okay, what the hell. Just promise me one thing?" She waited for Laura's nod, then said, "If we get stuck in Donner Pass, my body's not on the menu."

CHAPTER 23

John Thomas giggled as he watched the two puppies squirming on the blanket in the large cardboard box. Their eyes had opened days ago and they were trying to gain control of their limbs, tumbling around their limited territory. John Thomas, delighted by their grunts, petted their small heads, laughing as the sounds changed to tiny growls.

"John Thomas, I don't wanna go," Lucas said for the third time. He stood next to his kneeling brother, on the verge of slugging John Thomas for emphasis.

John Thomas, thinking that the puppies might be hungry again, wondered if he should call Reina in from the backyard. "It'll be okay, we'll go someplace where there isn't so much snow."

"I don't care about snow. I wanna stay here."

"We can't, Lucas. Everybody's going." John Thomas rose and went to the back door.

Lucas followed, saying, "We could stay here alone, just like we did before, in the other house."

"We can't." John Thomas opened the back door and called Reina.

"Why?"

"Because, we just can't, that's all. We gotta go with Katie and Laura and Jo—"

"Why?" Lucas interrupted.

Reina trotted in and John Thomas shut the door behind her. "Because." He started following Reina into the den, but Lucas grabbed his wrist, digging his fingers in.

"I'm gonna stay here," he declared furiously.

John Thomas shook his arm. "Stop it, Lucas. That hurts, let go."

"No." Lucas defiantly tightened his grip. "I'm staying. And you're staying, too."

"What's going on, guys?" Eli said as he came into the kitchen. "Hey, Lucas, stop that. Let go of him."

Lucas, eyes narrowing mutinously, crossed his arms on his chest.

Ignoring him, Eli ruffled John Thomas's hair. "You guys get your stuff out of the den while I move the puppies to the car, okay?" John Thomas trotted obediently from the room. Lucas followed, resentment evident in every movement of his body.

Donner Pass was snowed in. Snow packs on both sides of the road formed walls higher than the roof of the Suburban and the passageway sometimes narrowed to a single lane. Laura moved into an icy pullout barely large enough for the SUV and waited, engine idling, for Josiah or Eli to give the all clear over the CB radio. Poking her head out the window, she craned her neck to see how much farther the single-lane stretch extended. She saw the first of a slow line of oncoming cars.

"I can't tell where it widens. There's a curve ahead."

"This is really getting old," Kate muttered as she watched the cars crawl past them. They'd left the city four hours ago and already she missed the bustle and distractions.

"Here comes the last one. Green sedan," Eli said over the CB.

Laura waited for the sedan to pass before easing back onto the road. Within minutes, it widened to two lanes. The leapfrogging method they were using was time-consuming, but it was better than constantly backing up their vehicles for oncoming cars on the narrow stretches.

Catherine spoke into the mike. "Boys, if we could stop at a facility, rather than the next mere widening of the road, I'd be grateful."

Shortly thereafter, they spotted a solitary gas station on a slight rise ahead, to the left. One car was parked near it, an old jeep, and it was obvious from the number of tire tracks and the flattened snow that others had stopped, though the station itself was abandoned. Parking some distance from the jeep, everyone spilled from the vehicles, stretching and stamping their feet. Despite the bright sunshine and brilliant blue sky, an icy breeze instantly reddened their cheeks.

Catherine pulled a packet of toilet-seat protectors from her pocket and extracted singles of the papery tissue, handing one each to Laura and Kate.

"Jesus, Catherine." Kate grabbed hers and stuffed it into her pocket. When Josiah and Eli laughed, Kate blurted, "Couldn't you have waited 'til we got to the restroom, for chrissakes?"

"Don't be silly," Catherine responded. "My goodness, for someone who continuously peppers her speech with scatological references, I am surprised at such sudden modesty."

"Yeah, well, when I say shit, I say shit; I don't say I'm gonna go *take* a shit, damn it." She turned and stomped away. Catherine said loudly, "Does everyone have toilet paper?" Without turning around, Kate threw her hands up in the air and shouted a wordless cry of aggravation. Laura caught up with her and, looking at each other, they burst into laughter.

"Can you believe her?" Kate said, grinning. "I

thought she was too proper to even *think* the word 'toilet,' much less shout it in the middle of a parking lot."

"Well, above all else, she's practical. I guess we should've expected it."

"Next thing you know she'll be passing out rubbers."

"A little late, in my case."

"It's never too late, honey, because—" Kate broke off as they rounded the corner of the building and saw a woman emerging from the restroom twenty paces away. A handgun was held close to her waist, pointed at them. The woman stared at them with red-rimmed eyes. Encased in bulky clothing, her brown hair straggled from beneath her knitted cap in thin tangles.

Kate cleared her throat. "Hey, listen, we just wanna use the bathroom."

"Where's my girl?" the woman demanded. She raised the gun, and gripped it so tightly the black hole of its muzzle quivered. "Give me my girl back. Give me my girl!"

A man's voice echoed from behind the door to the men's room. "Donna, I'm comin' out, hold on, it's just me openin' the door." The door swung inward and a bone-thin man stepped out in front of Kate and Laura, facing the woman. "Put it down, Donna, come on now, honey."

"Gary! It's them. Gary, they've got my girl!"

"Shh, no, it's not them, honey, they don't have our girl," he said soothingly, looking briefly over his shoulder at Kate and Laura. "Come on now." He walked forward as he spoke and gently took the gun from her grip as she stared into his eyes.

"Are you sure, Gary?" she whimpered. "Really sure?"

"I'm really sure," he assured her, pocketing the gun and hugging her to him with one arm. "Come on, now, let's move on." He turned her toward the jeep just as Catherine, followed by the men and boys, rounded the corner.

"It's her, Gary!" Donna screamed, pushing herself away. "She's got my girl." She pointed at Catherine. "Give me my girl."

Gary pulled her back and repeated his calming words, his brief tone of exasperation quickly smothered.

Laura swallowed, not daring to move. The poor woman must have lost her daughter to the blackout. "That's Catherine," she said. "She's with us." Then, wanting to sympathize, she added a lie. "She lost her girl, too."

Donna gave an anguished cry and collapsed against Gary, clutching at his coat.

Kate whispered, "Nice going, Laura."

Dismayed, Laura said, "Maybe we should go back to the car."

The woman broke away from her husband and pushed herself between Kate and Laura, to grab Catherine's arm and search her face with frantic eyes. "Did you see them?" she asked Catherine. "Did you see them take your girl? I seen them take mine. They snatched her right from my arms. It happened so fast. I was holding her. She's just a little thing, just a beautiful little girl." She crumpled to the ground, sobbing into her hands.

Gripping his wife's arms, the man raised her gently and wrapped her in his arms as her sobs diminished to a thin cry.

"Two weeks ago, it happened," Gary said to Catherine. "She was there alone, with our girl, and two women came up to her, telling her 'My, what a pretty baby.' Donna had no reason not to trust them—they were just women admiring her baby. Then one of them grabbed Kelly and the other pushed Donna hard enough to make her fall." His close-set brown eyes were murky with pain.

"Donna chased after them. But, in the time it took her to get to her feet, they were already out the door. Their car was right there, and they took off. She was close enough to touch the car and have it slide from under her fingers."

He squeezed his eyes shut and swallowed, his arms tightening around his wife. "I don't know how long she chased it; she doesn't remember." He met Catherine's unwavering gaze and shook his head. "East, that street was. You see what I mean? That street happened to head east."

Catherine nodded slowly. "Yes, I see," she said, and

her chin trembled.

Laura felt the infinite sadness of the couple's endless search in a random direction that was their only lead. She watched them walk to the jeep, their bodies leaning into each other in the age-old language of support.

At dusk, they finally turned into a likely driveway. The house, amidst pines, was dark, and the adjacent carport empty. They were subdued after the encounter earlier that day, in moods that had deepened into melancholy. Laura tried again to shake it off as Josiah and Eli emerged from the parked truck.

Getting everyone settled for the night in a strange house, preparing a meal, situating the boys and the puppies, encountering the possibility of no electricity or running water, seemed a daunting stream of exhausting chores after the tense day.

The work actually proved to be uplifting. The bustle, the animated voices, the boys and Reina underfoot, brought a feeling of normalcy and purpose. By the time the house had been explored, rooms assigned, bedding changed, generator found and started, propane heat turned on and the house warmed, and soup and sandwiches made and consumed, Laura felt herself again. By nine o'clock, the boys were tucked into bed without their usual protests. The noisy generator was turned off and the adults gathered in the living room. Candles and lanterns were disbursed along the mantle and atop various tables, and a small fire burned in a pot-bellied stove on a stone hearth.

For a while, conversation was limited. Laura considered going to bed but was delayed by the coziness.

"I don't guess they'll ever find her," Kate remarked, bringing the sad plight of the couple once more to everyone's mind.

"I wonder how long they'll keep looking," said Eli.

"The search is her hope," Catherine said, "and her downfall."

"Her poor husband," Kate said. "It was his kid, too, and he's stuck taking care of his crazy wife."

"I wonder how many people went nuts after the blackout," Eli mused. "Most people must've lost some family."

"Yeah," Kate frowned. "Maybe the TV shrinks are right about the second blackout, that it was a backlash, some kind of mass mourning."

Laura stared into space while she listened, but when the silence lengthened, she found that all eyes had turned to her. Their mixture of anticipation was comical. She smiled, held up her hands, and said, "Come on, what do you want me to say? I've already told you what I know." Even Eli, though profusely apologetic, had been openly skeptical.

"See how she doesn't say what she thinks it is?" said

Kate. "See how she says what she knows it is?" Smugly, she added, "Face it, Laura, you're hopeless."

"It's time we seriously consider our self-defense," said Catherine somberly. "Today could have taken a tragic turn. That woman, unbalanced as she was, could have easily shot Kate or Laura. We were completely unprepared."

"That was a fluke, Catherine," Kate protested. "You can't expect us to be armed all the time."

"That is exactly what we must do," Catherine said. "I suggest we avoid use of public facilities. It was wrong to suggest it and I would never have forgiven myself had it ended in tragedy."

"She's right," Josiah said. "What's the point in trying to find a safe home, away from the—*Shaitan*," he glanced at Laura, "if we don't assume strangers could be dangerous?"

"Even after everything that's happened," said Eli, obviously perplexed, "the world changed, the death and weirdness, it's hard to think differently." He met Josiah's gaze. "You know?"

Josiah nodded sympathetically at his friend. "Yeah, I know, Eli. But we really don't have a choice. Things *are* different."

Kate groaned. "We train ourselves to be assassins and no one gets near us. We live the rest of our lives with no one to talk to but each other."

Laura laughed. "We just need to screen people,

Kate. Besides, I think we make a nice group. I wouldn't mind hanging out together, forever." She willed herself not to look at Josiah.

Kate grinned. "Together, forever, that's okay by me, as long as you promise that we won't have to forsake all others. No offense, but I'm still a young and, whaddya-callit—vital—woman. If the four of you chase off every eligible man, I'll go nuts."

The discussion stalled when the children's awareness of weapons became a question.

"We demand they don't touch our guns," Eli insisted.

"We keep the guns hidden," Kate muttered. "If that little monster knew we had loaded guns, he'd shoot us all."

By now, everyone knew Kate's view of Lucas, and her reasons for it. Even Josiah, who'd barely interacted with either child, now kept watch on Lucas.

Laura, thinking how often Lucas appeared unexpectedly in a doorway, found herself becoming wary. The boys' room was at the end of the hallway. *They can't hear anything,* she thought. *We've been talking quietly.*

"Kate's right," Josiah said. "Our best option is to keep guns out of sight. If the time comes, we'll deal with it then."

"You guys ever notice how Josiah keeps score?" said Kate, having endured enough serious discussion. "Kate's right," she mimicked, chalking the air with her finger,

"Catherine's right"—another slash—"Eli's right"—slash. She paused, forefinger aloft and gave Laura a pitying look. "Sorry, honey, I can't remember if he ever gave you any points." Her expression dissolved into innocence. "Or does he do you privately?"

Laura's cheeks flamed. "Jesus, Kate," she sputtered.

Kate's gibe at Laura surprised Eli. Yet, a glance at Josiah brought confirmation. *So that's how it is,* he thought. *Laura? How did I not know?* He rose and made a show of stretching tiredly, knowing he wasn't pulling it off. He was all angles and jerks. "Time to hit the sack," he said, then glanced at Kate and Catherine. "How about it?"

Kate rolled her eyes. "Oh, brother. If that's not—" a look at Josiah changed her next words, "—an invitation, then I don't know what is." She rose, and jokingly pinched Eli's cheek. "But not tonight, honey. I'm beat." Waggling her fingers over her head, she said, "Good night, all."

Catherine shook her head as Kate flounced out. "Irrepressible," she said. "Josiah, you must teach me the look you gave her. She's exhausted my skills." With a small smile and a nod, she left, and Eli trailed behind her.

Waiting until the last door clicked shut, Josiah laughed softly. "Kate's a piece of work," he said. He walked over to Laura and held out his hand.

Laura placed her hand in his, heart pounding in her

ears. He did want her. As their hands touched, she felt the silky heat of his flesh on hers, a sensation of erotic warmth. *My God. And that's just his hand!*

He drew her up and they stood, eyes locked. His face lowered to hers and their lips touched. They sank to the couch, lost in a universe of two.

CHAPTER 24

DAYS LATER, EXHAUSTED FROM THEIR GRIM JOURNEY, Laura and the others found a place to call home. The strangers they'd encountered were suspicious, aggressive, often frightening. The weapons and ammunition they'd taken pains to find had been worth the trouble. Being unarmed was now unthinkable.

They came upon the old farmhouse in the late afternoon of a cold, overcast day that had been full of tense encounters, shouted warnings to move on, and brandished shotguns. Tired and hungry, they cautiously rounded the last tree-lined bend of a long dirt road and saw the large house in a small clearing. It had all the signs of having been abandoned.

The old house was a mile off the main road, in a sparsely populated section of Butte County, in northern California. The rambling two-story, solid structure had an attic and a deep, wrap-around porch. An orchard lay south of the house, and vegetation indicated good soil.

It took them several days to unload supplies, sanitize the house, and settle in. They set up generators and primed the well pump to restore use of the water system. In an overgrown clearing below the north side of the house, they found the decomposed, scavenger-ravaged body of an old man.

Josiah and Eli wrapped the grim remains in an old tarp and, late that afternoon, buried it far from the house. Kate and Laura sat on a knoll and watched the men disappear into the woods with the body. The January sun cast a pale, cold light, sharpening the clear air so that distant snow-covered peaks of the Sierras stood in perfect relief against the dark thunderheads hovering over them.

Laura had watched Josiah until he and Eli disappeared among the trees. She savored thoughts of their night together, of his skin against hers, but her heart ached.

No matter how often she replayed their discussion the following morning, she couldn't understand why he'd retreated from her. *You're so beautiful,* he'd told her, *such a beautiful person, but we can't do this again. I'm sorry.*

She'd been speechless, the closeness she'd felt now suspect. Awkwardly, she'd probed for an explanation, but none of his tender words helped her understand.

Maybe he'd felt the depth of her emotion—she hadn't tried to hide it—and that was why he'd retreated. She knew Josiah, and the thought that he might be frightened by commitment left her feeling flat.

Maybe it was the baby, she thought, *another man's child, coming between us.*

Gazing still at the point of the trail where she'd last seen Josiah before he and Eli vanished with their burden, she wondered how far they'd go before they found a place to lay the poor old man to rest. How far into unknown forests they would all have to travel.

Josiah tramped through the brush, shoulders bowed beneath a heavy weight; not the corpse, he barely felt that brittle load of bones and shriveled flesh. The weight came from Laura's gaze from atop the knoll. He moved quickly to put a screen of trees between them.

He'd actually convinced himself he and Laura could come together casually. *Dumbshit,* he berated himself. *You did know better.* Truth was, he'd indulged himself, at her expense. He'd had to see what the wild tug he felt would become. And it had surpassed any speculation.

But, shit. The way she'd looked at him—both during and after—she might just as well have put her heart on a platter and thrust it before him.

Even though he wanted Laura as much this very minute as he had before, he knew he'd tire of her, eventually.

And the breakup would be messy, putting a strain on everyone. He had to think of the group and, mostly, Eli. Eli was comfortable here, with them.

Shifting his grip on the tarp, he ducked under a branch, warned Eli of it, and emerged into a small clearing.

As Eli stopped next to him, Josiah knew Laura's future played a part in his decision. He liked and respected her, didn't want her hurt, and he wanted to keep it that way.

Laura. Friendship. Not like Eli, but still, nothing but friendship.

Laura, no longer able to see Josiah, looked down at the wet grass.

"I wonder if the old man lived here alone," she said to Kate. She wanted to stop thinking about Josiah. Friendship was the only possibility now. Perhaps it could be fixed later.

"Maybe," said Kate. She stared down at the narrow, wooded valley below them, then up to where it widened toward the foothills, and farther yet to the distant mountains. The mild weather that had allowed them to leave Reno continued, leaving the foothills brilliant green with new growth. "The house is too neat for any of those kids in the photos to have lived here," she added.

Framed photos had covered the walls, tabletops, and

fireplace mantle. She, Laura, and Catherine had carefully packed them away, speculating on their identities.

"Sad," Laura said.

"Aw, come on. The guy's probably thrilled he didn't have to stick around after the shit hit the fan. Anyway, by your reckoning, we're probably sitting on him right now." She yanked up a fistful of weeds and shook it. "Go find somewhere else to reincarnate, you old turdball."

She frowned at her handful of weeds, picking through and discarding them, until there was only a single, purplish-gray one left. "Hey, Laura, look at this." She thrust the oddly shaped and colored bit of vegetation in front of Laura's eyes.

Laura pushed Kate's hand back for a better perspective. "And?"

"Look at it. The weird spikes? They've got little suction-cup thingies on them."

Laura shrugged. "So what? Maybe it's one of those insect-eating plants. What are they called?"

"Insectius eatemupus? Crap, how would I know?"

Kate placed the weed on her palm and examined it closely. Suddenly, she yelped, startling Laura.

"What?"

"Damn." Kate shook her hand upside down, flapping it wildly. The weed remained stuck to her.

"It's got some kind of sticker. Ow. Shit." She grasped the weed at its root with two fingers of her other hand and pulled gently. Laura scrabbled to her knees and leaned close. At the place where the plant stuck on Kate's palm, three of the tiny suction cups were firmly flattened against her skin. "Fuck, it burns!"

She yanked the weed off and tossed it aside. On her palm, one tiny purplish saucer remained, along with two perfect circles of flared red where the others had been attached. "Goddamn!" She scratched at the remaining sucker with a fingernail until it curled into a ball and dropped off.

They hurried to the house, Kate blowing on her palm and shaking her hand.

The evening meal was subdued, everyone exhausted. Kate's wounds, three perfect red spots of inflammation, had been displayed and, as they sat in the living room, children upstairs in bed, she reapplied the medicated ointment Laura had selected.

Catherine sat in the matching armchair opposite Kate, both angled toward the fireplace. The room was lit with kerosene lamps, candles, and the fire Eli was tending as he sat cross-legged before the hearth, idly nudging the burning wood with a poker. Laura snuggled beneath an afghan on the couch and Josiah, a kerosene lamp in hand, inspected bookshelves at one side of the fireplace.

Muffled rumbles of thunder occasionally broadened into deep booms.

"Are you certain there weren't any more?" Catherine asked again.

"For the zillionth time, Catherine, yes." Kate didn't bother looking up.

"No need for that tone. Although you've looked, it's improbable that just one plant would grow in such a large area."

"I know, I know," Kate muttered. "But it's not that impossible. Seeds can be carried by wind or birds. Maybe it flew in from Golden Gate Park."

"Does it still hurt?"

"That goop took most of the burn away."

Eli turned and looked at Laura. "Don't you come from this area?"

"Not quite," Laura answered. "We lived farther northeast."

"And you never saw this weird plant?"

Laura shook her head. "And I'm sure I would've. We kids would have been warned about something that could hurt us like that."

Josiah selected a book, crossed the room, and sat on the floor with his back against the couch.

Catherine thumped her cane on the floor beside her chair. "It's time," she said decisively. Assured she had everyone's attention, she nodded. "It's time we come to some conclusions, the first of which is that Reina's puppies must be disposed of."

"What?" Laura exclaimed.

"What do you mean, 'disposed of'?" Eli asked.

Josiah stared intently at Catherine. She met his gaze and said, "You've noticed, haven't you?"

He nodded.

"Noticed what?" Eli asked.

"They're not normal," Catherine said.

"Normal how?" Kate sounded confused. "They're four weeks old. How can you tell they're not normal?"

"By observing Reina. She has to be coaxed with treats to stay in the box while the puppies nurse. And I cannot blame her a bit. They behave like demons. Her reprimanding nips have no effect, and, despite the availability of several swollen teats, the two pups always fight over the same one. They're vicious and revolting."

"Pups do that, don't they?" Eli asked.

"Not to that extent," Catherine stated. "They're far more competitive than normal, particularly with a healthy mother. They show threatening abnormalities and we must not allow them to mature."

"You want us to kill them?" Laura asked in disbelief.

"Yes. However, I don't expect you, or anyone else, to do it. It was my suggestion. If you'll occupy the children tomorrow, I'll take care of it."

"You've been itching to shoot something ever since

we met," Kate said.

Catherine sniffed. "I won't be wasting our ammunition on them."

"Then how—"

"I'll take care of it, Catherine," Josiah said, looking up from his book.

"I still don't get it, Catherine," Eli said. "What do some weird plants have to do with puppies?"

Catherine was about to speak when the storm broke with fury. Instantly, the room was filled with sounds of the downpour on the roof and sharp reports of drops gusting against the windowpanes. Looking at the shade-shuttered windows, they listened without a word spoken until, moments later, the sound steadied into heavy winter rain.

"As you all know," Catherine said above the sound of the storm, "I am a firm believer in science and have little patience with conclusions drawn from hope or emotion. However," she gazed sharply at each of them, "strange events seem to be changing this world. And the pace is not slowing." She leaned forward on her cane. "We can no longer afford the luxury of awaiting information before we decide on a course of action. Despite risks, we must draw premature conclusions if we want to survive."

Rain and snapping fire was all that could be heard. Josiah closed his book and set it aside. Laura pulled the afghan tightly around her legs. Kate looked silently at nothing.

"Okay," said Eli to Catherine. "So you're saying that

we do the puppies now so they can't hurt us later?"

Catherine nodded.

"What else?" he prodded.

"Kate's hand," Catherine said. "The plant that injured her is toxic and none of us is familiar with it. If it's natural, we simply avoid it. But, if it's unnatural, the change is most likely some reaction to the blackout. We must act as if the second possibility is the true one."

"What kind of reaction?" Kate asked.

"Mutation," Catherine responded. "Natural mutations—those that account for species' survival—are minor, gradual. Gross mutations rarely survive. Yet we now have evidence of two gross mutations, the puppies and the plant, that are surviving. I say again, the world is changing."

Laura thought of Reina's litter: two stillborn, one deformed, and two . . . vicious?

"I don't get it," Kate said belligerently. "The damn plant could be natural. Why blame it on the blackout?"

"Kate, dear, you must try to understand." Catherine's voice was gentle. "What is at stake now, as we make all decisions, is our survival."

Kate's indignation grew. "Are you saying man-eating plants and deformed monsters are going to start popping up all over the place?" She jumped from her chair. "Laura already thinks *Night of the Living Dead* is real, and now you're bringing in *Alien* and *Attack of the Killer*

Tomatoes. Listen. Things will get back to normal. We just sit tight and wait it out. That's all." She threw herself back into her chair.

Catherine thumped her cane on the floor. "That's not all," she said sternly. "What happens when we run out of food?"

"We get more." Kate glared at her.

"And when there's no more to be gotten?"

"We hunt. Forage."

Catherine said very softly, "And what if we're only able to find inedible animals, and toxic plants?"

Frustrated, Kate blurted, "Then we're just fucked, I guess."

Catherine nodded gravely. "But we don't want to be. So we assume the worst now, and plan ahead."

Kate glowered. "What are you going to plan for if everything's gonna be mutated? Hell, even Laura can't plan on her ba—" She clapped a hand over her mouth, horrified. "Oh, shit. Laura, I didn't mean that."

Laura stared back at her, white-faced.

"Nonsense." Catherine barked in the tense silence. "I never said everything was mutating."

"Reina's pups." Laura was pale. "Two stillborn, one deformed, and the two surviving ones no . . . good. That's five out of five."

"Laura—" Kate began, uncertain of what to say.

"Why shouldn't we suppose that everything will

mutate?" asked Laura, fighting back tears.

"Don't worry about your baby, Laura," said Eli. "Everything'll be okay."

"No," Laura said. "Everything's not okay. Everything's really, really wrong."

Everyone spoke at once, but Laura stopped them.

"Listen to me!" she cried. "I know none of you believe what I told you. But it's all fitting together.

"What if something broke during the blackout, when the barrier between the physical world and Us came down? What if We can't get through anymore?

"If We can't get through, We aren't controlling genetic combinations. Things are still reproducing biologically but without guidance."

"If that's true, Laura," said Josiah, "everything will randomly mutate into extinction."

No one could think of anything to say to that. In the silence, they once again became aware of the violent storm. Lightning flared through the window shades and thunder shook the house. The downpour was steady, with occasional sharp gusts lashing rain against the windows.

Catherine cleared her throat. "I believe I'll have a sherry."

"I'll get it," offered Eli. "I think I'll have some, too. Anyone else?" Kate and Josiah said yes. Laura was drying her tears. "Give me a hand, Laura." He tugged her off the couch and guided her to the kitchen.

When they came back with the sherry, Laura smiled her appreciation to Eli, who'd talked ceaselessly while they were in the kitchen to lure her from her dreadful thoughts. But, as she curled herself back into her corner of the couch, she found herself again confronting her latest discovery.

The way in was gone. Life, as they knew it, was no longer being born.

What was taking its place?

CHAPTER 25

THE STORM RAGED AGAINST THE HOUSE THROUGHOUT the night. By 4:30 a.m., Laura felt she hadn't slept at all. Snuggled beneath her blankets, she listened to the deluge. No wonder primitive people had personalized the elements; her own heart tried to match the rhythm of the fury lashing through the darkness. Lightning flared as tree branches whipped loudly against the old house. The sudden brightness and wild sounds made her feel vulnerable, cratered a pit of loneliness within her.

She flung back the covers and dressed quickly in jeans, cotton turtleneck, thick sweater, wool socks, and sheepskin slippers. Quietly, she padded down the stairs of the sleeping house. In the roomy kitchen, she lit the kerosene lamp on the dining table. The table's rough wood, polished to a sheen with years of use, reflected the glow.

She stoked the fire in the old cookstove, filtered

water into the kettle, and found a cup, spoon, honey, and tea. Shivering, she dragged a worn rocker closer to the stove, then sat with her tea in the stove's ring of warmth and replayed last night's thoughts.

We *can't get through anymore.* She was certain. The understanding was visceral.

She found it difficult to believe she was the only one who remembered the knowledge that had burst upon the world, and yet, she wondered. During the months past, not one person had offered any similar version of her own experience.

Sipping her tea, she noticed that a curtain was hanging slightly askew, exposing a wedge of dark pane. She stared at the small slice of darkness patterned with silvery raindrops, an intrusion by the wild fury outside. For an instant, the storm and darkness seemed unending, a scene that would remain unchanged as the world died. Quickly, she jumped up and straightened the curtain.

Laura warmed her hands on her cup as she rocked in the old chair, battling the thought of life severed from its source, the terrible implication to her child. *Will its eyes be empty?* Her only hope was that her child had been conceived before the barrier had fallen—and been replaced by a barrier against the life force. The slim hope hinged on one question: Did life begin at conception?

Babies must have been born since the blackout. But babies don't do much in the first few months. Would anyone notice anything missing if they weren't looking for it? Would such young eyes reflect that horrible emptiness?

Motion in the doorway startled her. John Thomas appeared, blond hair tousled, shivering in his pajamas. Reina drooped sheepishly at his side, head down and ears back.

"Couldn't you sleep either, John Thomas?"

John Thomas shook his head. "Too loud. I think the rain's breaking my window. Can it do that?"

Laura smiled reassuringly and held her hand out to him. "Come here, John Thomas."

To her surprise, he climbed into her lap. She folded her arms around him, flushed with pleasure at his unexpected trust. It was always Kate he chose to snuggle near.

"Warm enough?" she inquired.

He nodded and curled himself against her. Reina collapsed to the floor next to them with a soft grunt.

"It's a dark and stormy night, all right," said Laura, with an extra hug, "but I've been through lots of storms and I've never seen a window break. But if it does, we'll fix it."

"Do we have extra window stuff?"

"I don't know, but we could get some."

He snuggled tighter. "What if we couldn't get any more glass?"

Hearing the tremor in his high voice, Laura realized he was seeking absolutes and would continue questioning every solution until he heard something undeniable. "Well then," she declared, squeezing him gently, "you see that big pantry door there?"

He twisted, saw the heavy wooden door, and nodded.

"We'll take that door right off its hinges," she said, "and we'll put it over the broken window and nail it to the wall with five hundred and forty-seven big, fat nails. How's that?"

John Thomas giggled. "That might work."

Laura laughed. Resuming her rocking, she hummed an old tune from her childhood, one she'd used to sing to her younger brother, Conrad. As she hummed, cuddling John Thomas, she thought about Conrad. Where was he now? How was he surviving this new world? She knew how ill-equipped Conrad was for anything harsh. He was made for happy times, for laughter and parties, where his easygoing nature caused people to let him coast along.

Sadness trembled through her humming.

Kate's loud yawn preceded her through the doorway. When she appeared, in her too-large plaid robe, its belt loosely tied, Laura silently indicated John Thomas was asleep.

Kate whispered, "Oops, sorry."

"He fell asleep a little while ago," Laura whispered. "Would you make a place for him on the couch?"

Kate nodded, and Laura listened to her movements in the living room. Kate was stirring up the banked fire and adding kindling. Laura eased out of the rocking chair. Although John Thomas was small and thin for his age, his limp weight was awkward. She carried him to the now-blanketed couch and covered him with the throw Kate handed her.

At first, Laura and Kate whispered as they added logs to the fire, but it soon became apparent that John Thomas was sleeping soundly.

"How long have you been up?" Kate asked.

"Since 4:30. John Thomas came down about an hour later. He was scared the storm might break his window."

"It sounds like it might break the walls, too." Kate rose and stretched, then placed her hands at the small of her back. "Man, what a night!"

"I was surprised to see him. Usually he goes to you when he's scared."

"Yeah, well." Kate grinned at her. "He probably found my door locked."

"Locked? Why?"

"Company." Kate winked. "Josiah dropped by last night. Hey, I don't suppose you started some coffee?" She disappeared into the kitchen.

Pain seared Laura's heart, again and again. It hurt to breathe. Josiah and Kate? How?

A locked door.

Thoughts of Kate and Josiah, together, assaulted her; Josiah's hands on Kate, Josiah's eyes on Kate, Josiah's gentle words to Kate. Pain twisted through her stomach into her throat. She pressed her temples to push the visions out of her mind. She couldn't function with those images inside, but she couldn't think about anything else.

Why had Kate done this to her? She knew how she felt about Josiah. How could she not? A dozen memories: Kate's knowing winks behind Josiah's back, Kate teasing her about Josiah, Kate looking sideways, her innuendos . . .

Kate bringing her pregnancy to everyone's attention.

Had Kate done it deliberately? She'd thought, at the time, that Kate might have been using her pregnancy as an excuse not to leave Reno. Now she wondered if Kate had just wanted Josiah to know.

If the ugly suspicion were true, it meant a mean-spirited Kate had tried to sabotage any chance of romance she might have with Josiah. She couldn't fathom such a betrayal.

She forced herself to acknowledge that she had noticed Kate's attraction to Josiah, and ignored it. Kate may have done the same thing with her. She'd never told Kate about their night, more than a week ago, or confided her feelings, fearing that Kate would blurt it out. Anger and self-pity welled within her.

Was Kate the reason Josiah had stopped their

relationship from going further? Was Kate the one he'd wanted all along?

She was almost four months pregnant. Even though Josiah had known before they'd slept together, maybe he'd had second thoughts or feared that he would be expected to act as the baby's father. But he gave no indication of misunderstanding her that thoroughly. In fact, so many of the little things he said showed her that he truly understood her. Her thoughts twisted and tumbled, her heart ached, and visions of Josiah entwined with Kate blinded her with tears.

"What are we going to do when we run out of coffee?" Kate complained, coming back into the room with a steaming mug.

Laura grasped the fireplace poker and busied herself with the fire. She kept her face averted and surreptitiously wiped away her tears as Kate settled herself into an armchair.

"Think the storm's gonna last all day?" asked Kate innocently.

Laura shrugged.

"Sure seems like it. Great, huh? A whole day of being cooped in with the troops."

Laura stiffened.

Kate noisily sipped her coffee. "Something wrong, kiddo? Don't you feel good?"

"I'm all right."

Kate set her coffee on the hearth, reached out and gently rubbed Laura's shoulder. "Honey, I'm sorry about what I said last night. I can be so stupid, saying whatever pops into my head, but I really didn't mean it. Your baby's going to be just fine. Really."

Laura felt completely abandoned. Suddenly, it was too much; their life force cut off from entering the world, earth repopulated by mutated organisms without souls, the unknown condition of the child in her womb. And her forever-love, Josiah, choosing someone else. Tears spilled from her eyes, and her mouth trembled.

"Aw, honey." Kate's voice wavered and her eyes watered at her friend's distress. She gathered Laura in her arms. "Don't cry. It's okay. Everything will be fine."

Laura endured the embrace, listened to meaningless words. There was no comfort in them, none to be found in the forsaken world. Even love had been snatched from her. And not just Josiah. There would be no bonding with a soulless infant. She was alone.

Conrad was all she had left on the planet. Where was he? Hot tears filled her world.

CHAPTER 26

Mohammed sat in the copilot seat and watched every move Mack made. He watched the dials and gauges in front of him and listened to the changing tones of the engines. If he learned to fly this plane, he could escape. Tension knotted his stomach and fear contracted his throat.

The thought of flying the plane terrified him, but Mack terrified him more, a terror that never left him. Not since the horror in the bloody kitchen, when he'd finally decided to flee from Mack. But Mack never stopped watching him. Every movement of Mack's body spoke of a readiness to whirl around and seize Mohammed.

Tension mounted every day, the feeling of being cornered by something huge, menacing. Deadly.

Chin to chest, from the corner of his eye he watched Mack's hands on the yoke. Muscular hands. Long fingers. Wiry tufts of black hair at the base of each finger. Mack was watching him. He slid his glance away from Mack's hands, down to his own. It was all he could do to keep them from trembling.

How many days had it been? Days of flying and circling, landing, and refueling. Stealing cars and venturing into towns. Everything they did was at Mack's direction, and under Mack's cold scrutiny. The idea of losing himself in a crowd, or of dashing into the countryside, was smothered by Mack's watchfulness. His neck could be snapped with one quick twist of Mack's powerful hands. And sometimes he felt Mack was waiting for just that.

The only time Mack left Mohammed and Conrad alone was in the plane, when they were parked on empty stretches of open tarmac. Mack would disappear into a distant hangar. He sometimes thought that Mack just hid himself and watched to see if Mohammed would run. And then Mack would follow, and *snap!* That would be that.

As they approached another landing strip, on the edge of a midsized airport, Mohammed noted the land below. Flat ground stretched, all reds and browns, in every direction, with big rocks, maybe small mountains, scattered in the distance. There were no foothills. The craggy humps rose suddenly from the flat land, as though they'd been randomly set down by a giant at play. Smoky haze clung to the western horizon, tinged orange by the late afternoon sun. An occasional glitter in the haze indicated a city crouched within.

Mohammed watched as Mack banked the plane into a slow descent toward the isolated airport. His own hands ached to grip the copilot control before him as it moved in concert with Mack's adjustments. Anticipating the touchdown, he tensed, and then they were swaying along the runway.

"I'll never get used to that," Conrad shouted with relief over the decelerating engine noise. Since the first takeoff, he'd refused to sit up front and instead huddled miserably in the back, enduring each takeoff and landing.

Mohammed, fixing a smile on his face, twisted around, gestured a thumbs-up to Conrad, and wondered whether this parody of normalcy was fooling Mack.

Conrad laughed. "Ali, you're a natural for this flying stuff. I bet you'd go nuts at Disneyland."

"Yah, Conrad, sure," he said, neither knowing, nor caring, what Conrad was talking about. Mohammed could not understand Conrad's ease with Mack. Did Conrad not see what Mohammed saw in Mack's cold eyes? Did he not feel the same paralysis of will?

Mohammed needed to understand Conrad, because he had to decide, soon, if he would take Conrad with him when he fled. That decision rested on Conrad's worth.

Had he been in his own country, Conrad would have been a simple problem; he would spit on him rather than try to define him. Once betrayed, shame upon you;

twice betrayed, shame upon me. He should have nothing more to do with Conrad, but . . . He might overlook opportunity if he abandoned Conrad. He was in an unknown land, among unknown people. Better a known enemy than an unknown friend.

As the plane rolled to a halt, the answer came in Conrad's favor: Conrad was not evil, but weak. Weakness, on a perilous journey, was not quite as dangerous as a malicious nature. It was a lesson of his nomadic youth. "Where are we, Mack?" Conrad asked as Mack cut the engines.

"Wyoming," Mack replied, then told him and Mohammed to stay put. Jumping out of the plane, he strode the deserted grounds toward a nearby hangar without looking back.

Conrad came forward and dropped into Mack's empty seat. He peered out the windows. "Wyoming? This isn't how I pictured Wyoming."

Meaningless words flowed past Mohammed. He had understood Conrad's question to Mack, but Mack had answered with a strange word. When Conrad repeated the word, it must have meant he had some sense of where they were in this vast country. The mountains, rivers, forests, and grasslands, the innumerable cities, towns, and roads over which they'd flown—so confusing.

Glancing at the distant hangar, he wondered how long Mack would be gone this time.

His heart jumped and he sucked his breath. Now? Was he ready? Could he do it?

He gauged the distance to the building. Could he start the plane, turn it, get it past the curve on which it now sat, and over to a runway? All before Mack could dash out? His breath was rapid as he looked at the building, the fuel gauge, the starter, Conrad.

Conrad was in the pilot's seat.

For all the duplication of the controls before him, Mohammed hadn't the faintest idea whether they worked, and he had no intention of finding out. Mack flew the plane from the other seat. So would he.

Mohammed was frantically aware of the passing seconds. What would Conrad do when he suddenly started the plane? Would he stop him? Ruin his plan? Once Mack knew that he was thinking of taking the plane, he would never leave him another opportunity. He might decide it was time to kill him. Mohammed knew there was no time to guess at Conrad's reaction, no way to quickly explain. Conrad must be left behind. Another glance at the hangar. Still no sign of Mack.

"Conrad," Mohammed croaked. He felt his lips stretch into a smile. Conrad turned to him with his usual mild courtesy. "Conrad. Piss, hah?" Mohammed gestured at the door.

"Nah, I'm okay," Conrad said.

Mohammed, sick with tension, shrilled, "Piss,

Conrad. Piss. Out! Out! Out!" He waved frantically at the door.

Startled, Conrad started laughing. "All right, Ali, don't get your turban in a twist! I thought you were asking if *I* had to go." He swung his legs out the door, stepped down and turned, a hand on each side of the cockpit opening. "Say it like this, Ali: *I* have to piss. You want to learn English, don't you? Say *I* have to piss."

Mohammed's eyes became slits and he erupted in a volley of guttural curses as he clambered into the pilot seat. Fool. Jackass. Brainless flea. Mohammed could have exited the plane from the other door. Stupid camel turd. He wanted to scream at Conrad to back away so he could close the door.

Instead, he clenched his jaw and held Conrad's gaze as he repeated, "*I* have to pi—"

Conrad's head turned, and Mohammed looked to see what had caught Conrad's attention. It was Mack, coming from the shadowed interior of the hangar. Mohammed's stomach flipped. Disappointment flooded over him. He slumped into his seat and ignored Conrad's urgings to piss before they took off again.

Mack, however, decided they would camp for the night. Gesturing Conrad back into the plane, he leaped inside and taxied the craft to the edge of the tarmac, where he parked a few yards from its lip.

Mohammed beheld the dry brown land. Its simplicity,

from the earthen tones and stubborn plant life, to the distant craggy outcroppings, spoke of home. Despite the tension that vibrated his thin body, he was uplifted by the vast stillness. He stepped off the hot blacktop, onto the warm brown dirt, and soothed himself with the primal expanse.

The mellow afternoon light shifted toward evening and the ground shadowed to darker shades. Distant rugged mountains became highlighted with warm tones in the oblique rays of the lowering sun. He breathed deeply, his bony chest expanding to draw the majesty into his own small existence. "Allahu Akbar," he whispered.

Something large hit his back and nearly brought him to his knees. Stumbling forward, heart in his throat, he was certain the moment he'd expected had finally come. He whirled around, one hand on his turban, and saw his rolled sleeping bag lay at his feet, the surprise attacker. Mack lounged against the side of the plane, watching him.

"Mecca's thataway, pardner," Mack said, pointing opposite the setting sun.

One glance into Mack's glittering eyes showed . . . what? An evil plan? An evil end?

"Hey, Ali, come on." Conrad's voice jolted Mohammed.

Mack walked to the other side of the plane. Mohammed drew a shaky breath.

"We're setting up camp the right way," Conrad said. "Campfire, barbecue—the works. Get your butt over here and help me."

Mohammed picked up his sleeping bag and went to Conrad's side on legs that trembled with every step. A small comfort, having someone between him and Mack. Minute by minute, the fading light was being absorbed, and the air chilled. He clung to the spaces through which Conrad moved, keeping Conrad between himself and Mack, as he helped set up camp. He was certain that Mack meant to harm him, tonight.

His bowels turning to water, he cast another desperate glance into the increasing darkness. Praise be to Allah, but in all that open space, there was nowhere to run. The irony numbed him.

When Mack killed him, it would be over. He would not go to the other place because that path had vanished in the blackout. Something dreadful now blocked the ancient path, the way home to the soul-living. The night the madwoman had approached him with her eerie, sing-song insanity, he had known this with certainty. Faced with his own death, he'd known with awful surety that all those who died now were simply gone, unable to return to the energy-life.

He had to stay alive. Perhaps, some day, the path would reopen, but he had to live now, to see that day. Mack could send him into a void from which there was no returning.

In the moonless sky hung countless pinpricks of

light. Conrad and Mack sat cross-legged near the grill and ate hot pieces of meat. Mohammed, in Conrad's shadow, only nibbled. His churning stomach would not tolerate food. He awaited his fate, clutching the only weapons he had, his fork and a dull table knife.

Mack saw Mohammed shrink into the shadows, tuck his feet away from the fire. Amused by Mohammed's fear, of the way he clutched his puny fork and gripped his useless knife, Mack betrayed nothing. He held his steak in his hand, smacked his lips, licked the juices from his fingers, then chewed off another bite. The fire warmed his face, his chest, his knees. And at his back, he could feel the massaging waves of Mohammed's terror.

Let his fear grow until he snaps. Maybe Ali would do something to provoke him. He raised his piece of meat for another bite. Just as his teeth closed, he imagined Ali's thigh. Eyes bright and sharp, he bit hard, and chewed slowly. Ali could be a toy for quite a while.

Beneath his excitement, Mack felt annoyance because Conrad just didn't get it. He began to explore and exploit the annoyance, because tonight he was going to let all of it out. And if it went the way he thought, this *thing* inside made manifest, the annoyance would evolve to anger, the anger into rage, and the rage into delicious ice-hot power.

Conrad would learn. And Ali would watch.

What would this *thing* do to Conrad? He couldn't

wait to find out.

Conrad unfurled his sleeping bag near the fire. Mack waited for Conrad to trigger annoyance. Then Conrad glanced at him and smiled, and the firelight accentuated the Laura-like features Conrad shared. Anger boomed through Mack. Laura should be here. He'd asked her, and she'd refused. And there was Conrad with his Laura-face, mocking him.

Anger speared into ice-hot rage, skittered to the edge of exquisite pain, then thrust him into the whirling dark vortex beyond. He flung his head back, spread his arms, rose to his feet. He was steel. He was turmoil.

There was no subtlety to his attack.

Conrad's involuntary shout quickly became cries of fear and pain. Mohammed, lying stiff a few feet away in his own sleeping bag, was engulfed by Conrad's panic, then frozen by Mack's voice speaking directly to him over Conrad's thrashing body.

"Stay put, Ali Baba," Mack threatened. He punched, quick and hard, at Conrad, just under the point where the ribs met. Conrad's body spasmed, coiled to one side, and Mack grabbed Conrad's waistband and thrust the pants downward with strong jerks. His voice growled with excitement. "Move one inch, you little shit," he warned Mohammed, "and I'll rip your fucking throat out." He pinned Conrad's flailing arms and began his vicious rape.

Lying within arm's reach of Mack, Mohammed didn't move. The universe stretched above him. He could hold no thought. All but terror was sucked from his mind, the anticipation of his own fate. Conrad's cries and Mack's grunts sounded suddenly very far away.

Morning chilled Mohammed's face. He lay still, feeling the coldness. Something was wrong but the night had shrouded his thoughts. He strained to hear a telltale sound, but silence thrummed against his eardrums. His eyes swiveled and he saw red coals in the fire pit, indicating recent attention. Mack?

Every cell shocked to attention. Silence was replaced by the pounding of his heart as he remembered the night's violence.

Bolting up, he looked around the campsite. All was still. The coals glowed silently. Conrad was inert, huddled in a sleeping bag close by. Mack was nowhere to be seen. Mohammed scrambled out of his sack and crouched, like an animal scenting danger.

He finally saw Mack, far across the tarmac. Daylight was not full and it was only Mack's motion that alerted Mohammed. He tried to determine if the evil man was approaching or retreating.

In a few seconds, he saw Mack was heading toward

the terminal. With a ragged sigh, Mohammed was suddenly aware of both bladder and bowels pressing for relief. Scrambling to his feet, he moved a few steps to one side, hurriedly scratched a shallow hole in the dirt, and relieved himself. After covering his mess, he squatted near the heat of the coals and watched Mack disappear into a distant building.

He knew this was his chance. Even with time to warm the engines, Mack could not possibly cross the distance before Mohammed managed to begin the takeoff. Once the plane began to roll, Mack could not catch him.

Mohammed was startled to see Conrad staring blankly at him. The bag covered him to the nose and he neither moved nor blinked. Mohammed cleared his throat and said, "Hai, Conrad."

No response. Was Conrad dead? Mohammed looked for the slightest movement of the bag. "Conrad?" he said hesitantly.

The bag moved and Conrad moaned, though his blank stare remained unchanged. Mohammed looked again at the faraway terminal. Still no sign of Mack. He turned back to Conrad's haunted expression and knew he couldn't leave him. He searched his limited vocabulary, as a panicky sense of urgency drove him to Conrad's side. Conrad's eyes widened and he shrank away as Mohammed neared him. Mohammed ignored the flinching response. There was no time to coax, soothe, or worry about injuries.

"Conrad," he said. "We go. Now, Conrad, *now.* Come." He tugged at Conrad's arm beneath the bulky material. A strangled sound erupted from Conrad and his head twisted wildly, panic distorting his features.

"Mack gone," Mohammed hissed. He gestured across the slowly lightening airfield, his chest tight with need to explain their opportunity to flee. He pointed at the plane and then between the two of them. "Go plane fast, *fast.* Come, Conrad."

Grimacing in fear, Conrad looked at the plane and shook his head.

Mohammed fumbled with Conrad's bag, located the zipper, then struggled as it snagged on the material. Bent to the task, he continued his goading. "Conrad, out, out. Fast." He glanced hurriedly over his shoulder at the building into which Mack had disappeared. It was no longer dim. He located the doors but could detect no movement.

Conrad finally stirred, dragging himself out of the bag like a man swimming through mud. Mohammed yanked on Conrad, knowing that every move must be painful to him, but feeling the lightness of his own body. Alone, he could zoom like a hummingbird to the plane, but at Conrad's side, burdened by the weight of Conrad's arm across his small shoulders, he could only stumble forward. Mohammed threw one last nervous glance across the airfield just as they reached the plane and his view was cut off.

Flinging open the passenger door, he pushed and heaved Conrad, who groaned in pain, up and into the seat, then scrambled after him, shutting the door as he clambered over Conrad. He looked through the windshield as he flung himself into the pilot's seat. Clear, still clear. He straightened his skewed turban.

Inspecting the controls, Mohammed's hands trembled. This was his one and only chance; either he converted his observations into skillful movements, or he failed—to crash, or worse, to fall back into Mack's murderous hands. Mohammed had no doubt that an attempted escape would provoke Mack's full fury. He eyed the gauges and dials. He and Conrad were at his mercy and Mack had no mercy. They succeeded or they were both doomed.

Placing one trembling finger on a switch, he squeezed his eyes shut and tried to think. Again he looked at the empty airfield—and suddenly felt the weight of a hand on his arm. His heart nearly exploded.

"Aiiii! Conrad," he croaked breathlessly, staring at him.

"Suitcases," Conrad whispered.

Suitcases? They had no more need to worry about Mack's stupid suitcases. Then Mohammed hit his forehead with his palm, uttering curses at his own stupidity. No! They must leave the suitcases behind. He had to throw them out of the plane, or Mack would be forever on their trail. He was obsessed with them and would never let them be taken.

Mohammed sat, unwilling to leave the safety of the cockpit in order to remove one suitcase from each wing compartment. Maybe he would just toss out the third one, in the aisle behind him. Leaping from his seat, he grasped the bag's handle—knowing nothing of the priceless diamonds sewn into its inner lining—dragged it forward, and pushed it out the door. He reseated himself and shut the door. What was Mack doing? Surely he would appear any moment, coming at them with his monstrous ground-eating gait.

Mohammed had no sooner latched his door than Conrad shouted hoarsely, "Suitcases! Ali. Hurry. In the wings, Ali. Go!"

Mohammed saw Conrad's wild-eyed hysteria. Spittle bubbled at one corner of his mouth and flew from his lips as he fumbled at his door, moaning.

Mohammed knew precious moments would be lost trying to help Conrad back into the plane.

"No!" he yelled and grabbed Conrad's arm. "Sit. Sit. I go, I go!"

Conrad slumped into his seat as Mohammed jumped to the ground and scurried behind the wing, undid the catch, opened the compartment, grasped the suitcase handle and nearly fell over when he swung it out.

Dropping the bag, he shut the compartment and ran around the plane to the other wing. Just as he snapped the compartment open, he heard a muffled shout from Conrad and thumping on the door. Conrad didn't realize that the suitcases were being taken out, Mohammed thought, as he reached for the last bag.

He yanked the bag out and, as he bent to shove it away from the plane, glanced toward the terminal, and froze. Mack was striding away from the building.

Mohammed saw Mack pause and use one arm to shade his eyes as he stared in their direction. Mack shouted, then he was running. Mohammed wailed with fear. He scrambled on all fours under the wing, up and through the door, over the bruised and frantic Conrad, and into the pilot's seat. Too frightened to glance through the window at Mack's ground-covering lope, he fastened his gaze on the gauges and switches and began the starting sequence. Engines turned over, rumbled, caught, then coughed in rough misses.

Conrad babbled nonsense and his hands smacked his own lap in rapid staccato, urging Mohammed to hurry, hurry, hurry!

With unbearable anxiety, Mohammed, turban askew, hand on the throttle, waited, listening to the engines, knowing that until they changed to a smoother pitch, he could not put the plane into motion. The engines would die.

And so would they.

The pitch changed. Mohammed's right hand eased the throttle forward even as he saw Mack, almost upon them, running hard now, close enough for Mohammed to see the rage in his eyes, the furious twist of his mouth. The engines revved louder, and he pedaled the plane into motion, turning it. Now Mack was visible only through Conrad's window. His heart almost leaping from his chest, Mohammed eased the plane into a roll, as Conrad shrank away from the window framing Mack's fury.

They needed more speed. He pushed the throttle another notch and his stomach dropped when the engine choked. After an enormous backfire the plane lurched, accelerated, and then they were bumping over pits and cracks in the blacktop, headed for the runway. Fifty yards away, twenty, ten, he had to slow down, to turn onto the runway.

Mack was behind them, but where? How close? He slowed, eased into a right turn, ears so tuned to the engines that the strange pop he heard, followed by a metallic ping, didn't register. He was calculating where to stop, to rev the engines high enough to begin the sudden race toward flight, when the sound came again: a gun; bullets hitting the plane. No time for proper sequence. Pick up speed as they went; hope the engines continued, the runway was long enough . . .

He glanced between instruments and runway, peripherally aware of the blurring ground, the sensation of acceleration. He stopped thinking about Mack. Gripping the yoke, he held his breath, tuned to the coming moment.

Colors and noises blended as he held the shuddering plane on course. When he thought the moment had come, he pulled the yoke back, just as he'd seen it done many times, and felt the plane lift. A sudden smoothness filled his hands, and then he was riding the air, correcting the slight dip of one wing, then the other, and tilting to a steeper climb. His blood sang and his body swayed to the gentle bucks of air currents. He flew the plane higher and farther, until he felt the plane was no longer a projectile in space, but his space above the earth, his world in the sky, in which he sat, free. His small body filled with exultation and he burst into laughter as he leveled the plane and scanned the clear blue morning sky with shining brown eyes.

He grinned triumphantly at Conrad.

Conrad's face was stark white, his mouth open, his eyes dark and wide. Sweaty strips of hair clung to his forehead and his hands twisted together, white-knuckled and trembling.

"Way cool, hah, Conrad?" Mohammed grinned wider, his twelve-year-old voice high with excitement.

Conrad managed to shut his eyes and draw a breath. When he opened them again, they had brightened, as though, emerging from the brief darkness, relief had finally come. His smile, no longer sickly, was twisted a bit by pain. When he spoke, much to Mohammed's satisfaction, his voice held admiration.

"Way cool, Ali. Way, *way* cool. My God, I can't believe it." Conrad saw the ground far below and swallowed hard. "How'd you do it? When'd you learn to fly, Ali? Christ, we could have gotten away before—before last night." He shook his head and with shaky hands rubbed his eyes, gently, then harder. He cupped his face in both hands, hunched his shoulders, and then he was crying, hard and loud, and gulping for air.

Mohammed looked at the blue sky that contrasted so clearly with the earth tones of the strange land below. Distant craggy outcroppings bled angular shadows cast by the rising sun. The drone of the engines filled the spaces between Conrad's harsh sobs.

With great care, Mohammed banked the plane into a wide turn, an exploratory maneuver. He concentrated on feeling every vibration, dip, and buck of the plane as it rode the air. He had no destination; he simply put the sun behind him. As with the desert, this was a straight course. He thought that he'd figured out which of the strange dials indicated direction, but its shifts were erratic. He preferred his own sense of direction, a gift of the wind and shifting sand that had been handed down by so many generations before him. He did not know where he was, but every inch, every moment, added to ancient points of reference.

In the stillness of the sky, he was revisited by a memory of the night just before the world had changed; squatting on the bank of the watering hole, the silk-soft dusk of the desert around him as he listened to the movements of the camels, his little sister's voice calling to him through the darkness.

Hammudi, she'd called, *Hammudi, yehla, yehla.* Then the great blackness had come. The camels had moaned their sudden distress, and then his small sister was crumpling to the sand amidst trampling hooves.

He swallowed the ache in his throat and wished he knew if little Aida had been quick enough to slip back to the place of soul-living. Or had she been lost in the same instant the barrier had slammed shut?

He wished he could find words for the questions that plagued him. Why had he gone with Mack, left his homeland and lost the capacity to fully communicate with another human being? At home, he might have been able to find a person who remembered. And one who could have told him if Aida was safe, if there was any hope of reopening the way.

How could he ever return to his homeland? This plane would not cross the immense ocean. He tightened his grip on the yoke, to keep his longing from turning the plane into the sun, to the east, to home.

Conrad's sobs dwindled to moans, then ceased. He

rubbed tearstains from his cheeks and wiped his nose on his shirtsleeves. A last, shuddering sigh subsumed memories that would hold him captive forever.

"Where are we going, Ali?" Conrad asked.

Startled from his lonely thoughts, Mohammed cried out and jerked the yoke. The plane shot upward, and both of them shouted in surprise. Mohammed quickly pushed it back, overcompensating, and the plane nosed down with a sickening lurch.

"Aghh—shit!" Conrad yelled.

Spitting curses, Mohammed tried to regain control. Exaggerated movements had caused them to climb, then plunge, so he pulled back slowly on the yoke. Too slowly. He lost one engine, and his heart slammed into his throat as it sputtered into silence. The plane abruptly tilted to one side. Fighting panic, he struggled to level the wings, pulling steadily back on the yoke. He leveled the plane, only to find they were still losing altitude. Frantically, he replayed the landing sequence in his mind, and the missing components: a runway and two working engines.

Conrad shouted and jabbed at the side window, gesturing from the dead engine to the control panel. "Start the engine. Start the fucking engine!"

The words suddenly made sense. Mohammed discarded his assumption that the plane had to be parked to be started and immediately shut down the fuel supply to the dead engine. Agonizing seconds passed before he tried to restart, bringing them ever closer to the ground.

As the earth rushed toward them, he could wait no longer. Praying to Allah, he flipped the switch and pushed the button. The warm engines came smoothly to life and Mohammed coaxed the plane to gain elevation. He held his breath as they continued to ascend, then let it out with a triumphant cry. He looked at Conrad. They both grinned, giddy with relief.

An hour later, only moments after landing, they were arguing.

"Never again," Conrad said, gripping the dash as the plane came to a stop. "I swear to God, I will never again set foot in a plane as long as I live." He patted Mohammed's little shoulder hard and shook his head. "I don't know how you did it, Ali. Goddamn it, you were great. But, no shit, man, you need a whole lot of practice before I ever go up with you again, not that I would ever, ever go up again. Let's get the hell out of this deathtrap and find a car."

"No car. No-no-no!" Mohammed protested. He jabbed his finger at a gauge. "Fuel, Conrad, fuel." His hand made an upward swoop. "Up-up-up, we go, plane."

"Are you out of your fucking mind?" Conrad stared at Mohammed in amazement. "Are you nuts? We barely made it down. We're driving. In a car. On the ground!" He flung his door open.

"Plane!" Mohammed shouted, banging the yoke with his hand.

"Car!"

"Plane!"

"Car, Goddamn it. Agh, fuck it!" Conrad said, twisting away and jumping the short distance to the ground.

"Ahh, fuck it you, too!" Mohammed yelled after him.

Conrad gasped when his feet hit the ground, jarring his sore body. Leaning back against the plane, he wondered what damage Mack had done to him other than the obvious. His kidneys were throbbing. And he couldn't breathe right. Were his ribs broken?

Anger shook him from the worldview he'd been ready to accept again, now that the worst was over. It was the mindset that had moved him through life, self-sure complacency, the false security of a life without previous injustice.

But an entirely new anger boiled within him, standing there on the hard ground, his back against the metal of the plane, his eyes closed. His bruised body was not him. Yet it belonged to him. And Mack had used him, used it. A moan escaped his throat. Hearing himself, he blinked, and saw Mohammed standing before him, turban firmly in place.

"Hai, Conrad." Mohammed squinted at him. "Okay,

hah?" He pointed with exaggeration at his own backside. "Okay, hah?" he repeated with jabbing motions at his rear.

Conrad looked away but was unable to escape the shame, or the knowledge that Mohammed had witnessed it.

Mohammed danced before him, performing a mime of jutting butt and jabbing finger, his voice high and insistent. "Okay, hah? Okay, Conrad?"

"Stop it!" Conrad exploded. "Stop it!"

Mohammed straightened, feet planted, arms akimbo, and stared at Conrad. "Okay, hah?"

"Okay. Fine. I'm fine—just dandy, Goddamn dandy, you fucking idiot. Now let's get the fuck out of here." He marched away and Mohammed marched after him.

PART III

CHAPTER 27

YEAR 6, POST-BLACKOUT

KATE SLOUCHED IN THE PASSENGER SEAT, ARMS CROSSED for warmth. She hated nights like this. Overcast sky. No moon. No stars.

C'mon, Josiah, she thought. How long could it take to take a leak?

The bushes on both sides of the road were barely visible and the woods behind them were black. That huge cave bear they'd been hearing rumors about could be in there, or one of the creepy two-headed snakes. Or those Goddamn beady-eyed wolverines that just came at you like—

Something rustled to her left. She peered through the darkness. Josiah? Or something else? She clenched her jaw.

Darkness erupted with gunshots.

Kate's heart froze. There was a yell, the sound of snapping brush and leaves. She snatched her gun from the floorboards and scrambled into the driver's seat.

A lurching figure broke free of the bushy darkness on the passenger side of the jeep. Her throat tightened in panic.

"Go!" Josiah yelled.

Kate leaned over and flung open the passenger door, then started the jeep. A shot popped from the woods.

Josiah, nearly at the jeep, faltered, sagged, and stumbled on. "GO!" he rasped as he fell inside. A rifle cracked, a voice shouted, and Josiah cried out in pain. Kate thrust the shift into gear, floored the pedal, and spun in a storm of dust onto the road, a handful of Josiah's jacket clutched in her fist to keep him from rolling out the door. Careening down the road, she didn't let go of him until he had both feet inside and had yanked the door shut.

Risking a quick glance, Kate saw Josiah was covered in blood, and slumped, unconscious, against the door.

"Laura, do stop pacing," Catherine instructed. "You're making me dizzy."

"Sorry," said Laura. She crossed to the front window and peered into the darkness. The room glowed with candlelight, and the muted laughter of children came from the den they'd built over the back porch. "Where are they? This is just like Kate, making us all crazy."

Laura couldn't quite understand why she felt so tense. This wasn't the first time Josiah had been gone for an extended period. Eli and Josiah had once talked themselves into a foray all the way to San Francisco, a three-week adventure that, near the end, had left those at home counting the minutes and watching the driveway.

And when they finally did return, they were not only safe and intact, they were bubbling like schoolchildren with all kinds of exciting stories of their adventures, stories to be told around the fireplace for some time to come: Eli about the untenable contrast between farm life and city life (he definitely preferred the former), and Josiah about the professor of a class he'd once audited, a brilliant Chinese physicist and theoretician who had brought substance, rather than faith, to things unseen in the universe. Josiah had been excited to find Dr. Chang in the bustling city and felt an unaccustomed delight in introducing to one another the only two men he'd ever respected.

"It's not like Josiah," said Eli, joining Laura at the window. He'd insisted he felt well enough to join them. Five days of isolation in the attic sickroom was enough. Though still weak, he was no longer contagious and needed to be with the others, sharing his worry.

Laura crossed the room and placed a hand on his

arm. "I know," she said softly.

He squeezed her hand in sympathy. No one suspected the depth of their friendship, cemented five years ago in one afternoon of intimacy, a strange, out-of-context interlude.

It had been a bad summer for her, a time when Kate's and Josiah's relationship had intensified and was difficult for her to witness. She'd walked to a sun-filled mini-meadow in the woods, not far from the house, a spot she frequented when she wanted to be alone. She'd been surprised to see Eli sprawled in the golden weeds, head buried in his bent arms.

She'd almost left, but hesitated when Eli noticed her.

"Laura?" His voice had been as warm and soft as the afternoon.

She'd walked over, knelt down beside him, and, inexplicably, burst into tears.

Instantly sympathetic, though perplexed, Eli scrambled to his knees, put his arms around her, then held her, stroked her hair, and said nothing.

His tender solicitude undid her. Emotions spilled from her and she poured out her secret: her love for Josiah, her pain at seeing him with Kate. Eli hugged her close and brushed away her tears with his thumb, as though she were a child. He kissed her hair.

Lifting her face to the comfort of his lips, she pressed herself to him with unexpected trust.

They made love with ease, an exchange of comfort that was part of their familiarity. It was odd—friendly and satisfying in a quiet, peaceful way. Afterward, they lay close, listening to sounds of the forest, watching the blue sky framed by treetops.

Though they'd never repeated that intimacy, the affection they'd so expressed for one another deepened their friendship in a way that was different from all else. The memory of that afternoon was one they both cherished.

"Quiet," Catherine suddenly commanded. She cocked her head.

Jarred into the present, Laura heard the faint sound of an engine, growing stronger. Several minutes would pass before the vehicle made the final curve onto the driveway.

"Laura, get the guns," Catherine said.

"Why? It's the jeep. I recognize its sound."

"Perhaps," Catherine said grimly. "Get the guns. Quickly!"

Laura hurried to the gun cabinet, her mind whirling with fear Catherine had invoked.

"Eli," Catherine snapped. "Alert the children."

Eli rushed from the room. Laura unlocked the cabinet and removed a rifle, two handguns, and clips and ammunition.

The children knew what to do, she reassured herself. The thud of the trap door shutting meant they were under the porch, now the floor of the den, in the enclosed area that had been weather-sealed and camouflaged. They'd built an emergency exit to the yard, and Laura fervently hoped they wouldn't now have to use it. She imagined the children scurrying through woods full of mutated creatures, and fear for her daughter nearly eclipsed her thoughts. *Lily.* Lily, whose beautiful brown eyes had, from her first moment of life, reflected her precious soul.

Eli rejoined them and, weapons in hand, they took up positions, Laura and Catherine each at a front window and Eli dashing upstairs with the rifle into Kate's bedroom, where he squatted to one side of the central window overlooking the driveway.

Laura listened to the sound of the jeep. It was traveling fast. She glimpsed the headlight beams scattering through the woods lining the road. Any second now, the car would turn into the driveway.

The jeep burst from the trees and ignored the curved driveway that circled the grassy grounds in front, its high-beams pointed directly at the house. Horn blaring, it sped over the grass and came to a jerking stop mere inches from the front porch steps.

"Don't move," Catherine hissed just as Laura stepped away from the wall.

The driver's door opened, and a shape tumbled out into the night, shouting. Kate's voice! Something was terribly wrong.

Laura and Catherine reached the front door

simultaneously. Kate threw herself against it from the other side, banging and shouting. Eli clattered down the stairs as Laura flung open the door. Kate tumbled in, wild-eyed.

"He's hurt bad. Hurry!"

Laura's world became a muffled fog. They all hurried down the steps. Through the open door of the jeep, Laura saw Josiah, slumped against the passenger door, eyes closed, mouth slack, arms limp. Blood soaked his shirt, pants.

Eli, Kate, and Laura struggled to get Josiah out of the car, up the steps, and into the house. Groans slid from Josiah's unconscious lips. As they settled him on the couch, Laura's and Eli's frantic questions overlapped Kate's answers.

"Enough!" Catherine barked. "Laura, get the medical kit. Eli, get hot water. Boil more and make sure the stove stays lit. Quickly."

Eli hurried to the kitchen and Laura dashed up the stairs.

"Clean rags, Laura," Catherine called, then turned to Kate. "Kate, scissors from the kitchen drawer. And get clean sheets and blankets." She bent over Josiah and gently lifted one eyelid, then placed her fingers against his carotid artery. "How long ago?"

"About two hours."

"Scissors, quickly."

Josiah had been shot in his right shoulder, left thigh, and left foot. The bullet that had entered slightly beneath his collarbone had left a gaping exit wound beneath his shoulder blade. The other two bullets remained lodged. As Laura and Catherine cut his clothes away, Eli went outside to start the generator. On his way, he opened the trapdoor and hustled the children out, tersely telling them that Josiah had been hurt and they needed to stay in the den. Back in the living room, he clustered several lamps onto the high table behind the couch.

To keep herself busy, Kate stoked the fireplace as she told them what had happened. It was a short story. With a last savage poke at the blazing logs, she hurried back to them.

"Goddamn those assholes!" She tried to peer between Laura and Catherine at Josiah. "How bad is he? Is he gonna be all right?"

"I don't know." Catherine said grimly. "I think I can remove the bullet from his thigh, but not the one in his foot." She handed several instruments from the medical bag to Eli and instructed him to immerse them in the pot of boiling water on the stove, then douse them with alcohol. She took out a small vial of Demerol and a syringe. "I once was a nurse," she muttered, to everyone's surprise.

"What sidetracked you?" Kate asked.

Catherine sniffed. "What else? A man. That which has, as you put it, sidetracked women throughout the ages."

"You told us your Harold was a prince," said Kate, eyes fixed on Josiah.

Catherine sighed. "His name was Howard and, yes, he was a prince." She drew Demerol into the syringe. "And awfully good at that which sidetracks us."

Kate reached past Laura and brushed a few damp curls from Josiah's glistening forehead. "I've been in love a jillion times and I still did what I wanted."

Laura tried to ignore Kate's proprietary gesture and concentrated on sponging Josiah's shoulder wound. "At least," she said, "the bullet didn't stay in here."

"Let's hope the damage it did on its way through can be healed," Catherine said.

"I wish I'd shot back," Kate said, straightening up.

"That would have only been a waste of valuable time," said Catherine.

"You did good, Kate," assured Eli, giving Kate a quick hug.

Two hours later, Catherine had removed the bullet from Josiah's thigh and his wounds had been cleaned, disinfected, and bandaged. He lay, drugged, beneath a mound of blankets. Although they were exhausted, no one suggested sleep. Eli found a bottle of sherry and poured them each a drink. They grimly toasted to Josiah's recovery, and none of them voiced their shared concern over the bullet still lodged in his foot.

"I totally forgot about the kids!" exclaimed Laura. "I better get them to bed."

As soon as she entered the playroom, Lily and John

Thomas hurried to her, Lucas trailing behind them. Reina's ears perked and her tail thumped the floor.

"Is Josiah okay?" asked John Thomas. His voice had begun changing the last few weeks, and it faltered now. Laura was struck anew by how much he'd grown, seemingly right before her eyes. The shy young boy was now a gangly, gentle adolescent.

Lily grabbed her hand. "Can we go see him?"

Lucas crowded next to her. He, too, showed worry, teeth anxiously nibbling his lower lip in a way similar to Josiah's.

"He's hurt very badly," Laura said. "We've helped him as much as we can and now we have to see if his body can heal itself. You can see him, but he's sleeping, so you have to be very quiet." They all nodded solemnly. "All right, let's go, and then it's off to bed."

She led the parade into the living room, and the children clustered around the couch.

"Poor Josiah," John Thomas whispered, voice cracking.

Lucas patted John Thomas's arm. "He'll be okay," he said. Laura smiled, feeling an unaccustomed tenderness toward Lucas. He had changed in the last few years, becoming nearly a model child, yet she still didn't feel the same warmth toward him she did for John Thomas.

Lily hadn't said a word. She stood so still she didn't seem to be breathing. After a moment, she raised her eyes to her mother's. "Can I touch him?"

Laura nodded. "Only on the head, Lily. Very gently."

Lily raised her hand to her mouth, kissed her fingers, and placed them briefly on Josiah's brow. She looked sadly up at Laura. "He's purple/hill, Mommy. It would be awful to not have purple/hill."

Laura smiled. Lily had begun making up multiple-word adjectives and nouns almost from the day she'd started talking. "We won't lose purple/hill. Come on now. Bedtime."

By the next morning, Josiah's foot was swollen, the skin red and stretched to near transparency, looking ready to burst. Erratic bands of red reached past the swelling. During the night, fever had caused delirium.

In the early hours, Laura sat by his side, bathing his face and neck with a cool cloth.

Eli came out of the kitchen with more cold water. His arms trembled as he exchanged the pots, and Laura was concerned he might be relapsing into his recent illness.

Catherine, in a chair at the foot of the couch, straightened from her position over Josiah's foot and dropped a soiled cloth into a plastic bag. The flesh at the inner arch of Josiah's foot was puckered and discolored. Using the last of the fresh damp rags, she gently pressed more pus from the wound. Laura and Eli held Josiah while he groaned and jerked from side to side. Catherine wiped the area clean, then placed a gauze pad smeared with antibiotic ointment over the open wound and gently rewrapped the foot.

Josiah, eyes closed, moaned and arched the small of his back, then fell limp, breathing raggedly. Laura replaced the already-hot cloth on his forehead with a cool one.

"This can't continue," Catherine said. She picked up the plastic bag of soiled rags and closed it with a firm knot. "Josiah needs proper medical attention."

"You know our only other choice is the hospital in Reno," said Eli. "Christ, Reno! How would we deal with the Brotherhood? And moving Josiah over those roads, avoiding ambushes—" He broke off, breathing raggedly.

"Josiah may die en route, but he will certainly die here."

"No," Laura said. "How can you say that? Eli's right, Reno's too risky. And Josiah's strong. We can take care of him, keep cleaning and draining his wound. Load him up with antibiotics."

Catherine's expression was sad but determined. "No, Laura. Our antibiotics are old, possibly useless." She paused, then added, heavily, "Josiah may have gangrene."

Laura's stomach twisted. "Gangrene?" she whispered. "Are you sure?" The word carried hopelessness. The certainty of Josiah's death.

"I'm almost certain," said Catherine.

"Goddamn it!" Laura shouted, jumping to her feet. "If you're not sure, how could you say something like that?" Her body trembled in fury.

"What?" Kate asked, descending the stairs in robe and slippers. "What's going on?"

"Goddamn it!" Laura whirled away from Catherine and attempted to brush by Kate.

Kate grabbed her arm and felt Laura's quivering anger. "Holy shit." She looked at Catherine and Eli. "Which one of you got Laura to cuss?"

"There was purpose to my words, Laura." Catherine's tone of entreaty halted Laura.

"I shoulda known it was you, Catherine," said Kate.

Catherine ignored her. "Laura, please. I wish to apologize for my abruptness."

Kate nudged Laura forward. "Hurry up, kiddo, before she changes her mind."

Laura reluctantly went to stand before Catherine, who took her hands in her own.

"My dear," Catherine said with simple sincerity, "I didn't know. I'm sorry."

Laura knew instantly what Catherine was saying: she had just now realized the depth of Laura's feelings for Josiah. Laura forced back tears. She'd learned to live with the constant ache of her unrequited love. It was sympathy she couldn't withstand.

"Great," Kate said, oblivious to undercurrents. She sat in a chair next to the couch and placed her hand on Josiah's brow. "Jesus Christ. He's burning up!"

"Yes," Catherine said. She squeezed Laura's hands and released them. "We've been discussing moving him to the hospital."

"Are you nuts?" Kate grabbed a fresh washrag and dipped it into the cold water, wrung it out minimally, and let drops fall on Josiah's dry lips.

"Catherine thinks it's gangrene," said Eli bleakly.

Laura knew how deeply Catherine's words must have struck Eli. Still fighting tears, she went to hug him.

"Gangrene!" Kate exploded. "You got to be kidding, Catherine. Wasn't that wiped out a long time ago? He must have been vaccinated, for cryin' out loud."

"No," replied Catherine, without reproach.

Laura stifled a hysterical giggle and exchanged a look with Eli, his mouth twitching with laughter. Her giggles escaped, then she burst into tears, hands covering her face.

"What the hell's going on?" Kate said uneasily.

"It's been a long night," said Catherine. "Kate, gangrene is the necrotic condition—death—of flesh, caused by infection. I said earlier that Josiah may have gangrene. I should have said gangrene is inevitable. To stop gangrene could require amputation."

"Amputation!" Kate exploded. "Chrissakes, Catherine."

"If the affected portion of the body is not removed," Catherine continued over Kate's protest, "the decay continues until the host is dead . . ."

Kate erupted from her chair and ran to the stairs.

"Kate?" Catherine paused.

"Be right back," Kate said, dashing up the stairs.

"Gotta get dressed." Over her shoulder, "What the fuck are you guys waiting for? Eli, get the Suburban. Hurry." She disappeared up the stairs.

CHAPTER 28

Eli was still far too ill for a trip, and Catherine could neither drive nor help physically move Josiah. Both would remain behind with the children; Kate and Laura would take Josiah to Reno.

The Suburban was fueled and brought out with filled gas cans in its rooftop storage. The vehicle consumed so much gas they seldom used it, though it was kept in good repair. Its red exterior and chrome bumpers had long ago been sprayed green and black for camouflage.

They turned the rear compartment into a bed for Josiah. Food, water, medication, clothing, weapons, and ammunition were loaded, as were tire chains, and the HF ham radio and antenna. Kate hadn't called after Josiah was shot because erecting the ancient radio and large antenna took time. The old radio and its antennae were a last resort, always kept hidden.

They carefully put Josiah to bed in the Suburban, head

near the front seat so his condition could be monitored.

Laura felt as if something had been forgotten. A sensation of wrongness filled her.

She was leaving Lily for an unknown amount of time. What if she couldn't get back? If their home was attacked, Catherine was old and Eli was sick. What if Eli got worse? Only Catherine would be left to protect the three children. And if Catherine had another stroke, the children would be alone.

Laura gazed at Lily, standing by Catherine on the porch, her delicate face framed by waves and curls of black hair, her little body clad in jeans and yellow sweater.

Lily stared back at Laura, trying hard not to cry.

"Oh, Lily," Laura said in a whisper and rushed to her, lifting her and kissing her soft cheek, her silky hair, one perfect ear peeking from her curls. She felt Lily's arms fold around her neck, a tiny kiss on her own cheek. "You be good, sweetie, okay?" Laura murmured. "Listen to Catherine and Eli and stay close to the house."

Lily nodded, then looked at Laura, her small face full of worry. "Stay away from the dark/stinks, Mommy." Dark/stinks was her name for the many mutant predators that lurked in forests and fields.

"I will, baby." Laura kissed her nose. "Don't worry. I'll be fine."

Lily's worry vanished, replaced by curiosity. "How do you know?"

Laura felt she'd never get used to the way Lily took everything so literally.

"Because I'm careful and when people are careful they can avoid bad things. Okay?"

Lily nodded and Laura set her back onto the porch between Catherine and Eli. John Thomas stood close to Kate, his eyes dark with anxiety. She stroked his cheek, smiled reassuringly, then ruffled Lily's curls. "Don't worry, kiddo. I'll take care of your mom."

Lily gave her a dubious look, then tugged her hand until Kate squatted to eye level.

"Kate," Lily said, frowning, "the salty/prickles aren't careful. They're"—she grimaced in frustration—"they're green/jumpy/orange. Don't let them out, okay? Be pine/bubbles like most times."

Kate pulled Lily in for a hug and rolled her eyes at Laura. "Sure thing, kiddo." Then she rose and grabbed John Thomas in a fierce hug. He was taller than she now but still a child in her arms. His voice cracked when he said good-bye.

Laura climbed into the driver's seat and Kate closed the rear doors, then hopped into the passenger side.

As final farewells were called out, it dawned on Laura. "Where's Lucas?"

Heads swiveled, punctuated by shrugs, and Laura, putting the car into gear, called out, "Say good-bye to him for us."

Kate stuck her head out the window as they rolled down the driveway. "Don't worry, Lily-pie; I won't let the pickles out."

Lily stamped her foot and yelled, "Prickles, Kate. Salty/*prickles!*"

With a final wave, Kate rolled up her window. "Where does your kid come up with that shit?"

Laura managed a laugh as she turned onto the dirt road and glanced into the mirror one last time. The figures on the porch were still waving.

Kate leaned over the back of the seat and checked Josiah. "Do you really think he'll get gangrene?"

"I just don't know. How's he doing?"

"I think he's sleeping." She placed her hand on his forehead. "He's still awfully hot."

Laura, concentrating on avoiding the ruts and holes in the road, said, "Get the map and let's figure out some alternate routes, just in case."

Kate spread the map on her lap. "We can forget 20 East as a detour; that hasn't been open in years. Probably never will be, either. We can drop down to 80 and get as far as Grass Valley or Shantytown if we want to try cutting to 89. The only other option is to hit 395 way farther north and take the long way in. 'Course, the longer the route, the more chance of blockades or ambushes." She rattled the map. "Maybe we should just try to get into Sacramento. It's closer."

"Forget it." Laura eased the Suburban from the dirt road onto the blacktop, such as it was. Years of neglect had left every driving surface full of cracks, potholes, pits. Driving was tense and required constant attention. "Sacramento's a hellhole, you know that."

"Yeah, but—"

"We couldn't get past the first street, much less to a hospital, which have probably all been destroyed, anyway. You weren't there, Kate. You didn't see what it's like; it's not a city, it's a nightmare."

"It was two or three years ago you and Eli were there," Kate said stubbornly. "Maybe it's better now."

"How? Nobody in their right mind would go there. It's nothing but a gang town, full of criminals and—*Shaitan*." True to her expectation, Kate blew a sigh of exasperation.

Kate still believed *Shaitan* were simply people who'd been driven insane by the second blackout. Hell, she'd been through it herself. She knew what a supreme act of will it had taken to remain intact beneath that heavy shroud of dread and despair. "Look, honey," she said, impatiently, "this is Josiah's life we're talking about. *Shaitan* don't have superpowers. Don't start on all that soulless shit now."

Laura refused to get drawn in. "Sacramento's off-limits. Even Catherine and Eli didn't consider it an option."

"We can't get into Reno unless we join their damn

Brotherhood." Kate said determinedly.

"We'll play along for as long as it takes to get Josiah well. At least Reno's regulated and we won't have to worry every time we go out on the street."

Kate rattled the map, lips pressed tight in silence.

Trying to ignore the tension between them, Laura worked at avoiding the worst potholes in the two-lane highway as she wondered whether their group's unanimous decision to remain in California had been wrong after all. In the six years since the blackout, California hadn't stabilized the way other states had, although they'd heard life in other states wasn't a picnic, either.

The nation was now fragmented in a way that had been unforeseeable. Montana, Idaho, and Oregon had formed a loose coalition of their own and, in doing so, had isolated Washington from the rest of the United States. The states east of the Mississippi were closely allied, excluding Florida, which had declared itself a Catholic religious sovereignty. In Year 2, following the blackout, Georgia, Alabama, Mississippi, and parts of Louisiana and Tennessee formed a Christian fundamentalist alliance. The Midwestern states, though never formally declaring themselves separate, nevertheless established new trade protocols with the east, the northwestern states, and the newly enlarged Florida, now called Greater Florida.

Religious mania swept the nation, and the rest of the world, and post-blackout events kept everyone off balance.

Survival was a daily struggle, further complicated by the onset of plant and animal mutations.

This last development crushed any possibilities people would return to more temperate religious beliefs. People cowered in prayer, bound by the hope that belief would spare them, as nothing else seemed to.

During Year 2, agricultural experimentation in the Midwest united it with the Washington, D.C., government (which still had jurisdiction over all the weaponry) and resulted in control of several strains of base-crops. While Greater Florida was coming into being, the Midwest struggled to replant hundreds of thousands of acres, first denuding it of wildly mutated growth. The numbers who died of starvation in the early years remained unknown.

California was a renegade state, peopled by anarchists of every description whose politics unified them in only one area: the rejection of any form of government. Pocket communities had regained electrical power, but the state, as a whole, remained off the grid. Its once-extensive hydroelectric system had been sabotaged beyond repair during ensuing years. Power plants were vandalized and numerous dams destroyed by explosives. Many Californians were convinced that the blackout had been caused by the U.S. government. These self-named Free Thinkers thought government, corporate greed, and self-serving politics had destroyed the world.

People who were convinced they knew the cause of the blackout collaborated, and disagreements over myriad belief systems caused ever-deepening fractures between groups. Even those who agreed spiritually disagreed on how mankind should now proceed. It was a time of new rituals, new religions, and untried social structures.

As communities argued, traffic between communities slowed. Travelers became wary of entering unknown territories; ignorance of local laws often carried terrible punishments. Those who crossed posted areas—where signs claimed restricted scavenging rights—were at grave risk. Foragers who crossed uncertain lines went as heavily armed groups, or as fools.

Well, we aren't fools, and we are heavily armed, Laura thought as she worried about the scavenging boundary not far ahead. Though the population of the territory they had to cross was scattered and mostly benign, aggressive bands of men policed it. As they crossed the invisible boundary, Laura's anxiety increased. Their Suburban was packed with supplies and they had a lot to lose. Most important, time. An hour's grace, for Josiah, might mean the difference between amputation and death.

She tried to force herself to relax. It was a long way to Reno.

"How're you doing?" Kate ventured. It had been a long silence between them.

Buoyed by the tacit offer of truce, Laura felt stirrings of optimism. She smiled at Kate. "Maybe we're worrying about nothing."

"Uh-oh," Kate said, staring straight ahead.

They had just topped a hill. The road dipped, then rose again. At the top of that rise sat a vehicle, centered in the road.

"Maybe it's empty," said Laura, but no sooner had she spoken than doors on both sides of the distant vehicle opened. Two men emerged, one from each side. Both men gripped rifles.

"Shit," Kate said.

Laura's heart raced. The road leveled off and she drove at a steady pace as they started up the incline toward the men. The open, rolling countryside, dotted with oaks, had no dwellings.

"Do you recognize them?" Kate asked.

"I don't think so. But we could mention Charlie—they might know him." Charlie was a man they'd once met on an excursion through the neighboring territory.

"For all we know, Charlie's dead," Kate muttered.

The ground leveled and Laura stopped twenty feet from the truck. She saw the glint of a .357 Magnum that had appeared in Kate's lap. "Give me the flag," she hissed.

Kate snatched a square of folded material from the glove box and passed it to her. Laura shook it out, then rolled down her window and thrust it through, holding it up by the two upper corners. The white linen, painted with a fat red cross, hung limply.

"We're headed for Reno," she called out. "We have a sick man."

Agonizing seconds ticked by as the men, rifles trained on them, considered her words.

Laura hoped they would be afraid of contagion and let them pass. Her stomach knotted with tension. They could shoot and loot, but she hoped these men wouldn't risk the odds that she might be bluffing them.

The men exchanged a few words, then removed their caps and used them to cover their mouths and noses. One man lowered his rifle a bit. "Go around," he shouted angrily. "Fast!"

Laura tossed the makeshift flag to the floor and steered off the road. The slope canted them to the left as she struggled to get the Suburban past the truck. For an instant she was sure they would be shot as they drew alongside them, then they were past, and she fought to get the Suburban back onto the blacktop. At the edge of the asphalt, she pressed the accelerator, and they slewed onto the smoother surface.

She disregarded all but the worst of the pock-marked surface and held the speeding car to the road, wanting to get far away, fast. Kate shouted at her to slow down.

"Check Josiah," Laura said, easing off the accelerator. The rearview mirror showed the other truck's doors were closed and it was far behind them. A slight curve in the road and then it was gone. Laura breathed easier. Kate scrambled to her knees and leaned over the back of the seat, while Laura scanned the foothills ahead.

"Aw, shit," Kate exclaimed.

"What? Is he all right?"

"You little shit," Kate yelled. "Get out here."

Laura braked to a stop. "What—" Following Kate's angry glare, she saw movement in the mound of clothing and blankets in the rear. Her mouth dropped open as Lucas appeared.

Kate slammed her fist on the seatback. "Goddamn it."

"Lucas, what are you doing here?" yelled Laura.

"I swear to God, I'm gonna beat the shit out of you, you little—"

"What are you doing here?" Laura repeated. Hastily, she scanned the area around them. They were far too exposed to deal with Lucas right here. Within minutes, she had them off the road and turned into a grove of oaks, where she maneuvered them into concealment.

Kate, one hand on Josiah's brow, glowered murderously at Lucas. Laura turned her attention to Lucas as well. He was scrunched into the farthest corner, staring back at Kate. His innocent expression appalled Laura.

"You think this is some fucking joy ride?" Kate spat.

"Kate," Laura cautioned.

"Don't give me any shit now, Laura, this is serious.

What the fuck are we supposed to do with him? We don't have time to take him home; we're stuck with him." She turned to Lucas. "I have a good mind to let you find your own way home." Cursing with rage, she ordered Lucas out of the car.

"What are you doing?" said Laura, alarmed.

"Out. I want him out!"

"We can't just leave him here."

"We're not gonna leave him here," Kate snarled. "I just want him out of my sight before I kill him. We need to figure this out."

"We don't have a choice."

Lucas reached for the door handle.

"Never mind," Kate shouted at him. "You stay here. Laura and I are getting out. You just sit there, you understand? You just sit there and don't make a fucking peep."

Lucas nodded and settled back, his innocent expression unchanged. Laura couldn't comprehend it; that look was horribly, dreadfully wrong.

Kate snatched the keys from the ignition, and Laura followed her as she stomped angrily to the edge of the grove. Near bushes at the base of a large oak, Kate squatted on her haunches. Laura sat cross-legged beside her, careful to keep herself hidden from the road.

Kate whispered angrily, "What're we going to do, Laura?"

"His face, Kate. Did you see his expression?" Was

Kate feeling the same fear? Something macabre was so suddenly apparent in Lucas. No, not suddenly, Laura thought, fearfully. *It's always been there and I've refused to see it. When did I stop wondering about him? My God, he became a model child. How? Why didn't I notice?* All her earlier distrust of him came rushing back.

"What did he hear, Laura?" Kate whispered urgently. "What did we say that he could use to betray us in Reno? We talked about fooling the Brotherhood. Do you think he heard us?"

Laura couldn't shake the image of Lucas's innocent expression. Any other child would have shown guilt. Remorse. "I don't know. Does it matter? He could make anything up."

Kate swore. "What're we gonna do? Keep him gagged? It won't work. He'll make noise during the border search and that'll be the end. Kidnapping. That's what he'd make them believe."

Kidnapping had become the most widespread, and most harshly punished, crime. Healthy, well-formed children were at a premium ever since the mutations began. So many grossly deformed infants had been born since the blackout that many people had stopped having children. But not everyone had access to birth control, so babies were inevitable.

Society evolved new rules—varying by communities. In some, abortions became as commonplace as sex while, in others, they were forbidden. There were also communities that demanded reproduction, that saw the births as the only method of gauging God's anger. Which woman's healthy child would signal an end to the punishment? Grotesque children were often the result.

Normal children were fiercely coveted.

Attention was focused on the children born immediately after the blackout, before widespread mutations had become evident. These seemingly normal children became the most highly prized members of their communities, their welfare of utmost importance. But their specialness didn't last, once the *Shaitan* were named.

Shaitan, who slaughtered indiscriminately, whose hideous natures were beyond comprehension. Whose appearance was linked to the second blackout. *Look at the eyes,* people warned one another, dreading to see that terrifyingly dark, sucking emptiness.

And then it was identified in the eyes of babies. The bloodbath that followed was the worst catastrophe unleashed by the blackout. Vigilantes searched for *Shaitan* children—any child born after the blackout—and killed them. Worse, innocent children who were small and appeared to be the right age were killed, along with the hysterical parents trying to shield them.

By Year 6, young, normal children were at a premium, and committing the crime of kidnapping resulted in gruesome public death.

Laura and Kate exchanged anxious looks. Was Kate right? Would Lucas betray them, claim he'd been kidnapped?

"He's *Shaitan*," Kate spat furiously. "He's always been Goddamn *Shaitan*. We should have left him back in Reno, when we were first trying to figure out what to do with him, when we knew something was wrong with him."

"He can't be *Shaitan*, Kate," Laura said firmly. "It's not in his eyes. Besides, I thought you didn't believe in *Shaitan*."

"I'd believe anything about that little fuck," Kate sidestepped. "He's not normal and now he's dangerous to us—to Josiah."

"He really fooled us all," Laura said uneasily. Kate had tolerated him only for John Thomas's sake. Despite her exasperating stubbornness, Kate was dependable in a crisis, and now it was clear her early recognition of something strange about Lucas had been right. He might already have cost Josiah the small window of survival.

The air throbbed with danger.

"Should we kill him?" Laura heard herself say. Stunned, she pressed both hands against her lips.

Kate stared at her, shocked. Then, grinning hugely, she thrust her face at Laura's. "Who are you and what have you done with my Laura?"

"God, Kate, I can't believe I said that."

"Maybe you read my mind." Kate looked away and added, flatly, "That's probably what we should do, but we both know that neither of us can do it." Rising, she said, "Come on, we gotta go."

"But we haven't decided anything."

"We've got to go. We'll just have to wing it."

That evening, while Kate and Laura set up camp in a small clearing, Lucas ducked into the bushes. Moonlight flickered through the trees on patches of snow. He moved until he was hidden but near enough to observe Kate and Laura. He would have preferred to remain in the car and play his new game, but the women were too close to it for the game to be safe.

Finding a tree near a clump of undisturbed snow, he followed their movements while he scooped snow into his mouth. Relaxing, all expression left his face. His eyes gleamed darkly as he settled into his true self.

He'd discovered his new game unexpectedly, just after Kate and Laura had left him alone in the car. No, not quite alone. With nothing to do, he'd turned his attention to Josiah, drawn by his groans. Crawling to the space near Josiah's head, he watched the sweat gleam on his face, saw the heated redness of his skin and the pain that contorted his features. A flush of power pumped through Lucas, leaving him light-headed; here was a body, at his mercy. He could do anything he wanted.

Placing a finger on Josiah's bandaged shoulder, he'd pressed down and been rewarded by Josiah's convulsive moan as his head thrashed from side to side. Lucas had glanced furtively around, prompted by years of caution.

He'd played the game, exploring other pain centers, for as long as he'd dared, until he'd seen the women returning. Then he'd scurried back to his corner, breathing hard, heart thumping with wild beats of erotic pleasure, his first. Unable to regain control of his features, he'd buried his face when the women reentered the car.

The memory of the game filled him as he hid in the bushes. Eyes glazed, his breath quickened as he relived the intense pleasure, and his hand explored the throbbing in his lap. Mouth open, face slack, he clutched himself, rubbing, pushing, discovering new surges. His painful grip pounded harder and harder, until an explosion burst through him and he cried out, overcome with pleasure.

"Lucas!"

Someone had called his name, and he shuddered, trying to reorient himself.

"It's okay," he gasped, unable to keep the tremor from his voice. "Just—just a, a squirrel. It scared me, that's all."

Laura and Kate tried to sleep, curled into their sleeping

bags on the hard ground. With no extra bag for Lucas, they'd given him the two-man tent and spare blankets and ordered him to bed after he'd eaten a silent meal of a sandwich and water. His expression of smiling gratitude had filled Laura with disgust.

The car creaked with Josiah's restless movements. She and Kate had stopped responding to his moans and delusional babbling, finding they were helpless to ease him further. After tending to his wound and giving him Demerol there was nothing more they could do. The odor from his infected foot was unbearable.

They would now have to travel over the wintry pass with the windows open. Laura slept fitfully through the last three hours of the night.

CHAPTER 29

LAURA EASED OFF THE ACCELERATOR AS THEY NEARED the California/Nevada border. There was little traffic on the road and snow at the shoulders lay in dirty patches. Most of the vehicles she saw were parked and had the Brotherhood logo on their doors: a big red fist clutching a gold lightning bolt. The Brotherhood preached that Jesus Christ now walked the world, but crucifixion would not be his fate this time, not with the Brotherhood ready to kill those who were counter to their holy purpose.

Seeing uniformed and heavily armed guards, Laura tensed as she came to a stop at the patrol kiosk.

Kate pinched Lucas, sitting between them, and whispered harshly, "You say one word, you make one fucking move, and I swear you will die."

Lucas nodded solemnly. It had taken him some time to settle on the appropriate expression, but he was certain he'd gotten it right.

As Laura watched one of the guards march toward them, she rehearsed the Brotherhood greeting and response she'd seen on the broadcasts they'd occasionally watched. The Brotherhood channel broadcast twenty-four hours a day, but none of the programming had ever shown the border patrol.

The guard stopped two feet from her open window, semiautomatic weapon in hand. He wore a khaki uniform, pressed, starched, and adorned with medals and patches, beneath his open, three-quarter length overcoat. His cowboy hat looked incongruous but displayed the Brotherhood logo.

"The Lord walks," the guard pronounced, eyes direct and steady.

"Amen," Laura responded.

"The Lord walks among us," he said, tone subtly rising.

"Hallelujah!" Laura forced enthusiasm into her voice, willing herself to act for all she was worth.

"As once He rose, now hath He descended."

"Hallowed be that ground."

"What say you to Him, Sister?"

Laura opened her mouth and her mind went blank. *What say you to Him, Sister?* She couldn't think, could only hear the question. What was the response? *What say you to Him, Sister?* Her scalp prickled and she closed her eyes, hiding her sudden fear from the guard's piercing gaze.

Kate, hand on Laura's leg as she leaned across Lucas,

responded loudly, "My soul is Thine, O Lord."

Laura's eyes flew open and the guard was staring at her, ignoring Kate. He gestured at Laura with his weapon. Get out, his motion said.

"Wait," Kate pleaded, still straining across Lucas's and Laura's laps. "Brother, listen."

The guard's attention flicked to her. "She's exhausted, Brother. She's been up all night, praying for the Lord's help. Look. Her husband is dying. We bring him to the Brotherhood, those who have taken the Lord into their hearts and from whom He will not turn."

Laura felt a wave of surprise at the cadence of Kate's words, authentic with religion.

The guard hesitated, then thrust his head through the open window to peer over Laura's shoulder. Assaulted by the thick smell of tissue decay rising from the rear, his face wrinkled in disgust. Just as he jerked his head back, he noticed Lucas, half hidden by Kate. The sentry's expression sparkled, as though he'd just uncovered a treasure, and he spoke to the guards behind him with excitement.

"Sister Donna!" he yelled. "Over here." A figure broke from the knot and hurried over, weapon at the ready. The young guard stepped to the side, giving his partner an unobstructed view to the interior. "It's your pledge, Sister. We can cover for you if you want to take him now."

This guard was dressed identically to the other, but

her coat collar covered the lower half of her face and the brim of her hat obscured her eyes. All Laura saw was a red nose and a few strands of white hair. What did the other guard mean about taking him now? All that kept Lucas from betraying them was his position, pressed between herself and Kate, and Kate's empty threat.

"How old are you, darlin'?" the old woman asked Lucas, tipping her hat back. Her eyes were greedy, as though she could barely restrain herself from snatching Lucas away.

"Donna?" said Kate, in hesitant recognition.

Puzzled, Laura wondered what dangerous game Kate was playing.

"Donna," Kate said with certainty. "It's us. Don't you remember?" Still straining across Lucas, her body hiding a vise like grip on his thigh, she smiled enthusiastically at the woman. "I know it's been years, but"—her smile faltered and her voice became gentle—"did you ever find her, Donna? Your little baby girl?"

Memory of the long-ago scene jolted Laura: the near-deserted rest stop, the woman pointing the gun at them, accusing them of stealing her child, the husband . . . Gary. Gary stepping between them and his crazed wife.

Sucking in her breath, she saw, in the three-quarter view, a trace of the woman in her memory. Donna's hair was now white, and her face etched with lines, but her expression was the same, the intensity, the greed. The way her eyes narrowed in suspicion of Kate's words.

"Kelly was a *Shaitan*-child," she said in a dismissive tone that chilled Laura. "But I don't remember you. If you'd known Kelly, you'd have known her spirit was taken by the second blackout."

"Praise the Lord," Kate said, switching gears, "for taking her, Sister Donna. Surely He blessed you with a sign of His coming, removing the unholy from your arms. We're truly saved now, for He has led us to one of His favored people."

Laura could see the effect of Kate's words on the woman, how her eyes gleamed at Kate's suggestion of her favored status. A slyness then crept across her features, both puzzling and alarming Laura.

To the other guard, Donna said. "I'll take them in, Brother Jimmy." She pointed to a parked jeep and instructed them to follow her. "We'll fill out the pledge papers at my house, it's not far."

"Sister Donna," Kate said urgently, gesturing at Josiah. "My friend's husband is so ill. Can we take him to the hospital first?"

The woman hesitated, squinting suspiciously at Josiah. Kate added firmly, "His sickness led us to you. He has placed us all in your hands, Sister."

"What's wrong with him?" Sister Donna asked. Her nose wrinkled at the stench of decay inside.

"He was shot by heathens," Kate answered firmly.

The woman nodded. "Then we'll go to the hospital."

With Lucas between them, Laura and Kate barely spoke as they followed Donna's jeep into Reno. As Laura drove, her thoughts felt smothered by their predicament.

The old woman had them at her mercy. They knew nothing about her, and Laura couldn't shake the strange look she'd seen cross the woman's face. They traveled now in the wake of Donna's unknown agenda.

As they followed Donna along the South Virginia Street exit, Laura considered turning off at a side street and fleeing, but abandoned the thought. There was too much traffic, and every vehicle she saw had a Brotherhood logo on its doors. Their camouflage-painted Suburban was conspicuous. And their mission was to get Josiah to the hospital.

Once Josiah was in competent hands, they could turn their attention to Sister Donna. And to Lucas. She wished they'd caught him before they'd left home, though now that she understood his true nature she was glad he wasn't anywhere near Lily. As they drove toward St. Mary's hospital, she remembered wanting to kill him. The truly unthinkable.

He's a child—John Thomas's brother.

He's not a child. He's an amoral sociopath.

He is Life. We have to find a way to help him.

She followed the jeep onto the hospital's emergency entrance driveway, fervently hoping they were there in time to save Josiah, wondering if Lucas would betray them all. She barely heard Kate ordering Lucas out of the car with them.

For all her trepidation about Sister Donna, Laura was thankful for her presence during the admission procedure. Without her, the red tape might have been insurmountable. The registration counter was long and curved, manned by four gowned and capped personnel. The large lobby teemed with people standing in lines or sitting in plastic chairs lining the walls or clustered in muttering groups. Everywhere she looked, the Brotherhood logo was displayed on posters, clothing, paperwork, caps, and scrub uniforms of admissions clerks, nurses, and doctors. Even the gurney that came for Josiah had the logo on its sheets.

It had been a long time since Laura had been with so many people, so much noise and bustle. The surrealism was heightened by the exaggerated piety of nearly every sentence being spoken. "Jesus walks" was a greeting, a benediction, a farewell, a pause in conversation.

The laborious paperwork done, Josiah was wheeled away with suddenness, time only for a brief farewell touch. Then they were outside and Laura tried to regain control of her breathing, lose the feeling of suffocation, still her inner quivering.

She grabbed Kate in a fierce hug, pressing her face into her curls, and Kate whispered assurances about

Josiah, as much to reassure herself as Laura.

"Maybe I should take the boy with me the rest of the way," suggested Sister Donna, impatient, eager.

"No," Kate said. She put her arm around Lucas and pulled him close. "He's a comfort to us, Sister. Let us pray together while we follow you."

Sister Donna nodded curtly and hurried to her jeep. "Come on, then."

Once again they were on the freeway, headed back in the direction from which they had come.

"I wonder how long till we hear something," Laura said. When she'd expressed concern about leaving the hospital so soon, the clerk had sternly assured her that the Lord guided the hands of the surgeon, and Laura's duty was to pray, not to question.

"It's in His hands, our lord whatshisname, hollowed-out be his face. Christ! I'll never say that name again, I swear to God. If He took a step for every time one of those freaks said 'He walks,' He'd be in China already. They don't hafta crucify Him this time. They're *walking* His ass to death."

Laura laughed reluctantly.

"That damn militant logo everywhere. And with all this walking shit, they probably got rid of all the crosses and tacked up an old pair of Nikes."

"Nikes!" Lucas laughed.

Kate and Laura stiffened at his voice. Before leaving

the hospital, they'd reestablished the backseat and Lucas was belted in behind Kate.

"Nikes," Lucas repeated.

Laura looked at him in the rearview mirror. He looked like a normal child, on an outing with adults. The extent of his pretense astounded her. Did he really think to just brazen his way back into their good graces?

Kate rummaged through the glove box and pulled out a compact CD player and headphones. They'd gotten it for Catherine on their first journey. She'd said music calmed her, and it had. Kate plugged an adapter into the lighter receptacle, pushed Play and turned up the volume until even Laura could hear music from the headset.

"Vivaldi. So that's where that CD was," Laura said.

Kate unbuckled her seat belt and turned backward in her seat. Just before clamping the headset over Lucas's ears, she demanded, "Keep this on 'til I say different." She resettled herself with the player on her lap where she could monitor the volume.

Hoping they were free of Lucas's eavesdropping, Laura and Kate spoke in whispers, following Sister Donna at sixty miles per hour over surprisingly well-maintained roads.

"What do you think she wants?" asked Laura.

"I don't know. She looks at Lucas like she wants to gobble him up. Maybe she never got over losing her baby. She'd shit bricks if she knew how whacko Lucas is."

Laura checked the mirror and saw Lucas gazing out the side window, hands in his lap.

"It'd be a hell of a lot easier if he *was Shaitan*," Kate continued. "We could just snuff his ass."

Laura couldn't bring herself to utter agreement.

"He's been a weird little shit from the start," Kate muttered, "but now, he just points due spooky. What's with this angel-face shit?"

"I know—it's as if he thinks if he pretends everything's normal, he can make us believe it, too."

Kate shook her head, bewildered.

Sister Donna's turn signal began to blink. "Looks like we're finally getting off the freeway," Laura said.

"We can't ditch her 'til the hospital calls us," said Kate. "If we sign the pledge, maybe she'll leave us alone. But we'll have to find a place to stay."

"The pledge process might be more complicated than we expect," Laura worried.

"I'll handle it," Kate assured her.

Laura remembered Kate's ease at the border. "You sounded like a real believer." She followed the jeep along an avenue carved into rolling, dry grasslands. Behind them, to the southwest, the freeway climbed into the mountains. The road ahead curved toward the foothills and the Truckee River, and Laura saw a scattering of houses amid a sparse, well-established pine forest.

"I told you I was raised in the stuff."

"Right, until you were fifteen. I never realized how much it influenced you, the way you usually talk."

"Ha. Yeah. Well, my parents were progressive Southern Baptist. A lot of Baptists are against having women ministers. My folks wanted me to be the preacher son they never had."

They made a sharp turn into a driveway and, after a short, steep climb, the driveway ended in a flat parking area in front of a garage, near a neatly kept ranch house. Laura set the brake. "A preacher?" she said, turning to Kate.

Kate grinned. "Hold that thought. We're back on the wing." She pushed Stop on the CD player and got out of the car.

Donna emerged from her jeep.

Kate held Lucas firmly by the arm as they followed Donna through a side entrance into the house, stepping into the kitchen. Without removing her overcoat, Donna gestured for them to sit at a breakfast table. She set a kettle of water on the stove, turned on a gas flame, and, with practiced moves, began to fix tea and sandwiches.

Unrecognizable sounds came from elsewhere in the house. The thought that it might be Donna's husband, Gary, gave Laura some hope. Gary had been a stable influence when they'd confronted Donna long ago.

One of the intermittent sounds became louder, muffled by closed doors. Laura thought it sounded like a wail, and exchanged glances with Kate. Donna, whose back was to them, had her head cocked toward the door.

"We'll eat in a minute," said Donna. She walked toward the inner door. "I'll go fetch the papers. Phone rings, answer it, might be the hospital, though I doubt they'll be calling soon." She shut the door loudly behind her.

Kate whispered, "Did you hear that?"

"I heard it," Laura whispered back. "What did it sound like to you?"

"Like an animal or something."

Kate leaned closer. "If there are any question-and-answer parts in the pledge, let me do the talking. You just repeat what I say. Stay like this," she demonstrated a bowed prayerful attitude, "and act like you're tired and worried and not really thinking straight because of Josiah."

"That won't be hard," Laura said. "Those might not even be real doctors at that hospital."

"Of course they're doctors," Kate said. "What do you think they—oh, Jesus," the color drained from her face. "You mean faith healers?"

"I saw knives and things," Lucas interjected helpfully. Kate and Laura looked at him and he nodded.

Scalpels, Laura thought. She almost smiled at Lucas but jerked her attention away.

When Sister Donna came back, she carried a sheaf of papers in one hand. She set tea and buttered bread on the table, then joined them.

"Let us pray," she demanded.

After the meager lunch, the pledge process seemed interminable. Following lengthy prayers, Sister Donna began the question and response Kate had anticipated. Laura, head bowed, voice tired and whispery, repeated every one of Kate's careful responses. Laura was amazed at Kate, who quoted Bible passages, citing chapter and verse, often engaging Sister Donna in tangential religious dialogue. As the numbing process wore on, Laura's mind wandered to Josiah.

It had been almost three hours since they'd left him at the hospital. She wished the phone would ring yet dreaded what she might learn. One part of her bargained with God and another part mocked her simplistic petitions.

Laura had only been peripherally exposed to the concept of God. As a child, she'd asked the usual questions: Who was God? Where was He? Did He really make everything and know what everyone did? The idea of such an authority was at once comforting and threatening. Her parents had no answers. They'd simply told her they didn't know; when she grew up, she could decide for herself what to believe.

At age six, Laura decided she'd inform God of her interest right away, just in case. The God she'd imagined was more like an invisible friend and she developed her own way of chatting with Him, though her prayers were hardly more than negotiations bolstered by evolving diplomatic skills.

God, she prayed now, like a child, *let it be just a foot, please. More would be unfair.*

"Amen," she heard Lucas say. With trepidation, she realized Donna had turned her attention to Lucas.

"The Lord walks among us," Sister Donna said to Lucas, her eyes alight.

"Hallelujah," Lucas responded.

"As once He rose, now hath He descended." Sister Donna nodded encouragingly at him.

"Hallelujah. Blessed be that ground," Lucas crowed.

Sister Donna laughed in delight and stroked his hair, then gently pinched his cheek. "Very good, darlin'," she praised. "Now, how about a cookie?"

Kate glanced at Laura, face hard, eyebrows raised. Sister Donna gave Lucas a handful of cookies and told him to go play on the backyard swing while the grown-ups talked.

Laura glanced out the window. They were atop a slight hill with several houses below, widely separated, each with its own small plot of land. All appeared to be deserted, shabby, showing years of neglect and weather damage. There were no signs of any people.

Donna distributed the papers she'd brought in earlier and explained how each copy would go to a different department at the central office. She pointed with a stubby, nail-bitten finger at places requiring signatures. As they began to sign, she fumbled in her khaki pants pockets to retrieve several entangled necklaces that she placed on the table. Each thin silver chain bore a small fist clutching a lightning bolt.

From a large envelope, she pulled several folded Brotherhood logo decals and laid them on the table.

The strange intensity filled Donna's eyes. "There's evil in this world." They nodded, and Donna stared intently at them, back and forth, the silence lengthening. Laura's unease grew. Now what?

"Listen close," Sister Donna whispered harshly. "The Brotherhood, it's not the true way."

Laura and Kate sat stunned. What was this new twist in an already bizarre maze of superstition? Was this a test of some kind?

Donna's jaw clenched; her hands trembled.

"What do you mean, Sister Donna? He walks among us," said Kate, hoping to choose the right lines in this new drama.

"Four, five years ago," said Donna in a hushed, secretive voice, "the Brotherhood was a real church with a real preacher. That was Reverend Perry, that was. Reverend Perry, he's still head of the church, but things have changed, ever since Brother Em joined him. He's the leader now, and he is a snake; a daemon is what he is." Her hands shot out and gripped each of theirs. She spoke rapidly, spitting her words out like a lariat to snare them.

"Reverend Perry used to preach about the goodness

of God and the evil of Satan and about us needing to fight together for the Lord. Reverend Perry, he didn't quarrel with the other churches, he just tended his own flock. Then Brother Snake shows up and things became real different." Faster and faster her words came.

"Everything changed. Brother Em, he started fighting with other churches. I mean real blood battles. There were killings, lots and lots of killings. My Gary died fighting. I couldn't go out, I was pregnant. But my Gary went out one day and never came back."

Her face twisted and Laura felt her stomach tighten. Why was Donna telling them all this? Betraying her true thoughts of the Brotherhood, in which she was enmeshed, to two complete strangers? She felt her fingers growing numb in Donna's tight grip.

"The Brotherhood preys on *Shaitan*. Brother Em brings that evil right into church, makes a blood spectacle of it."

"Lord have mercy," Kate said.

Donna nodded emphatically. "That's not all. They use *Shaitan* evil in their rituals. In God's own house!" A feverish light burned in her eyes. "Anyone not pledged to the Brotherhood is *Shaitan*, according to Brother Em."

Laura swallowed hard, understanding the trap they had walked into. It had just, near audibly, snapped shut.

"That's not the worst of it," said Donna. Shoulders hunched, she whispered, "What they do to *Shaitan* children in church is an abomination."

Kate frowned. "Where are they finding *Shaitan* children?"

"They breed 'em." Donna hissed.

"They what?" exclaimed Laura.

Donna nodded vigorously. "It's the truth, so help me, God." She turned to Kate. "Jesus led you to me, Sister Kate. I can protect your boy!"

Kate held Donna's gaze as she slowly withdrew her hand from Donna's grasp and, just as slowly, rose from her seat. Obviously, Donna thought Lucas was her son, an honest mistake, given Kate's proprietary manner with him that hid whispered threats, furtive control. She said nothing, buying time while she considered how to use the error to their advantage.

Donna, mistaking Kate's silence for suspicion, pressed Kate back down into her seat. "Listen to me! They'll take your boy. There aren't many *real* children left. It's the reason Brother Jimmy called me to you at the border. I've had to play their game; I *had* to, with Gary gone, and my own boy to protect."

Laura's head was spinning. Lucas was their bargaining chip? The reason Donna was emboldened to take them into her confidence?

"You have a boy?" Kate asked. "How old?"

Sister Donna stared at Kate. "Almost four."

Kate and Laura exchanged looks.

"He's not *Shaitan*," Sister Donna proclaimed. "He's different, but he's not *Shaitan*. I know it."

Probably deformed, Laura thought, remembering the thin wail they'd heard earlier.

"What does the Brotherhood do with *Shaitan*?" Kate asked.

"It used to be, they just killed them, but not in the church. Reverend Perry preached about cleansing the evil, but then Brother Em came, and he started a bunch of rituals and ceremonies that brought people into the church. Everyone began pledging to the Brotherhood. Everyone wants to see the *Shaitan* die! They pack the church for the ritual killings. And big offerings are required to witness the cleansing."

Fear shone in her eyes. "They torture the *Shaitan* until evil almost explodes their awful eyes, then they sacrifice them on the altar. Mind you, I'm all for killing these soulless spawn of Satan, but the Brotherhood's not stamping out the evil, they're sending that evil straight to God. Sacrificing 'em on the altar like that! *Shaitan* can't be purified. They go to heaven as evil as they came into this world. I know that as sure as I know anything." Sweat beaded on her face and she suddenly slumped in her chair.

"I've hidden little Samuel all these years," she whispered. "The Brotherhood demands all newborns. Brother Em's got them all convinced that *Shaitan* evil is limited, and the faster they can empty it, the better. He personally handles all the baby sacrifices. Even other churches let him have those."

She shook her head vehemently. "They're not getting Samuel," she said in a hard voice. "He's not *Shaitan.* I knew that Kelly was; not at first, but I knew. Kelly was eight months old when the blackout came—and the second blackout. Back then, 'course, nobody knew evil had spilled into the world, and I lost Kelly a week after—almost lost my mind as well. But after the second blackout . . . well, I knew. Kelly wasn't the same, not her eyes.

"But little Samuel's no *Shaitan.*" She glared.

If Donna's version of the Brotherhood was true, thought Laura, everything in this place was demented and dangerous. Perhaps Donna was right about little Samuel, too. Maybe Samuel was like Lily, a child with a soul. Maybe there were others, souls that had somehow managed to bridge the disruption in time and space.

"Why don't you take Samuel out of here?" Kate asked Donna.

"It's not that easy," answered Donna, pinning Kate with a look. "I need help."

Now we come to it, thought Laura.

"You want our help," Kate stated.

Donna nodded eagerly. Spittle flew as she spoke. "Yes. I can't do it alone. I can't handle Samuel by myself, not and get us past the border. And not to keep him safe afterward."

Kate raked fingers over her head, sweeping back her curls. "What do you want us to do? We've got Josiah in the hospital and, from what you've said, we're gonna have a heck of a time getting out of here with Lucas."

"That's just it, you see?" Donna interrupted. "I help you with Lucas, and you help me with Samuel. I got it all worked out, and I've been waiting for the right people to help me. I prayed on it every day and my prayers have been answered." She clasped Kate's hand and looked at Laura. "You're the first ones to come with real belief of the old churches and the truth of the Lord. The Lord led you to me."

The telephone rang, startling all of them. Sister Donna jumped up to answer it. "Don't worry," she said to Laura. "The Lord is watching over us." After a few words on the phone, she handed it to Laura, then left the room, this time leaving the door to the hallway open.

Laura held the phone so Kate could listen as well. The female voice said Josiah was out of surgery and that the doctor would like to speak to her as soon as she could come. Laura asked what had been done but the woman would add nothing, repeating only that Laura needed to speak with the doctor. Frustrated, Laura thanked her and ended the call. "Let's go," she said to Kate.

They grabbed their coats from the chairs and Kate called down the hallway where Donna had disappeared.

"Sister Donna! We gotta go."

"Hold on," called Donna.

She walked down the narrow hallway toward them, tugging a small form behind her. As she stepped into the kitchen, she brought the boy next to her. "This is Samuel," she said.

Laura and Kate stared silently at the Neanderthal child.

CHAPTER 30

THEY WERE UNEASY ABOUT LEAVING LUCAS, BUT SISTER Donna convinced them it would be too risky to take him.

"He'll be okay," Kate insisted for the third time, before they were even out of the driveway. "Look, even if he does blow our story, Donna needs us too much to turn us in."

Laura grimaced. "She's crazy. We can't trust her."

"She may be crazy but I don't think she's loony. She's just trying to save her kid."

"What was your take on him?"

"Don't know. I could barely see eyes under that caveboy forehead of his. How about you?"

Laura shook her head. She did have an opinion, a strong one, but not one Kate would want to hear. Samuel was a true-to-form throwback, a real Neanderthal. The mutations now plaguing the world weren't random, after all. They were evolutionary reversals, limited only by the genetic memory of all the DNA combinations that had already existed before the blackout. *We direct evolution; we create every new life-form. If We can't get through, no new forms can be created. Everything that's born now is either malformed according to pre-existing patterns, or de-evolved. Nothing can be new.*

Is this the proof I need for someone to believe me? She nearly blurted her thoughts but, knowing the argument that would follow, bit them back. *I need more than little Samuel. We've seen odd creatures, none recognizable. Only an expert could tell.*

"Our exit's next," Kate said, interrupting her thoughts. "You better slow down."

In the thick of Reno traffic, Laura was thankful for the Brotherhood logos Sister Donna had applied to the Suburban. The ubiquitous logos were a sign of unity that, given what they now knew, were necessary for their survival. At the same time, they made her feel alienated, severing any sense of connection she might have felt toward the humanity peopling the town.

"This is creepy," Kate said as Laura pulled into the hospital parking lot. "Are you feeling what I'm feeling?"

Laura killed the engine. "It's really bad," she said.

They looked down at the logo necklaces they wore.

Dr. Carlson's words were terse, but his eyes were kind. In a small waiting room, he gestured them to be seated. He was about forty, Laura estimated, old enough to have been practicing medicine before the blackout.

Josiah's leg had been amputated just above the knee. Dr. Carlson outlined his reasons for the more radical procedure by citing the complications that might have resulted with a lesser option. Laura barely heard, lost in memories of Josiah: striding down the slope behind the house, springing effortlessly up the stairs, entering a room with the grace of a cat.

Sadly, she imagined Josiah waking in the hospital bed, not yet knowing that part of him was gone. Her vision blurred and tears spilled as she refocused on the doctor's voice.

"—for a week at least," he was saying. "By then we should know that the antibiotics have done their work. Barring complications, he could be released then, but once the leg has healed, we must try to find a prosthesis and discuss his future care."

He placed his hands on Laura's shoulders. "I'm sorry."

She nodded, remembering that Josiah had been admitted into the hospital as her husband. "Thank you," she murmured. "For everything. Can we see him now?"

"He's heavily sedated, in ICU. He must remain isolated for at least a day, to reduce the risk of infection. I'm sorry."

Laura looked at Kate, whose face was drawn, freckles sharp against her pale white skin.

"There is something you can do," the doctor suggested. "You can pray. The Lord hears our prayers. Jesus walks, sisters."

They sat numbly in the Suburban.

"The fucking Lord walks, but now Josiah can't," Kate said in defeat and anger.

"When I was little, I asked God for a Barbie," said Laura listlessly.

"Did you get one?"

"My mother thought Barbies were ridiculous."

"She was a feminist?"

"I don't know. She popped us kids out and went back to her horses, like the rest was up to us. Mom was crazy about her horses. She babied them and let us run wild. We kids had a lot of freedom and took care of each other." She laughed halfheartedly. "We came up with some wild meals. I remember one week we ate nothing but hot dogs on crackers, and oranges smeared with jam.

Then my older brother, Tony, decided to cook a chicken. He was about eight. I was six, and Conrad, two or three. Tony stuck a frozen chicken in a pot of water and let it boil for hours. When it started falling apart, he set the pot on the table. We picked pieces off and dipped them in ranch dressing, peanut butter, mustard, ketchup, and chutney. I think we had every jar we could find out on the table."

"Sounds messy."

"All our meals were. Every time Mom would come into the kitchen, she'd say, 'We don't have kids, we have an infestation.' Dad would just clean it up and she'd go back to her horses. When Conrad was little, and somebody would ask, 'What are you kids up to?' Conrad would say, 'We're not kids. We're a 'festation!'"

She'd given up hope of ever seeing Conrad again and, now, the sadness of that loss mingled with her sadness for Josiah. She reached blindly for Kate's hand and they sat quietly, comforting each other with small pressures of their clasped hands.

Laura felt drained of the urgency that had prodded her since their journey began, unable to formulate a plan for the coming days. She couldn't move past the moment when Josiah would learn of his condition.

Dusk fell and the parking lot lights came on. They talked quietly about not returning to Donna's house, too exhausted to pretend, or be suspicious. But there was nowhere else to go.

And Lucas was there.

"Do you think everything Donna said about the Brotherhood is true?" Laura asked. "Sacrificing babies on altars?"

"Only *Shaitan* are being born. What's the difference where they kill them?" Although Kate didn't believe Laura's theory of soulless *Shaitan*, she did acknowledge that all new births were mutations, mental as well as physical. Her face wrinkled in disgust. "The shitty thing about it is that the women are getting pregnant on purpose. Chrissakes. Breeding for killing! That's sick."

Dreading seeing Donna again, Kate smacked a fist on the seat as Laura drove out of the parking lot. "How are we going to get through the next few weeks? Shit, maybe it's lucky we did run into Donna. At least she's against the sacrifices." She suddenly grinned at Laura. "You wanna tell me again what a good thing it is we didn't go to Sacramento?"

"I swear to God, I'll never leave home again," said Laura. "If we make it back."

A week later, they were more involved in the Brotherhood than they'd ever have thought possible. Donna insisted they attend services, and that they meet

Reverend Perry. Anyone not attending services could be construed as being *Shaitan*.

"He knows you're here," she'd said stubbornly. "If we don't do everything by the book, then there's gonna be questions. I don't want him thinking I might be hiding *Shaitan*. I've worked too hard. I've got my boy to think of—and you've got yours."

Donna was fiercely protective of her child and pathetically eager for signs of their approval and acceptance of him. They took great care to treat him well and interact normally with him despite his oddities.

It was more than Samuel's appearance that was startling. He only gestured and made noises, mostly grunts and growls. Usually placid and compliant, when thwarted he would emit piercing wails that were muted only by his soundproofed room. Although the subdivision where she lived was deserted, Donna had installed the soundproofing as a precaution.

Their nonchalant attitude toward Samuel soothed Donna enough for her to believe that everything was as she wished. Otherwise, Laura knew, Donna would never have left Samuel with her when she went off with Kate. Not to mention having left Lucas behind, as well. Donna considered Lucas a hostage, just as Laura and Kate had suspected, to ensure their compliance with her plans.

If she only knew what we really think of Lucas, Laura thought as she watched the boys on the monkey bars.

It was her first time alone with Samuel, her first chance to scrutinize him openly, without Donna's constraining presence.

They had not disabused Donna of her notion that Lucas was Kate's child. It would never have occurred to them to claim Lucas as their own, but it was obvious now that he would have been taken from them otherwise. And that would have been his opportunity to betray them, a betrayal that would end badly for them. Very badly.

Another edge given them by Donna's assumption of Lucas's value was that if immediate escape became necessary, they could abandon Lucas rather than risk their lives for him. *He's Donna's hole card,* Laura thought, *and we're not playing the same game.* She couldn't help but pity Donna. *Poor woman, just trying to survive.*

The boys had abandoned the monkey bars and were crouched near the fence. Laura guessed they'd found an anthill or a bug. *Boys and bugs, that's one thing that hasn't changed.*

She looked at Samuel's crouched, compact body. Even dressed as he was, in plaid shirt and loose overalls, his broad shoulders, thick chest, and long arms couldn't be concealed. His massive head was emphasized by the haircut Donna had given him, painstakingly shaped to approximate that of any other small boy. It revealed his sloping forehead, heavy brow, and chinless face. Even a hat could do no more than perch ridiculously atop his big head.

She and Kate had soon learned why Donna needed their help to smuggle Samuel past the border; not only were his wailing tantrums unpredictable, but his metabolism was sufficiently different to make sedatives dangerous for him. Donna had told them she'd once, hoping to quiet him, given him a small dose of cough syrup with codeine, and had almost killed him. She'd even tried binding and gagging him, but the gag couldn't be made secure enough to prevent his furious roars. So she needed someone to act as a decoy for any noises Samuel might make when they passed checkpoints. Not even Reverend Perry could get past checkpoints without stopping and showing identification.

As soon as Donna and Kate had left in the morning, Laura had sent Lucas out to the swings but kept Samuel with her in the kitchen. Nervously, she'd knelt down before him to look into his eyes. Samuel stared back at her, without reaction, his dark pupils sharp and unwavering, like a cat watching for the next movement of something that held its interest. Laura searched his eyes, barely breathing, seeking the swirling blackness even as she braced for its terrifying appearance.

It wasn't there. She got up from her crouch, and Samuel's massive brow tilted back as she rose. Smiling, she said, "Cookie, Samuel?" He grunted loudly, patted his hand on his mouth, and turned to the cabinet where Donna kept his treats.

As she watched the boys now, still fascinated by whatever they had found, she tried to assess what she'd learned in little Samuel's eyes, his innocent, animal-like gaze. Was Donna right about Samuel? Donna claimed to have recognized a change in her eight-month-old daughter, Kelly, and this, Donna believed, gave her a real standard of comparison to judge Samuel as not *Shaitan.*

If Samuel was not *Shaitan*, the Way was not completely shattered; souls were getting through. If Samuel was *Shaitan*, his eyes, unlike others, didn't betray him.

A movement caught her attention: Samuel, reaching to the ground, one hand after the other, plucking up things that he stuffed into his mouth. Lucas intently watched him.

"Samuel." Laura sprang from her chair and sprinted across the yard. When she reached Samuel, she dropped to her knees and grabbed his arm to stop him from feeding himself what he'd found.

Beetles. Laura saw the tiny black legs waving between Samuel's fingers on its shelled body. With a roar of rage, Samuel swept her to one side with his other arm, the large beetle still firmly between his fingers. Laura scrambled forward and grabbed his wrist before he could put the beetle into his gaping mouth. He turned, snarling, and tried to twist his arm from her hand. Prepared this time for little Samuel's startling strength, she stood up to gain leverage.

As Laura pulled Samuel to his feet, she knew she needed to keep him off-balance. She moved quickly toward the house, shaking his arm to release the struggling beetle from his grip. He grunted loudly and she braced herself for the keening wail that was sure to erupt any moment. Just before they entered the side door, the beetle dropped from his fingers. She yanked Samuel into the house, and almost shut the door on Lucas, who had followed them.

Laura held Samuel by one arm, her heart thudding. Hoping to avert Samuel's inevitable tantrum, she looked down into his contorted face and loudly called his name, then, in desperation, screamed, "Cookie!" The next instant burned itself into her memory.

Samuel opened his eyes to focus on Laura, and she saw swirling black, vile intent amassing within the child, his pupils dilated atop a boiling sea of pitch-black lava. Laura was nearly paralyzed by the malevolence. The next instant, the dark whirling ceased so completely, Laura stood transfixed, holding her breath, as she confronted the now-placid, heavily browed face of an innocent, four-year-old Neander-child.

"Better give it to him," Lucas said. The amusement in his voice was disorienting.

"Huh?"

"The cookie. Better give it to him. He seems to be pretty hungry."

That afternoon, as Kate drove them to the hospital, Laura told her what happened.

"He's definitely *Shaitan*," she concluded.

"Of course he's *Shaitan*."

"Donna seems so sure he isn't."

"So what? You think cave-babies are immune to the virus?"

"You actually think people are *Shaitan* because of a virus?"

"It's as good an explanation as any."

"No," Laura said absently. "If it was a virus, it would have mutated long ago."

"Maybe it is mutating, but we don't notice anything past the *Shaitan*."

"No," she repeated. "Things are mutating backward." That notion had been gnawing at her all week, causing her to utter it without thinking.

"Because of the cave-kid? Just because he's a throwback doesn't mean everything is. That would mean *Shaitan* are throwbacks, too, and I know they're not in the history books."

Laura had come to a familiar impasse with Kate. Yet, strangely, she didn't feel the usual dread at entering an argument with her. *It wasn't my opinion I needed Kate to accept,* she realized. *It was me.* Had she really, all this time, believed their friendship to be so fragile it couldn't withstand disagreement? *My God, I even gave Josiah up to her without a fight.*

Kate glanced at her. "Are you gonna tell me that *Shaitan* are in the history books and I missed class that day?"

Laura laughed, resolved to pursue self-realization later. It was enough, for now, to know she didn't need to fear speaking her mind. "No, *Shaitan* are new. But they're not new life. They're from some different source."

Kate groaned. "Not that again."

Laura shrugged. "Until I can figure out if there's a way we can get the Path back, it doesn't matter what anyone believes." There. She'd said it.

"The Path." Kate snorted. "You talk about it like it's some kinda backwoods trail, with real dirt and twigs and rocks and shit on it."

"More like an energy path, but complicated, because it involves conversion of energy into matter. Not just matter." Laura nodded. "But soulmatter. Organic life. More a quantum trail."

"You're not mad at me," said Kate, surprised.

"Why should I be mad at you?"

"Come on! Every time this shit's come up before, you'd get pissed off at me. Like I'm stupid and you've got all the answers."

"I never thought you were stupid," Laura said

quietly. "I get upset when you act like I'm delusional. You've decided it's something religious, so I'm suspect. You've made me scared to talk about it because I don't want you to think as little of me as you do religious fanatics." She blinked back sudden tears. "I really need you to be my friend."

Kate abruptly pulled to the wide shoulder of the highway. Not looking at Laura, she drew a deep breath, as though steeling herself against something, then said, "I used to be one of those religious nuts." She closed her eyes. "I know what it's like to believe in something so much it takes over your whole life. You walk around knowing that you're witnessing miracles, so you try to get others to see them, too. You feel like every breath you take is divine, and when you're with other people who feel the same way, it's a kind of heaven.

"You're never alone, because you feel God is in you, supporting every move you make. And you don't fear death because you know some day you'll be with God."

Laura sat very still. She heard resignation—and pain—in Kate's voice, and knew something terrible was coming.

"So one day me and my little sister, Carrie, were crossing the street, and she got hit by a car. She was just half a step in front of me. I sat in the street holding her. Her head was smashed and there was blood everywhere. I prayed like I'd never prayed before." After a pause, she added, tonelessly, "I was fourteen and Carrie was eight.

"I pleaded for God to make good on the promises I'd heard my entire life, that people could be healed if you believe. I called in all the favors for having been a good servant. I prayed with every ounce of faith I had. I was convinced that He would listen.

"Carrie just watched me, all broken up, bleeding. I knew she was counting on my relationship with God, counting on me to have God save her life." She glanced at Laura.

Laura didn't know what to say, but her eyes burned with sympathy.

"Carrie didn't die, but she didn't get better. When she got out of the hospital, my folks put her bed in our living room. It became like a shrine. I was always there, praying. My parents told everyone that Carrie would have died if I hadn't been with her. At first, I believed that, too.

"But Carrie never got better. She was paralyzed from the neck down, couldn't talk, but she never took her eyes off me, never lost hope when I was near her. The more she believed, the more unsure I got. Finally, I couldn't feel anything but failure. For months I didn't sleep because of nightmares, and I couldn't eat.

"My fifteenth birthday, I went downstairs to Carrie like I did every morning, and . . . all of a sudden, it was all just gone. The faith, the belief. Half a step was the difference between Carrie getting hit instead of me. If it was a test of faith, God blew it, because nobody could've believed stronger than me. And in that minute, I knew: Faith was bullshit and so was He.

"I looked at Carrie and she was staring at me like she always did, her faith just as strong.

"I got so Goddamn mad. My whole life looked like one big stupid lie. People were living to please something that didn't exist. All the praying, all the believing—lies. My knees buckled and I hit the floor."

Laura found her voice. "Oh, Kate, how horrible. It's no wonder you—"

"No," Kate barked. "That's exactly why I never tell anyone. I don't want people thinking, 'Now I understand Kate.' I hate that. I am more than just that, and I won't be boiled down to psycho-babble."

Laura nodded guiltily. "Why did your parents think you'd be a preacher?"

"I was good," Kate said simply. "Not virtuous good. I was good with the Bible. I could understand the metaphors and explain them like they were my own."

There it was. The skinny girl in Laura's imagination, accepted as a prodigy by her religious community, speaking with the charismatic energy she still had today. There was Kate, stripped of years, denuded of cynicism, peeled down to latent talent, innocent passion.

"You must have been something," said Laura.

"Yeah, I was something all right; I was part of deceiving people. It makes me sick to remember things

I said that made other people victims of the bullshit."

"But you—"

"But I was raised in it, it wasn't my fault, blah, blah, blah."

Laura held up a hand. "Let me finish. You can't blame yourself. You were just a kid."

"I told you I ran away at fifteen. Well, I ran away that day, my birthday. I didn't say anything, didn't leave a note, didn't even say good-bye to Carrie."

Tears mixed with defiance.

"I tried to force myself into the living room once more, but I couldn't do it. Carrie, she knew I was standing there but couldn't turn her head. And I couldn't go in." Her voice dropped to a husky whisper. "I hated her." Her face twisted, holding back tears. "She was nine years old and paralyzed and I hated her for my failure, so I walked out."

Kate drew a shaky breath. "I never even called for five years. When I finally did, my mom hung up on me. I found out later that Carrie had died the week after I left."

Kate wiped her nose and smiled crookedly. "Shit, it's been twenty-something years."

"I'm so sorry."

"Don't be. I only told you about it because of what we were talking about. *Shaitan* and religious nuts and that shit." Kate shifted into gear and pulled onto the empty highway.

"But at least, with your experience, you can understand why people can become involved in religion," Laura said, phrasing her words tactfully.

"Not really. I was only fifteen, but I figured it out, even though it would've been easier not to. I could've told myself that sometimes God says, 'No.'" She banged the steering wheel. "It's a fucking cop-out. People fucking cop out. I wised up. So can they."

"Do you see me as a religious nut for believing in my epiphany?" Laura asked cautiously.

Kate laughed, "Sorry, honey, your story sounds just like others I've heard. People who believe in miracles will believe anything.

"But I love you anyway," she added, shifting abruptly into her whimsical self.

Josiah's recovery was so swift that Dr. Carlson, as one might expect, called it a miracle. Laura and Kate visited Josiah daily at the hospital, but visiting hours were short and strictly enforced. They hadn't been there when Josiah had regained consciousness and was told of his amputation. By the time they saw him, Josiah had dealt with the loss in his own solitary way.

Laura knew immediately, could see in his expression and the lazy smile with which he greeted them, that he'd adapted to his fate. A rush of love filled her.

"Welcome back," she said, touching his hand.

Kate lightly stroked his cheek. "Hi, kiddo, how're you feeling?"

Josiah grinned. "Pretty spacey. Drugs, I guess."

"Aw, you're just hungry," Kate said. "You've lost weight."

"Chopping off body parts will do that." Josiah raised his head. "What's the word on this place?" he whispered. "They said you'd be coming, but I wasn't sure who they meant. They keep talking about my wife and a Sister Donna."

"Laura's your wife," Kate whispered. "We'll explain later. Donna's . . . well, we'll explain that later, too. We're in Reno and—"

"That much I figured," Josiah said.

"Josiah, listen. The Brotherhood's way heavier than we understood from their broadcasts."

Laura saw the doorknob turn, nudged Kate, and said loudly, "Praise the Lord. Thank you for hearing our prayers."

"Amen," Kate said as a nurse entered the room. "The Lord walks, Sister," she greeted her politely.

When Josiah was released from the hospital and safely in the Suburban, he finally heard enough to connect the hurried bits and pieces they'd told him during visiting hours.

Laura drove slowly, taking side roads at a whim to delay the return to Donna's house.

"The town's crammed with people," Kate said. "Hotels aren't even hotels anymore; they're like huge communes, people living in all the rooms. The old Play 'N Pray Casino is headquarters to the Brotherhood. There's about fifteen or twenty preachers, besides Reverend Perry, and each of them has a couple of sidekicks. Perry's sidekick is some guy called Brother Em, who Donna says is a real piece of work."

"Remember that huge, round bowling alley?" Laura asked. "They've turned that into a hydroponics plant and it's not the only one. It's really amazing how organized the city is. They have power plants outside of town that generate enough electricity to run everything, plus extra that they sell to the army base in Carson City."

"Actually, the army base is Carson City," Kate corrected. "There are no civilians there, we hear. The Brotherhood doesn't allow any traffic between here and there. The border shit they've set up in that direction is crazy—fences, barbed wire, sentry towers, land mines—you name it."

"What about I-80 east?" Josiah asked.

"Patrolled. All the highways have border crossings—80, 395, 445—but nothing like the one blocking 395 south to Carson City. We tried 445 one day. We showed the patrol our papers and said we were headed to Pyramid

Lake, but they wouldn't let us through. Wanted to know why we didn't have a pass from headquarters."

"What happened?"

"We pretended we did have a pass, asked them to look through the papers again. The guard was pretty nice but he still wouldn't let us through without it. 'Jesus walks'—hah. Even He couldn't walk out of this place without a pass. They're sure anyone trying to get out is *Shaitan*."

Josiah's concern grew. "Is this Jesus supposed to be in Reno?"

"Nobody knows, but everybody seems to think He must be," said Laura. "It's how they account for everything that happens."

"Why the tight borders? Why keep people in who don't want to stay?"

"Like I said," Kate said. "Anyone who wants to leave must be *Shaitan*. Perry says the idea came direct from God during one of their chats. The *Shaitan*, according to his sidekick, Em, come from some finite pool of evilness. The sacrifices on the altar are supposed to gradually reduce the pool to pre-blackout size."

"Getting into Reno, to the Brotherhood," Laura explained, "is easy. The patrols let everyone, except army personnel, in, and put them on a list so they can keep track of them. They don't let army in because they can't keep them without the government coming down on them."

"The Brotherhood is splintered into a bunch of

sects," said Kate, "and membership competition seems to revolve around the most *Shaitan* sacrifices."

"Where are all these *Shaitan* coming from?" Josiah asked.

"I've wondered, myself," said Laura. "Maybe they're not all *Shaitan*—just victims. Like the old witch hunts."

"But the eyes—" Josiah began.

"From what Donna's said about the torture that goes on before the sacrifice," said Kate, "anybody would end up looking crazy. And on the altar, only preachers are close enough to see."

Josiah became unnaturally pale.

He's so tired, Laura thought. She checked her watch and saw he was overdue for his medication.

Spotting a freeway on-ramp, Laura merged into traffic. As she sped toward Donna's, she told Josiah about Samuel, including a new theory she hadn't mentioned to Kate, that *Shaitan* learned to conceal the dark emptiness in their eyes. If others believed this, it supported the practice of torture to get *Shaitan* to reveal themselves.

Why did it matter that *Shaitan* could keep their nature from showing in their eyes? Kate wanted to know. The eyes boiled as soon as they were angered.

"What if they're not as easily provoked as we thought?" asked Laura. "What if some are not as uncontrolled as we think?"

"What would that mean, Laura?" Josiah asked.

Their exit lay only a few miles ahead.

"I'm trying to define them. If we know what they are, what their source is, maybe there's a way to stop them from being part of everything that's being born."

Kate laughed and shook her head. "Back to the Path, kiddo?"

Laura smiled. There was no sarcasm in Kate's voice. Impulsively, she squeezed Kate's hand. "Something else," she said. "If they can hide it, maybe you're right about Lucas being *Shaitan*, Kate."

"Lucas?" said Josiah, surprised.

"I've never seen it in his eyes," Laura said. "And that's thrown me. It never occurred to me that he could hide it."

"But why haven't they all learned to hide it?" Josiah asked. "To protect themselves."

"Maybe a lot of them did," said Laura. "But I think whatever makes them *Shaitan* makes them crave the hunt, even if they're the hunted."

"Self-preservation," Kate said suddenly. "Everything's born with that instinct."

"Yes!" Laura said. "Self-preservation is triggered by fear, and they have no fear. That's part of what's so terrible about their eyes."

"It has to take time to learn to hide it," Josiah said, shifting uncomfortably. "To even learn that they should."

Laura exited the freeway. Slowing for the curved

boulevard, she said, "Time is exactly what Samuel's had. Four years."

"Well, shit, that lets Lucas out," Kate said. "It couldn'ta been more than a month after the blackout that we found him."

There was disappointment in Kate's voice. She'd been feeling vindicated in her dislike of Lucas.

"Not if he'd been born *Shaitan*," Laura said.

"But—" Josiah started.

"We assume that the evil of the *Shaitan* is new," Laura interrupted, turning into the driveway. "But if it's the flip side of life, it's always been there. Only, instead of trickling into the world the way it used to, maybe the blackout let it pour in."

CHAPTER 31

Donna gave her bedroom to Josiah and Laura. "It's the biggest bed in the house," she said, waving away Laura's protests. "Good mattress. Can't find nice mattresses anymore. I'll bunk with Kate and Lucas and you two take the big bed." She drew Laura aside and whispered, "He'll need your comfort to get over missing that leg."

Laura thanked her, feeling heat in her cheeks. She avoided Josiah's eyes as she and Kate helped him to the bedroom.

As soon as they were alone in the room, Kate groaned. "Shit, Josiah, I shoulda said you were *my* husband. Not that I want to jump what's left of your bones. I just hate being in the same room with Donna." She flipped back the covers of the freshly made bed.

Josiah grinned, reaching for the glass of water and an oxycodone Laura held out to him. "You're so sentimental, Kate, it just warms me down to my toes. All five of them."

Kate grunted. "Funny, ha-ha. You're not the one who'll have to listen to Donna's sermons when the lights go out."

"So how'd I become Laura's in the first place?"

They eased Josiah onto the bed, and Kate removed his shoe.

"Because of the border guard," Kate told him. "If I'd known how easy it was to get in to Reno, I wouldn't have bothered. He was probably just going to preach, but I thought he was going to haul her off 'cause she doesn't know a fucking thing Biblical. It just popped out of my mouth."

Josiah's green eyes were clouded with pain. Laura helped him into a clean pajama top, then guided his head gently onto the pillow. She and Kate eased off his pants and pulled the covers over him.

Josiah sighed. "You did good, Kate. Maybe people who don't respond right become sacrifices . . . more to recognizing them than meets the eye. You did good." His lashes fluttered, and when his breathing steadied, Kate and Laura slipped from the room.

Josiah's schedule of medication placed his last dose an hour before bedtime. He was always deeply asleep by the time Laura carefully entered her side of the bed, where she would lie, exploring the irony of his nearness. On the fourth evening, after Josiah and the children were in bed, Donna said it was time to make plans. She brewed chamomile tea and met Kate and Laura at the kitchen table, full of eagerness.

"I put in for my scouting permit months ago," she began as she poured their tea. "The permit came through this morning. The Lord is with us."

"What's a scouting permit?" Kate asked.

"The Brotherhood doesn't just wait for *Shaitan*. Scouts can go out and search the countryside for them."

"You need a permit?" Laura asked.

"It's special." Donna nodded vigorously. "Like I told you, I'm a senior sister, and I've been applying every year, for years." She bowed her head. "It's not been easy, living here."

Kate touched Donna's gnarled hand. "Sister Donna, can we all get out on your permit?"

Donna's eyes flew open in alarm and she clutched her chest. "No! That's not the way. We'll do it in stages, so it won't bring the Brotherhood down on us," she said nervously.

"Scouts go out two by two—a scout and a deputy. The deputy spreads the Word while the scout brings people close. When the deputy starts in about *Shaitan*, riling the crowd, the scout keeps a close eye for possibilities. It's tricky, bringing the *Shaitan* in without them suspecting anything. The scout tempts the *Shaitan* with lies about Reno, street fights, murders, evildoing. Sometimes the *Shaitan* just gallop in.

"The fastest way to become a scout is to become a deputy first, but I couldn't leave Samuel alone. Sometimes, they're gone for weeks. I don't know what I'd have done if my scout permit had come through before you came." She shook her head. "The Hand of the Lord," she said in quiet amazement.

"Deputies," Laura said, "don't need permits? You can deputize whoever you want?"

Donna nodded. "Of course, they have to be approved by the church, but that doesn't take much."

"Reverend Perry?"

"Any Brotherhood preacher. Reverend Jasper could do it."

Laura had dreaded encountering Reverend Perry again. She recalled their first meeting, when Donna took them to the Play 'N Pray. His zealousness was almost lustful. He was a man she would have avoided even before the blackout.

"So are you going to deputize me or Sister Laura?" asked Kate.

Donna shook her head. "Too complicated. Brother Josiah."

"What?" Kate exclaimed. "Why?"

Donna's eyes were hard. "Think about it. You've been here long enough—you think they're gonna deputize breeding-age women? They've got their eye on you two, especially you, Kate. You're not married *and* you're a breeder."

Laura realized with suddenness. "Lucas."

Donna nodded. "Me, well, Samuel was a hard birth and something went wrong. I did it here, alone, and I'm glad because they would have taken Samuel. A year later, when I was tested, it turned out I couldn't have more children, Praise the Lord."

"But what if Josiah hadn't made it through the operation?" asked Kate. "You said you had a plan before that."

Donna nodded. "I did. But it meant one of you being a man. That wasn't as good as having Josiah. Any preacher'd deputize him in a minute, what with his honest eyes and his affliction. This works well. You're both smaller and easier to hide. We'll make two runs. First, we'll smuggle you, Kate. You and Samuel. We'll find a hideout on the California side and leave the two of you there, then come back for Laura and Lucas. We'll have to wait a few days before we come back, long enough to make it seem like we've been scouting."

It was apparent that Donna had given thought to the details of their escape, by separating Kate and Lucas in the first run. Laura didn't know if Donna was just being careful or if she was still suspicious of them. Kate would be free with Samuel, but Lucas was still Donna's hostage.

"Sounds like a good plan, Sister Donna," said Kate.

"Let's pray."

They joined hands and bowed their heads as Kate

led them in a prayer, asking God to watch over them.

Then Kate dropped their hands. She slowly rose to her feet.

Laura watched Kate transform. Her face shone. Her eyes glowed. Her gaze pierced them. She flung her arms up, her head back, and shouted, "Praise the Lord!" Her voice reverberated. She stabbed a finger at Donna. "Do you feel Him, Sister?"

Laura saw Donna's mouth open, her eyes gleam with belief. "I do. I feel Him." Sudden tears glistened in her eyes.

"And do you feel Him?"

Kate had abruptly shifted to her. Amazing, how her eyes burned. Laura managed to say, "I do," and added a weak, "Hallelujah."

Kate went on at some length.

Laura saw Donna's lips moving, her cheeks glistening with tears, and finally, Kate said, "Amen."

Donna looked respectfully at Kate. "There are a lot of good people here, misled, don't even know they've been led away from God."

"Satan," Kate said sadly.

Donna regarded Kate with new awe that had shifted the balance, Laura realized. Laura now understood Kate had been laying the groundwork for weeks.

"How soon can you deputize Josiah?" Kate asked with new authority.

"He's already registered to the Brotherhood, but

he'll have to attend meetings—when you think he's ready," Donna said. She removed a billfold from her back pocket and shoved it into Kate's hand. "We can fill out the information on him now."

Kate pulled folded papers from the billfold and rifled through them.

"That's my scout certificate." Donna pointed one out. After Kate smoothed the sheet, Donna indicated a spot halfway down the page. "That's where Josiah needs to sign, in front of the preacher."

Kate scanned the sheet. "This right, Sister Donna? You're forty-two?"

Donna nodded, uncertain.

"A very young forty-two, Sister," Kate lied.

Donna returned a bashful smile.

Laura lay awake, still amazed by Kate's performance. She felt shame at playing on Donna's belief. And now they were stuck with Donna and Samuel. *Forever?* Donna would never survive, alone, with Samuel. *Two Shaitan in our house, Samuel and Lucas. What will we do?* She turned restlessly onto her side, wishing for morning.

During the next two weeks, awkward in the role of true believer and distracted by Josiah's presence in her bed, Laura found commonplace situations difficult. The doctor wanted to know what she thought of Josiah's state of mind, and Laura had groped. How should she be feeling? What did she feel? Did Laura think Kate might lead a prayer meeting after dinner? asked Donna. Laura shrugged, trying to hide her confusion. She had lost her ability to assess and to react appropriately.

She felt like she was floating, and traveled the days on autopilot, driving Josiah to therapy, babysitting, running errands, not thinking. Pretending to pray. Watching Kate manipulate Donna. Sitting through thrice-weekly sermons at Donna's church. Barely sleeping at night.

When they'd first arrived, Donna had taken a leave of absence from work, but the day after Kate's performance, Donna had resumed her role in the Brotherhood.

"I have to go back to work, we all have to attend church regularly, and we need to get Lucas enrolled in Sunday school," said Donna. "We have to show him off more, so people don't get anxious. People are greedy for children. Thank the Lord, he's small for his age. If they knew he was eleven, they'd put him in the breeding program." With disgust, she added, "Brother Snake runs that program. Says preparing the young needs his personal guidance."

CHAPTER 32

Reverend Perry stood before a mirror and adjusted his string tie, carefully holding its silver clasp and smiling at his reflection. A work of art, that clasp. Brother Em said its medallionlike facing was easily five or six hundred years old.

Reverend Perry, looking in the mirror, faced his own vanity. "Caught you again, you old bastard," he chuckled. He knew it was only by the Lord's grace that he was able, but he felt no pity for those poor souls who would never understand.

He walked out of his bedroom, through the large suite, to his study. His penthouse consumed the entire twenty-sixth floor of the Play 'N Pray Casino. Lush carpet, sumptuous furnishings, and museum-quality art went unnoticed, until he entered his study and closed the door to his favorite room.

The shelves held only Bibles, old and new, acquired

over the years. And his Jesus collection. Replicas of Jesus were on every shelf and table, every inch of wall. Statues of Jesus, Jesus bookmarks, Jesus trays, even a narrow Jesus fountain between his desk and the window.

He smiled and sank into the leather chair at his desk just as his desk intercom buzzed.

He pushed the button. "Jesus walks."

"Praise the Lord," his secretary, Olivia, responded. "Brother Em is here."

"Send him in." He leaned back, steepled his fingers, and waited.

A minute later, Brother Em entered the study.

"Jesus walks," said Reverend Perry.

"Praise the Lord," Mack Silby responded. His smile was fierce and his eyes were chips of ice. He sat, leaned back, and placed his crossed ankles on Perry's desk.

Ignoring the boots, Reverend Perry kept his attention on Mack's face. "I've been hearing things again," he said, pressing his lips into a thin line.

Mack's smile remained unchanged, and he said nothing.

"The girl was twelve!" Reverend Perry's voice was grim. His fingers laced, white-knuckled. "Raped. Slashed. Beaten." He slapped the desktop. "It has to stop."

Mack silently let the angry words fade.

Perry's gaze slipped from Mack's cold eyes. Brother Em, like all the rest of them, was God's instrument. He packed the church with followers. Brother Em, Perry had to admit, brought the congregation together in an indisputable way. Memory of the last sacrifice flashed through Perry's mind. Even he, at the height of Brother Em's thunderous calls for Satan to reveal himself, had found himself glancing into shadowy corners. Even the nonbelievers, those members who attended only to witness the sacrifices, became unsure of their disbelief when Mack stood at the pulpit.

He sighed and slumped back in his chair. *God shall judge him, not I. All I can do is try to guide him.*

"I mean it, Mack," he said quietly.

CHAPTER 33

DONNA SUGGESTED IT MIGHT BE A GOOD DAY TO HAVE Josiah deputized. She smiled at Kate when she spoke, as though offering her suggestion for Kate's approval. She wasn't disappointed; Kate responded warmly with an impulsive hug.

"You think so, Sister Donna?" Kate beamed. "Has Reverend Jasper seen him in the pews often enough to recognize him?" she asked, knowing the answer. They'd all taken pains to make Josiah's presence obvious, slowly helping him down the length of the center aisle, taking seats as close to the front as possible.

Kate had fretted the passing days, monitored Laura's opinion of Josiah's condition, of every word the doctor and therapist said, the delay for his prosthesis, the initial fitting, the readjustments. The hospital was not well supplied. Every staff member let Josiah know it was by the grace of the Lord that his prosthesis was so close a fit.

He'd worn it home the week before Donna's announcement.

Kate had resisted Donna's urgings to enroll Lucas in Sunday school by saying she could not bring herself to expose her son to the perversions of the Brotherhood. Donna's worry about this one thing was making them all uneasy. Clearly, they were creating suspicion by not sharing Lucas with the congregation.

The morning Donna said it was time to deputize Josiah, Kate told her she would enroll Lucas, and smiled at the relief on Donna's face.

Arm around Donna's shoulders as they walked toward the Suburban, Kate whispered, "Surely you see the Lord's hand in this? It's time for us to put your plan into action."

Donna's eyes shone, both at the praise and the hope.

"Lucas shouldn't have to go to more than one or two classes before you come back for him and Laura," said Kate. "You're off work Tuesday, right?"

Donna nodded.

"Then Tuesday it is. Can you arrange for scouting leave?"

"I'll do it."

It was Sunday. The instant they stepped into the church, they knew something was diffcrent. The atmosphere was charged with anticipation. Kate grabbed Lucas and stepped close to Josiah, protectively sandwiching him between herself and Laura. They all moved to one side of the doorway, their backs to the wall while they watched Donna move through the crowd to find seats.

"Who's that?" Josiah asked, looking toward the pulpit.

As Kate and Laura strained to see, Laura's lungs emptied. "Oh, my God," she rasped. Mack? *Mack? It can't be,* she thought wildly.

"What's wrong?" Josiah said.

"What is it, Laura?" Kate hissed, leaning across Josiah.

Laura swallowed, shocked. "It's . . . Mack," she croaked. "Lily's father."

"What?" Kate squeaked.

Josiah focused on the tall, cloaked figure at the front of the church. Lily's father?

None of them noticed Lucas's avid interest, his small tongue darting across his lips. Lucas hardly felt Kate's hands on his shoulders. He didn't know how to use this new information, just that it meant something huge to the grown-ups and, therefore, something huge could be done with it. Somehow, sometime.

"Come on," Josiah said. "Donna's waving. She found seats."

Laura felt a gnawing horror in her stomach as she slid into the pew, closely followed by Kate, then Lucas, then Josiah, on the aisle. She ducked her head and peeked through her hair at Mack, standing near the altar with the Reverends Jasper and Higsworth. *What is Mack doing here?* In the same robes as the two preachers? Her dread had little to do with Mack's apparent role in the church. It was all about Lily. Lily was hers. It was unthinkable that a stranger might somehow lay claim to her daughter. And maybe try to take her away. Her fists clenched. She needed to get out of the church before Mack saw her, and Lily would be safe. She peeked at him again. Would he even remember her?

Crushed against Donna, Laura saw distress in Donna's face and gave a questioning look.

"Brother Em," Donna whispered, indicating Mack. "There's gonna be a sacrifice."

Laura's heart pounded. Mack was Brother Em? The man Donna called Snake? The man who headed the Brotherhood's breeding program? She nudged Kate and whispered the news.

Kate tensed and examined the robed men grouped behind the pulpit. The rustle of the settling congregation absorbed whatever they were saying to each other. She gripped Laura's hand.

Noticing Donna's own white-knuckled hands, Laura reached over and folded one into her own. She felt a warm squeeze before Donna abruptly jumped up in response to Brother Em's amplified, thunderous call. The crowd rose and shouted their responses to his urging. The ritual had begun.

Brother Em ranted unlike any other preacher they'd heard. The energy he exerted was frenzied, and the crowd shouted back with feverish anticipation. Laura trembled as fury pulsed through the overcrowded room. Her blood seemed to run hotter beneath the surface of her skin. It pulsed wildly in her throat.

The hypnotic urging of the crowd was almost irresistible.

She dug her fingernails into her palm when she heard a thin wail beneath Mack's thunder and the crowd's fury. *A baby,* she thought, and her hot blood turned to ice.

The congregation came to its feet when Mack stepped into the aisle, the infant held high, showing it to those on one side, then the other. He screamed for Satan to pit his power against God. People cringed when he dared the Devil to come forward. As Mack passed, each row became silent, people craning to see. Raising the crying infant back and forth, he neared Laura's row. His furious eyes raked the congregation.

Then his eyes found Laura's, held them with terrible intensity. Nausea swept over her at his flicker of recognition. He raised the child with a nearly imperceptible nod, demanding her to look. The baby's tiny, red, wrinkled face trembled with hungry cries. Only a few hours old, she thought, hearing its small voice. Flooded with memories of Lily's first moments of life, she thought, *too young even for tears.*

Her legs went limp and she collapsed into the hard pew. Kate clutched Laura's arm, but all Laura heard was the cry of the newborn filling the air.

"Listen to me. Listen," Kate whispered. "It's *Shaitan*." She squeezed Laura's arm. "It's not Lily."

Laura tried not to look at the altar but couldn't resist. The newborn dangling by its heels, the shapes of the hellish clergymen. The knife plunged, sliced a cross into the torso of the squirming infant, and Laura's strangled cry was lost in the roar of the crowd. She rose on watery legs with the others when the congregation bellowed. Mack vanished through a dark doorway on one side of the altar.

Laura sank into numbness as people flowed into the aisles, excited, eyes glowing. Mack—Brother Em—sacrificer of infants, his intense gaze directed at her; recognition. He would know Lily had been born after the blackout. She fought the panic, the need to flee. From Mack. From whatever he had become. From any possibility he could learn of Lily.

She stood numbly between Josiah and Kate as Donna led Reverend Jasper to them. She listened to Jasper's saccharine praise of Josiah for embarking on Jesus's work. Jasper and Josiah signed Donna's scouting permit, and Laura bowed her head as the reverend blessed their efforts. They pushed through the crowd, out to the parking lot.

As Kate drove, Laura thought, *It's almost over. We*

can go home. She felt a light-headed giddiness. Relief. She'd never have to see Mack again.

Josiah, next to her in the backseat, nudged her. "Penny for your thoughts," he said.

She involuntarily laughed, feeling love for him. "You offered me a yen once. Is that less than a penny?"

Josiah draped his arm around Laura's shoulders.

"It won't be long now, will it, Sister Donna?" Josiah said.

His possessive arm around her was for Donna's benefit, Laura realized, but that didn't diminish the comfort it gave her.

None of them noticed the tall figure in the shadow of the church's rear entrance, his eyes following their progress out of the parking lot. As the Suburban disappeared from sight, Mack Silby visualized Laura's face and overlaid an image of Conrad. His eyes flared black, convoluted shadows.

He remembered Conrad. Oh, yes. The sensations of that long-ago night in the desert were so crisp/cruel he could taste them. None of the tortures he had inflicted on others had ever reached the exquisiteness of his experience with Conrad. His first.

And here was Laura. She had betrayed him, denied him. Like Conrad had betrayed him, left him stranded.

They both deserved any suffering he could devise.

Mack began to ache with anticipation. He fought the urge to throw back his head and howl, to snarl furiously. The frenzy he was feeling needed to be let out. But he knew that if he ever completely let go, he would not come together again.

He stood shaking in the shadows, face contorted, fingernails gouging his palms. Lucid moments were becoming harder to maintain. He had watched *Shaitan* lose that battle, in spectacular bouts of self-destruction, ripping at themselves in clawed frenzy, tearing their own flesh with feverish need.

He did not know what he was. That he was, that was all that mattered. To be or not to be, that was his battle. The skill was to ride sensation to the brink, then leap beyond the plunge. But the promise of the plunge was exquisite, increasingly difficult to resist.

As he stood, panting, in the shadows, he vowed: He would find Laura, follow her to Conrad, recapture that first sensation. He would have them both and kill them both, in the worst way he could devise, devouring their pain and terror. And whoever was with them would only augment his feast.

CHAPTER 34

KATE HURRIED DONNA INTO THE HOUSE. THE EXTENDed service and Kate's detour into a busy gas station to fill the car's dual tanks had made them later than usual. Donna was overdue at the guard station.

Laura watched Lucas sprint around the side of the house as she held the car door open for Josiah. When Lucas disappeared, she was struck by the normalcy of it all. She heard Kate offering to retrieve Donna's freshly pressed uniform from the laundry room and Donna calling her thanks as she hurried into the house to release Samuel from his confinement.

Samuel. No, things were not normal.

Josiah, holding his crutch, met her eyes. "Strange, isn't it?" Josiah remarked, glancing at the house.

"Any Sunday in America," Laura agreed, warmed by the congruity of their thoughts. "What do you suppose Lucas was thinking . . . at the church?"

Josiah eased himself to the edge of seat. "I guess that depends on whether or not he really is *Shaitan.* If he is, then he probably got a kick out of it. If not, it's another trauma to add to whatever it is that makes him so different."

"I think he is," Laura said slowly. "Ever since I saw *Shaitan* in Samuel's eyes and realized it could be hidden, I started seeing Lucas as *Shaitan* . . ." Her voice trailed away.

"I know." Keeping his full weight on his good leg, Josiah arranged the crutch under his arm. He stood close to Laura, his voice low. "We can't do anything unless we're certain. Even then," his voice softened, "a piece of you wonders if he could be helped, if we could get rid of the *Shaitan* and keep the kid."

Her heart leaped. She'd barely acknowledged that thought herself. Did Josiah have some kind of hope? Eagerly, she looked at him. "Could we?"

"You're the kindest person I've ever met, Laura. But we're not in a kind world. Never have been. If he's *Shaitan*, he has to die." He touched her cheek gently with one forefinger.

Laura lowered her head. Her cheek tingled where his touch had trailed.

As they entered the kitchen, sounds funneled down the hallway: Kate urging Donna, Donna's muffled response, drawers opening and closing. Josiah seated himself at the table and Laura began preparing lunch. Donna hurried into the kitchen, Kate on her heels.

"Don't forget to sign out for a leave of absence," instructed Kate, holding Donna's coat. "And do it before your shift ends, not when you get there."

"What's the difference?" Donna asked.

"That way," explained Kate, "there won't be time for them to try to juggle schedules. They'll just have to work with what you put down."

"But—"

"Come straight home for our celebration," Kate rattled on. "A nice big turkey with all the fixin's."

Donna smiled. "Sounds good, Sister Kate."

Kate opened the refrigerator, snatched a bag out, and shoved it into Donna's hands. "Lunch. Now hurry." She hustled Donna out the door.

Kate watched from the doorway as Donna trotted to the jeep and climbed in. She waved as the jeep rolled down the steep driveway, taillights flashing. Then Kate—chin down, head cocked—stood at the door for an entire minute.

Laura noticed Kate's stillness, and glanced at Josiah. He, too, was watching Kate, his eyes hooded. Seconds passed.

Kate suddenly spun to face them.

Laura jumped. "What?" she exclaimed involuntarily.

Kate grinned. "We're outta here." In three steps, she was at the table, pulling papers from her back pocket and slapping them on its surface. "I got them. Her papers, the scouting permit. We'll be eight hours gone by the time she gets back."

Laura was stunned. All these weeks, while she'd been resigning herself to the burden of Donna and Samuel, Kate had been planning on leaving them?

She grabbed Kate's arm. "We can't leave her."

Kate's expression turned to stone.

"She's depending on us," Laura pleaded. "Kate, please. We can't abandon her. She's given us—"

Kate wrenched her arm from Laura's grip, refolded the precious papers, and shoved them into her back pocket. "How much do you think she'll trust us, once she knows we've been lying? The whole shit-line I've been feeding her? She'd turn on us so fast it'd make your head spin.

"We gotta get out of here alive, Laura, and stay alive once we're out. I'm not going to risk taking her crazy ass and that *Shaitan* of hers."

"She's not crazy—you said so yourself."

"Look." Kate leaned into Laura's face. "She can't even see that her own kid's dangerous. Every time he has a tantrum, it's right there in his eyes. And she's hard-line religion. Evil. Satan. Hellfire—it's all real to her. She's been going along with all those . . . sacrifices . . . that she's sure are sending the unholy directly into heaven—and why? To save her mortal ass and her cave-*Shaitan*. How the fuck is she going to atone for that? I'm thinking that once she finds out we're phonies, we might look like a good bargaining chip with God. I'll be damned if

I'll let that happen."

Laura and Kate stared at each other. "You can't know that's what's going to happen. We shouldn't just walk out on her, it's not right."

"Get over it," Kate suggested gruffly. "We're saving ourselves."

Their gazes locked. *You should know about saving yourself, Kate, you abandoned your own sister,* Laura thought. And Kate's face abruptly became hard, as though she'd seen Laura's thought. Laura lowered her eyes, unable to retract what hadn't been spoken.

"Let's move," Kate said harshly. She brushed past Laura.

Josiah patted Laura's shoulder. "It's not a kind world, Laura." He went after Kate.

The Suburban was packed. The backseat had been flipped forward and its backrest was poised to be lowered so that it would be flush with the rear compartment. Once it was down, the shallow space beneath it would be barely large enough for Laura and Lucas to lie hidden, squeezed together.

They would travel on I-80 east to Winnemucca, through flat desert, past a border manned by the Brotherhood. At Winnemucca, they would take

Highway 227 northwest into the southeastern tip of Oregon, then cut back down into California. It was a long detour, but the road to Carson City was heavily patrolled and the route west, over Donner Pass, was where Donna worked.

Standing by the SUV, Laura dreaded being confined beneath the seat. What was taking Kate so long? Luring Samuel to his room with a box of cookies should have been easy.

Josiah came out into the brightness, holding his unused crutch in one hand. Under one arm he had his sleeping bag and, under the other, a bag of food. Laura noted improvement in the way he moved with his prosthetic.

"What's Kate doing?" she asked.

"Filling some extra water jugs," replied Josiah. "It's going to be stuffy under that seat. You going to be all right?"

"Do I have a choice?"

"Guess not." He stepped closer to her. "Laura," he said, and she heard the gentle lowering of his voice she'd often noticed when he spoke to her. Her heartbeat quickened. Because of their one night together? Or did he think her more fragile than the others? *Kind,* he'd said. Was that all she meant to him?

"I know how badly you feel about leaving Donna," Josiah continued, "but Kate's right; there's too much risk. And Donna's plan of splitting us up is no good. This way's better."

Laura guiltily looked away. For all her championing of Donna, she did feel relief. She hadn't wanted the burden of Donna and Samuel.

Kate hurried from the house with plastic jugs that she placed in the rear of the Suburban. She banged back doors shut. "Let's roll," she said, then yelled, "Lucas. Let's go!" They all looked at the corner of the house, around which Lucas should appear.

"Lucas!" Kate called again sharply. Muttering a curse, she trotted toward the backyard. They heard her shout his name once more. Moments later she reappeared, white with fury.

"The little asshole," she cursed.

"What—" Laura began.

"Gone," Kate spat. "Hiding—whatever. Fuck! Come on, let's go."

Josiah hit the roof of the Suburban with the side of his fist.

"We've got to find him!" Laura protested.

"No time," Kate said. "I haven't seen him since we started packing. He could be anywhere."

The knoll atop which they stood overlooked the scattered neighborhood below.

"We won't find him," Josiah said grimly. "He could be in any of those houses, or in the woods. Cars. Garages." He clenched his jaw.

"No," Laura blurted.

Kate's hands clenched. "I swear to God, Laura, if you start your shit, I'm gonna fucking—"

"No," Laura said. "Don't you get it? We've been worried that he'd betray us. This is it. If we don't find him, he'll give us up to the first person he sees."

"Exactly." Kate cried. "Our only chance is now. We've got to go. We've got to be across the border before he finds someone to tell."

"Get in, Laura." Josiah held the door open.

Laura glanced at the empty neighborhood. With Lucas left behind, Donna would know they'd abandoned her.

"I'll be right back," said Laura. She ran toward the house. In the kitchen, she found pen and paper, and scrawled: *Donna, we're so sorry,* then put the note on the refrigerator, under a Jesus-shaped magnet.

Without Lucas, lying under the seat wasn't bad. She had more room, and Josiah had used a two-foot section of broomstick to prop the back of the seat at a slight angle. She was ready to yank the length of broomstick aside at the slightest warning from Kate or Josiah.

They rode in silence. Miles later, it dawned on Laura that Donna would know they'd betrayed her, even without Lucas; Kate had stolen her papers and permit.

Lucas watched the Suburban leave, then rose from behind a broken window. The house he'd chosen, bordering the main street two curved blocks from Donna's place, smelled of rodents and mildew. A trail down the hill behind Donna's led to the house.

As the sound of the Chevy faded, he congratulated himself on finding the shortcut, getting away. Being smarter than all of them.

Drawn from the yard by commotion, he had heard enough to know they were leaving—without Donna. He'd witnessed them packing the truck and realized the time for freedom had come.

He only regretted he couldn't somehow hurt Kate before leaving, for all the things she'd said, all the times she'd threatened—for not being fooled by him the way the others were. He hated that about her—hated that, no matter how good he was, she didn't buy it.

A time would come when Kate would be at his mercy, he vowed. Someday Kate would meet the real Lucas.

He left the smelly house and climbed back up the hill, every cell of his body singing with freedom. Of all the scenarios he'd imagined, this hadn't been one. Free and alone. He could do anything, go anywhere.

It felt strange not to have to be on guard, he thought,

munching cookies at the kitchen table. Even times back home when he was by himself, he was guarded; John Thomas or Lily or one of the grown-ups was always near. Alertness was part of his life; self-control had gone hand-in-hand with the persona of an enthusiastic, well-behaved child.

Keeping an innocent expression on his face had become such a habit that he now frowned deliberately and let his face become real. Then he heard a muffled thump, and froze.

In the split second of registering the noise, he realized the sound was Samuel. He'd forgotten about Samuel. Lucas's heart slowed. With predatory stillness, he thought about Samuel, with no one around to protect him. He slipped down the hallway and put his ear to Samuel's locked door.

Images flooded him: Samuel on the floor, terrified, bloody, writhing. Lucas pictured knives, skewers, the hammer that lay in the kitchen drawer. He looked at the key beneath the doorknob. Silently, he retreated. Nothing could be done without a plan.

He scanned the kitchen, the knives on the wall behind the stove. Samuel was strong. And quick, really quick, even though he looked weird and clumsy. It would have to be a surprise. He couldn't simply open the door and confront him. The sound of the turning key would be enough to alert Samuel. On the other hand,

Samuel wouldn't be expecting violence. The sound of the key would mean release.

Scowling, Lucas tried to predict Samuel's reaction. Samuel was different.

The more Lucas thought, the angrier he became at Samuel. He clenched his fists, outraged that his long-awaited freedom to do anything he wanted was being challenged by confusion.

His need to prey upon Samuel became hot, single-minded. His hand plunged to his crotch, kneading the heat.

His blood raced, spurred by the massage. Fire burned through him, searing a path of anticipation. He could almost smell the blood, hear the screams, the groans, the . . . car?

Car! He jumped up, erection shriveling, mind racing. They couldn't be back. It wasn't fair. He pressed against the wall near the window and inched aside the curtain.

It wasn't them.

A red sports car purred up the driveway and parked in front of the garage. Poised to flee, Lucas waited to see who would emerge.

The car's door was still closed. He had time to unlock a back window and climb out before the stranger got to the house.

The car's door swung open. Brother Em! What was he doing here? There was no time to lose. He'd seen the way Brother Em looked at him in church that morning.

If Brother Em found him here, he'd be trapped! Again.

He dashed toward the room he'd shared with Kate and Donna. Passing Samuel's room, he glanced at the lock, then stopped so suddenly he had to steady himself.

The front doorbell rang. Lucas stared at the key in Samuel's door.

He grinned, his panic gone. Why not let Samuel answer the front door, Samuel greet Brother Em? In fact, why not hide somewhere and watch Brother Em meet Samuel? The worst that could happen was the man would take Samuel away. At least he would still be free; even if Brother Em spotted him, he'd have his hands full with Samuel.

In fact, Brother Em might sacrifice Samuel right on the spot.

The doorbell rang again as Lucas unlocked Samuel's door. This was going to be really good.

Lucas pointed Samuel toward the front door and Samuel ran and opened it. Then Lucas watched, hidden behind the kitchen door, a show beyond his wildest imaginings. Brother Em did things to Samuel that took Lucas's breath away with voyeuristic envy. And when Samuel's last tortured groan had gurgled into silence, his twisted, mangled body still, Brother Em found Lucas in his hiding place as if by radar.

But Lucas, ever resourceful, had something to offer in exchange for his freedom.

Lucas knew Brother Em—Mack, Laura had called him—was Lily's father. He'd known right away that he'd overheard something huge. Now he congratulated himself on having recognizing its importance; Mack showed obvious glee at the information.

Mack needed him to lead him to Laura. And Lily.

As Lucas and Mack left, they passed through the kitchen and Lucas saw the note Laura had left on the refrigerator: *Donna, we're so sorry.* Chuckling, he plucked it off, trotted back to the living room, and stood over Samuel's mutilated body. He would have liked to have put the note on Samuel's breast, but blood would have soaked it. Instead, he lodged it in Samuel's coarse black hair, and, with regret at not being able to see Donna's reaction, he ran out and jumped into the car next to Mack.

CHAPTER 35

"There it is," Kate said tersely.

Laura knocked the propping stick to one side and was instantly aware of every square inch of her tiny space, of the odors and dust rising from the old carpet beneath her face.

"How far?" she asked.

"A couple of miles," Josiah said. "How are you holding up?"

"I'm okay," she said.

Minutes of tense silence passed, then Laura felt the car slowing. As motion ceased, the sound of the idling engine echoed through Laura's cramped space. She strained to hear Kate's exchange with the border guards.

Familiar greetings. Kate chatting with the guards. Their voices friendly. The rustle of stolen papers she handed over. Grains of dirt on the carpet inches from her eyes. This was it, the high-risk instant; if either of the guards knew Donna personally, they were doomed.

More conversation, still friendly. And then they were moving. She drew a shuddering breath. They'd done it.

Hours later, in the very northwesternmost tip of Nevada, they camped in a hidden hollow not far from the road. The area had never been more than sparsely settled, thousands of scrub-covered acres and countless ranges separating one ranch from the next. Stars shone brilliantly in the moonless sky. The lonely immensity was breathtaking.

Sitting around a small campfire, they ate chicken sandwiches and drank filtered water. Their enormous relief mingled with anticipation of their return home. When they doused the fire and crawled into their sleeping bags, conversation fell to whispers in the star-filled utter stillness.

Laura wriggled into a comfortable position in her bag on the ground. Her head cushioned by a jacket, she studied the stars and remembered the images in which she'd been immersed during the blackout. The moment was intensely private, despite her friends' closeness.

Over time, the emotional impact of the epiphany—of being engulfed by near-infinite comprehension—had faded to memories of memories. *I remember the euphoria but I can't feel it anymore.* How would it be for everyone to move through every moment of their days in such bliss? *Our souls would shine like stars in our eyes.*

She wove her thoughts into the drifting pattern of stars. *Our souls would shine like stars.* A half-formed connection drifted past her consciousness, but she couldn't focus. *Stars burn out,* it whispered, and faded. Her eyelids fluttered, and she slept.

And woke in time to see the last of the stars fade into the morning light.

She lay quietly, watching the day materialize. Knowing the night sky was still out there, just beyond the dawn, was not the same as seeing it. *Just like my epiphany. Knowing it's real isn't the same as feeling it.* She recalled having a similar thought before she'd fallen asleep and tried to remember it. What leaped to mind, instead, was a new connection made while she slept. She bolted upright. The blackout had been an error.

"Oh, my God."

Laura started noisily breaking camp, impatient for Kate and Josiah to wake.

Kate stirred, tousled curls framing a sleepy face. "Quiet, already!"

Laura continued packing.

"I want my mattress," Kate muttered, sitting up. She shoved Josiah's shoulder. "Get up, Peg Leg. The ship's a-sailin'."

Josiah groaned, stretched his arms. "Thanks for hiring the handicapped, but I quit."

"Can't quit," Kate said, crawling out of her bag. "Against the rules."

Josiah gave Kate a pitying look. "Rules don't apply to quitters. That's the whole point of quitting."

Kate shoved her feet into her boots. "It's too early for this." She stomped off to relieve herself behind nearby boulders.

Later it was Laura's turn to drive and she was glad to have something to do while she considered her latest understanding. She drove, listening to Kate and Josiah exchange inanities.

When a lull occurred, Laura was ready, and announced, "I realized something new this morning. The blackout was an accident."

Kate snorted. "No shit, Sherlock."

Laura smiled. "I think We were trying something new and it went wrong. Instead of what We expected, the blackout happened."

"If I remember correctly," Josiah said, "you originally thought that the soulworld was trying to connect with this world, but They managed to plug in only for a few minutes and everyone blacked out and woke up not remembering any of it."

"And here we are," said Kate, "still unplugged."

Josiah leaned forward and swatted Kate lightly on the head.

"Hey! What was that for?"

"For acting like a turd."

"Laura knows what I think about all that crap."

"Everybody knows what you think about it," Josiah said easily. "But the rest of us don't mind talking about it. It's interesting, and if you're so against it, why don't you try finding holes in the argument?"

"Okay. What made you decide," Kate asked Laura, "that trying to connect up to this world wasn't the purpose after all?"

The star-filled night sky flashed into Laura's mind. "I've never been able to explain," she said, "the incredible feelings that were part of the blackout. The word 'euphoria' comes close, but it was more, continuously explosive and for a long time. Unimaginably beautiful—almost unbearable."

"The ultimate orgasm?" Kate suggested.

"No."

"Better than that?"

"Different, Kate. It was—"

"Oh, give it up, already."

Laura tensed. Kate's tone was no longer sarcastic, playful. She sounded malicious. Laura immediately remembered the silent exchange they'd had yesterday, which had ended the argument over abandoning Donna.

She'd tried to convince herself that it had been her imagination, that Kate had not sensed her disparaging comparison to Kate's abandonment of her sister. *How am I ever going to fix this?*

"What about the feeling caused by the blackout?" asked Josiah, choosing to ignore the undercurrents.

Laura cleared her throat. "It's too big for us," she went on. *I'll work it out with Kate later.* "Our bodies can't maintain that kind of high; we'd burn out. Like stars going nova. That's what killed so many people during the blackout, other than accidents, of course. It's why hardly any old people are left. Another minute of it would have probably wiped us all out."

"Interesting," said Josiah.

Laura slowed the car to avoid a small slide on the road.

"If the blackout was an error, what was the experiment?" asked Josiah.

"The kind that's been going on forever; an experiment to create a new life-form."

Kate dropped her pique and jumped back into the conversation. "There've been zillions of new species and zillions of errors. We wouldn't be here now if the world went black every time there was a screw-up."

"Blackouts didn't happen every time," Laura replied. "But evolutionary changes did."

"Dinosaurs," said Josiah, enjoying the discussion.

Kate hooted. "Even I know dinosaurs were wiped

out by a meteor. It changed the weather on the entire planet. Nothing hocus-pocus about it."

"That was when We changed direction. We could have brought the dinosaurs back, but we went mammal instead."

"Mammals already existed during the dinosaur age," said Josiah.

"Yes, but dinosaurs were dominant. Too many of Us were trapped. Dinosaurs were a dead end. We wanted more."

"More what?"

"More ability to reason, with complexity. To exist without having to spend all our waking hours fueling the body."

"Snakes and alligators," Josiah said promptly. "A crocodile might eat only once every few months."

Kate turned to him. "Where do you pick up this shit?"

Laura laughed. "Still not enough brains. Reptiles function by stimulus-response. They're hopeless as pets. No emotion. Maybe emotion's a by-product of reason. As soon as an animal can think, 'If I do this, then I can get that,' it begins to feel."

"How do you know a snake doesn't feel?" Kate demanded. "Maybe it sees a mouse and thinks, 'If I go after that, I can eat and I like to eat. I like mouse.'"

"No," Josiah said, "Laura's right. If a snake is hungry, it'll go after a mouse because it's triggered by the stimulus, not by thought. If it isn't hungry, the mouse is safe."

"I think that's what the blackout was—a break in evolutionary progression," Laura asserted. "We're on the brink of an entirely new direction."

"We who?" Kate scoffed. "A few weeks ago you said that everything's mutating backward, that nothing new's being born."

"The blackout was an accident. Something went wrong and now We can't get through anymore. Once We figure out how to get through again, things will be different. Really different."

Kate patted the air, warding off any more talk. "You're driving me nuts."

Josiah wondered what had happened between Kate and Laura to cause this latest friction. It ran deeper than usual, because Kate was behaving like a wounded animal. Josiah was surprised to find himself feeling sorry for her. It was her defiant strength that attracted him to her. She needed no protection. She needed nothing from him.

Laura, he knew, was dangerous. She'd caused such a confusion of emotions when they'd had sex, he'd had to force some distance between them. He'd loved before, and recognized the symptoms.

At nineteen, his love for Aleesha had lasted exactly five weeks. It had taken longer to stop being her possession, something he'd never before experienced, and never intended to again.

Although he regretted not having made love again with Laura—he still remembered it and wanted her with unabated intensity—he felt he'd made the right decision. Laura was a good friend, the kindest woman he'd ever met. Having her become needful of him, and expectant of receiving his own needs in return, would eventually have destroyed his affection for her.

Josiah had lived for years believing that love, that grand emotion of songs and stories, was but an over-hyped biological impulse. It was a joke.

When he met Eli, he realized friendship was the true apex of human experience. And for Josiah, that revelation had given a meaning to life where none, other than self, had existed before. Friendship didn't banish loneliness, but it was worth protecting, because it provided balance against isolation.

In the six years since the blackout, while the rest of humanity struggled to survive, Josiah had found contentment. He was living in a sanctuary of friendship, and he would die rather than foul it.

An hour later, near the peak of the steady climb over the final mountain before they would begin the descent into Oregon, Laura rounded a curve and slammed on the brakes. Tons of dirt, rock, and debris blocked the roadway.

The excess had cascaded into the canyon on their left. The road was impassible, the barrier immovable.

They looked at the steep hill on their right, the canyon on their left, the chaos of earth and rock in front of them, the empty curve of road descending behind them. Laura switched off the ignition.

Kate spoke first. "Lunchtime."

Laura set the brake. Although the road was fairly level where the slide had settled, the car was still on the hill and the road sloped behind them.

Josiah and Kate went to the back of the car and rummaged through the supplies, selecting the most perishable items for their lunch.

Laura walked back down the road and scanned the treeless hillside for the easiest way to climb to the top. From the top, she hoped to be able to determine a way to detour cross-country without having to backtrack too much. The land wasn't as mountainous as the I-80 corridor through the Sierras; the surrounding elevations here were like huge treeless mounds, but they were definitely in high country. Nights would be cold.

She could hear Kate and Josiah laughing, interrupting each other, adding the word *flambé* to everything.

Scanning the hillside for the thin line of an animal trail, abrupt weariness, wrapped in anger and sadness, flushed through her.

She looked at the curve ahead, the point at which

the road disappeared. *I'm tired of understanding and not being understood, tired of being careful of Kate's moods. I don't want to be happy for her when it's Josiah who makes her happy.*

She was almost at the curve.

"Hey, Laura!" Kate called. "Food's on."

Laura waved without turning around. "I'll be right back." She went around the curve. Hugging the hillside to make sure she was out of sight, she sat down in the dirt, pulled her knees to her chest, and let her tears flow.

When she raised her head from her knees, her sadness was heavy. Berating herself as she stood, she used her shirt to wipe her face.

What could she say, after six years? Her eyes prickled with another rush of tears. *I can't say anything,* she thought, as she always did. Josiah, like her memory of her epiphany, was just out of reach.

She tucked her shirt back into her jeans and turned her face into the coolness of a westerly breeze.

After lunch, they found a trail to the top of the hill. Josiah had difficulty climbing the slope with his artificial limb, and he held Laura's hand as she slowly moved ahead of him. Kate, impatient to reach the top, bounded ahead.

The trail leveled to a broad, flat expanse of sparse

greenery dotted with boulders and smaller rocks. Josiah sat on a rock to rest, and Laura walked toward the edge of the flatness. The earth's vitality stretched in every direction, dipping and rising, exuding rock formations, spreading into valleys and plateaus, erupting into distant peaks. The horizon clearly showed the planet's curvature. It was magnificent.

"We should call home," Kate suggested, coming to stand beside her. "We might be able to raise them from up here."

Laura was suddenly flooded with thoughts of Lily and the others.

"I'll go for the ham radio and antenna," said Laura.

Kate's laugh drifted back. "I'm already halfway there, kiddo," she said, disappearing down the trail.

Josiah watched her go, then turned back to Laura. "What's up with you and Kate?" he asked.

Laura shrugged. "It's a long story," she said. "Part of it's hers. I'd like to tell you, I'm just not sure if Kate . . ."

"That's all right. Obviously private."

"Not in my case. But, maybe Kate's."

"Sure, don't worry about it." Josiah changed the subject. "You remember the first time you told me about your epiphany?" he asked. "Sitting in the casino bar?" Laura nodded. "The thought crossed my mind then that what you were saying could be interpreted as a . . . messianic kind of message."

"Whoa." Laura forced a faltering laugh.

"And I thought how strange it would be that the rest of us would fall into our roles as disciples."

They stared at each other.

"I'm anything but a messiah." Laura looked away. Falling into Josiah's eyes was so easy.

She turned to stare blindly at the horizon. *You idiot.*

Josiah, realizing Laura wasn't going to say anything else, continued, "Kate's always had an attitude about religion, but she's never acted so defeated about it. In case you haven't noticed," he teased, "I'm probing."

"Right. About stuff you just told me was private and none of your business."

He nudged her playfully. "I never said it was none of my business."

She nudged him back. "Well, it isn't."

Josiah leaned his head against the rock and scanned the sky. "Remember how many jets there used to be?" he asked, suddenly pensive.

"Mm-hmm."

His face was tilted skyward and she was struck by his vulnerable expression.

"For a long time," he said quietly, "I thought things would eventually get back to normal. But we seem to be getting farther away from where we were. Maybe we're too far now to ever get back."

Laura heard loneliness in his voice.

Suddenly she came to her knees and cupped his face in her hands. "It's okay, it'll be okay. We'll find a way, I know we will."

He gazed at her and she found herself falling into his eyes. She kissed him without thought, pressing her lips softly to his. And kissed deeper, and he responded. He wrapped his arm around her and pulled her tightly against him.

It was a catch in time: no ground, no rock, no sky, just warm emotion and sharing. Yet, when Laura felt his hands slide to her arms and gently push her away, she understood.

He loves me. Just moments ago, she'd thought she'd never have his love and now knew it had always been there.

"Why are you afraid to love me, Josiah?"

He looked directly at her. "I like you too much," he said.

"Explain, please."

"Have you ever been in love before?"

"No."

"I have. Love takes all those feelings that should last a lifetime and burns them up in a flash. You and I can either be friends slowly together, or we take the fast ride and burn it all up."

"I don't think love can be used up," said Laura, choosing her words with care. "I think it's infinite—no beginning, no end." *We've always been connected. Before we even knew each other,* she now understood.

Impulsively, Laura grabbed his hand and asked, "Remember the first time you ever saw me?"

Josiah laughed. "How could I forget a scared crazy person with a gun."

"Do you remember your first impression of me?"

They both watched her playing with his hand, bending the fingers gently.

"I don't know." Josiah paused. "Same as I think of you now, I guess."

She squeezed his hand. "Me too. I see you the same now as I did when we first met."

Josiah laughed. "Obviously, this means something to you." He withdrew his hand from hers, making a show of using it to scratch his neck.

"It does. It'll start meaning something to you, too, once you think about it. Try to think of anybody else you've ever met that seems the same after you got to know them. The same as your first impression of them. It's always different. Like thinking of two different people. But when you really love someone, they're the same, because you recognize them right away. The love is already there. No beginning, no end."

She could see Josiah was uncomfortable. *He thinks I'm full of shit, but he doesn't want to hurt my feelings.* A rock clattered in the distance, announcing Kate's return.

Laura rose, smiled, and turned away, feeling the old

familiar ache. *Even now, knowing that he loves me, it still hurts to think of him with Kate.* She walked to the edge of the hilltop and waited for the grandeur of the vista to absorb her petty pain.

Eli's excited voice responded almost immediately, with rapid-fire questions, and brought huge grins from them.

"Come in. Over." His tone suddenly filled with anxiety, fear he'd lost them after hearing only their greeting.

Josiah pressed the mike button. "Yo, Eli. In answer to your first five questions, we're holdin' on. In answer to your last twelve, we're holdin' on, man. Over."

Background noises were indistinguishable before Eli spoke again. Josiah pictured Eli hunched over his mike, pressing the send switch.

"Roger," Eli finally said. "Over."

Grabbing the mike, Kate admonished Josiah, "Except for our location, I don't think we have to worry about what we say." She pressed the mike button. "Hi, Eli, it's Kate. Everything all right there? Over."

"Katie?" John Thomas's excited voice cracked over the set. "Katie, hi! When will you be home? Are you okay? How's Josiah, and Lucas, and Laura?" There was a click, then silence, then, "Over."

"We're all fine," Kate said without hesitation. "We'll

see you soon, maybe three days—five, max. Could you put Lily on, honey? Over." Kate handed the mike to Laura as Lily's high voice shouted, "Hello! Hel—" was cut off, then abruptly on again, "—ello? Mommy? Hello?"

Laura laughed past the sudden lump in her throat. "Hi, sweetie. I miss you so much."

Laura and Lily talked for several minutes, then Catherine came on. Eli interrupted Catherine and a few minutes later, John Thomas was on again. Kate deflected his request to speak to Lucas, but when he asked again, Josiah took the mike.

"John Thomas, you remember how sick I was? Well, they had to take part of my leg off, buddy, so I'm moving slower than usual. Those stairs we have at home are going to be hard for me right now. So, how about you and Lily do me a favor? Over."

There was a short silence during which it was easy to imagine the others back home absorbing the news of Josiah's condition, then John Thomas, sounding both sympathetic and eager to please, answered, "Sure, Josiah. Me and Lily can do anything for you. Over."

"Thanks, buddy. I'd like to switch rooms so I don't have to go up stairs. I'll take the den, and you kids use my room for a while. Could you switch stuff around? Eli can help you with the heavier things. Over."

"Okay. Me and Lily'll get started right away. Is there anything else you want us to do? Should we leave the TV in there for you? Margie and Carol stopped by last week with a bunch of DVDs. We traded 'em some of our old ones."

"And some of Mom's jam." Lily added, shouting directly into the mike. The sporadic visits of those two distant neighbors, beginning a little over a year ago, were momentous for Lily. They were the only strangers she'd ever met.

There was a pause and then Catherine said, "In most circumstances, I don't speak for the others, but I must say we are all happy to hear you sounding so well, Josiah. We feared the worst, and now feel inexpressible relief. Be well, my boy, and we'll see you soon."

After some scratchy, muffled noises, Eli spoke. "We're going to sign off and start planning the party. It's been too quiet around here without you guys. Be careful. Don't let something happen when you're so close to getting home. Over."

"You got it, Eli," Josiah promised. He felt a need to let Eli know how he valued him but couldn't think how to say it. Finally, he said, "You take care, too," and paused before adding, "Over."

It took four hours to find a way around the blocked pass and finally rejoin the road, long after it had dropped from the heights. The journey across foothills had been rough, and by the time Kate finally bounced the car back onto blacktop, they were exhausted from bracing themselves. Kate and Laura cheered, but Josiah was in too much pain.

He heard the women discussing whether to push ahead or to begin searching for a campsite or abandoned ranch house. Laura mentioned something about their route skirting the county of her hometown. Eyes closed, Josiah fought the urge to massage phantom pain from his missing leg. His energy depleted, he asked to stop, get water, take some medication.

A sudden fuzziness overtook his mind. He became lost in a fog, struggled to open his eyes, bring things into focus, and heard a muffled sound. It came again, closer.

"Josiah."

Laura's voice? The fog dissipated, leaving his lips tingling.

"Josiah?" Laura prodded. His eyes opened. Disoriented, he looked into Laura's face, wondered about the dimness of the light. He was on his back, on the ground.

"Hi, there," Laura said.

"Don't tell me I passed out."

"How are you feeling?"

"Weird."

"Are you in pain? We couldn't give you anything while you were . . . not passed out."

He smiled faintly. "I hurt all over."

Kate squatted down, holding a cup in one hand and a pill in the other. "Can you sit up?"

He did, with Laura's help. "Where are we?" he asked. Kate placed the pill in his mouth and held the cup to his lips.

"A barn in the middle of nowhere," Laura replied.

"The house is burned," Kate added, "but this barn's in good shape."

The configurations made sense to Josiah now, the rafters high above, the slits of faint light between wall boards. Through the open doors, he saw the fading glow of dusk.

"We spending the night here?"

"Good a place as any," Kate said, walking away. "We found bone-dry wood, so we'll have a small fire and hardly any smoke."

The Suburban was in the barn, its rear doors open. Kate unloaded supplies.

Laura told Josiah to rest while she helped Kate. His thoughts drifted to Eli, the urge earlier, to tell Eli—what? That he valued their friendship. That, before Eli, he'd never had a real friend.

The need to express this kind of emotion was new to him. His actions had always spoken louder than his words. But, for some words, there were no comparable actions. For all his belief that every person needed to make himself and not blame others, he had overlooked one basic element: communication. Not of ideas, but feelings. More specifically, feelings that connected people.

He'd never even told Eli how great it was that Eli seemed to understand him. Such a small thing to say, but he pictured how Eli would look when he told him. The pleased smile, as though he'd just been praised. And then he saw something in himself he'd never recognized: presumption. Like a cloak of superiority, as though people should be pleased by his praise. "You pompous ass," he muttered to himself. The revelation embarrassed him more than he could have expected.

He flung his head to one side, as though to escape his thoughts, and found Kate facing him, eyebrows raised, a load of wood in her arms. "You talking to me?" she asked.

He grinned. "Depends on what you heard."

"Hey, Laura," she called back into the barn, "Josiah's talking to himself. Should I make the fire right here? And put him in it?"

"Sure." Laura's voice drifted forward.

Josiah's pain was fading, and he relaxed. Laura's question haunted him: *Why are you afraid to love me?*

He wondered if there was a way to explain it to her. He remembered the hilltop, and Laura's kiss. Never again, he vowed. He wasn't about to lose Laura's friendship in order for her to know what he already knew.

He wondered if Eli could help. He'd never spoken to Eli about Laura, but until just a few hours ago, he'd thought Laura was satisfied with their friendship. Something in Laura had changed this afternoon, and it was putting pressure on him he didn't like.

He sank back onto the sleeping bag, deciding to talk to Eli about things he should have said long ago.

Hundreds of miles to the south, Lucas shivered in his sleep, curled at the base of a fir tree, with only his jacket for warmth. Mack stared into the darkness, his back against the jeep, a wool blanket wrapped around his shoulders.

He was finding it difficult to focus on his plan, though he didn't wonder why. Frowning in concentration, he ticked off the points again.

He had several five-gallon containers of gasoline. He had water, food, guns, and ammunition. He had his lovely, sharp, silent knife. The kid would provide directions. The kid said Laura wouldn't be going over Donner Pass because she'd ditched Sister Donna.

That meant Laura would take a long detour. And, just to make sure she did get home and into his trap, he had issued border bulletins, signed by Reverend Perry, that she was to be passed. Amazing, the things he could get Perry to do, just by promising a little restraint.

Mack smiled, anticipating the sweet rage that would soon fill his heart. Finally finding that weasel Conrad and finishing him; getting Laura, who had betrayed him again.

She had his daughter and hadn't told him. What was the kid's name, again? Lily.

Six-year-old Lily. What a lovely age.

CHAPTER 36

Laura was torn. The urgency she felt to reunite with Lily, to once again hold her in her arms, warred with her need to know about her brother, Conrad. Had he ever made it home? They were just a few hours from her hometown, but it lay in the wrong direction.

Kate and Josiah convinced her that the detour to her childhood home was reasonable. Josiah calculated it would delay them only half a day.

"Who knows if we'll ever be up this way again?" Kate added sincerely.

Laura was touched by their thoughtfulness, but the two urgencies continued their tug-of-war.

Birthdays had no meaning for Mohammed. Time was not the measure of a man's life. Amongst his people, a man might say "I was this tall during the year of the great winds." Time, for nomads, flowed like sand, one grain into the other; the journey from one destination to the next was life and its measure.

Mohammed was approximately fourteen by the time he and Conrad ended their journey. To travel so far was to be a man.

When he and Conrad arrived at the house in which Conrad had grown up, and settled there, Mohammed experienced an unease he could not define. The stability he'd never before experienced bred restlessness. But he worked hard and prayed regularly. In those first weeks, he did far more work than Conrad, but this inequity didn't trouble him. Conrad was in mourning.

The first thing they'd seen, as they'd turned onto the long dirt driveway, was Conrad's family's Land Rover. It rested, smashed and crumpled, against one of many massive oak trees. Hungry scavengers had plundered the bodies within, but enough remained to tell the story.

Three partial skeletons, strewn in and around the vehicle, bespoke the awful fate of his parents and brother. Mohammed, having heard much about Conrad's family, needed only to count skulls and see Conrad's stricken face.

Remembering Conrad's stories of a sister who had moved to a distant city, Mohammed wondered if he should offer the condolence that Conrad was not alone but, out of respect, said nothing.

Mohammed's mother had died, he'd seen his own sister killed, and he now lived with the belief that their path might have shattered the instant before they could reunite with paradise. At least Conrad was spared that terrible knowledge.

It was a long, grief-stricken walk down the dusty road, toward the white-shingled house at its end. Because of its remote location, it had not been ransacked. The cellar was well-stocked with canned and packaged goods.

Starting the generator was all Conrad had done that first day. Once the pump had been primed and the fully fueled generator started, clear well water ran through the pipes.

Mohammed familiarized himself with the house, barn, and outbuildings. He walked fence lines and crossed enormous pastures, slid down hidden gullies, and followed deep streams that emerged into lush meadows and meandered in shallow ribbons amidst open grassland.

The high, rich plateau, with its open sky, appealed to Mohammed. Far in the distance, two snowcapped mountains loomed, one to the northeast and one to the southwest. Large, spreading trees spotted the meadows.

During some of his solitary treks across Conrad's land, he glimpsed a herd of horses, always in the distance. He deduced that the horses could only mean there was a measure of safety to be found here—they were alive; nobody was hunting them for meat.

Twice in their long journey from southern California

to Conrad's home in the northeast, they'd ridden on horses found grazing in fenced pastures. Conrad was a good horseman, and Mohammed found such travel akin to his life as a camel boy, though not only were horses more companionable and tractable, they smelled better as well.

Their first two mounts had been shot out from beneath them by a roving band, who'd then insisted they share the meat. Mohammed had been mollified by that token of justice.

Their second two mounts, however, were stolen from them at gunpoint by a couple with two children. Mohammed had been furious at the theft, and urged Conrad to avenge the wrong; the only laws Mohammed knew allowed them to slit the throats of robbers. But Conrad spoke of the children's hardships and held that no debt was owed.

"Agh!" Mohammed had spat to one side in disgust.

The smaller child had been about Aida's size. But she'd looked nothing like Aida. So why did he think of his dead sister? And why, in thinking of her, had be become so angry?

"Bara imshi nayik!" he'd screamed at Conrad.

"Don't know what you just said," Conrad had said, "but you've said it plenty before. What's it mean, anyway?"

"It mean," Mohammed had explained furiously, "Go fuck yourself."

Conrad's surprise turned to laughter. "You've been

saying that to me all this time and I never knew it?" He waggled Mohammed's turban. "Little shit! Teach me how to say it."

"No!" said Mohammed. And then he'd laughed, too.

A week into their overland journey, Mohammed tried to talk to Conrad about the blackout but didn't know enough English. He frustrated himself and confused Conrad, but he didn't give up. Mohammed learned a few more words every day.

The next talk was in the bunkhouse of a large ranch in Arizona, eighty miles from the nearest town. The old man who lived alone in the big house nearby had hired them for a few days in exchange for room and board.

"Conrad, big talk, hah?" Mohammed had begun.

"Sure, what do you want to talk about?" Conrad said.

"Talk about how—no, why—here. Now."

"Why we're here now? It's as good a place as any."

"No, no!" Mohammed shook his head. "Not today, many, many days."

"I don't know how many days we're staying, but the deal I made with the old man—"

"No, no! Not here." Mohammed smacked the bunk on which he sat, cross-legged. He waved his arms around. "Here. All. Why all here now."

Conrad rubbed the stubble on his cheek. "You want to talk about the meaning of life? Shit, Ali, I don't have any answers. Nobody does."

Mohammed watched him intently, then pounced on the one useful word he hadn't understood. "Life?"

"Yeah, life—everything. Well, not everything, but everything that's alive."

"Alife?"

"Alive. Um, let's see—breathing." Conrad breathed in and out, exaggeratedly. "I breathe, you breathe, we're alive. Everything that breathes is alive. Life."

"Life. Yah, hokay." Mohammed filed the word away. He couldn't think of a gesture for the concept of change. He took another tack. "I in Tunisia."

"You *were* in Tunisia. Now you're in America."

"I *were* in Tunisia. Now I in America. In Tunisia, I do camel work."

"Right."

"One day," Mohammed held up a finger, then suddenly yelled, "Pow!" and crumbled to one side.

"You were shot?" Conrad exclaimed.

"No." Mohammed hit the mattress with his fists. "Not shot. Everything, pow!"

"There was an explosion?"

Mohammed tensed. "Explosion?" he asked tentatively.

"Yeah, pow." Conrad threw his arms up. "Fire. Bang!"

Mohammed shook his head. "No fire, no bang."

Conrad sighed. "I don't know what you mean."

"I need word, Conrad."

"I know. You need a word for something that

happened in Tunisia. Did it happen before or after the blackout?"

"Blackout?"

"When everything changed."

Mohammed looked blank.

"When everything—" Conrad suddenly understood. "Everything pow. Blackout."

"Blackout," Mohammed repeated. "Hokay. What in your head when blackout?"

"I don't remember. Nobody remembers."

"I know," Mohammed stated, thumping his chest.

"You know?" Conrad quirked a brow. "Okay, Ali, how did the blackout happen?"

"Not how, not why . . . *what*. I know what blackout is. It big, Conrad. BIG."

"Yeah. The whole world."

"More big."

"What do you mean, more big? Like the whole universe? You can't know that."

Mohammed didn't understand everything Conrad said, but he heard the scoffing tone.

He remained silent and Conrad fell asleep.

Gradually, over the next months, Mohammed brought Conrad to understand his belief that every living cell was soul-energy come to the physical plane. But Conrad called it a far-fetched theory.

By the time they were settled in California, in

Conrad's old home, they no longer talked about the blackout. Mohammed gave up; Conrad stubbornly refused to discuss it. Worse yet had been Conrad's insistence that nobody remembered. Mohammed's experience was his alone and could therefore never be fully shared.

The small town several miles north of Conrad's home was not empty. It was many days before they knew they weren't alone. Of the town's original 267 inhabitants, only a handful remained, but others had come to the tiny town, most of them under thirty. They'd quickly established their own set of rules, and, more significantly, beliefs.

Six years after the blackout, the town was a community of Free Thinkers committed to living as one with the mother earth, her bounty, and each individual's worth. They were intolerant toward intolerance but couldn't recognize the inherent contradiction.

Mohammed had little difficulty adapting his own religious practices to the pagan rituals of his neighbors. When they circled and chanted to nature and each other, Mohammed knelt, facing east, and prayed to Allah. The amusement they invoked in him had elements of contempt and theirs of him, an unspoken condescension. Mohammed preferred the solitude of the ranch and continued living there, even after Conrad moved to town.

Three years after they'd arrived, Conrad had married one of the Free Thinkers, a pretty girl in her late teens. The whole town joined the celebration, a ceremony conducted with songs accompanied by bells and wind chimes, and involving exchanges of garlands and self-written poetry. Feasting and dancing continued into the night, and the new couple moved to the bride's house in town, where they took up residence.

Mohammed had bicycled home alone that night beneath a bright full moon. It wasn't until he'd stepped into the quiet house that the importance of Conrad's marriage struck him; Conrad had pledged himself to another. Mohammed was free, his fate no longer tied to Conrad's.

It had been strange at first, living alone. Conrad had filled the place with too many people and too much noise. When it suddenly ceased, Mohammed found the silence that remained to his liking.

At first, Conrad and his wife, Fawn—a name she'd chosen—came often to help with chores, usually accompanied by three or four others. But Conrad eventually spent most of his time immersed in the socialism underlying the commune's thinking, and he gradually came to treat the ranch with detached fondness. A year later, he referred to it as Mohammed's place and his visits dwindled further.

Now eighteen, Mohammed was accustomed to seeing no one for weeks. Standing at the sink, he washed his few dishes, feeling the warm, soapy water on his work-hardened hands. He glanced out the window and down the long dirt driveway at the pink and white blossoms of apple trees lining its length.

A vehicle appeared at the end of the driveway. He strained to recognize it through the dust. Townspeople rarely used cars. The camouflage-painted Suburban rumbled into the yard and stopped. Three doors opened.

He recognized Laura instantly from the many photographs he'd seen of her. Stepping out onto the porch, he raised an arm in greeting. "Hello. Welcome home."

"Hi," Kate chirped, appraising the dark, handsome young man approaching them.

Laura squinted at him. "Hi," she said. "I'm sorry, but do I know you?"

Mohammed smiled, a flash of white teeth in a brown face. "I am called Ali. You are known to me through Conrad."

Laura's hands flew to her mouth as she turned toward the house. "Conrad? Oh, my God, he's here?

He's all right?"

"He's fine. He and his friends are at The Hill." Mohammed pointed at a low distant hill to the northwest, the closest high ground, "preparing for the Festival of Stars. They will return soon." He beckoned toward the house. "Come inside. Please."

Kate introduced herself and Josiah while Laura wandered through her childhood home, touching everything—walls, pictures, furniture, even unknown items. She toured rooms and hallways, heard again the familiar creak of the stairs as she climbed to the second floor, inhaled the familiar smell of the old house.

Her bedroom was the same. Her stuffed animals and baby dolls were still on the dresser. She thought of Lily and knew she would take these treasures to her. And as many family photos as she could. Conrad could go with them when they left. They'd be a family again.

Mohammed placed food and drink on the table and they all talked nonstop throughout the meal. Having heard of Free Thinkers, but never having met any, they were intrigued by Mohammed's description of the community.

When Mohammed briefly left the table, they had a whispered exchange about Lily's birth date, and, after some quick calculations, they established a pre-blackout birthday for Lily that wouldn't be inadvertently contradicted by Conrad. No one had mentioned Lily or the *Shaitan*. It didn't occur to them that the town's minimal contact with the outside world left their knowledge of *Shaitan* to be based on little more than inaccurate myth.

Mohammed had never connected these mythical stories of *Shaitan* with Mack. He'd lived so close to Mack in those weeks after the blackout, feared him so intensely, that Mack could never be a myth. He and Conrad had never once mentioned Mack's name after their escape and Mohammed didn't know Conrad still woke to terrifying nightmares, sweating and shaking.

The townspeople used solar- and wind-powered energy but avoided all communication technology, such as radio and television, to be free of all the contamination endemic in pre-blackout times. Media ranked as a major contaminant.

Among the many oddities adopted by his neighbors, this was one that both perplexed and amused Mohammed; having lived in a closed society during his early years, he remembered his tribe's hunger for news whenever they had camped near towns.

Conrad had explained it to him. According to Conrad, televisions, radios, newspapers, and magazines had submerged society in fads and ads and trends that falsely shaped thinking and opinion, and molded the public into chaotic clay. In this way, wealth had been funneled to the already wealthy and made debtors of the poor.

When Mohammed rejoined them, Josiah asked for news of the rest of the world. Reno had given them little that wasn't distorted by the Brotherhood's agenda.

But Mohammed didn't have much to offer and, seeing Josiah's disappointment, explained the ban on radios and TV. "They don't want to be consumers and line the pockets of the wealthy. It seems they can only accomplish this by not listening at all."

Kate laughed. "They're sounding loonier by the minute. Oh, well, at least they aren't religious."

"But they are," Mohammed said.

"One of the first things I asked was if there was any church stuff going on here and you said no."

"You asked about preachers, God, and prophets. These people do not pray to God or Jesus, but they do worship. The earth mother, Nature, is their God."

"Well, shit, that's all right. It's not a death cult, like Christianity."

"Death cult?"

"Yeah. Worshiping the dead, like Christians do with Jesus Christ. He's been dead for over two thousand years, for cryin' out loud. Death cult."

Mohammed averted his eyes. He knew about Jesus, the prophet. Like the prophet Mohammed, Jesus had relayed the words of Allah, but instead of being given the respect that his own people accorded to the prophet Mohammed, some Christians worshiped Jesus Christ as if he were Allah.

Kate was one who not only rejected the prophet Jesus but went to the extreme of disrespecting him. He glanced at Laura and Josiah. Were they as dismissive of the prophets as was their companion? With some regret, he decided he would be cautious of his new guests.

Laura's heart raced as, through the kitchen window, she watched Conrad and his wife approach the house. She flung the door open and screamed, "Conrad." He froze, then mouthed her name as she flew down the stairs, into his arms.

Their words collided as they hugged, overwhelmed after so many years of separation. He cupped her face with his hands; she stroked his hair; they hugged, broke apart, and hugged again.

Conrad introduced his wife, Fawn, and Laura introduced Conrad to her friends; then they went into the house they'd played in as children and began the slow process of reconstructing interrupted lives.

Mohammed, Josiah, Kate, and Fawn sat on the large porch and talked. Fawn was a slim young woman with brown hair that framed her pale face. As Josiah questioned her about the community, it became clear their interests were basic: farming, preserving food, and harnessing nonpolluting energy.

Kate ventured a question about their beliefs.

"The life-force is all around us," Fawn said. "We try

to stay in balance with it."

"Are there special . . ." Josiah chose a word carefully. ". . . things you do?"

Fawn nodded. "You guys should join us tonight at the Festival of Stars. It's awesome. We create energy among us, tap into the Mother-energy." She waved a slim arm. "It's all around us and it's . . . focused, see? It's got direction."

Mohammed, hearing the familiar words, remembered his excitement when he'd first gained rudimentary understanding of his neighbors' beliefs, thinking they mirrored his own secret knowledge. When that burgeoning hope was crushed, so was he. The force they talked about sprang from the earth. Furthermore, they ascribed good and bad to it, and they splintered it into characteristics they then assigned to trees and rocks and whatever else caught their fancy.

"We've found the way to ride it. It's complicated to explain . . ."

"I'll bet it is," muttered Kate.

Not so complicated, Mohammed thought. *Once the fermented drink kicks in.*

"Because we're part of it," Fawn went on, unfazed. "See, if we just stayed with the part that's in us, we couldn't flow with the part that comes from the source, and provides."

"Sounds schizophrenic," Kate joked.

"You have to let go of the part, to find the whole,"

Fawn said seriously.

Josiah placed a hand on Kate's knee with warning pressure. "Can anybody do it?" he asked.

"Oh, sure!" Fawn responded with enthusiasm. "Would you like to try?"

"No, thanks," Kate said, ignoring Josiah's lightly pressing fingcrs.

"We've had a pretty long day," said Josiah. "Some pretty rough weeks, actually. We need to leave early tomorrow."

Kate stood, stretched, yawned loudly, and glanced at the house. "Laura and Conrad must in memoryville. Hey, Ali." She turned to the youth. "Why don't you show me around? My ass aches from sitting."

Mohammed pushed himself away from the post. "Certainly," he said. He went down the porch steps and into the yard. He'd noted the sarcasm beneath Kate's comments to Fawn, despite her earlier dismissal of the local community's beliefs as harmless.

Kate followed him. "Why is everyone in the conversion business?" she complained.

"What means 'conversion'?" Mohammed asked, walking.

"Trying to get people to think the same way you do."

Mohammed nodded. "Each follows his own fate." He shrugged. "Allah will judge."

Kate glanced sidelong at him. "Allah, huh?"

"Yes." His smile was a flash of white teeth in dimpled parentheses. "But don't worry, I won't seek to—"

"Convert?"

"Yes. Convert. Your fate is your own."

Kate blew a sigh. "Fair enough." She glimpsed movement in a pasture beyond. "Horses!"

Mohammed told her about the herd, his beloved charges, while they moved toward the pasture, his delight melting his reserve as he explained the characteristics of each horse. His sudden boyishness reminded Kate of John Thomas, which made her happy.

By the time they returned to the house, plans were under way. Conrad and Fawn, who'd left to attend the festival, would accompany them home. Conrad wanted to meet his niece, Lily, and spend more time with Laura.

Excitedly, Laura had suggested building Conrad and Fawn a home near the main house. But Conrad had adamantly refused to leave his own community, so she'd urged him to at least visit. He'd suggested that they all relocate to the ranch and join the Free Thinkers. Laura rejected the offer, knowing that if her group ever moved, it would be toward technology, not to more isolation.

Conrad agreed to a visit but left the final decision to Fawn. Fawn was enthusiastic at the idea that Conrad—and she—had a niece and surprised Laura with her decisiveness; she announced plans to negotiate for one of the community's vehicles and some of their hoarded gasoline. Fawn was hardly passive, as Laura's first impression had indicated.

When Kate and Mohammed returned, Laura excitedly told Kate about Conrad's decision to visit.

"Conrad is leaving?" Mohammed asked.

"To visit our home and meet my daughter," explained Laura.

"Ali should come along," Kate said. "Wouldn't Catherine get a kick out of him?" She turned to Mohammed. "Catherine's an older lady who lives with us, Ali. She'd love to meet you and hear all your stories."

"She is an elder?" Mohammed asked.

"Yes, she's an elder," Josiah said.

"This village is awaiting an elder," said Mohammed.

"Why?" Josiah inquired.

"They are strange. My people revered elders for the knowing that comes with much seeing, yes? Elders were sought out by those who wished guidance. These people wait for an old one to find them."

"Maybe Catherine's exactly what they need." Kate laughed. "She'd blow out their mumbo jumbo in no time flat. They'd be begging her to leave."

Mohammed smiled despite himself. Surely one should not speak of an elder this way, but Kate's irreverence seemed playful, like a child.

"This elder, she is truly wise?" said Mohammed.

"Truly." Laura giggled.

"Then," Mohammed announced, "I, too, will go. I have important questions for your elder."

During dinner, Laura, absorbed in thoughts of Lily and Conrad, imagined their meeting. Josiah, his leg throbbing, ate quietly. Kate, wanting an early start, fretted over whether Conrad and Fawn would be punctual.

Mohammed wondered about the elder, Catherine. Did she remember Allah's gift to them of the ability to create and design their very existence? This was not written in the Koran, yet it was true. He didn't know why the knowledge had been given to him, only that it was incomplete. And fate was leading him to the elder, Catherine.

Mohammed, mindful of his duties as host, asked Laura politely, "How old is your daughter?"

"Seven."

"Ah. She was born then, before the blackout."

"Of course she was," Kate jumped in. "She's not *Shaitan*."

Mohammed looked puzzled. "Why do you say this?"

"Because she was born before the blackout."

"I don't understand."

"Ali," Josiah said, carefully, "don't the people here know about *Shaitan*?"

"There are stories, but they are just stories."

Laura leaned toward him. "Are there babies in the village?"

Mohammed smiled and nodded. "Oh, yes, many

babies, many children."

"Jesus Christ," Kate said.

"Oh, fuck," Josiah said.

Mohammed was confused. Did the unwell ones bother them? Not all children had infirmities; many were well-formed. At first, Mohammed had thought Allah was showing displeasure at the community's infidels, but as village hunters went farther, and brought back tales of strange creatures, it became apparent change was widespread. Perhaps the soulworld was straining to create a new life-form, one with the ability to rejoin the otherworld and show the rest of them the way.

"In my land," he said, "children are a blessing. In this village, also."

Laura shook her head. "Almost everywhere else, they're being killed. The children being born now are not normal. Most people try not to have them."

Mohammed's eyes were wide. "This is not right. It is very fucking bad! There is but one God, Allah, from Whom all blessings flow." He shoved his chair violently back and sprang to his feet. "What you say is an abomination."

They listened to his footsteps pound up the stairs, the slam of a door.

"And I thought he was the only normal one in this bunch," Kate remarked.

Josiah shook his head. "Poor guy. Stuck in a foreign country, isolated from everyone else, so he has to figure everything out himself. He must have been what—twelve? —when the blackout hit?"

"At least he didn't end up in Reno," said Kate.

Laura was astounded. "They're having babies. I wonder how many there are."

"Enough to start a *Shaitan* daycare center," quipped Kate.

"We have to warn these people," Laura started.

Josiah interrupted. "It won't do any good. I heard enough from Fawn to tell you exactly what they'll say: 'We must celebrate difference, for it comes from the Source, yada-yada.'"

"I wonder if Ali'll change his mind about coming," Kate said.

"Conrad and Fawn have got to live with us," Laura said, worried.

Josiah nodded. "Don't say anything until we're home."

"What if Fawn's already pregnant?" Kate asked. "What if Ali says something about baby killers? Somebody better go talk to him." She stared at Josiah.

Josiah went slowly up the stairs using his crutches, having removed his prosthesis before sitting down to dinner. In the upper hallway, he leaned against a wall and wiped sweat from his brow, then continued to Mohammed's room and knocked.

Mohammed opened the door, his expression impassive.

"Can I come in? I need to sit down."

Mohammed hesitated, then nodded and swung the door wider.

"Thanks." Josiah eased himself into a chair. "This one-legged business is hard. Gets tiring."

"Yes," Mohammed said. He sat on the bed facing Josiah.

"It's like this, Ali," Josiah said. "We can talk straight, man to man, or we can talk circles, player to player. What'll it be?"

"How we talk," replied Mohammed, "will be determined by the subject, yes?"

Josiah's eyebrows rose. "Kate's right. Catherine will like you," he said. "If you haven't changed your mind."

"I wish to go, yes. I am very eager to speak with your elder. But, I also do not wish to go if people beyond this place are killing children. There is no hope in that." He raised his chin. "I was wrong about this village. It is true they do not speak Allah's name, but at least they revere His gifts. Perhaps my fate lies here, after all."

"If it's your fate to meet Catherine, you should go with us. Otherwise, you'll have to make the trip alone, later." He paused. "If your fate lies here, your return is assured."

After several moments, Mohammed nodded solemnly. "I will go with you," he said, and added firmly, "then I will return."

"Good. Now can we talk about this other thing? This thing that's wrong with the babies?"

"No," Mohammed said decisively.

"Why?"

"Tomorrow we will begin a journey together. It is good to start in agreement, yes?"

Josiah laughed. "Okay." With his crutches, he rose awkwardly. "One more thing. If we're not going to talk about it now, let's wait until we get to my home."

Mohammed tilted his head questioningly.

"I don't want you talking about it to Conrad or his wife until you and I talk." He saw wariness in Mohammed's eyes and shook his head. "Ali, it's simple. Laura wants to spend time with her brother. She hasn't seen him in years. She doesn't want anything to mess up his visit. Understand?"

He waited for Mohammed's nod, then nodded back. "Good."

It took them two days to get home. They kept to the roads as much as possible and detoured around the larger towns. Much of the land was eerily empty of people, and they were halfway home when they came upon a series of small, one-street towns that looked suspended in time, modern Pompeiis, layered with overgrown vegetation rather than lava and ash.

They drove slowly along the main street of the first town, full of lonely images: A bench smothered in weeds and the skeletal remains of a body; a dilapidated storefront, screen door propped open by stacked boxes; an old grime-covered car drawn up to the single pump of the town's only gas station, the fuel nozzle still in the car's intake. Skeletons sprawled amongst thriving weeds.

The second town was nearly the same. Stray gusts raised dust, flapped rags, and ruffled leaves, leaving nothing changed in their wake. Tangles of vegetation were the only life, no birds in the trees, no mice scurrying along cracked foundations. Only untended gardens and undisturbed skeletons.

It seemed the area had been infected by some virulent organism. Miles later, they saw their first bird. They traveled for hours before they felt safe enough to stop and make camp for the evening. Gathering close to the campfire, they spoke in hushed voices of the eerie scenes they'd passed.

The strong resemblance of Conrad and Laura was noticeable to Josiah. Strikingly similar in appearance, they also shared many gestures and expressions. Even their questions shared a breathless quality, one he found appealing in Laura but not in Conrad. Conrad, he decided, lacked Laura's sincerity. Conrad was a small-time player.

Josiah began to realize there would never be a child whose fingers could be compared to his own, whose eyes would be as green as his, or whose voice would sound similar. He felt a tug of sadness. He'd never thought of having children; that he should do so now, when it was no longer possible, was unlike him. For years he'd called others fools for replicating themselves, and now he was regretting his own lost opportunity.

CHAPTER 37

Mack watched the house from a screen of bushes. He had a clear view of Lily, reading a book on the porch swing, though, from this distance, he couldn't make out her features. It didn't matter. She would look like Laura and Conrad.

Things Lucas had told him allowed him to revise his plan. His breath was loud in the stillness of the surrounding forest. *Breathe slower.* No rage, not yet, he warned.

According to Lucas, the Suburban was always garaged. Mack had already verified its absence. Laura wasn't home yet.

According to Lucas, Laura spoke often of Conrad and said she'd one day like to make the trip back to her childhood home. Lucas remembered the name of her hometown and Mack had found it on the map. It was possible, he decided, that Laura, escaping from Reno, had detoured there.

The children had a hiding place beneath the floor of the den.

Strangers were met with rifles.

No one in that house knew Mack was Lily's father.

And Lucas had talked a lot about Lily and Laura, enough to give Mack awareness of previously unexplored opportunities to thrust Laura into new realms of terror.

His icy blue eyes watched Lily as she disappeared into the house. He would have Lily, then Conrad. Laura would watch everything. Then he would have Laura.

Mack was in the front yard when Eli saw him through a window. Adrenaline shot through Eli as he hissed a warning to Catherine, who was reading. Catherine snatched two loaded weapons from the cabinet, and Eli herded Lily and John Thomas through the trap door in the den. Reina leaped down after them.

He hardly had time to straighten the rug over the trap door before the knock sounded.

Eli and Catherine pointed their guns as the man identified himself through the door as Mack Silby, an acquaintance of Laura, Kate, and Josiah, from Reno. He asked to speak to any of the three.

Eli answered through the closed door. "They're not home," he said. "What do you want?"

"You mean they're not back from Reno yet?" Mack exclaimed. "How's that possible?" He lowered his voice, full of concern. "I left Reno hours after they did. I know I didn't pass them on the road."

Eli and Catherine strained to decipher Mack's mumbling and heard enough to exchange a worried look.

"Well, listen, folks," Mack said loudly. "I brought Lucas. He's safe with me."

At this, Eli opened the door. "What are you talking about?" he asked. "Lucas is with them."

"No," Mack said. "Lucas is asleep in my car." He'd left the car, he explained, hidden in the trees. "The world is so strange these days," he added. "Can't be too careful. There was trouble with the Brotherhood, and Lucas was separated from them. I told them I'd bring him along."

"They didn't say anything about leaving Lucas behind," Eli said warily.

"That must be why they didn't put him on the radio when John Thomas asked for him," said Catherine. She looked sharply at Mack. "They did not mention you, though."

"Radio?" Mack inquired. He glanced casually past them, assessing the interior of the house. "Well, great." Mack clapped his hands. "We can clear this up, right now. Call them, they can vouch for me, and you can tell them Lucas is all right."

"They don't keep the antennae up," Eli explained.

"But they got out of Reno all right?" Mack asked, then

added fretfully, "I know I didn't pass them on the road . . ."

Eli and Catherine exchanged looks. The man's concern seemed genuine. Relenting, they allowed Mack inside.

"They said they took a safer alternate route out of Nevada," said Eli.

"Good thinking," said Mack. "Bet that was Laura's idea. She's one smart woman."

Eli set his shotgun aside and took the armchair opposite Mack. "That she is."

Catherine set the safety of her handgun and slipped it into the large pocket of her house-smock. She moved to the sideboard, where a pot of tea sat on a tray. "Our conversation with them was brief," she told Mack. "Eli and I were unable to understand this Brotherhood. Perhaps, Mr. Silby, you might enlighten us?"

"Happy to," Mack agreed. "I've lived with the Brotherhood for years." He gestured at the room. "Not used to seeing a house without religious symbols."

Catherine lifted the tea tray and faced him. "I hope it doesn't offend you. We understand that the Brotherhood is quite . . . devout?" She bent at the waist and held out the tray.

Mack smiled and reached for a cup. "That's putting it mildly. In fact, I told Laura it was a good thing she hadn't brought Lily. It's terrible what they do to kids born after the blackout."

Catherine froze. *Lily's true birth date? Never.* Eli,

with a strangled sound, pushed himself from the depths of his chair and reached for the shotgun.

Unaware of what alerted them, Mack reacted instantly. Snarling, he flung his hot cup of tea into Eli's face and upended the tray Catherine still held. Catherine fell backward, spilling scalding tea on her chest. In one motion, Mack unsheathed his huge knife and swung at Eli. Catherine's last impression, as her head hit the floor, was dismay at the knife.

Mack lunged toward Eli, and Eli threw up his arms in defense, stumbled against the armchair behind him, fell to one side. Eyes wide with shock, he saw the knife lift from his chest, covered with his blood. *Not like this,* his mind screamed. The knife plunged downward, and he jerked to the left, but everything around him moved so quickly, and his reactions seemed so slow.

Blood sprayed in Eli's eyes.

Mack's arm pumped, stabbed, sliced, butchered. Flesh chunked, tattered, ran red. Lost in rabid predatory rage, he felt only hot power as he plunged his knife repeatedly, though there was no life left in the mangled body.

When, finally, he stopped, chest heaving, the room remained out of focus for several minutes. Then he saw the corpse beneath him was unrecognizable. The old woman was still unconscious. He looked at the door of the kitchen. Beyond it was the den. The hidden lair.

And Lily.

CHAPTER 38

It was afternoon when Kate pulled the Suburban into their driveway. Conrad's gray Toyota followed. Leaning forward, Laura couldn't wait to catch her first glimpse of home. They broke free of the trees at the last turn.

In just moments, they'd be reunited with Lily, Eli, Catherine, and John Thomas.

The house, large and sturdy, lay ahead: its front porch, its steps down into the yard. And Catherine, slumped on the top step. Laura's laughter suddenly curdled.

Catherine sat to one side of the top step, leaning heavily against the banister rails, a shotgun in her lap.

They stopped and Catherine straightened with visible effort. Staunch, solid Catherine suddenly appeared a frail, worn woman.

"What the hell?" Kate said. She and Laura jumped out and rushed up the stairs.

"Lily?" Laura questioned frantically. But Catherine

shook her head. Trembling, Laura sank down at Catherine's feet.

"What happened? What's wrong?" pleaded Laura.

Josiah had followed without being aware he'd used his crutches. Conrad's Toyota pulled up and the engine stopped.

Catherine stared at Kate and Laura, licked her dry lips, then locked gazes with Josiah.

"Catherine?" Josiah questioned. His stomach was an icy pit. In the deathly still air, the buzz of insects throbbed against his ears.

"Josiah," said Catherine, voice cracking. Her lips trembled, and Josiah knew Eli was dead.

"How?" he said, his voice empty of expression.

"We buried him yesterday, near the vineyard, John Thomas and I."

Anguish lodged in his throat and he shouted, "HOW?"

The house door opened and John Thomas stood framed in the doorway, his face gaunt, eyes red rimmed.

"Katie?" cried John Thomas. He flew into her arms, buried his face in her neck, and cried. She hugged him tightly and cried with him.

Laura, wrapped in her own arms, sobbed, bent over at the waist. Catherine raised her hands and wept into them. Conrad and Fawn stood, pressed together, in front of their truck.

Mohammed stood near them, head bowed with respect to the tragedy of this homecoming. Josiah had told him enough about Eli that he'd looked forward to meeting him. Now, Mohammed mourned the real loss of this soul, Eli, for only Mohammed knew of the ultimate place into which Eli had passed. A suffocating fear came every time he thought of the new meaning of death to this world.

Josiah didn't cry. He stared at Catherine, grief suspended, aware only of an intense rage.

Catherine's face was hidden by her long, wrinkled fingers. She still had something left to tell Laura, but didn't know how, didn't have the strength.

Laura, face smeared with tears, went to Josiah. There was a confusion of voices and movement that meant nothing to him. He swallowed and flexed his hands and concentrated solely on controlling the rage that expanded every vein in his body.

Somehow, they were all in the living room. As the others clustered in twos and threes, he sat alone in an armchair, trembling, and distantly wondered why Catherine still hadn't answered his question. Ali sat on the floor, Conrad and Fawn on the couch, holding hands. Kate sat with John Thomas, cuddling him, her hand stroking his hair, both still crying. Laura wept into her hands. Catherine stood next to her, face drawn in pain.

Josiah thought of Eli, buried near the vineyard. The

vines had been Eli's special project. He'd become so absorbed with them over the years that they'd all teased him. An entire bookcase was devoted to Eli's books on grapes and winemaking, scavenged on many trips. Josiah's gaze wandered to the books, looking suddenly so forlorn, each worn copy leaning upon the next. His throat ached.

The thought of Eli, under the ground, in the darkness that had terrified him, made Josiah's anger swell, his grief grow.

Yet he could not cry.

Eli is dead, he thought. *He was dead yesterday while I was miles away, thinking about things to tell him. He was alive only in my mind. The conversation will never happen . . .*

He looked around the room, met Laura's gaze, and looked away.

Wiping her tears with the heel of a hand, Laura wished she could comfort Josiah. If only she could make him understand that Eli wasn't truly lost . . . but now wasn't the time.

Laura assumed Eli had succumbed to a fatal relapse of his illness and wondered how Lily was taking it. She had loved Eli so much. Did she really understand what had happened? She was so young.

"Is Lily asleep?" she asked Catherine, who seemed to diminish further in size.

Laura caught her breath, suddenly terrified. She stared at Catherine and all sound ceased. Everyone focused on Catherine. John Thomas pushed his face into Kate's shoulder and wailed.

With unimaginable frailness, Catherine whispered, "Forgive me, Laura."

The last of Josiah's reality shattered.

"What do you mean?" Laura shrieked, grabbing Catherine's arm.

"She was taken." Catherine's voice broke. "He took her. He . . . killed Eli and took Lily." She raised a trembling hand to her face.

"Who?" Laura screamed. "What are you talking about? Who took her? Where?"

Catherine shuddered. "He said his name is Mack Silby and—"

"What?" Kate yelled.

"That motherfucker!" Josiah roared.

Conrad cried out and Mohammed wailed.

Josiah turned in time to see Laura crumple to the floor.

CHAPTER 39

Kate and Mohammed lifted Laura. They had barely placed her limp body on the couch when she unexpectedly lunged back up, hysterical. Kate restrained her, shouting at her, but Laura was frantic.

"Let me go!" she screamed, crazed with fear. "Let me go. No time. Find her!"

Mack. The culmination of all evil. *Shaitan.* Lily's father. A child murderer. Eli's killer. Lily, trapped in his terrifying presence.

She had to go *now.*

Kate and Fawn sat on either side of her, holding her arms. With a sudden snarl of rage, Laura wrenched her arm from Kate's grip. Fawn flung her arms around her waist.

"Stop it. Let her go!" Josiah shouted.

Startled, Fawn's arms dropped.

"I'm leaving," said Laura, and she moved toward the door.

Josiah gripped her arms. "You'll need help."

Laura's body trembled with adrenaline. "I need guns," she proclaimed. "All of them. I've got to go. I can't wait anymore."

"I'll go with you," said Josiah.

Kate jumped up. "Me, too."

Laura's face twisted with anxiety. "This is taking too long. I've got to go."

Catherine's voice rang out with its old authority. "Don't be foolish. You have no idea where he's taken her."

Laura clutched herself in a hug, jittering from foot to foot.

Catherine turned to Mohammed. "Young man, what is your name?"

Startled by the sudden attention of the elder, he stammered, "Mohammed."

Kate shook her head and muttered, "Mohammed? Mohammed Ali?"

"I am called Ali," Mohammed said to Catherine. "My name is Mohammed."

"Very well, Mohammed." Catherine pointed at the kitchen door. "That is the kitchen. Fetch the large blue jar from the refrigerator." Mohammed hurried across the room as Catherine pinned her gaze on Fawn, sitting on the couch. "And your name?"

"Fawn."

Catherine nodded. "And yours?"

"Conrad."

Catherine's chin notched up and she stared down at Conrad. "Yes," she said, almost to herself. "I see it now. You are Laura's brother."

Conrad nodded. Catherine drew a deep breath. "Amazing," she said softly, then waved at Laura and Kate. "Sit down, girls. There must be a plan."

Laura twitched anxiously. "He must have taken her to Reno. I have to—"

"Sit down," Catherine commanded. "I was given instructions by that evil man. If you wish to see Lily, you must control yourself. You will not leave until morning." Mohammed had returned to her side, holding a large blue ceramic canister. "Thank you, Mohammed." Catherine popped the lid and retrieved several small pill containers. Peering at the labels, she dropped all but one bottle back into the canister. "A glass of water now, please." Mohammed moved quickly.

Kate tugged Laura to an armchair, then glimpsed John Thomas, huddled miserably on the couch. "Come here, honey." Kate hugged him close. "We'll get our Lily back. I promise."

"And Lucas, Katie. He's got Lucas, too," said John Thomas.

Kate stiffened. Lucas. That was how Mack had found them. Lucas had indeed betrayed them . . . all of them. Forcing warmth into her voice, she said, "And we'll get Lucas back, too." *I'll rip him to shreds.* "How about you brew us up a pot of tea?" She gently nudged him toward the kitchen.

Catherine convinced Laura to take a mild sedative. "You must calm down. You'll need your strength." Laura swallowed the two pills and Catherine resumed her seat.

"He did not take Lily to Reno; he took her to San Francisco," Catherine said, then explained Mack's orders.

He would call every morning, over the shortwave, until Laura answered. They were not to try and follow him. He was very precise with his threats. When he reached Laura, he would give further instructions.

Catherine then told them how cleverly they'd been deceived.

"I must have hit my head on the floor. When I awoke, I was bound, saw what he had done . . ." Her mouth trembled and she fought for control. "Reina, too."

John Thomas had reseated himself next to Kate. He clutched her tightly. Catherine recalled his first days at Laura's San Francisco apartment. He'd been Kate's small, thin shadow then, traumatized, clinging. Now, seeing him re-immersed in terror, haunted by the same images she had of Eli mutilated, Reina's entrails torn from her body, she damned Mack Silby, his incomprehensible evil.

Mack had easily found the children, almost as if

he were directed to them, hidden beneath the enclosed porch. John Thomas tried to hold Reina as he and Lily huddled in the dark musty space, but Reina had charged the instant Mack had lifted the trapdoor.

John Thomas said Reina had been so brave, savaging Mack even as he slashed her again and again.

"I had to help her, Catherine, I had to," John Thomas had cried, explaining why he hadn't fled with Lily through the escape hatch, into the woods. Catherine had held and reassured him. Reina had been trying to save them so, of course, he had to do the same for her. Inwardly, she screamed at the foolhardiness of that decision. John Thomas had managed neither to restrain Reina nor lead Lily to safety and now blamed himself. Though bruised by repeated blows from Mack, John Thomas's guilt was far more painful.

"Reina tried to save John Thomas and Lily," Catherine told the group. "And John Thomas matched her bravery. He tried to help Reina."

Kate enfolded John Thomas's shaking body. She understood the implication of Catherine's careful words: John Thomas had been Lily's last hope of escape. But, by trying to save Reina, he had sealed Lily's fate.

Her eyes met Laura's. John Thomas needed Laura's forgiveness. Catherine and Josiah knew it as well.

It hurt Laura to breathe. Lily and John Thomas could have run into the woods, up into the massive oak hundreds of yards within the safety of the forest. *No. That didn't happen. Oh, God, why didn't that happen?* Moving on rubbery legs, she went to the couch, fell to her knees, and pulled John Thomas from Kate's arms into her own.

"Oh, John Thomas," she assured him, through tears, "it's not your fault. He is a terrible, evil man. I'm so glad he didn't hurt you more." John Thomas's back and thighs were blackened with bruises from Mack.

John Thomas slumped in Laura's arms, his breath coming in shallow gasps. Catherine placed two bottles of Eli's homemade wine with glasses on the table and requested that Fawn bring cornbread and honey from the kitchen, and turn off the teakettle.

Kate began lighting lamps. Mohammed drew the drapes against the twilight. Josiah asked John Thomas to start a fire, and while John Thomas knelt at the hearth, Josiah spoke to him quietly.

As Laura watched, she felt lightheaded and remote. The pills Catherine had given her had dulled the stabs of panic.

The others appeared to move in slow motion, drinking wine, ignoring the food. Kate seemed to float across the room to hand Josiah a glass, firelight splintered on the glassware. Eli's absence fell upon Laura without warning. He was not there to pour, to hold a glass to the light, to quiz them about color, scent, density. Eli was back with the soulworld, his fear of death put to rest. *I told you it was all right, Eli. I told you.*

Kate tried to feed John Thomas a piece of cornbread, but he balked after one bite. Catherine said he'd slept less than an hour since Mack had gone. So Kate helped John Thomas upstairs, and he was asleep by the time she tucked the blankets around him.

Catherine resumed her story, and Laura found her anxiety mounting once again. Catherine spoke of regaining consciousness and seeing Mack holding Lily tightly while he barked his instructions. Laura was sickened by thoughts of Mack's hands on her child.

"His demands. They are barbaric," said Catherine, faltering.

"For God's sake, what does he want, Catherine?" cried Laura.

"He wants Conrad, in exchange for Lily. Did he know you were going to visit Conrad?"

"Hell, no!" Kate exploded. "We wouldn't have told that fucking monster anything. We didn't even know we were gonna see Conrad."

"He wants Conrad?" Laura interrupted, confused. She turned to her brother. "You know Mack?"

Conrad nodded, his face pale.

"He's the man who flew the plane that took us halfway across America," explained Mohammed. He nodded for Conrad to speak, but Conrad didn't. Mohammed had never told anyone what Mack had done to Conrad; that was Conrad's burden.

"I didn't know Conrad was to be here," said Catherine. "And yet, here you are. How could he know you'd be here?"

"Fate," said Mohammed quietly.

Everyone looked at Conrad. "No," he whispered. "I can't."

Laura gasped. "Conrad, please. We'll make a plan. He won't get you. But I need you to help me get her back."

"I can't, Laura, you don't understand what he did to me, what he—" Conrad's eyes fell. "I can't . . . I'm sorry." He rushed into the kitchen and shut the door, but they could hear him vomit, over and over.

Fawn started to follow him. "I don't know," she said helplessly. "He's never said anything to me." She went into the kitchen.

They turned to Mohammed, who was sitting on the floor, but he kept his gaze on his hands in his lap.

Kate sat close to Laura and put an arm around her. "We'll get her back, even if that sonofabitch won't help. We'll leave as soon as the bastard calls, and we'll get her back."

Laura's eyes burned. "If he's hurt her, I swear I will kill him."

"I believe you," said Kate. Restlessly, she stood, then crossed to Mohammed. "You know something we don't.

Why does Mack want Conrad?"

"Easy, Kate," said Josiah.

"I don't know," Mohammed answered her truthfully. "How is one to know the thinking of an evil man?"

"Shit." Kate dropped cross-legged to the floor next to him.

"What did Mack do, Ali?" Laura asked. "Conrad said Mack did something to him."

"This is for Conrad to tell," Mohammed said firmly. He was distracted because the elder, Catherine, had said something that had confused him, in part because he hadn't fully understood her words. But it had to be important because, by her account, it had been the turning point for her and Eli's actions toward Mack. And it had something to do with Lily.

"A question, please?" he entreated Catherine. She nodded.

"What is meaning of *post-blackout?*"

Catherine pursed her lips.

"It doesn't matter," Josiah told her. "Mohammed and the others don't know about *Shaitan*."

Kate huffed. "They know Mack—at least, Conrad and Ali do."

"Post-blackout," explained Laura suddenly, "means after the blackout. Lily was born after the blackout, not before, like we told you."

"Ah." Mohammed turned to Kate. "You lied, then."

"Damn right," said Kate. "How was I supposed to know you live in a nest full of *Shaitan* kids and don't even know what they are? Listen, kiddo, Mack's *Shaitan*, and there's a shitload of others just like him. *Shaitan*—that's a name someone else made up for those things, not me.

"Everything born after the blackout is *Shaitan*." She leaned her face into his. "Except Lily. You need to know this. Lily is no *Shaitan*."

Mohammed shrugged. "Yes. I understand," he said. His thoughts whirled. Mack was evil. That was certain. Kate and the others believed that same evil was now spreading into this world. He felt immeasurably depressed. The elder—Catherine—must also believe this, so she could not possibly know what he knew. The soul-force was Allah's gift. It was not possible for anything to be born without this force impelling them into existence, creating the very matter they inhabited.

The elder's gaze still rested upon him.

"We do not know, for a fact, Mohammed," said Catherine, "that everything being born is like Mack Silby. However, in many places, people slaughter every child born after the blackout. That's why we've told no one Lily's true birth date. We know she is not *Shaitan*. We do not know why she seems to be the exception."

"It's because of the epiphany," Laura said stubbornly. "I remembered. Remembering protected her somehow."

"Epiphany?" Mohammed repeated the strange

word. His body tensed. "You remembered . . . what?"

"Don't get her started," Kate said, then slapped her knee. "Fuck me! Sorry, Laura. Go ahead, honey, talk all you want. I'll shut up."

Laura shrugged. "Doesn't matter."

Kate said quickly, "Laura thinks—I mean, Laura's sure—the blackout was caused by this . . . revelation that hit everybody at once. Everybody suddenly knew everything. There was no more, um—barrier—is that right, Laura? —that kept us from knowing what things are like after we die." She mistook Mohammed's increasingly odd expression as disbelief.

"Yeah, I know," she said hastily. "And there's a lot more—about souls and cell-life and all kinds of shit, that really, kinda . . ." She faltered.

Josiah said, "It makes so much sense I wish I could believe it. Eli—" He stopped abruptly.

Mohammed jumped up, chest heaving. "You know," he said to Laura.

Kate grabbed his arm. "Take it easy, she's not an infidel or anything."

Mohammed shook his arm free and turned a look of fierce joy upon her. "She remembers!" he cried. He squeezed his eyes shut, fell to his knees, and prostrated himself. Arabic prayer tumbled from his lips.

Kate gaped at him.

Mohammed sat back on his feet and stared at Laura.

"I, too, remember," he told her. "I thought no one else did."

Laura gasped. "You . . . remember? The epiphany?"

"I do not know this word," he grinned, "but I remember the vision that came during the blackout."

Laura raised a trembling hand to her mouth.

"Holy shit," Kate said. "I don't believe this. You mean—"

"Many people claim to remember," Catherine interrupted. She nodded a plea to Kate to diminish the drama. "We're overwrought. It's not the best time to discuss it."

Laura's eyes were feverishly bright, her face splotchy; her body trembled. Kate also saw that Laura, focused on Mohammed, hadn't heard Catherine.

"Let's take a break," suggested Kate.

"No." Laura protested. She crawled across the floor to sit with Mohammed. "Tell me what you know," she demanded.

"All of it," he nodded eagerly. "All of it is Us. We—"

"We made it all, from the first cell—" Laura's voice shook.

"And the next, and every different form from then—"

"We direct. We—"

"—create!" Mohammed beamed joyously.

"It's all Us."

They clasped hands.

Kate turned to Josiah and Catherine. "Holy shit!

Will one of you explain this?"

"Kate," Josiah said. "A little more wine, please?"

She snatched the glass from his hand. "Okay, only first—"

"For Laura, too," instructed Josiah.

Kate grumbled, "Fetch the wine, Cinderella, sweep the hearth, Cinderella." She moved swiftly to the sideboard.

"Laura," said Catherine.

Mohammed and Laura were engrossed in each other.

"Laura!" Catherine said louder.

Laura turned to her. "Do you see now? It's all true."

Kate got Laura to sit back on the couch and handed her a glass of wine. Catherine, admonishing Mohammed to give them a moment, placed one hand on Laura's brow and took her pulse with the other, asking if the pills she'd taken earlier had had any effect. Laura described her momentary calm, now gone.

Catherine sighed. "Our medications have exceeded their expiration dates."

"We have some prescriptions from Reno," Josiah offered. "They're in the car, in the cooler."

Kate was already moving. "I know. Fetch the cooler, Cinderella." Mohammed watched her leave, then turned a puzzled look on Josiah. "Cinderella?"

With a small smile, Josiah said, "A legendary maiden, fair of face and tiny of foot."

"Ah. Like Kate, then."

Josiah snorted into his wine. "Yeah, sure."

Kate brought the cooler and Catherine found sleeping pills as well as Josiah's personal prescriptions. Kate took the cooler to the kitchen and was startled to see Conrad and Fawn, sitting at the table. They'd slipped her mind.

Kate transferred the medicines to the refrigerator, then glared at Conrad. "You're a real chickenshit," she said, and marched from the room.

"Josiah and Catherine are coming with us," Laura told Kate. "They're going to help us get Lily back."

"Of course we are," Catherine said.

"Catherine won't let me and Ali talk about the epiphany," said Laura.

"Don't exaggerate," said Catherine. "Lie quietly, now. You and Mohammed will have time."

The drug was strong and Laura was thankful to feel her terrible fear and worry blunted. Drowsily, she let herself feel the happiness of knowing the epiphany was shared by another. There was so much to talk about.

She slept.

CHAPTER 40

JOSIAH WAS THE FIRST TO WAKE. HIS EYES SNAPPED open and he was slapped by the awareness that Eli was dead and Lily was the captive of a madman.

The grief jerked him upright. The things he'd wanted to tell Eli would remain unsaid.

He imagined how terrified Eli must have been, as death—Mack—came at him.

He remembered how much Eli had dreaded the idea of his own death. Of life dancing on without him . . . forevermore without him. An unspeakable sadness filled Josiah.

Sitting on the bed, in the darkness, he finally understood why Eli had tortured himself with regret about the inevitable. In his sorrow, he bound his thoughts as closely as he possibly could to his friend and, for the first time, felt Eli's terror of being denied forever a presence in the universe, a loneliness so unbearable it immobilized his world. Josiah gasped a breath, shattering the vision.

He lit the candle on the nightstand and attached his prosthesis, mourning for Laura, who would wake to the same smothering awareness. Lily gone. Eli dead.

Looking around the room, he saw that a transfer of his belongings had been completed. His old backpack lay in the corner.

He'd carried that backpack with him everywhere in the months following the blackout. It was worn, stained, misshapen. A reminder of those first months in which his and Eli's friendship had formed and strengthened. He picked it up and opened the plastic catch, trying to remember what was inside.

Smoothing the bedcovers, he upended the backpack and stared at the jumbled result: a tattered paperback map book, pencils and notebooks, trail mix, a knife, a Power Bar, a miniature tape recorder, four packs of Trojans, a tube of sunscreen, a jar of aspirin, medical tape, matches. And a small pouch.

He'd forgotten about the pouch. Suede, dyed a brilliant turquoise, tiny white and yellow beads encircled the drawstrings that closed the top of the pouch. He'd found it in an abandoned store the day after the blackout, the day he and Eli had wandered through the ravaged city, and had shoved it into his pocket. He hadn't remembered the pouch again until that night, in the empty house in which they'd taken refuge. Feeling it in his pocket as he'd sat down, he'd pulled it out. Eli had suggested that he hang it around his neck, like an Indian medicine pouch. Collecting powerful "medicine" could be fun, Eli had said, then, with a laugh, he tossed him pocket nail clippers as his first totem.

Josiah blinked away hot tears.

The next day, Josiah began to fill the pouch with useless, evocative objects, compiling a minor time capsule—something that would relate a sense of the time those objects were important. Every time he'd added an item, he'd codified a vague promise to himself not to look in the bag but to save it for some future date.

Sitting on the bed, he tried to remember what was in it. It hadn't been that long. Only six years since the blackout. Six years of knowing Eli.

He tentatively opened the pouch, then spilled the memories from it. Eli's pocket clippers. A small photo of three children he'd removed from the hand of a dead woman. The yen he'd offered Laura, payment for her thoughts. A delicate gold chain necklace he'd found, limply draped over a wreckage-strewn curb.

A newspaper clipping. He unfolded it carefully. A grainy black-and-white photo of a fireman being awarded a medal.

A miniature cassette tape.

Josiah remembered fishing the tape out of the trash can where Eli had thrown both it and the small tape recorder, the third day after the blackout. Josiah thought the tape was from Eli's grandmother, speaking from a time that would never return, and had never listened to it. Josiah had saved it for Eli, who might one day regret having discarded it.

Now Eli was gone, but Josiah would not let something meaningful to Eli be lost.

He picked up the small recorder from the bed, inserted the cassette, and pushed Play. Nothing; the batteries were dead. He found spares in his dresser drawer, reloaded the recorder, and heard the spools whir. Sitting on the bed, he waited to hear Eli's grandmother.

But it was not a female voice.

It was male and it was unintelligible. Disappointed, Josiah thought even this small way of honoring Eli's memory had been snatched away. He watched the spools spin and heard nothing but gibberish. No wonder Eli had thrown it away.

But that didn't account for the look on Eli's face when he'd pitched it into the can. A look Josiah vividly remembered. It was the emotion he'd seen twisting Eli's face that had caused him to save the tape.

Josiah listened more carefully. The voice pitched higher, until it cracked. There was heavy breathing. Then, a single word, spoken in a sob. The hairs on Josiah's neck prickled. *Eli?* Was that Eli? He stopped the tape, rewound it fractionally, then replayed it to catch that one word, straining to make it out through the sobs.

"Unbelievable," the voice said. Josiah replayed it. "Unbelievable." It *was* Eli. Heart racing, Josiah let the tape continue.

For an hour, Josiah barely moved—at times, barely breathed—as he listened to the entire tape, not even trying to make sense of the garble, intent on the parts that were clear. When both sides of the tape finally finished, he sat, overcome, shaken. It was clear that Eli had recorded these words immediately upon regaining consciousness after the blackout. The second side of the tape, which was almost entirely intelligible, was full of his impressions of what he was seeing and hearing as he looked at the destruction on Doyle Drive in front of him and the Golden Gate Bridge behind him.

Hands trembling, Josiah flipped the tape back to the first side, pushed Play, knowing now that this side of the tape held the very first words Eli had spoken just minutes after regaining consciousness.

He listened over and over to the confused passages, Eli's nearly incoherent revelations, and was eventually able to understand that Eli was describing his mind's images and emotions. His words tumbled in broken sentences, like someone's impressions of a vivid dream from which he'd just woken, a dream so full of visual and emotional detail he was unable to keep up with the story line, dropping one thought to grasp another before it faded.

No wonder Eli had thrown the tape away, Josiah

thought. Eli had recognized his own voice but not his own words. To himself, he must have sounded terrifyingly insane.

Listening again and again, Josiah was finally able to make sense of the unrelated snatches, at times fantastically descriptive.

It was Laura's epiphany.

Laura had spent the night on the couch deep in a drug-induced sleep. She awakened slowly, her body sluggish, mind heavy with despair. She sat up, wrapped her arms around her knees, and rocked with grief, her desperation welling. There was nothing she could do right now to help Lily.

"Laura." Josiah stood in the doorway.

Startled, she looked up.

"What is it? What's wrong?" she whispered, thinking, *Oh, God, I can't take anymore.*

Josiah, dazed, limped slowly to the couch. "It's true," he said. "It's real—epiphany—that's really what happened during the blackout. I believe it, but it's so—unbelievable."

Laura looked at him uncertainly. *Is he trying to make me feel better?*

Josiah saw her wariness and shook his head. "I

found an old tape of Eli's."

Josiah told Laura about Eli's garbled descriptions that corroborated everything Laura had always said. Eli had forgotten it all, just as he and everyone else had. Everyone but Laura and Mohammed. "It's no wonder," Josiah said, "Eli threw the tape away. Hearing it must have scared the hell out of him.

"I don't think he even tried to figure out what he'd said on the first side," Josiah continued. "And the second side—where he explains what he's seeing—sounds so unemotional; horrible accidents, deaths, relayed in this casual voice that sounds like he's just reading a menu." Josiah sadly shook his head. "I should have listened to it years ago. Everything would be different now. Eli might not be dead. And Lily—"

Laura flung her arms around him. The turmoil of emotions in her, so many of them dreadful, left her barely able to function. She clung with all her might to this moment of hope, of love. It was an incredible instant, one she'd imagined for so long; sharing the truth of the epiphany with Josiah.

After a moment, she slowly pushed away from him.

"Everything would have probably happened the same way," she said. "Except our conversations would have been different."

"Eli's all right," Josiah said, awed. "He knows now that there is no void. No end."

Laura smiled at his joy. "I tried to tell you that yesterday."

Mohammed's voice startled them.

"But, no, Laura," he blurted, walking in. "The path home is gone. I thought you knew this." Then his face lit up and he cried, "Are you saying it's been fixed?"

Laura caught her breath. "What do you mean? It was always there—it's the way in that's gone, not the way out."

Stunned, they simultaneously realized they were both right. There was no more way in. There was no more way out. Laura dropped her face into her hands and Mohammed fell to his knees.

Josiah looked from one to the other in disbelief. With a roar, he launched himself at Mohammed.

Locking his hands around Mohammed's throat, he pulled him to his feet. "He's safe." He shook Mohammed furiously. "Laura said he's safe!"

Laura jumped up and grabbed one of Josiah's arms. "Stop it. Josiah!" She pushed him, screamed into his face.

Kate, in rumpled plaid pajamas, pounded barefoot down the stairs, shouting, "What the fu—" She jumped the last three steps. Squirming between Josiah and Mohammed, she grabbed two fistfuls of Josiah's hair. "Cut it out. Let go!" she yelled, shaking his head.

Catherine, who had followed Kate, stopped mid-stairs. Her kimono robe was belted tightly and her gray hair, free of its pins and netting, flowed, uncombed, over her shoulders.

"Stop this at once," she commanded.

Laura, pulling at Josiah's arm with all her strength, stumbled backward when his hands fell from Mohammed's throat. They stared at Catherine and couldn't remember ever having seen her emerge from her room without every hair in place.

Catherine, erect and satisfied, sniffed and said, "Breakfast in ten minutes." She turned and went back up the stairs.

"What the hell's going on?" demanded Kate.

Josiah shook his head. He stared at Mohammed, who looked gravely back, rubbing his neck.

"It is the truth," Mohammed said. "I do not make truth."

Laura gently touched Josiah. She saw tears in his eyes.

Josiah limped away, paused, turned to Mohammed. "Where is he, then?" he asked. "Is he . . . lost?"

Mohammed replied softly, "I don't know."

They listened to Josiah's uneven footsteps passing through the kitchen, the den door clicking shut.

Laura sat on the couch.

Kate asked, "What's Josiah talking about? Who's lost?"

"Eli," Laura whispered. New fear for Lily pounded in her chest.

"Eli's not lost." Kate's voice cracked. "Eli's dead, Laura."

"Yes," Laura said.

"But, what . . . ?" Kate turned to Mohammed. "Explain this," she commanded.

"The Path is gone," he said simply.

"The Path? Wha—oh, Christ!"

Laura watched Kate and felt pity. *Three of us now know the truth.*

Kate marched into the kitchen, muttering curses.

Josiah stayed in his room, and the rest picked at their breakfasts. Laura didn't eat. She held a glass of water with both hands, forcing small sips. Conrad sat opposite her, between Fawn and John Thomas, but Laura was unwilling to look at him.

Kate and Catherine urged John Thomas to eat more, trying to draw a few words from him. Kate threw frequent glances at Laura.

Conrad and Fawn murmured to each other, but Mohammed ate silently. Occasionally, his fork hovered over his plate with a peculiar stillness, then, with a grunt, he would resume eating.

Conrad pushed his chair from the table with an unintentional loud screech. "I—I guess Fawn and Ali and I will shove off. If you need some help getting stuff together . . ."

Kate grabbed her plate to begin clearing the

table. “Don’t do us any favors, bucko.” She snatched Mohammed’s plate, not noticing he wasn’t finished. The dishes clattered on the tile counter.

Conrad turned to his sister. “Laura, please, you’ve got to understand.”

“She understands,” Kate interrupted, grabbing Catherine’s and John Thomas’s plates. “She understands Lily’s with the fucking *Shaitan* King, and you’re leaving.”

John Thomas’s voice trembled with anxiety. “Katie, are you going with Laura? I want to go, too. Please don’t leave me here again.”

Kate hugged John Thomas. “Honey, we’re all going.”

“I will go, too,” Mohammed said quietly.

Kate nodded. She glared at Conrad. “Leave, already. The sooner, the better.”

“Get off my case,” Conrad said angrily. “You don’t know shit.”

“I don’t have to know shit!” Kate yelled back. “Get the fuck out of my house!”

“What a bitch,” said Fawn.

“Go back to your fucking Source, Mrs. Shit—your fucking *Shaitan* nursery.”

Catherine stood up. “Have done,” she barked.

Everyone froze. Conrad began to say, “It’s not that I—”

Catherine sliced her hand through the air. “Enough.”

Josiah stepped into the kitchen.

“Conrad,” said Catherine tersely, “despite your sister’s

pleas and your niece's dire need, you refuse to help. We all fear that dreadful man. You've chosen not to share your personal encounter, leaving us to conjecture. This does not promote our sympathy. After all, you are obviously alive and whole."

Conrad flushed, gripped a chair with shaking hands. "Just because I'm not . . . dead . . . or missing a leg, doesn't mean I'm not—"

"He raped you," Josiah said matter-of-factly.

"Fuck you!" Conrad screamed, shoving his chair violently against the table. "You don't know a fucking thing!"

Josiah said derisively, "Worse things can happen, dude."

Conrad's face contorted. "You cold bastards," he stammered. "You've even fucked up Laura."

Laura stared at him, pale and expressionless.

"Why are you looking at me like that?" Conrad's voice pitched higher. "You always understood—"

Kate exploded. "Lily's her kid, for Christ's sake!"

"Like I said, Conrad," Josiah continued, "there are worse things than what Mack did to you. Like doing the same thing to a little girl."

Laura's moan was lost beneath Conrad's shout. "No! It's the same. Would you ask her to face him again after he did that to her?"

"Get him out of here," Laura whispered hoarsely. "Get him out of here."

Fawn grabbed Conrad's hand, pulled him to the

door, urged him through, then paused to face them. "He is right. Every life is precious to the Mother and she wouldn't like one being sacrificed for another."

Kate marched up to Fawn and slapped her viciously across the face.

Aghast and in pain, Fawn fled after Conrad.

"Laura." Josiah held a hand out to her. "Can I talk to you?" She nodded. "In there." He indicated the den.

The sound of Conrad's truck faded as Josiah led Laura out of the room.

"She's falling apart," Kate whispered. "Maybe I oughta go in there."

"She needs Josiah," Catherine said. "I hope he understands how much."

Kate glanced at Mohammed. "You drive, Ali?" Mohammed nodded. "Okay, you and John Thomas take the Suburban around back, gas it up, and check the oil. Keys are in it." Mohammed nodded and they left.

"What do you think's going on in there?" asked Kate, following Catherine into the living room.

"Love," said Catherine. "She's lost Lily; she's lost Conrad."

Kate shook her head. "She's got to hate Conrad now."

"Perhaps. But she still loves him." Catherine paused. "In much the same way she still loves you, despite your relationship with Josiah."

"What are you talking about?" Kate's voice wavered.

"Laura loves Josiah and you sleep with him."

Kate stared at Catherine.

"You can't possibly say you weren't aware of her feelings."

"It's none of your business," Kate snapped, looking away.

Catherine nodded. "Perhaps. You know Laura won't fight you for him, Kate," said Catherine softly, "though she needs him far more than you ever will."

Kate was silent.

Catherine nodded. "You knew," she said, gently.

Kate searched Catherine's face. "Why are you trying to make me feel like shit?"

"I'm not," Catherine said. "Laura needs Josiah. And Josiah needs Laura even more."

"Josiah's got a mind of his own."

"Josiah is a strong man," Catherine agreed. "However, one of his attributes now also seems to be his worst limitation. His sense of responsibility. His insistence upon being culpable for his own actions."

"What's wrong with that?" asked Kate blankly.

"Nothing. But Josiah fears having someone depend upon him for something he may not be able to provide. He doesn't know that true love does not take, it gives." She sighed and added, "I do know his relationship with you provides him a safety zone."

"Shit," Kate finally said.

Catherine drew Kate down on the couch next to her. "I'm sorry. I believe Josiah loves Laura every bit as much as she loves him. You must let him discover that."

Kate leaned into the comfort of Catherine's arms, but she remained stiff. "This is really stupid," she said. "It's not like I love Josiah. It's just . . ."

Catherine hugged her tighter. "This is a difficult time for us all," she soothed. "We feel helpless, facing so much tragedy. We all love Lily dearly, but Laura's is the grief of a mother. We must be strong for her. And for Josiah. Because Eli was his first friend."

She held Kate's face between her aging hands. "Don't feel guilty, Kate, about any anger or resentment you may feel. And don't act on those emotions. Please. You are such an excellent person."

Kate's lips trembled. "You think?"

Catherine chuckled. "I know," she said. "Good gracious, I know."

CHAPTER 41

LAURA AND JOSIAH SAT ON HIS BED. THE BLANKNESS in her eyes was daunting. *Hold on, Laura,* he thought, and heard Eli's voice in his mind, *Holdin' on, Josiah, holdin' on.* He'd never felt so out of control, so vulnerable. He held her hand gently, helplessly.

The items he'd spilled from his backpack were still scattered on his bed. He picked up the yen and placed it in her hand.

"Do you remember?" he asked.

Laura stared at the coin in her palm. Her fingers trembled. "Yes." She struggled into the present moment. "I wondered if you were talking about the coin or yourself when you said 'a yen for your thoughts.' I didn't know if you were flirting." Her fingers curled, hiding the yen.

"I probably was."

She looked into his eyes. He was as she'd always

known him. She felt his presence so fully. Then he touched her, a featherlight stroke of a forefinger, beneath her chin. She felt them coming together but couldn't bring her shattered self into focus: Lily, the void that awaited them all, Eli . . .

"Eli and I had a motto," he said quietly. "*Hold on,* we'd tell each other. Hold on." He gathered Laura tenderly against him. "Hold on to me, Laura," he whispered. "Let me hold on to you." And his tears finally came.

Time seemed to stop. Laura concentrated all of herself into the moment of being with Josiah. This small moment contained infinity.

They kissed cautiously, feeling its electricity spread through them. The universe of their kiss dilated, until infinity could not contain it. Small involuntary sounds rose from Laura, urging Josiah closer, and when there was no more space between them, he urged her closer still.

Josiah swept the clutter from the bed, and they tore at each other's clothing, their bodies flushed. Josiah's prosthesis fell upon the floor.

Their hands explored each other. Skin tingled, eyes lost focus, and when their bodies would no longer contain their power, they tumbled into thunder.

Holding each other tightly through subsiding waves, awareness of their world returned: the bed, the tangled sheets, their heavy limbs. Josiah moved to ease some of his weight from Laura, but she clutched him tighter, emptying her lungs, ready for a breath of new life.

Faces close, small smiles, gentle kisses, silken touches.

"I love you," Josiah whispered. "I love you," he said again and kissed her with such tenderness, tears filled her eyes.

She cupped his face and said, "I love you. I will love you forever."

"Forever," Josiah repeated.

When Laura and Josiah emerged from the den, neatly dressed and combed, the kitchen and living room were empty.

"Where is everyone?" Laura wondered aloud. They heard a thump from above, then John Thomas's muffled voice calling out. Kate's voice, equally muffled, answered.

"Upstairs," Josiah answered. He reached out and stroked Laura's hair.

"What are we going to tell Kate?" Laura asked.

Josiah shrugged. "What's to tell? She'll know."

The world slowly regathered itself within them, tragedies and circumstances regaining their holds. They embraced.

The sound of a throat being cleared ended their hug. Kate stood on the bottom step of the staircase. "I finally talked Catherine out of a suitcase," she said, "but she's not too happy with the duffel bag. Says everything's gonna get wrinkled. I said, so what do you think this is? A Goddamn tour of the continent? You want I should find you a Goddamn steamer trunk?" She swung around the newel post and brushed past them toward the kitchen.

Laura put a hand on Kate's arm, stopping her. "Kate," she began.

Kate whirled and grabbed her in a crushing hug. "You don't have to say anything, kiddo. It's okay. All that's important now is Lily."

Mack's call came two hours later. They were all packed and gathered in the living room, waiting. Laura sat, willing the shortwave set to speak. When it finally did, she jumped.

Mack's voice, once so familiar to Laura, now held only cold malevolence.

He growled a street address. Writing it down, Laura demanded to hear Lily.

"Mommy?" The fear and hope within that one word sent Laura flying apart. Josiah pulled her to him before she could fall.

CHAPTER 42

Lily was a generous child. Like most children, she collected objects, but, unlike other children, Lily used her things to create something new. These creations she would give away. Somebody was always receiving something from Lily.

Her gifts were never random. It was how she related to others. It was how she showed them that she knew who they were. The bouquet meant for Catherine could never have been given to Laura, for Laura's bouquet was an entirely different creation. The carefully shaped rhinoceros, made from the red clay scooped from a deposit near the creek below the house, was formed only for Josiah. Lily always had several projects under way, her creativity driven by a need to express things for which there seemed to be no words.

At times, she'd feel a strange tickle/itch in her throat as she strained for a description of what she was perceiving.

The first time she heard the expression "on the tip of my tongue," she began using it liberally, with one slight change. "It's on the tip of my insides," she'd groan in frustration, unable to communicate her perceptions.

When Lily was very young, just learning to talk, she didn't know that some of the things she was already groping to express had no words. By the time she was four, her vocabulary was exceptional, yet many words she wanted eluded her. She had a phase, lasting about six months, when she became unsettled, often verging on tantrums. Everyone was perplexed by this behavior—unusual for her—but no one grasped the frustration that lay at the root of it. Lily wanted different words and nobody seemed able to provide them.

At four and a half, Lily finally accepted that certain sensations had no words, but she didn't realize the concepts she was trying to verbalize were unique to her. She began making up phrases, putting words together in odd ways that approximated what she wanted to say. Adults found her phrases charming but didn't realize they marked a transition in her understanding. When Lily murmured, "I love you, stubble/blossom," to Kate, Kate would laugh and kiss her. Lily presented Catherine with a scrap of board over which she had glued an assortment of stones, all smooth and within millimeters of the same size, and said, "This is for you, heart/meadow." Catherine had accepted it with grave pleasure.

Had Lily known the word "empathy," it would have proven to be as woefully inadequate a word as all the others. It wasn't that she was able to relate to feelings of others; it was that she was able to see the inner images people had of themselves—the sense of self that is as integral to every person's inner eye as their features are to those who see them. To Lily, others' self-images had a presence that hinted of color and sound, that had odor and texture, but were both more than that, and not that at all.

Lily had no guide to this extra sense only she possessed. The rainbow of information she received had innumerable shades and colors for which she had no words; even its arc was indescribable. So she poured her frustration into generous creations because she had to; she wasn't big enough to hold it.

On her fifth birthday, Laura had laughingly captured Lily as she ran past in the front yard, face hot and sweaty. Lily had twisted from her grasp, body taut with the need to finish her current project. "Not now, Mommy. I need peace," she'd implored, frantic to be on her way. With a quick kiss, Laura had sent her off, smiling at just another of Lily's strange sayings. But Lily had meant exactly that, for it was only when she had completed something and given it to the person for whom it was meant, that she felt, for a moment, at peace. Understood.

Of all the people in Lily's life, only Lucas had never received a gift meant just for him. She gave Lucas things, but those things she gave were, to her, meaningless. She had never grasped the meaning of Lucas. At first, his elusiveness bewildered her and she became frustrated. Later, the lifelessness of creations begun for him seemed threatening, unpleasant, edging into fright. She found herself dreading to begin a gift for him, so she gave up.

When Mack had grabbed Lily, the sensations that had abruptly overwhelmed her were far worse than his blood-bathed hands and arms. Terror unlike anything she'd ever felt froze her mind. She could not process the fiery chaos emanating from Mack. Her brief struggle ended when she went into shock, unable to contain the loathsome agony of knowing all that was this evil man.

She didn't remember being carried from the house, then flung into the backseat of Mack's jeep. The rumble of the engine finally penetrated her mind fog, followed by the sight of Lucas, peering over the front seat at her. His presence meant something, but she could not think.

The jeep sped over holes and ruts. Lily stared at the back of Lucas's head until a hard jolt threw her against the door. The sudden physical pain caused her to burst into tears. She wrapped her arms over her head and cried hysterically, unable to cope with the suffocating terror.

It was Lucas, turning to grin at her, that caused her to focus through blurring tears. Lucas. Sudden hope burned through her. But when her vision cleared, she saw the grin Lucas wore was a rictus in a flat, cold face.

"Hello, Lily," he said, then turned away. Lily's scalp prickled. Lucas had changed, terrifyingly. The boy she'd known—his facial expressions, his movements, even the tone of his voice—was gone. In their place was a spontaneous cruelty that seemed to pulse. Gone was the cleverly devised persona with which he'd fooled everyone, and confused Lily.

The meaning of Lucas that had for so long eluded her was now revealed. And it bore a striking resemblance to the thing driving the jeep.

The jeep bucked, jumped, swerved, and sped, and the seat belt cut into her lap. Her side banged against the door every time the jeep hit a rut. Where was her mother? Had she been near enough to see this car leaving? Lucas was here and Lucas had been with her mother.

Lily stretched and twisted, trying to look over the back of her seat at the road behind them, but the seat was too high, and her head wouldn't stop bouncing. She sagged down and pressed herself into the corner as the jeep careened onward.

Mommy will come, she told herself stubbornly. She fought to not become more afraid. It was dark. She'd never been by herself after dark. Chaotic emotions pulsed around her. Tears pooled and her throat ached. *Mommy will come,* she whispered to herself.

CHAPTER 43

San Francisco glittered in the early morning sun. As the Suburban moved down the Waldo Grade, on the approach to the Golden Gate Bridge, Josiah took one hand off the steering wheel and squeezed Laura's knee. "Almost there," he said.

Sitting between Josiah and Catherine, Laura stared at the city across the bay, unable to remember how it once looked. There used to be more skyscrapers. The pyramid-shaped TransAmerica building was gone. Houses still covered the hills, clustered thickly, but there were large, blackened gaps.

Distant building-covered blocks, checkered by dark gaps, sprawled all along the peninsula to the open ocean. Midway, the golden onion dome of the Russian Orthodox Church gleamed brightly above surrounding houses.

"My goodness," said Catherine, "I haven't seen this little traffic on the bridge in over fifty years." They were, in fact, the only car on the bridge other than a pickup truck far ahead of them, passing beneath the south tower.

"Look at all the boats," Kate said from the backseat. "Freighters and tankers and—holy shit! Chinese junks."

Mohammed, seated behind Catherine, saw the ocean, where the bay widened into deeper waters and the distant horizon. An outgoing tanker and several fishing boats dotted the blue-green coastal water. He unbuckled his seat belt and craned to see the ship-crowded bay. It had been years since he'd seen so much activity.

In Year 4, Josiah and Eli had risked a difficult trip to San Francisco, to see for themselves if the rumors of a thriving city were true. They'd traveled by motorcycle, retracing the route they had all used to flee after the blackout, and had returned home with news of a city changed almost beyond recognition; many of the skyscrapers that had once defined the San Francisco skyline were gone. Entire downtown blocks had been demolished, the rubble removed so the ground could be planted. Chicken farms were scattered throughout the city. Golden Gate Park was a huge cooperative farm, with plots of vegetables and grains interspersed among the few trees left standing.

They'd found the city to be dominated by an Asian population, with new, unwritten laws; justice relied on the perspective of the individual. Weapons abounded, though killing remained a serious crime, condoned only if the slain was a proven *Shaitan*. Clan systems thrived, networks of respectability with which everyone wished to affiliate; clan members protected each other and vouched for each other's good standing. Thus, *Shaitan* were quickly outed.

San Francisco's language had become a mixture of English and Chinese dialects. Non-Asians spoke Chinese as often as they could. A pidgin-English/Chinese was evolving.

The well-armed population crowded along the wharves, close to their source of economy. The bay was crowded with every possible configuration of vessel. Oil refineries in Richmond, on the eastern shores of the bay, were functioning, guarded by mercenaries. Tankers brought in crude oil from Alaska and Texas and left with the refined product.

"Where's the map?" Laura asked. She fretted over finding the address on Sutter that Mack had given them. The city was definitely different. Downtown would be different, and Sutter Street was downtown.

"Right here, dear." Catherine handed her the outdated map. She'd given up reassuring Laura that she knew the city as well as the back of her hand.

Kate turned to John Thomas. He was slumped

against his seat, staring straight ahead.

"Are you all right, honey?" she asked him. "You look a little pale."

John Thomas smiled wanly. "I'm fine." He couldn't explain the images fading briefly in and out of his mind. One of the images seemed to be of this bridge, but it was full of crashed cars and was accompanied by a nightmarish feeling. Another had a strange boxy look, but the sides of the box were opaque, like shattered windows, thick and somehow still whole. This image brought a suffocating sensation. There were others that made even less sense. Suddenly, he heard Lucas's voice as clearly as though his brother sat right next to him. "John Thomas," Lucas said. "John Thomas."

John Thomas sat up, darting glances at the others. That was weird. No one else looked startled, even though the words were so loud. Heart thumping, he wondered if Lucas, trapped somewhere in the city with that horrible man, had really called out to him and he'd somehow heard him in his mind. Lucas's voice had been too audible to be a memory. It had been real.

"What's going on?" Kate asked. She had heard it, then. But no, Kate was staring through the windshield. John Thomas followed her gaze and saw a diagonal line of orange cones angling across the lanes. Josiah was slowing down, steering to the far right lane. They were close enough to make out the figure of a person in the tollbooth toward which the cones funneled them.

"Checkpoint," Josiah replied.

"We gotta pay a toll?" Kate asked.

"I don't think so," Josiah said. He rolled his window down and braked by the booth.

The man inside, armed with a semiautomatic weapon, smiled at them. "Business, pleasure, or immigration?" he asked.

"Business," Josiah answered.

"Length of stay?"

"Hard to say." Josiah shrugged. "Long enough to make a few trades, short enough not to spend all our profits."

The man laughed, then bent slightly at the waist and ran his gaze over each of them. Straightening up, he waved them through. "Happy trading."

"Thanks." Josiah accelerated and, within moments, they were on Doyle Drive, heading toward the Marina district.

Laura swiveled in her seat. "You're still sure, Mohammed? You haven't changed your mind?" Her voice was tense and pleading.

"I am sure. I will not change my mind, Laura, don't worry."

Laura buried her head in her hands. "Oh, God."

The tension everyone had been rallying to ignore was breached.

Catherine harrumphed. "There's no point in second-guessing our plan. It's the best we can come up with and it will either work, or it will not. Uncertainty can only undermine us."

"So many holes in the plan," Laura agonized. "What if Mack's hidden Lily and we kill him and then can't find her? Or what if he's holding her so close that we can't get a shot at him before he realizes that Mohammed isn't Conrad? The hat just won't help. He'll demand to see Mohammed's face. What if . . ." She faltered, unable to say the awful words. *What if Lily's already dead?*

"What if everything works right?" Josiah interrupted firmly. "What if Mack does see Mohammed's face and Plan B works: he accepts Mohammed's offer to lead him to Conrad? What if Mack accepts Mohammed in trade for Conrad, like Mohammed said he might?"

Mohammed had told them the entire story of the night Mack had raped Conrad, of how sure he'd been that Mack had been going to come after him instead. He was certain Mack would have gotten him, had he not escaped with Conrad early the next morning. None of them understood why Mack had fixated on Conrad, and perhaps Mohammed as well.

Entering the Marina district, they were engulfed in noise and traffic. By the time they turned onto Bay Street, moving toward North Beach, they had slowed to a crawl, weaving through streets crowded with drivers, cyclists, and horse-drawn wagons. Pedestrians swarmed between the wheeled traffic, the sidewalks offering only narrow paths alongside the makeshift booths crowding their lengths.

"There must have been an earthquake," Catherine remarked. "Or several." She pointed out a few canted buildings, drawing their attention to the side of one particularly expressive two-story house. Large, dark cracks meandered along its pink stucco exterior, wide enough in places to expose wounded wood and plaster.

"Fires, too," said Laura. "I saw a lot of black, empty areas in the Richmond District when we came over the bridge."

"I suggest we try a different route," Catherine said. "It may be even worse on Columbus. Hyde Street should be coming up . . . yes, there, turn right."

"Hey, that's not Hyde," Kate said, squinting at the hand-lettered sign tacked atop the corner pole. "It says . . . oh. It's in Chinese."

"It is Hyde," Catherine said. "Turn, Josiah. A rose is a rose."

Josiah turned and, by the second block, was able to drive faster as the traffic thinned. Three blocks later, the street ended. He stopped and they stared at the excavated hill in front of them, long wooden ladders sprawled along its face.

"Goodness," Catherine said. "Turn left."

For the next fifteen minutes, no one else spoke as Catherine guided Josiah through a series of turns and detours, managing somehow to move southward.

"Are we still going in the right direction?" Laura asked worriedly.

"If the place is south of us, we are," Mohammed said.

"You said you've never been to San Francisco," said Kate.

"Indeed, I have not."

"Good sense of direction," Josiah said, turning right at Catherine's gesture.

Five minutes later, Catherine told him to stop. They were definitely downtown. Tall, dark buildings sat shoulder to shoulder along every street. "This is close enough," said Catherine.

"Where's Sutter?" Laura asked.

"The street directly in front of us," Catherine answered. "The address we were given should be about three blocks to the left."

"Here we go," Kate said. She scrambled onto her knees and began rummaging through a box behind her seat, handing items to John Thomas for distribution. "That's for Catherine," she said, handing him a dark shawl. "Josiah." She tossed a baseball cap over. "Me." A wig of glossy black hair, styled in a pageboy, landed on John Thomas's lap. "You." Another wig, also black, the hair shorter and unkempt. "Mohammed." A tan cowboy hat. "Mohammed." A tan London Fog raincoat. "Josiah." A knee-length, dark nylon raincoat. "And Catherine." She flipped around and handed Catherine a lap robe.

"I still don't like the idea of getting John Thomas

into this," Kate protested. She watched him fit his wig over his closely cropped hair, then bent her head forward, flipped her own wig on, and jammed her red curls beneath it.

Adjusting his tightly fitted cap of black hair, John Thomas said, "You know how good I shoot." His voice was determined, but his face was pale.

"That's another thing." She glared at Mohammed. "Why I ever agreed to . . ."

Mohammed, coat on, placed the cowboy hat on his head and said, "He is old enough to avenge his brother, who is in danger." No one had yet told Mohammed of their belief that Lucas was *Shaitan*. And it certainly couldn't be discussed in John Thomas's presence.

"Like Catherine said," Josiah added, giving his baseball cap a tug, "no point in second-guessing our plan. Two, two, and two. It's our best bet."

Laura and Mohammed would enter the building, Josiah and Catherine would cover the entrance, and Kate and John Thomas the rear. If there was no back exit, Kate and John Thomas would wait across the street, ready to help.

Laura sat tensely, waiting for everyone to start moving. *Get out get out get out,* she screamed inwardly, *let's GO.* Her nerves were raw, her thoughts ragged with the knowledge that Lily might be just a few blocks away. She felt the heaviness of the gun in her jacket pocket. If

Lily wasn't directly in front of Mack, she would shoot through her pocket. But she suspected Lily would be. It was how she pictured it. A shadowy room. Mack sitting in a chair, facing the doorway. Lily in his lap.

The scene played itself out: she and Mohammed entering the room; Mack ordering Mohammed to remove his hat; a snarl of rage when he saw his face. Laura yelling "Wait!" frantically shouting the words of Plan B, "Take him! He'll go!" but too late. Mack already shooting, Mohammed down, the flash of the bullet coming for her, knowing she couldn't shoot because Lily—Lily, oh, God—

"Laura," Josiah said. His hand covered her cold fists and she jumped. "I wish I could go in with you." His eyes were full of worry.

She shivered and leaned against him. "I wish you could, too."

Mohammed got out, went to the rear of the car and opened the back doors. Lifting out Catherine's old wheelchair—the one Laura had used to bring her home from the hospital the day after the blackout—he unfolded it and wheeled it to Catherine. Seated, she adjusted her lap robe to conceal her gun, then draped her shawl over her head in such a way that her face was hidden.

"Goddamn this leg," Josiah exclaimed as he watched Catherine's preparations.

Laura stroked his cheek. "You still wouldn't be able to go in with me. You're too tall. He'd know right away that you're not Conrad." Concern and love in their eyes, they exchanged a sudden, hard kiss.

Josiah and Catherine would make the first pass of the building, identifying it and getting as much information as they could. The wheelchair would help disguise Josiah; using it for support, he could conceal his limp.

Counting the buildings on either side of their target, Catherine and Josiah would continue around the corner to see about a rear access, then rejoin the others one block north and one west with their information.

Kate and John Thomas scrambled out of the car. With a last, fierce hug, Laura and Josiah followed them. The car was locked up and the six of them set off, Josiah pushing Catherine's wheelchair toward the corner of Taylor and Sutter while the others walked in the opposite direction, to the corner of Bush and Taylor.

Laura could barely keep herself from pacing as she and Mohammed waited on their corner. Josiah and Catherine had completed their mission and were headed back to the front of the building. There was indeed an alley behind the address Mack had given them, and Kate and John Thomas were hurrying toward it.

Her hands clenched. This was it. A few more minutes to allow the others to position themselves, then she and

Mohammed would confront Mack. *Lily, Mommy's here, I'm coming, baby.* Adrenaline thrummed through her. She had to calm down. Her teeth chattered.

Mohammed, finished with his silent prayer, raised his bowed head.

"Time?" Laura choked.

He shook his head. "It has only been a few seconds. Take a deep breath and let it out slowly."

She tried.

"Again, please," he directed. She took another, deeper breath.

"Again, slower."

At the end of her third deep breath, Laura had steadied a bit.

"Better," Mohammed said.

Laura nodded. "I never said thank you. You're doing what my own brother wouldn't do."

"It is Allah's will. For years I called upon Him to let me know if my little sister had returned to him. For years I knew only that the path home was gone. Allah answered my prayers. He led me to you and you answered my question. You had felt the emergence of your parents and brother on the other side during the long minutes of the epiphany. I know now, Aida is safe. It is my obligation to help you save your Lily."

Laura slowly shook her head. "You're not obligated. And the path back is broken now. I'll risk it, myself, to save Lily, but you—I have no right to ask you."

"It is time," said Mohammed. He pulled the brim of his hat lower and stepped off the curb. Laura followed him.

The building in which Mack waited had once housed a theater where plays were performed. Looking at its façade, Laura realized she'd once attended a performance there. The theater had been on an upper floor, the stairway old and cramped. Mohammed swung the door open.

She entered before him and they stood just inside the doorway, facing the empty lobby, letting their eyes adjust to the gloom as the door slowly clicked shut behind them. There was a long stairway at the far end of the lobby. A lit candle guttered atop the lower newel post, casting a feeble glow on the bottom steps.

Laura held her breath and clutched Mohammed's arm as she peered into the dark silence at the top of the stairs.

As they crept across the dim lobby, Mohammed grabbed the fat candle and held it in front of them. They started up the uncarpeted, wooden steps that creaked under their weight, the noise echoing in the stairwell. Laura's heart pounded faster with every step, knowing it announced them. She imagined Mack listening in the darkness above.

Struggling to remember the layout of the building, she quickened her pace. Mohammed kept up with her and the candle he held sputtered and died. He tossed it behind him, its thump swallowed by the noise of their climb.

There would be a landing, she remembered, a turn, more stairs, another turn, and then a few more steps to the upper hallway. They made the first turn, their vision impeded by darkness. She couldn't remember if the door to the theater would be to the left or the right once they reached the hallway. The small theater had few seats, she knew, tiered in semi-circles, just a section of balcony overlooking a small stage.

In the upper hallway, they saw the open door on their right. Two fat candles flickered on the floor on either side of the opening. Hazy, gray light came in from a dirty window at the end of the hall behind them.

Laura moved slowly toward the darkness framed by the doorway. She gripped the gun in her pocket. Mohammed abruptly grabbed her arm and she gasped and stopped. He pulled her to the wall, a few feet from the doorway.

"Call him," he whispered.

Laura pressed the side of her face against the wall, and called, "Mack? We're here."

He answered, his disembodied voice ominous, angry. "You're late."

"No," said Laura. "You said today." He hadn't specified a time.

"You're LATE!" he roared. It sounded as though he stood right inside the doorway.

It's the acoustics, Laura told herself. *He must be down on the stage.*

Mack laughed harshly . . . and applauded. *Now, Laura, MOVE.* She slid through the opening and into the dark theater. She saw the blurred outlines of the closest chairs, dimly lit by the flickering candles on the floor in the doorway. Her back against the wall, she groped deeper into the theater, behind the last row of chairs, straining to see the blacked-out stage below. She heard Mohammed's breath, felt a tug on her jacket as he tried to stay close.

"CONRAD!" Mack shouted.

Laura and Mohammed bumped together. She wondered, in the unexpected darkness, what they should do if they couldn't see Mack—go directly to Plan B? But how would Mack react, his demand thwarted at the outset? The darkness and the acoustics made it impossible to know his position. They couldn't observe his reaction. There would be no instant in which his movement would cue a counteraction. And where was Lily? Was she even in the room? Laura felt intense, fierce hatred for the man—the thing—who imprisoned her daughter.

She shouted into the black pit. "Where's Lily? You won't get Conrad until I have Lily!"

"DARE MAKE NO DEMANDS UPON ME!" Mack thundered. "I will slit her open and rip out her heart!"

Laura crouched and moved as Mack shouted, creeping

down the center aisle with Mohammed following closely. She drew the gun with her right hand as she stretched her left before her, finding the balcony railing. Clutching the cold rail, she crouched against the short wall it topped. Mohammed crouched beside her.

"You think I don't see you?" Mack said, his voice suddenly a soft, whispering caress. "Who's with you, hmm? Is that you, Conrad?" Wild laughter skittered from him and reverberated through the theater.

Houselights brightly erupted, then dimmed.

Laura saw the stage, empty but for Lucas, who was standing center stage in a spotlight. Her gaze froze on him for an instant, then darted around the theater. Empty. No movement. The darkness yawned blackly beyond the coned spotlight.

"Hello, Laura," Lucas said.

Where was Mack? Laura's finger twitched on the trigger of her gun. She couldn't stop staring at Lucas, the monster who had led Mack to Lily. Mouth dry, she raised her gun, cocked it.

"What are you doing?" Mohammed hissed.

Laura ignored him. Where was Mack? Still, she couldn't tear her gaze from Lucas. "You," she spat. "Kate was right about you."

"You should have seen what Mack did to Samuel," Lucas said as though she hadn't spoken. His child voice filled the theater. "There was so much blood. Remember those weird sounds Samuel used to make? You should've heard him when he got gutted. You should've heard him, Laura. You should think about how Lily's going to sound."

Blood pounded in Laura's ears. *Oh, God, where's Lily? WHERE'S MACK?*

"Conrad," Mack said, behind her.

She whirled, heart in her mouth. Mohammed gaped at Mack. There was a moment of complete stillness as Mack stared blankly at Mohammed, and then Laura saw recognition flare in his eyes.

"Ali!" Mack exploded. The gun in his hand wavered.

Laura didn't think. She raised her gun and fired. Her grip was too tense, and the gun bucked in her hand, twisting to the side and kicking her arm back. Her elbow cracked against the rail and pain zinged through her arm. The gun fell from her suddenly nerveless fingers. Her shot had gone wild.

Mack aimed his gun at her.

Lucas had been careful not to give away Mack's position while he kept Laura's attention on himself. Talking about Samuel had been a stroke of genius, he bragged to himself as he hurried off the stage. Now was his chance, finally. He heard Mack yell, "Ali!" and paused, wondering who that could be. He almost turned back. But no, it didn't matter.

He had to hurry. Lily was his now. All his, and he couldn't wait to try some of his ideas on her, things Mack hadn't let him do. He was angry at Mack for that, for stopping him from hurting Lily. It had been almost more than he could take, having Lily there, helpless, and not being able to do anything about it. And it wasn't as though Mack was protecting her. No, the only reason Mack had stopped him was because he liked frustrating him. He shouldn't have let Mack know how much he wanted Lily. As soon as Mack saw that, saw that need, he started jerking him around. *Asshole.*

His hand was on the doorknob of the backstage dressing room, where they'd left Lily, when he heard a gun go off. *Good.* He hoped they all killed each other. Hurrying into the room, he saw Lily right where Mack had left her, gagged and bound to a chair. She was his. He knelt at her feet, fumbling at the knots as he looked into her face. The cloth gag was tight over her mouth, her eyes big and terrified. Thrilled by her fear, inspiration hit him.

"Did you hear that shot, Lily?" he asked her. Her eyes got bigger. "Mack just killed your mother. She's dead, Lily." Immediate tears spilled down her cheeks. His heart pumped faster. *Oh shit, oh shit, this is great.*

He heard a loud clank, then a creak. Now what?

Quietly, he moved to the door, careful to keep himself hidden behind the frame. A shaft of daylight came from the back door of the theater, which exited into the alley behind the building. A figure slipped through and paused, momentarily outlined in the light.

Kate! What was she doing here? A surge of hatred shook him and he pressed himself flatter against the doorframe. A montage of images flooded his mind, tortures he'd devised for Kate. He'd fantasized them so often, the images were crisp and detailed.

The exit door, weighted to shut automatically, was closing, shrinking the shafted angle of daylight. Kate stood against the far wall, her figure fading in the diminishing light. Lucas squinted. She was moving away now, deeper into the theater.

Hurryhurryhurry. He rushed back to Lily and worked on the binding knots. There! Her legs were free. Now the hands, behind her. She was crying, snuffling behind the gag.

"Shut up!" he hissed. "We're getting out of here before Mack comes back. Shut up or he'll hear you."

There! Her hands were free. He snatched one and yanked her out of the chair, leaving her gag in place. She fumbled at it with her free hand as he pulled her, stumbling, to the door. Two shots rang out, loud, echoing. Perfect! Tightening his grip on Lily's hand, Lucas ran to the exit door, jerked it open, and dragged her through.

He was free.

"Lucas! Lily!" John Thomas cried out, and he snatched off his wig when he stepped from behind the trash Dumpster where Kate had left him.

Startled, feeling a crushing disappointment, Lucas turned to his brother.

Lily moaned, straining toward John Thomas as she tugged to get her arm free of Lucas, her other hand pulling at the tight gag. Her little chest was heaving, trying to get air, her nose too stuffed with crying, the gag too thick to breathe through. Then John Thomas was there, kneeling before her, wrenching it off her mouth. Gasping lungfuls of air, she flung herself at him, wrapped her arms around his neck and pushed her face against his throat, sobbing.

John Thomas hugged her close, then lifted her up as he stood, staring from Lucas to the back door of the theater. "What's going on?" He freed one arm and hugged Lucas briefly, stroked his head, then wrapped the arm back around Lily. "Are you all right, Lucas? I heard shots. Where's—"

"Mommmmy!" Lily cried waveringly, then tightened her arms around his neck and sobbed harder, loud, gasping wails.

"Quiet," Lucas commanded through clenched teeth. "Come on. We gotta go. Hurry. Before he comes." He moved down the alley, pulling at one of John Thomas's arms, both of which were crooked around Lily.

Nerves already taut from his endless wait, and now, having seen Lily gagged and hearing Lucas's warning, John Thomas's anxiety skyrocketed. He let himself be urged onward, but questions crowded his mind. What about Katie? Those shots? Was Laura all right? And Mohammed? Had Catherine and Josiah gone in, too?

"What's happening?" he asked as they broke into a trot. Even as they moved away from the building in which his people were dangerously confronting Mack, John Thomas knew he had no choice. He had Lily and Lucas. By some miracle, his brother, and Lily, who was as close to a sister as he would ever have, were with him. He had to keep them safe. Above all, he had to keep them safe. He couldn't, he *wouldn't* fail again. Lucas was running now. John Thomas abandoned his questions and ran after him, saving his breath for the sprint with his clinging, sobbing burden.

Lucas led them up one street and down another, through two alleys and around several corners. Finally, John Thomas could no longer keep up the pace. Gasping for air, he faltered, legs rubbery, arms aching from holding Lily. He tried to muster enough breath to call out to Lucas, but Lucas, twenty paces ahead, turned to check on him.

John Thomas leaned against a brick building. His arms were shaking. He would drop Lily if he didn't put her down. He loosened his grip to let her slide to the ground, but she immediately tightened her arms and legs around him. Chest heaving, John Thomas panted, "Lily, I can't breathe."

He felt her reluctance as she allowed herself to be set down. The instant her feet touched the ground, she pushed against him and wrapped her arms around his waist.

Lucas hurried back. "Come on, we've got to keep going. He'll find us!"

Lily whimpered, pressing her face against John Thomas and shrinking away from Lucas.

"Give me a chance to catch my breath," John Thomas pleaded. He glanced back at the last corner they had turned, fearful of seeing Mack. Lucas was right, they had to keep going. John Thomas examined the unfamiliar surroundings.

They were deep in the heart of downtown San Francisco, in a section that had been assaulted by earthquakes and fires. There were small cracks in the sidewalk and street and a long one in the foundation of a nearby building, a three-story stone structure that listed as though shifted off its foundation. Down the block, empty windows gaped in blackened buildings.

Then John Thomas became aware of activity around them. It had been there, in the background, all the while but, until now, he'd hardly registered the people, cars, and bicycles they'd been dodging. And the noise! A cacophony of horns, voices, engines, and bicycle bells now assaulted his ears, as though he'd just removed earplugs. He hadn't stood amongst this many people, been in the midst of so much noise, in years.

"Come on, John Thomas," Lucas demanded. "We've got to go."

"Where?" he asked desperately, unable to ignore the confusion around him. "If we go much farther, we'll never find our way back. We might already be lost."

"It doesn't matter," Lucas said. He stared at Lily, careful to keep the lust from his expression. The freedom he'd had, when restraint had no longer been necessary, when he could look exactly as he felt, had been intoxicating. Anger spiked through him; again, he had to wear the hateful mask of a putrid, pukey, Goddamn goody-goody. He grimaced, turned away from John Thomas and struggled for control.

Suddenly, he smiled. Of course. He didn't need to argue with John Thomas. He'd forgotten how easy John Thomas was to handle. Without comment, Lucas strode off.

"Lucas, wait!" John Thomas yelled.

Lucas quickened his pace.

"Lucas!" John Thomas bent to pick Lily up, then reconsidered and plucked one of her hands from its grip on his jacket. "Come on, Lily. Can you walk for a while?" He was already moving after Lucas.

Lily planted her feet and tugged back against his hand. "No, no, no, NO, NO."

John Thomas quickly dropped to one knee and glanced hastily around. "Shh. Okay, okay, I'll carry you. But you have to be quiet, Lily-o. There's too many people and—and you're a big girl, but—but you're still little." He fumbled his explanation, not knowing how to tell Lily that she had to be extra careful.

He'd been told the importance of placing Lily's public birth date prior to the blackout. He knew about *Shaitan* and *Shaitan* babies. He knew Lily wasn't *Shaitan* even if she was born after the blackout. But Lily didn't know anything. She didn't know she was really six and not seven. She didn't know other people might be dangerous if they knew. Until this very minute, he hadn't thought of it himself. He'd never been in public with Lily. None of them had.

Neck prickling, he glanced furtively at the bustling street. He had to be careful not to draw attention. They'd been here too long. Mack could be nearby. He picked Lily up, then scanned the block for Lucas. There. Lucas was waiting for them at the corner. Hugging Lily close, he forced himself to walk at an easy pace. No more dashing through the streets. They had to be careful.

Lily laid her head on his shoulder. Peeking through slitted eyes, she saw Lucas. She burrowed her face against John Thomas and moaned, "No, no, no," over and over.

John Thomas murmured everything was going to be all right, he wouldn't let anything happen to her.

Nearing Lucas, he said, "No more running, Lucas. Let's stop somewhere and figure out what to do."

"Soon," Lucas said after a pause. "A few more blocks first."

John Thomas nodded, his nerves wracked by fear of Mack. They crossed the street and headed up a hill.

"What's going on? What happened?" John Thomas asked urgently.

Lucas had his answer ready. "Laura's dead," he said.

Shock and grief ravaged John Thomas's face. His eyes flooded with tears, and he stumbled. Lily started crying again.

"Keep going," Lucas hissed. He walked alongside John Thomas, who held Lily tightly and gulped convulsively as he tried to deal with the blow. At the top of the hill, they turned right, John Thomas sniffing back his tears. Lucas, gleefully riding the emotional surges of John Thomas's pain, wanted more. He added, maliciously, "Kate, too. She got most of the way in, then he shot her."

John Thomas stopped. His entire body numbed. He shook his head, slow arcs of disbelief. "No," he murmured. "No, she can't be dead." It was too much. Reina, Eli, Laura, and—no, not Katie. She couldn't be dead. She might be hurt, but she wasn't dead. "No," he said, staring blindly at Lucas. "Katie has to be okay."

His arms tightened around Lily and he spun around. "We have to go back."

"No!" Lucas protested, grabbing his arm. John Thomas continued to walk and Lucas found himself being pulled in his wake. "Listen!" he shouted, thinking frantically. He ran in front of John Thomas. "You go, but leave Lily with me. You're right, Kate might be okay and she'll need your help. But you can't take Lily back in there!"

Lily tightened her arms around John Thomas's neck and wailed in his ear. He flinched, bumping into a woman who was hurrying by. She sidestepped him with a frown. Despite his turmoil, he remembered the need to keep from drawing attention.

He pressed Lily's head against him. "Hush, Lily. It's okay." There was a deep doorway in the building on his left. He ducked in, hurried to a far corner next to the door, and sat cross-legged on the cold tile, holding Lily close. Lucas followed.

John Thomas's thoughts tumbled as he tried to calm Lily. Knowing that she was grieving for her mother, as well as hurt by the ordeal with Mack, he despaired of getting her quickly calmed. He had to go back and help Katie. Lucas was right, though, he couldn't take Lily with him. And what about Josiah and Catherine? They must be helping Katie. But, no, maybe Mack had hurt them, too. Maybe he, John Thomas, was the only one left. The only one left to help all of them. He could feel his shoulder holster hidden beneath his jacket as Lily squirmed against him. Anxiety mounting, he tried again to gently pull Lily's arms from his neck, but she only gripped tighter.

This was impossible. The minutes were ticking by.

He'd never felt so torn. The need to protect Lucas and Lily was imperative. He felt it as a responsibility and as an instinct. He'd been Lucas's guardian for as long as he could remember. And Lily. His fierce love for Lily was unbreachable. He'd held her in his arms only minutes after she was born, had fed her and soothed her and played with her every day of her life. Her being, her spirit, was integral to his world.

But the others, too, were his family. Kate was his anchor, his guide, his parent. He'd never put his feelings for her into words, never acknowledged the obsessive compulsion with which he tied himself to her. He knew only that his world was at rest when Kate was near and had a subtle instability when she was not. Her absence tied tiny knots deep in his gut, so deep that he felt their tension only as a subliminal unease for which he had no words.

Catherine, Josiah, Laura, and Eli were all vital to him, merged into familial counterparts. He thought of Catherine as his grandmother, Josiah as his uncle, Laura as his aunt, and Eli—Eli had been his older brother, teasing, indulgent—and easy to talk to, about personal or embarrassing things. Eli was gone . . . now Laura, too. His heart ached with loss, twisted with fear for the others, burned with terror of Mack.

What to do? He sat on the cold tiles, hugging and rocking Lily. As terrified as he was of Mack, he had to try and help his family. At the same time, Lucas and Lily had to be kept safe, far away from Mack. He looked at Lucas, hunkered down in front of him.

He would do what Lucas had suggested, leave Lily here with him while he went back to help the others. It wasn't perfect. Lucas was just a child, but what other choice was there? And Lucas had already proven himself; he'd gotten Lily out of that building.

"Lily, listen, please, Lily-o," John Thomas said. He rocked and patted her. "Katie's hurt, Lily, I have to help Katie. You can stay with Lucas, he'll take care of you."

"No, no, no, NO NO," Lily sobbed into his neck. Her little fingers pinched as she clutched him. "Icefire/black, ICEFIRE/BLACK!" she wailed.

John Thomas sighed. This was no good. She'd never let him go. He squeezed his eyes shut against the pain of what he had to do next. It was going to be hard, she was so scared, so . . . small. But he had no choice. He might be the only chance the others had against Mack. Mack might have left them all, injured and bleeding, inside the building, while he pursued him and Lucas and Lily. When Mack didn't find them, he'd go back and make sure the others were dead. John Thomas remembered Mack's knife, slicing into Reina.

John Thomas grasped Lily's wrists in his hands and pulled them firmly from around his neck. In his best imitation of Catherine's no-nonsense tone, he said, "Lily, look at me." Her face was tear-stained, large brown eyes full of fear and pleading. He gentled his tone. "I'll be back as fast as I can. Lucas will take care of you. He—"

Lily screamed.

John Thomas's heart jumped into his throat. Shouting Lily's name, he clapped his hand over her mouth to smother her shrieks. But her body had gone rigid and her head twisted from side to side to escape his hand.

Lucas jumped to his feet. "Shut up!" he screamed. He grabbed a fistful of her hair and yanked her head back.

"Hey!" exclaimed John Thomas, shocked at Lucas. "What are you doing?" His hand flew from Lily's mouth and clamped Lucas's wrist. "Let her go." Lucas glared at him and John Thomas faltered at the flash of something dark, dark and dreadful in Lucas's eyes.

Mouth free, Lily screamed.

Unnerved by Lily's screams and Lucas's violence, and his . . . eyes, what had that been? Had he imagined it? John Thomas became aware of people in the doorway. More gathered behind them. There was shouting, but he couldn't understand the words. Loud, sliding tones barked and sang. *Chinese.* He'd heard Chinese on television, but never like this. The din became deafening in the echoing alcove. Adrenaline seared through him.

Lucas, seeing the people, released his grip on Lily's hair. Lily dropped heavily forward against John Thomas's chest, her head striking his chin. He held her tightly and struggled to stand. More people gathered, trying to see past those already in the doorway. A man pushed through the crowd and entered the alcove. His voice rose above the others and he jabbed the air to punctuate his rapid speech. The crowd quieted as they listened to the man's questioning.

John Thomas shook his head, lacking comprehension. A small, older woman darted in and stood close to the man. She peered, birdlike, at John Thomas. She spoke slowly, Chinese syllables of a different dialect, then smiled and raised her eyebrows, inviting him to answer. He shook his head again and shifted his arms around Lily in a protective gesture. Lily had stopped screaming, but clung to him as she stared at the strangers. Tear tracks on her face highlighted the dirt at their edges. Her dark hair was tangled, strands caught in the wetness of her cheeks.

In the silence that followed the woman's question, John Thomas realized that Lily was whimpering, a keening, unbroken thread. "It's okay, Lily," he whispered.

"Ahhh, Engrish," the tiny Chinese woman observed. She turned to the crowd, nodding and repeating,

"Engrish, Engrish," with every nod. A flurry of chatter broke out, but John Thomas didn't listen. Lily was saying something to him in a voice so small he couldn't hear her words.

"What?" he asked her, and was shocked by the face she turned to him. Her expression was of excruciating pain, her eyes drowning in tears.

"It hurts, it hurts, it hurts," she whimpered. "Make it stop, John Thomas, please." She burrowed her face against his shoulder, one arm covering her head, the other clutched around his neck. Wave after wave poured from the crowd, crashed against her unique perception.

"What is it, Lily?"

She wailed. He immediately heard the difference in her crying. It wasn't fear- or grief-crying, it was hurt-crying. He remembered the awful wrenching Lucas had given her when he'd pulled a fistful of her hair and gently rubbed the back of her head.

"Girrie okay?" the woman asked. Not getting a response, she raised her voice. "Hey, Boy! Girrie okay?" John Thomas looked at the crowd, thronging the doorway like a trap, and was filled with panic.

"Fine," he said to the woman, and walked into the crowd, arms protecting Lily as he twisted and pushed through. "Fine, we're fine," he muttered with every step. The tiny woman hurried after him, jabbering. Just as they reached the edge of the crowd, she grabbed his arm.

Startled, he cried out and wrenched from her grip. His feeling of suffocation became claustrophobia. Dark, enclosed images flashed into his mind.

Disoriented, he edged through the crowd. Voices rose. He couldn't tell if it was in dismay or anger. He almost stopped at their demanding tones, but his own voice suddenly filled his head. "RUN," it screamed.

As he leaned to sprint, a melody filled the air.

It rose hauntingly, a tinkling, simple tune. It stunned him, filled him with terror. He stood, transfixed, scalp prickling. The past six years melted away. In the forefront was only the terrifying, gut-wrenching tinkling that unlocked a nightmarish series of memories. Unable to hold on to reality, his arms numbed and went limp, his hands fell to his sides.

Lily slid downward with a sickening lurch, feet jarring to the ground. She looked up at John Thomas's face and couldn't comprehend what she saw, what she felt. Where was her John Thomas? What was happening? She stepped back and watched him slowly collapse, until he sat on the sidewalk, eyes glazed.

"John Thomas?" she whispered, frightened.

"Where's Conrad?" Mack demanded, his pistol aimed at Laura's head.

Laura's ears still roared from the blast of her gun. She saw Mack's lips move but couldn't hear him. She stared at his eyes. Red rimmed and raw, their ice-blue irises were thin rings around large pupils of sucking darkness.

"WHERE IS HE?" he shouted ferociously.

Deerlike, she froze, transfixed by the incomprehensible emptiness in the swirling black holes that were his eyes.

He cocked his pistol.

"NO!" Mohammed yelled, and his voice overcame the ringing in her ears. Mack's wild eyes jumped to Mohammed. Laura felt a snap, as though she'd hovered, and now jarred to the floor.

Mohammed pointed his gun at his own head.

"Only I know where Conrad is," he said to Mack. "You will put your gun down, or I will shoot myself."

Mack's face seemed to melt.

Laura gaped at the fluid contortions seizing his face. She realized it was just changing expressions, but the expressions were unlike anything she'd ever seen. The muscles twitched and froze independent of each other, mixing grimaces with smiles, squints with frowns; the mouth chewed with bared teeth, the tongue darted, eyes blinked, cheeks pouched, then hollowed, one nostril flared while the other pinched. His lips raised and lowered, flattened and widened.

And noises: grunts, laughs, wheezes, and growls, a keening wail, a shout. He leaped, jerked, twisted—an insane convulsion of movement, as though his very molecules were randomly exploding. His gun flailed wildly as his rabid, pounding paroxysm danced him closer to them.

Crouching, Laura shrank from his frenzy, her back against the short balcony wall, certain he would lunge at her any instant. She couldn't snatch her terrified gaze from him long enough to locate her gun, and suddenly he bared his teeth and brought a hand to his mouth.

Redness erupted, flowed down his chin. *Blood,* she realized, and couldn't understand its sudden appearance. Flinging his hand violently from his mouth, he grinned wildly, bent at the waist and plunged his face at hers, lips bared over a fleshy obscenity clenched between his teeth; his own forefinger, ripped from his hand, its end gleaming, ragged flesh and glistening bone. Plucking it from his teeth with his mangled hand, he bit it in half. She heard the knuckle pop, the crunch of bone as he ground his teeth together.

Horrified, she twisted her head aside, but he shoved his face before her, jerking in front of her again and again as she tried in vain to turn aside, stomach heaving.

Then his hand gripped her face, fingers pressed painfully into her cheeks, the dark void in his eyes mere inches from hers. "I TOLD you to bring CONRAD," he roared in fury. His fetid breath was hot, sharp with the iron smell of blood.

A deafening explosion flung him away from her and

she recoiled, warm blood spattering her face and chest. Mack's body slammed backward, collapsed over two chairs, and sagged heavily. Slowly, it rolled, then thudded into the aisle.

Mohammed held the gun he'd fired, muzzle down. Laura approached him, legs trembling, and took the gun from his hand. The weapon's grip was warm beneath her icy fingers. Returning to stand above Mack, she fired two more rounds into his body, though half his head had already been blown away.

Shen Lui pedaled his fish wagon slower as he approached the crowd, wondering what was going on. With any luck, he thought as he came to a halt, he might be able to sell the last of his fish, even those from yesterday. What an opportunity! He let the music play as he slid off the seat and set the brake. Hurriedly, he flipped up the icebox doors of the old ice cream wagon, unveiling the fish on their bed of ice.

John Thomas heard only the music, felt only the darkness it evoked, and was engulfed by deep terror.

Children-eaters. He was in a closet, hiding from the children-eaters. He was eight years old. Memories of burning bodies engulfed him as he passed out on the sidewalk.

Lily crouched close to John Thomas's limp body. Her

unique sense received new information, a John Thomas–knowing that was different from the past. Different, and yet, somehow not different. Brighter maybe. No, not brighter, what was the word? Her frustration rose. Her John Thomas was fuzzy/yellow/vanilla. This new shift in him bled soft/green and it sparkled. She didn't know how to arrange the newness in her mind.

Lily couldn't understand what was happening with her John Thomas–knowing, and with John Thomas.

She looked anxiously at the crowd of people and barely noticed the dimming of the clamor that had been assaulting her in pain-filled waves. The strangers talked and gestured. Some covered the lower halves of their faces with their hands, others hunched beneath their jacket collars. The ring they formed began to widen.

She glanced at Lucas only long enough to make sure he wasn't coming at her. His eyes tied ropes of disgust and terror around her.

Her toes were under John Thomas's ribs, her shins pressed his side. Too frightened now for tears, she nudged him gently, needing him desperately.

"John Thomas," she implored. "Wake up."

This was awful. She collapsed, sobbing, onto John Thomas.

The moment Lucas had been waiting for.

He now planned to tell Lily that Laura wasn't dead after all. She was just hurt. It wouldn't be hard for him to confuse Lily enough to convince her to go with him.

Hoping that whatever was wrong with John Thomas stayed wrong, he stepped forward but was stopped by an iron grip on his arm.

Whirling around, he barely kept a snarl from his face. The young Chinese man who held him yelled rapid-fire syllables at him. From within the crowd, the small woman who had earlier entered the alcove shouted at him. "No, Boy. Bad sick, bad."

Lucas now realized why people had covered their mouths and noses. Bad sick, the old bitch said. They thought John Thomas had some fatal disease. The crowd shuffled even farther back. The man who held him pulled him with them. The woman next to him grabbed Lucas's other arm.

Lucas fumed. Maybe he should kick, hit—break free. Then dash to Lily. Nobody would dare come near. He tensed his arms but felt the grips on them tighten. The man draped his free arm down along Lucas's neck and across his chest. *Shit. Fuck.*

Shen Lui stood by his fish wagon, one hand holding the icebox door. The crowd had stepped back from something in their midst. He craned to see until someone yelled "Stop. Sickness!"

Shen Lui froze. A body was on the sidewalk, a wailing child sprawled over it. He slammed the lid of the icebox, leaped onto his seat, and, standing on his pedals, he hurried away, taking the music with him.

John Thomas floated in thickness, a world his conscious mind had forgotten. But the forgetting that had taken place in a closet six years ago had been conjured by a traumatized mind. And now, bludgeoned by loss and terror, he plunged back through lonely darkness into that trauma. Phantoms chased him and he ran from them with heavy limbs. Children-eaters, CHILDREN-EATERS; like sharks, the terrifying phantoms swam in the thickness, with the crying and the dreadful music.

He had to move toward the hideous music to find the crying that called to him. The child who sobbed was important. He hurried, so slowly through this thick blackness. The crying became louder. The music . . . was fading. The crying. Was. Right in his ear.

His eyes fluttered open to a gray sky, and he felt a familiar weight on his chest. He hugged the familiarity. Lily. Dazed, he stared into grayness. Why was Lily crying?

"John Thomas?" Lily's tear-stained face, inches from his.

He blinked. "Hi, Lily-o. Did we fall down?"

John Thomas sat up as Lily babbled frantically. He tried to make sense of her words as he stared, dazed, at the ring of faces surrounding them. Reality crashed into him.

Mack, *Shaitan*. Protect Lily. Katie hurt. Eli, Laura, and Reina, dead. He scanned the crowd. And saw Lucas.

His body stilled, breath trapped in his throat.

Staring at Lucas, he felt only the feelings of his youth, his fear and abhorrence of his younger brother. All the rationales he'd applied to Lucas's behavior in the intervening years vanished, sucked out of him, and angry loathing spilled into the vacuum.

Lily tugged on his jacket, patted his face, needing his attention, to tell him.

"Lucas," she blurted. "He's icefire/black. Like that bad man who took me. Icefire/black, John Thomas."

John Thomas stared at Lily and understood. He looked at Lucas and saw loathsome empty darkness swirling in Lucas's eyes. Anger twisted through his fear.

Lucas, instantly aware of the change in John Thomas, didn't care. Savage heat filled him. He needed Lily's blood.

"*Shaitan*," he cried, thrusting a finger at Lily. "Her birthday is . . ."

But John Thomas was listening to something else: his father's last words, reverberating through the years. *"Watch out for Lucas."* And he knew, with certainty, what his father had meant.

When Lucas said the word "birthday," John Thomas was already drawing the gun from his shoulder holster. And as Lucas uttered his next word, the first bullet tore through his chest. The crowd screamed and scrambled away as the second bullet plowed into Lucas's forehead.

Kate, Laura, and Mohammed were waiting for a break in traffic when they heard the shots. Kate grabbed Laura's arm.

"Over there," she said, pointing up the steep street.

They ran, Mohammed pausing only long enough to make sure Josiah and Catherine, forced to move slower, still had them in sight.

They'd sprinted for blocks searching for Lily. Unable to find Lucas or Lily in the theater, they'd emerged to find John Thomas gone, as well. Clinging to the hope that John Thomas had somehow moved Lily to safety, they'd dashed back to the Suburban. But no John Thomas, no Lily.

The hill flattened onto an intersection and Laura, hands propped on knees, sweat running down her face, gasped, "Which way?"

"Look," said Mohammed. He pointed at a crowd at the far end of the block. They ran toward it.

The noisy mob snarled traffic. Laura hardly dared to hope, but then she heard Lily yelling, "No, no, no, NO."

Laura plunged through the mob, thrusting people aside.

"LILY!" she screamed as she burst onto an incomprehensible scene.

Lily clutched John Thomas as he gripped one of her wrists, while people tried to pull them apart.

"LILY!" Laura ran to her, dropped to her knees, and flung her arms around her.

"Mommy!" Lily collapsed against her.

Laura held her tightly. "I'm here. I'm here, honey." Ignoring the people yelling angrily at her in Chinese, she reached out to John Thomas and faltered at his dazed expression. Following his gaze, she saw what held his attention.

Blood pooled around Lucas, sprawled on the ground. There was a hole in his forehead, his eyes open.

I hope he rots in hell, she thought viciously, and tightened her hold on Lily.

"Holy shit," Kate said, thrusting herself between John Thomas and a man gripping his arm. "What happened, John Thomas?"

"I shot him," John Thomas confessed, his face pale.

"Oh, honey." Kate gathered John Thomas to her. "Are you all right?"

John Thomas's limbs quivered. He gazed mutely at Kate.

Three uniformed policemen arrived. One dispersed the milling people while the other two, one Caucasian, one Chinese, questioned the crowd in rapid Chinese. By then, Josiah and Catherine had arrived, followed by an ambulance, whose two attendants quickly removed Lucas's body.

The police arrested John Thomas, who was to be remanded to the juvenile authorities.

"Why?" Kate demanded. "The dead kid was *Shaitan*."

"Look, lady, nobody kills anybody in this city without accounting for it."

"But he was *Shaitan*, damn it."

The other policeman said, "This accusation must be verified by witnesses."

"We're all witnesses." Kate waved an arm at the others.

The young policeman shook his head. "Clan witnesses? Corroboration must come from a clan member."

Josiah spoke up. "We don't live here. We aren't part of a clan."

"Take it up with the courts." The policemen marched John Thomas to their car and seated him in the rear, hands cuffed. His face turned toward Kate and his desperate eyes stayed fixed on her as the patrol car pulled away.

"Now what?" Kate pleaded with Laura. The small band of people who had gone through so much together drew closer to each other.

"Now what?" repeated Laura numbly.

CHAPTER 44

The Richmond district was in shambles, mostly destroyed and deserted. Laura and the others needed temporary shelter, a place where they could sleep without fear.

Laura felt drained. In the backseat of the Suburban, cuddling her daughter, she tried to rid herself of images of the terrifying confrontation with Mack. His frenzy. The awful sound of bone crunching between his teeth. She had sworn everyone to silence about Mack being Lily's father. She never wanted Lily to find out. And clouding even her relief at having Lily safely in her arms again was the dreadful knowledge that, as long as *Shaitan* filled their world, Lily was in danger. They were all in danger.

Josiah drove slowly, with Catherine suggesting directions. Mohammed was silent.

Kate, in the backseat with Laura, hadn't said anything for a long time.

Josiah turned right, off Clement Street, onto 23rd Avenue. Most of the buildings on both sides of the street were intact but deserted, with minor damage showing. They chose a house and unloaded their belongings. Kate made a bed for Lily in a corner of the living room, while Mohammed built a fire in the fireplace and Catherine prepared a hasty meal from their supplies.

Kate could think of nothing but the image of John Thomas, framed in the window of the police car, staring at her. They had to free him immediately. But how were they going to find him? Where were the jails? Who could they get to help them? The cop had said something about clans.

"Kate," said Josiah, taking her arm and drawing her to the front door, "I know where to start."

"I'm going with you." She reached for the front doorknob, ready to sprint.

"No." Josiah knew how agitated Kate was and how difficult an agitated Kate would be to have at his side at this time. He needed the cooperation of strangers to navigate through the tight bonds of clansmanship governing the city and lead him to the one man who might help him. Where diplomacy was a must, Kate was a liability.

"What do you mean, *no?*" Kate said, outraged. "That's my kid out there!"

Quickly, Josiah explained his mission to find Dr. Chang.

Kate interrupted almost immediately. "*Doctor*

Chang? Chrissakes, Josiah, we need a lawyer, not a doctor."

"This is exactly why you're not going with me," Josiah said, containing his impatience.

Dr. George Chang, a physics professor, was a simple man, despite his intellectual and cultural background, and was the only teacher with whom Josiah had formed a relationship during his unofficial college class audits. When Josiah and Eli had visited San Francisco two years before, he'd made a point of finding Dr. Chang and introducing them—the only two men he'd ever truly respected. Now he could only hope Dr. Chang was still alive and would be willing to help.

Feeling the press of time, Josiah bluntly told Kate she would be a liability in his social negotiations. With grim determination he slid behind the wheel of the Suburban, Kate's protests and curses still ringing in his ears. Leaving her behind was definitely the right decision.

There was a rustle from the corner. "It's so good to have the child back," said Catherine, who rose to check on Lily. Laura, Kate, and Mohammed were busy swabbing down the kitchen, bathroom, and small bedroom that shared the same floor as the living room where she watched over Lily. No one was in the room to hear her murmured words, yet she was not abashed to speak them aloud. They gave voice to but a fraction of the emotion she felt at having Lily back.

As she neared the small mound of blankets and pillows nestled in a corner near the fireplace, she was startled into momentary immobility as Lily jackknifed up with a scream.

"ICEFIRE!" she wailed, eyes tightly shut. "ICEFIRE/ BLACK!"

Catherine painfully lowered herself onto the edge of the makeshift bed and gathered the child into her arms, uttering wordless, soothing sounds. Laura dashed into the room with loud, frantic inquiries, Kate and Mohammed at her heels.

"Just a nightmare, Laura," Catherine assured her as she relinquished Lily into Laura's arms. Lily's eyes were still tightly closed, but the tenor of her whimpers as she curled into her mother's embrace let them know she was awake, aware of her safe surroundings. At Laura's gentle questioning, Lily returned halting descriptions of her nightmare, her voice spiraling into high-pitched terror every time she uttered the word *icefire*. Catherine retreated into the kitchen and drew Kate and Mohammed with her, proposing they brew a nice pot of tea.

"What is this 'icefire'?" Mohammed wanted to know as the three of them sat around the kitchen table waiting for the kettle to boil.

Catherine made a helpless gesture of ignorance.

Kate frowned. "Don't take this wrong, Ali. Lily's fine, just like we told you before. It's just that she's got this little quirk, this weird kind of thing she does with words."

"What weird thing?"

Kate shifted uncomfortably on the hard oak of her chair. "She just . . . puts strange words together into clumps. She's been doing it for years. It's harmless; doesn't mean anything."

"The words don't mean anything?" Mohammed found that hard to believe. Who would bother to utter meaningless words?

Catherine rose to gather cups and spoons. "The words have meaning," she corrected, "when used individually. Lily, however, creates nonsensical compounds. Quite charming, really."

Mohammed's thoughts spun crazily as sudden intuition leaped among them: Lily wasn't creating nonsense with meaningful words; she was creating meaning with nonsense words. Hearing Lily's childish voice coming from the living room had reminded him of his little sister, Aida. But Aida had never made up funny words. Nor had she slapped a handful together trying to say something for which she didn't yet know the word. What if there were no words, in any language, for what Lily was trying to say?

Icefire. Lily understood something but had no language for it. That word had propelled her from a nightmare. She'd been Mack's prisoner. Mack was *Shaitan*. Perhaps icefire was *Shaitan*.

Catherine set a cup of tea down for him. He acknowledged her with a nod, a meager smile, and went back to his thoughts.

Laura had said that after the blackout things had mutated. Lily was born after the blackout. Was she a mutation after all? But Laura said all these mutations were reversals, forms that had, at some point in the past, existed.

Laura, though, had been pregnant during the blackout. During those minutes, the path had still been open.

Lily was a deliberate mutation, came the staggering thought.

Mohammed grasped his teacup, automatically blew over the brew, and took a swallow without a testing sip. The burning sensation that filled his mouth and throat overcame even the flame of his thoughts and he set the cup down with a thump, startling Catherine and Kate. He could only shake his head to their puzzled looks.

It was Laura to whom he needed to speak. He was bursting to tell Laura his thoughts about Lily, certain this was vital information. Both felt that, between them, they knew enough to figure out what was missing and, perhaps, learn how the Path could be fixed. Surely Lily's status as a deliberate mutation must have a connection to the very occurrence of the blackout and the resultant loss of the Path. Without the Path, everything would eventually mutate to nonexistence.

And earth would become, once again, just a lifeless rock in space.

Josiah stood on a pier of the small harbor at Fisherman's Wharf, gazing at the *Wil o' the Wisp* and the man standing on her deck. It was indeed a different world, Josiah thought, to have Chang, a man of such brilliance, fishing the sea instead of probing the universe. With surprised recognition, Chang greeted him warmly and invited him aboard. Josiah followed Chang down a set of narrow steps into the bowels of the sloop, where they settled themselves in a small, richly appointed salon off a tiny galley.

They chatted in the way of men becoming reacquainted, and Josiah waited for the right opening to put his case before Chang. He found, instead, a subtle reserve in Chang's demeanor that was disconcerting. As the minutes ticked by, the nuances of Chang's manner deepened and Josiah sensed not only reserve but an increasing resolve. Over what, Josiah wondered. It was almost as though Chang wanted something from him. Yet how could that be? Chang had no idea he'd show up at his docked home.

A moment later, a child appeared in the doorway,

and Josiah had his answer. She looked to be about Lily's age, which meant either that Chang was hiding her or that San Francisco laws protected children, *Shaitan* or not. Josiah, as an outsider, presented a danger to Chang and the child.

"Papa, it's time," proclaimed the girl, dressed in dark pants and a long-sleeved blue top, her shiny black hair plaited into a long, thick braid. Faint eyebrows rose upward when she spotted Josiah. Running lightly to her father, she cast Josiah a small smile and said, "Nice shweng fey."

Chang lifted his daughter onto his lap. "Feng Shui, little apple," he corrected gently. Su Ling smiled impishly. Chang caught and held Josiah's gaze. His chin tipped fractionally upward in defiance. "She sometimes gets her words mixed up."

Josiah nodded, his face expressionless while his mind raced for ways to use this new development. His enormous respect for Chang warred with his awareness that tools of deceptive manipulation had just been dropped into his lap.

"Tell me, little apple," Chang said, cupping his daughter's chin, "how are your lessons progressing?"

Su Ling pouted. "This morning, Madam Teacher made us do sums. It was very silly. She told us to carry numbers. Carry them where? I thought, but Ching Pao asked aloud the question in my head and got his knuckles rapped."

"You might have saved Ching Pao his punishment," Chang chided gently, "had you told Madam Teacher you had the same question."

Su Ling frowned. "Ching Pao should have his knuckles rapped. He's puddle/dung/foul."

Astonishment splashed over Josiah's face.

Chang's arms tightened around his daughter. "Sometimes Chinese words do not work for her."

Su Ling shook her head vehemently. "No, Papa, there is no—"

"Come now," Chang said, putting Su Ling on her feet. "You must gather your things for the Academy." The boat rocked gently as they walked down the narrow corridor.

Josiah's mind spun like a centrifuge, whipping aside the debris of half-formed plans and leaving a pure kernel of truth: he could tell Chang everything. *Everything.*

The man had a vested interest.

Laura tried to grasp that Lily might be a positive mutation. Mohammed had waited until her exhausted daughter had fallen asleep and been tucked beneath her blankets before gesturing Laura to him and, in a whisper, revealing his conclusions. His emphasis on Lily's word groupings as meaningful communication thrust new light on a peculiarity to which Laura had grown so accustomed she'd no longer taken notice of it.

All the gifts Lily created, she now realized, stunned, came not from an abundance of creativity but from a need to express something. To communicate.

This is for you. This *is* you.

Lily's words tumbled through Laura's mind, but this time it was as though a foreign language she'd been hearing for years suddenly began making sense. "Groping/sneeze/fiddler" wasn't the name of the necklace Lily had made for Kate; it had been Kate, Kate's essence, understood by Lily. And "Midnight/shaky/bubbles" hadn't been the wines Eli made; it had been Eli.

Dozens of examples jammed her thoughts. Lava/fountain/tide: Catherine. Cave/sparkle/throb: Josiah.

How hard it must have been for her. She was a sighted child amongst the blind. *And we have no clue what she's even looking at.*

Mohammed had to repeat Laura's name several times to regain her attention. "Try to understand," he urged, "what Lily could mean by 'icefire.'"

Laura was still dazed. The connection she'd made weeks ago resurfaced: the blackout had been the unintended consequence of the soul-energy's attempt to manifest a new evolutionary direction. And Lily was it. "How did you get from how she talks to her being a deliberate mutation?"

"I don't know," he answered truthfully. "Just as I

don't know how she gets these things-that-have-no-words. But we must try to understand icefire. What is it, Laura?"

Icefire? It was Mack. It was *Shaitan*. It was . . . conflicting.

"Chaos," she whispered. "Icefire, *Shaitan*—chaos. But chaos that is embodied."

"Chaos," Mohammed repeated. "Embodied chaos. Is that not . . . contradictory?"

"Yes," Laura said simply.

Kate stood in the doorway, fists clenched. She couldn't, she thought, stand listening to one more word of crap about what might be. John Thomas was in trouble. That was real, and all Laura was doing was rehashing her fantasy religion. Plugging the chinks of her new faith with even more thin air. Frustration mingled with her old, familiar anger and Kate turned away. Only John Thomas mattered now. She had to stay busy or she'd drive herself crazy. She'd clean the second floor rooms, she decided, starting with a room for John Thomas.

Catherine, who'd entered the room midway through Laura's and Mohammed's discussion, sat in an armchair near Lily's sleeping corner, unashamedly eavesdropping. This definition of *Shaitan* as embodied chaos fit quite well with thoughts she'd had long ago, when Laura had first insisted that *Shaitan* were of a force existing on the flip side of the universe.

Dark matter, Catherine had thought at the time, but she had said nothing. After all, the existence of "dark matter" was unproven, though many leaned toward the idea that it permeated the universe. Composed of unknown particles, undefined energy, the existence of dark matter could be inferred only by its effect on some stars. The rotational velocities of such stars evinced anomalies that could not be explained, and they roused scientific speculation of an unseen x-factor exerting an unknown force. They called it dark matter.

It was times such as these, Catherine reflected as she watched the intensity of the dialogue between Laura and Mohammed, that she missed her husband, Howard—her prince, as she'd often referred to him—with whom she'd engaged in so many stimulating conversations. Her flawed, brilliant prince, a student of many subjects, all of which he'd shared with her. Wearily, Catherine leaned back in her chair and closed her eyes.

"Maybe all the *Shaitan* will just . . . implode," Laura was saying hopefully. "Chaos can't be contained. Maybe that's why Mack went so crazy—that display of self-cannibalism . . ." She shuddered. "Chaos destroying the order closest to it—the body that contained it."

"What about those *Shaitan* you say have always been with us? Like Lucas? They don't do this, do they?"

"I think *Shaitan* born as infants have the advantage of adapting slowly since the bodies they come into are so much more limited." She paused, her own words jogging her onto a different subject. "Do you remember the . . . effort of breaking into this dimension?"

"Yes," said Mohammed. "It makes me shake inside. Jiggle?"

"Vibrate. Like oscillation—almost a tuning-in kind of thing."

"Yes. It was closing the . . . the loop . . . that made it possible."

"That's right. Good way to put it, Mohammed."

Catherine sat up. Closing the loop? Oscillations? She couldn't keep still over this one. "Laura, dear," she said calmly, "have you heard of string theory? Or, rather, M-theory, as it came to be called?"

Laura's blank expression was answer enough.

Catherine blanched. "I must lie down," she said.

Catherine sat, trembling, on the edge of the bed in the tiny bedroom off the dining room. String theory, evolved to M-theory, suggested that the tiniest particles into which matter could be reduced were not particles at all but loops of oscillating energy, and that their very oscillations defined their function. *We are not comprised of matter, but energy that is differentiated by its oscillation.*

So many of the things Laura had said all along had

made perfect sense to Catherine. The mere fact that bacteria shared common genes with the human species had been but one corroborating bit of information she'd tucked away years before. Regressive mutations. The missing components in babies born after the blackout—call it a soul, an essence, call it pudding, it didn't matter—whatever it was, it was indeed absent. And then Mohammed, with his matching epiphanic theory, the likening of *Shaitan* to chaos, the elusive universe of dark matter.

And now, the oscillations.

The instant she'd heard Laura mention oscillations, Mohammed speak of the loop, something had clicked. She could almost feel what they remembered, the energy source straining to gain entry into the physical dimension, splitting into ever smaller units, vibrating at incredible speeds, pulsing, oscillating, impossibly miniscule. Then closing the loop. And *poof.* A living charge within a molecule.

Her weariness vanished and she clasped her hands in her lap to still their trembling. After decades of laboring beneath the limiting belief that all things came to an end, she was infused with wonder and hope, happier than she could ever remember being.

A new thought loomed, smashing aside her joy. She grasped her cane but it slipped from her grip and clattered onto the floor. *Lily, Laura, Kate, the boys—all in terrible danger.*

Laura's epiphany was real. And Laura and Mohammed said the Path was gone. *All things will come to an end, after all.* A suffocation of heat, moisture, pressure. She clawed at her neckline. *No. It can't be.* There must be a way.

Reclining on the bed, she tried to calm down. She had to think quickly.

CHAPTER 45

LILY SQUIRMED IN HER MOTHER'S ARMS. AT FIRST she'd been content to nestle against her mother and watch Mohammed. He felt different than her own family and friends. She felt movement, fluidity she'd never encountered.

The urge to express the knowing filled her thoughts. She needed something long and smooth. A ribbon would be a start, but she needed . . . Maybe she could find something upstairs. She slithered from her mother's lap.

"Where are you going, honey?" Laura asked.

"Looking." Eyes gleaming, Lily went up the stairs in the foyer.

Laura turned to Kate, who hadn't stopped her restless pacing since Josiah had returned with the news that he'd accomplished his mission: he'd found Dr. Chang and had been successful in enlisting his aid. Kate had peppered Josiah with questions and he'd reassured her again and again that Dr. Chang would succeed in returning John Thomas to them. But Kate's patience was at an end.

"What's taking him so long?" she fumed. She strode to the window, yanked aside the drapes, and pressed her face against the pane to view the dark, deserted street.

Catherine appeared in the doorway of the small bedroom off the living room. She was convinced her little family, gathered in this room, needed saving. But there was more. If their other-dimensional source could not maintain corporeality within this universe, everything would be lost. She reclaimed her armchair. "Kate, dear," she said, "may I have a glass of water?"

While Kate was in the kitchen, Catherine announced to Laura, Josiah, and Mohammed that she, too, now believed in Laura's epiphany. She raised a hand to still the exclamations of amazement and requests for explanations for the reasoning that had brought her to their way of thinking.

"Did you listen to Eli's tape?" Josiah wanted to know. He had slipped it to her days ago along with the tiny recorder and a request to just listen to it, however many times it might take her to make sense of it.

She nodded. "Just now. However, I'd reached my conclusion before hearing it."

Suffused with joy, Laura knelt by Catherine's chair and embraced her. Catherine's expression, serene as always, held a new glow.

"What's going on?" Kate asked as she crossed the

room to hand Catherine her glass of water.

"Oh, Kate," Laura said, turning to her almost apologetically.

Catherine patted Laura's hand, saying, "Let me do this," and took the water from Kate. "Eli recorded a tape within minutes of the blackout," she began.

Realization swept across Kate's features. They were talking about Laura's Goddamned epiphany. Again. And, somehow, Catherine . . . "Aw, SHIT. Not you, too."

"The evidence has become overwhelming, Kate. Listen to Eli's tape and judge for yourself. And there are other considerations as well."

Deflated, Kate turned away and listlessly folded herself into a corner of the couch. "Yeah, sure," she muttered. "Whatever."

"Kate—"

"Forget it. Save your breath."

"Very well, then." Catherine fingered several pills from her sweater pocket and swallowed them with a large drink of water. It was time, she decided, to let them know.

"There is a way to fix this, to restore the Path," she began, to Laura's and Mohammed's surprise. Josiah leaned forward. Kate rolled her eyes but said nothing. Catherine took two more capsules with water, then related a summary of M-theory.

"Eleven dimensions," Josiah mused upon her conclusion, having long known of string theory. "Infinite universes, according to Dr. Chang."

Catherine nodded. "There must have been, at the moment of physical death, a release of energy from this dimension, back to the source-dimension. Laura and Mohammed believe the connection is gone. I believe it is just . . . scattered. And that something very elemental in us should recognize the singular oscillation it emanates, and thus find our way back."

Josiah frowned in thought. "You're assuming awareness exists at this most fundamental base."

Mohammed had followed Catherine's explanation with great difficulty and understood fully only after several requests for simpler definitions. "Does this not mean that the way will only be available to those who know they must struggle for it?" he finally asked.

Catherine smiled. "Yes." She then proposed that the peculiar matter/energy of *Shaitan* was the chaotic oscillation now blocking the return journey.

"Knowing this must be avoided, one of us may get through. And our very return is what will mend the path. The information we accumulate in our lifetimes is disseminated when we return. Just as Laura and Mohammed recalled galactic panoramas during the event and received inconceivable amounts of information, this 'realignment' will also become part of the body of realizations. The way in and the way out will be restored."

"You're right," Laura said slowly. "It really can be fixed."

"Yeah," Kate said absently. "If one of you croaks." She still wasn't convinced—or, refused to be.

Mohammed stared at her. Kate had spoken the truth. Someone who *knew* had to die to stop others from being sucked into the darkness of chaos.

Their attention was drawn to the staircase. Lily ran straight to Mohammed. "For you," she announced breathlessly, and thrust something into his hands. He held the oddly shaped creation in the palm of his hand. Blue ribbons crisscrossed it, forming an intricate weave that completely hid whatever it was composed of. The ribbon ends flowed like silk between his fingers.

"Thank you," he told her in a grave tone. He smiled into her merry eyes. *So like Aida.* A terrible thought lashed him. *What if Lily fell ill, lethally ill?* And she didn't understand about finding the way back? There was only one answer to that. Only one way to keep Lily safe and Kate, too, who denied understanding. They could not die first.

He looked at Laura and saw his conclusion mirrored in her eyes.

Josiah's arm tightened around Laura with the same realization.

"I'll go," Josiah said simply.

"No." She clutched his arms. "Don't say that." She must be the one to go. Not Josiah. She couldn't imagine the world without him in it. Yet how could she leave Lily?

Catherine could see that Laura and Josiah were struggling with their need to save each other. She let it play out, knowing that would make it all the easier for them to accept her own solution. She swallowed two more pills with the last of her water.

"Lily, dear," she said, holding out her empty glass, "would you refill this?"

Lily trotted into the kitchen with Catherine's glass. When she returned, Catherine suggested a project for her, something for John Thomas's homecoming. Lily whispered excitedly back, then had to squirm for release from a lingering hug. Catherine's tender gaze stayed on her until she disappeared up the stairs.

Kate listened to Josiah and Laura with growing alarm. That Goddamn Path. It was literally going to be the death of one of them. Knowing how completely Laura believed in her epiphany, she knew just how useless it was to argue. And now, even Josiah and Catherine were caught up in the fantasy. Sudden anger surged through her.

"Will you cut out this shit?" she yelled, glaring at Laura and Josiah. She whirled toward Catherine, pointing a shaking finger at her. "Chrissakes, Catherine, you started this. Fix it."

Mohammed silently slipped away.

He paused in the dimness of the hallway to look at his new friends one last time. Knowing his mission, he silently said good-bye. On the street, he would make his final obeisance to Allah. He would not go too far; they would hear the shot and know the need was filled.

Kate's chest was heaving. "Jesus Christ, Laura. You're Lily's mother. Do you really think she'll be better off with you gone?"

"Kate's right," said Josiah. "It makes more sense for me to go."

"No!" Kate cried. "It doesn't make sense for anybody to go."

Catherine raised her glass to her lips, but water trickled down her chin.

"Are you feeling all right, Catherine?" asked Josiah.

"Mmm, fine." This wasn't going to take much longer. Palming the last five pills, she hastily washed them down, then wiped trickles of spilled water from her chin.

"Catherine!" Kate hurried to her side. "What are you taking?"

Catherine smiled and patted Kate's hand. "Everything's fine now. I'll take care of it."

"SHIT." Kate dropped to her knees.

Josiah and Laura crowded next to Kate. Josiah cupped Catherine's wrist, fingertips on her pulse.

"What have you been taking?" Josiah asked Catherine.

"We've got to make her throw up," Laura instructed.

Catherine eased forward to peer past them at the

empty room. "Where's Mohammed?"

Kate grabbed Catherine's arm. "To the bathroom, *now.* We're getting this shit out of you."

With surprising strength, Catherine wrenched her arm from Kate's grip. "No! It's done. Where. Is. Mohammed?"

"Probably taking a piss."

"No!" Catherine's hands waved heavily. "Oh, he's going to . . . Josiah, get him. He's going to do it. I knew you two . . . but I didn't think, oh, how could I not . . ."

Josiah limped quickly out, calling Mohammed, knowing, even as he searched, that it was futile. Catherine was right. Mohammed had slipped away to take their lives into his own hands. And now they would lose both Mohammed and Catherine.

Mohammed would have gone outside to do it, thought Josiah. What was his reason? He hadn't known any of them long enough to . . . He had to find Mohammed before it was too late. It was obvious Catherine had planned her exit carefully.

Grabbing his and Kate's jackets from hooks by the door, he limped through the empty living room and stopped in the doorway of the small bedroom. Catherine lay on the bed, and Kate and Laura sat on either side of her.

"He's not in the house," he said, handing Kate's jacket to her.

She lifted a tormented face to him. "Catherine's . . . she's going to . . ."

"Find Mohammed," Catherine said, each syllable an effort. "Kate. Please."

Kate blurted, "But I don't want to leave you."

Catherine managed small smile. "You will never leave me, dear Kate. You are . . . burnt . . . into me. Forever."

Crying, Kate pressed a kiss onto Catherine's soft, worn cheek.

"Good-bye, dear," Catherine whispered.

Swiping at tears that would not stop, Kate wrenched herself off the bed and barged past Josiah.

Josiah gently kissed Catherine's cheek. "Thank you," he said, then searched for words of encouragement. Her theory of tuning in to innate vibrations had sounded plausible, but now that she actually hovered on that brink, he could only wonder at the how of it. Remembering the gluey, bleak horror of the second blackout, that ominous darkness she had to skirt, all he could utter was, "Hold on, Catherine, just hold on."

She smiled crookedly. "Don't worry. I'll . . . make it. I have perfect pitch."

Clever to the end, Josiah thought, and his answering smile, full of sadness and hope, was nearly undone by the grief that lay hard beneath it. He would miss the old woman far more than he'd ever expected.

"Laura," Catherine said, alone now with the young woman who'd changed her life and what lay beyond it.

"Tell me . . . what I shall find? I imagine . . . consternation. Many questions about . . . why we . . . stopped coming . . . back."

Laura tenderly stroked her hand as another piece of the puzzle slid into place. "There won't be any questions," she assured her. "That's our job here. People question everything. We question life itself and, therefore, the universe. On the other side, every returning essence is absorbed. It's where all the answers are saved."

"Don't tell . . . Kate," Catherine whispered.

"Why?"

"As long as there are questions, there will be . . . religion. The ultimate . . . irony."

Laura leaned close to hear her final, faint words.

"Look . . . for the . . . best . . . questions."

Mohammed knelt in the middle of the intersection of 23rd Avenue and Lake Street, as the last of his prayer drifted into the velvety silence. He prostrated himself one final time and felt a great peace. Very slowly, he sat back on his heels, and looked at the heavens splattered with millions upon millions of points of light. Stars. Suns. Creation.

"Allah is good," he whispered as he picked up the gun.

Kate heard Josiah shut the front door, but she didn't look back. "I'll go this way," she shouted. She hurried toward California Street. It was unthinkable. Catherine was dying. And all because of a stupid fucking idea. She could just kill Laura. And if it weren't for Mohammed, she could be at Catherine's side right now, holding her hand, not . . . not walking out on her.

She veered into the middle of the street to see both sides better and ran as fast as she could. Her harsh breathing and rapid footfalls echoed against the darkened houses.

A gunshot blasted through the night.

"Ali!" she screamed, and ran faster. Gasping for breath, she strained to make out the shadow in the middle of the upcoming intersection. "Ali!"

Mohammed listened to the echo of the shot he'd fired into the air. Surely they would have heard that. And hearing a second shot, they would investigate.

He placed the muzzle against his temple. And heard a cry. Without moving the gun, he turned his head and saw a shadowy figure rapidly nearing him through the surrounding darkness. His finger tightened on the trigger.

"Ali, stop!" Kate yelled. "Catherine did it. Catherine's dying." Kate dropped to her knees beside him. "We gotta hurry," she panted. "Maybe there's still time." With a groan, she grabbed his arm as she rose. They both ran. Mohammed, chin tucked and arms pumping, sprinted past her.

They were too late.

CHAPTER 46

"I CAN'T BELIEVE SHE'S GONE," KATE REPEATED numbly. Her deep grief was shrouded with resentment. "So Goddamn unnecessary."

Laura felt the words like a blow, but there was nothing she could say to prove Catherine didn't die in vain. It might be a long time before they would know anything. Mutations would have to stop. *Shaitan* must cease entering the world. Ironically, till then, she would need faith.

"It was necessary," Mohammed began but subsided at a glare from Kate.

A knock on the door shattered the tension. Kate ran to the foyer and flung the door open. With a cry of joy, she pulled a dazed John Thomas into her embrace.

Dr. George Chang, smiling politely, stood to one side

with his young daughter, Su Ling, while John Thomas was passed from one member of the household to another in a flurry of hugs and kisses. Lily attached herself to John Thomas with such fierceness, none could pry her clinging form from his. Josiah then introduced Chang and Su Ling and invited them to sit by the warmth of the fire. Even as they settled in, Kate fired questions at Chang and John Thomas, snatches of explanations overlapped, and John Thomas was gently told of Catherine's passing. Only then did Lily finally release her hold on him, allowing Kate to enfold her young charge in her arms, to share and ease his fresh grief.

Lily looked to the others and, for the first time, saw the little girl sitting quietly by her father's chair. Frozen in place, Lily could only stare, mouth agape. She'd never seen another little girl, never seen another child. Lucas, awful Lucas, had been the youngest person she'd ever been near, and he'd been six years older than she.

Both Josiah and George Chang watched the girls watching each other. Both knew this meeting was momentous.

Josiah, in enlisting his professor's aid, had told him everything he knew about Laura's epiphany, including her feeling that her daughter, gestating within her at the time of the blackout, was somehow special, invulnerable to its effects. Su Ling, too, had been in the womb during the blackout, Chang had revealed. Her mother had died giving birth, and Chang had hidden his precious child during the widespread purgings of those first years following the blackout.

When Josiah had heard Su Ling utter a clump of words in the midst of a remark to her father, his first thought had been, *Just like Lily.* He'd been amazed. Confounded. And immediately aware that Lily's odd way of speaking wasn't merely a quirk.

Standing next to Chang as they watched the rapt faces of the two children appraising each other, Josiah could almost swear he felt a frisson of charged awareness pass between the girls. He bent his lips to Chang's ear. "Laura thinks Lily's a deliberate mutation. There's something new here, George. And it looks like Su Ling's part of it."

George Chang caught his breath at the sight of his daughter's face. Always beautiful, his Su Ling now glowed. He glanced at Lily and saw her matching inner spirit similarly reflected. He blinked hard, several times. Was it just Su Ling's happiness he was seeing, or was it something else? Like Josiah, he could almost swear something palpable had passed silently between them.

Josiah, George, Laura, and Mohammed quietly discussed Su Ling and Lily.

"Even though there's no way for us to understand

how they're perceiving it," Laura said, "what they may be perceiving is a sense of self, how we each see ourselves." *While with us,* she thought, *our very conduits for sensing the world are also barriers to really knowing each other.* She glanced at Kate, wishing Kate could know how she saw her. The subtle rift between them would never have become a fracture.

"Lily and Su Ling always get true first impressions of people," she continued, grasping Josiah's hand in hers. "What will that mean for love?"

Would Lily truly love everyone, she wondered, love them in the way she herself loved Josiah? Or, maybe, love as the rest of them knew it was but the precursor to Lily's sixth sense, allowing only glimpses of another person's sense of self.

If Catherine had succeeded in fixing the path, then Lily and Su Ling were only the first of many like them. Human evolution would pass to the next phase.

"If one could know a person through their own eyes," said Dr. Chang, "it would be impossible to maintain prejudice. War becomes unthinkable." He shook his head wonderingly. "The world would indeed change."

"Katie." John Thomas tugged on her sleeve. They were sitting close together on the couch, across the room from the others.

"What, honey?"

He turned his face to hers, his eyes flat, dismal. "I shot Lucas."

"He was *Shaitan*, baby, you had to." She tenderly cupped his face, puzzled over his seemingly delayed reaction. "You did right, you hear? He wasn't a person, he wasn't really your brother—he never was."

"But Laura said Catherine went to fix the Path. Maybe it worked. Maybe whatever she did would have fixed Lucas, too. If I hadn't shot him, then he—"

"No." Kate looked deep into the eyes of the child she had come to love so completely, the boy who trusted her so implicitly. For his sake, she suddenly knew, she had to relinquish the defenses embedded solidly within her. She had to diminish them, scale them, and reach for the glimmer of hope she might use to help heal John Thomas. But she could not knowingly deceive him. The hope had to be real.

Taking a deep breath, something seemed to settle inside her. But it was more than a settling, it was also a letting go. And it felt good. "Lucas was from the dark, John Thomas," she said firmly. "*Shaitan* from before the blackout. He came by glitch, and there's no glitches on the Path. You see what I mean? Glitches can't be fixed."

Eyes full of trust, John Thomas nodded. Clasping his hand in hers, Kate drew him with her to join the others. John Thomas met Lily and Su Ling in the corner, where they sat on Lily's piles of blankets, and he let Lily pull him down beside her.

Kate stopped behind Laura and tapped her on the shoulder. "What say we rustle up a meal for this crew, kiddo?"

Laura smiled hesitantly. Was this a truce? Or something more meaningful? Kate nodded, smiled widely. The answer filled Laura with peace.

At her side, Josiah nuzzled her hair. "A yen for your thoughts," he whispered.

Laura could only shake her head, her heart too full for words.

EPILOGUE

THE FAMILY HAD GROWN. OR PERHAPS NOW IT WAS A new family.

And the world had changed.

Mohammed was gone. The boy, now a man, had decided to return to his homeland. It would be a long and arduous journey, filled with danger and excitement, but one he felt ready to undertake. Catherine's passing had indeed shifted life back on its course. No more *Shaitan* were born—at least, not into everything. Only the occasional glitches, like those that had conveyed Lucas and others like him into the world, still existed, as they always had.

As for those who remained together, Lily and Su Ling spent every waking moment communicating in ways none of the rest could understand.

Dr. George Chang and Kate had begun a fledgling relationship. Others in the family marveled, for it was the first time anyone had seen her sit and listen quietly, almost reverentially, to anyone, her freckled cheeks sometimes glazing with rose-tinted blushes.

Josiah and Laura were lost together, hidden in plain sight, speaking a language everyone knew, but in which none could participate.

And they all found themselves missing Catherine, recalling the fundamental guidance and indomitable spirit she had contributed, at one time or other, to everyone. Kate, especially, was fond of Catherine stories.

As for John Thomas, his world was full, his heart complete, no matter which small group he joined. Though he belonged exclusively to no particular pair, he fit well with them all. He could not know that this was the training he would need to become the leader he was destined to become. He looked forward to each day with a joy he could not explain.

If he could have explained it, he might have said that what he was experiencing was a new family, a new world. A new hope.